THE SILENCE IN THE SONG

BOOK ONE IN THE ILLUSION SERIES

ROBB WALLACE

HTTPS://ROBBWALLACE.CO.UK

ISBN: 978-0-9956873-8-7

To all those who dream and to all those who take action on their dreams, thank you.

A special dedication to my wife Donna, who I could not have done this without. Thank you.

To my family and friends who have given their time and energy to read and contribute to this project, my thanks is yours.

Special mentions:
To my father, you are a legend.
To the The Muscle Mole, The Tordoff, Dylan and Bones – thank you for your invaluable feedback.

Finally, this is a twenty-year project, a lot of things kept getting in the way but I made it. If you enjoy the book or even if you don't, please consider leaving a review on the platform you purchased it from. All links can be found at robbwallace.co.uk
If you pirated the book, please consider leaving a review, buying a copy, buying a few copies, sharing out the book on social etc. I am just a wee indie author following a dream, do the right thing.
For the artists, feel free to bring my characters to life. Contact me on social or via the web.

ROBBWALLACE.CO.UK IS THE CENTRE of my author brand. I have lots of content on this website, including information on all my books, including accompanying art and maps. There is also articles about being an author, marketing, SEO, as well as fantasy related articles like my long running Fantasy Author Interview series. You will also find links to my newsletter and all of my social channels.

robbwallace.co.uk

a   amazon.com/Robb-Wallace/e/B00NJW9XMW

f   facebook.com/robbauthor

g   goodreads.com/author/show/7980859.Robb_Wallace

y   twitter.com/robbauthor

▶   youtube.com/channel/UCHY58yjfyVnxY7ReEUc_CCg

d   tiktok.com/@robbauthor

○   instagram.com/robbauthor

CONTENTS

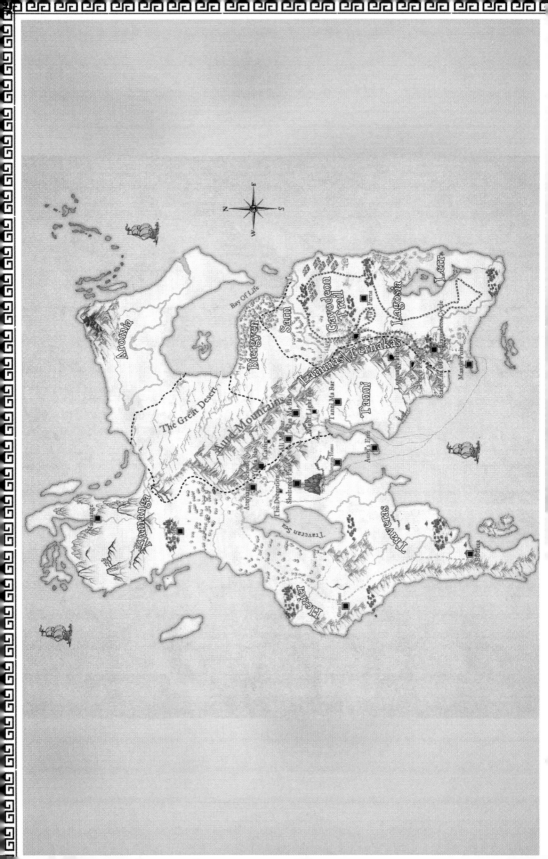

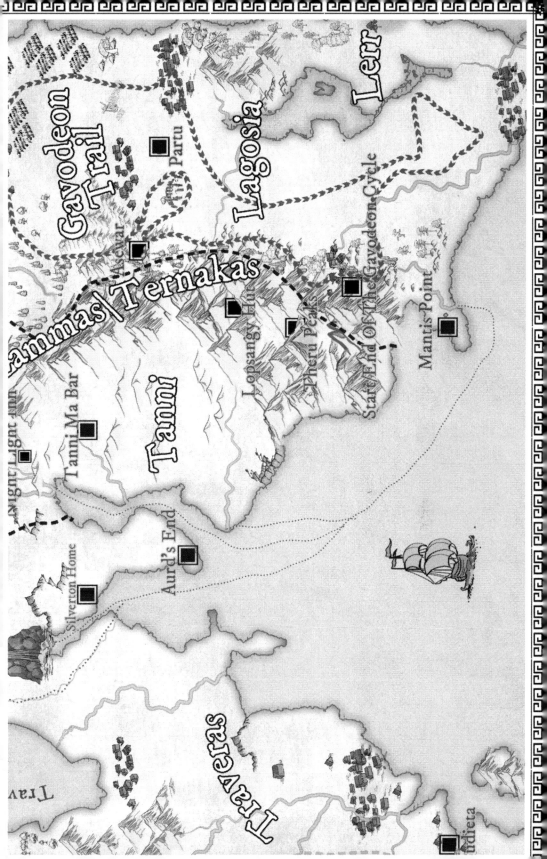

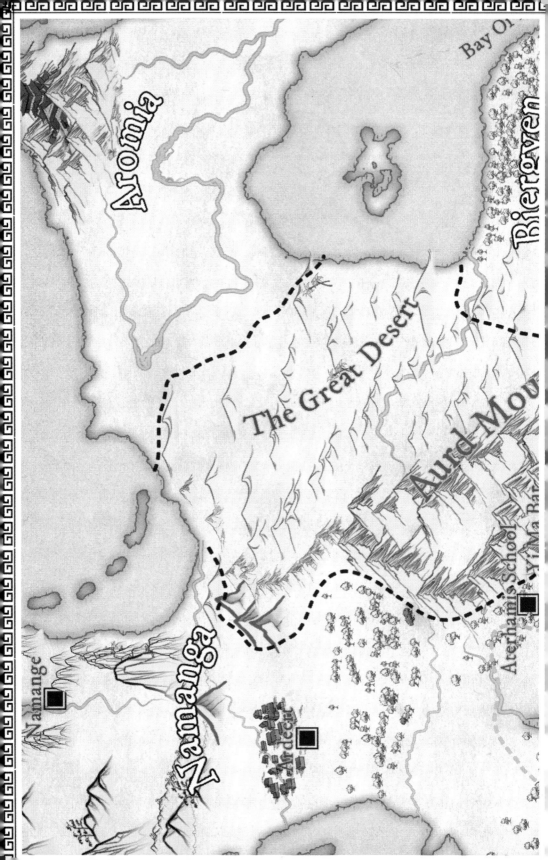

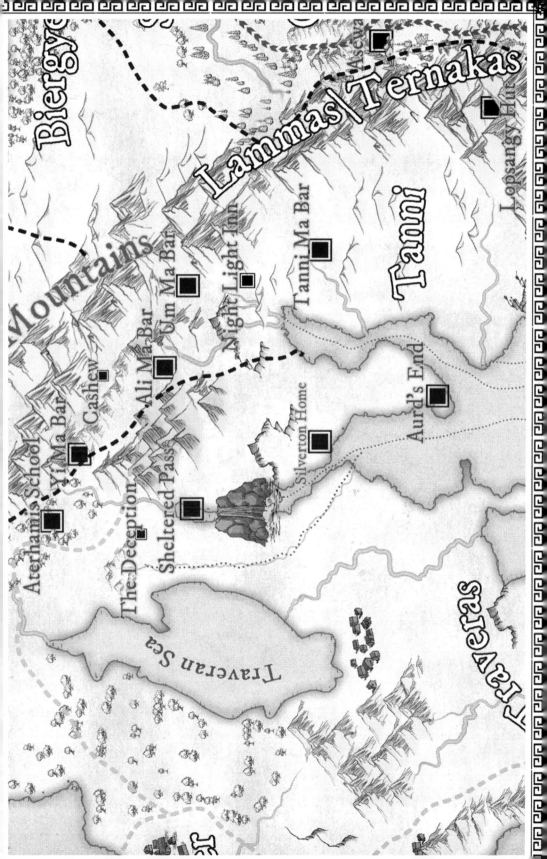

Biergyen

Sarn

Of Life

Lammas/Ternakas

Bar

ni

Asewar

Gavodeon Trail

Partu

Lopsangy Hut

Lagosia

Theru Peaks

art/End Of The Gavodeon Cycle

Lerr

Mantis Point

PROLOGUE 1

SUMMERIAN OFTEN REFLECTED ON his early years, uncomplicated days full of reading, debates, violence and sex. That was before he encountered the truth of how things really worked. He remembered that day clearly, the day the Anti Mass Voiders raided his home world. He recalls his discovery of them, their ability to wage physical war and a new form of energetic attack, simultaneously. He remembers the feeling of them feeding upon him as he battled them in the physical. He remembers them wiping out over eighty percent of his home world. He remembers the truths and half-truths the galactic Tenni Uh Akki government fed him and his family and the anger he felt towards the AMV. Those days were long gone, but the memories reminded him of his insignificance in the grand scheme of things, that he was as much a pawn in the game as these wretched souls that stood with him and against him this day. Yet he did what any warrior would do in times of war, he signed up to help. And here he was, playing his part as the immortal King. A glorified baby sitter, at the ass end of a far-flung galaxy, in this backward, uncivilised, technologically void, cesspit of a world.

***

THE TWO LEADERS STOOD face to face at the centre of the battlefield, the uneven ground beneath their feet untouched.

"I know what you are," said the Traveran King, Edvar. "The people here today may not know who or what they are fighting or why, but the historians of this world will one day write the truth."

"What do you know of the truth?" spat Summerian, the Namangan King. "The truth you think you know, the truth you think you have grasped, has been revealed a thousand times by thousands of your kin. Yet, your historians are still as ignorant today as they will be tomorrow. You are ants, insignificant pawns in a game you don't even understand, that you will never understand."

"I am one of the strongest overseers alive. I have touched The Nothing, I have glimpsed the truth of this life, of the illusion. And yet as I stand here, in your presence for the first time, I can feel your power. It confirms everything about you is true. You are not one of us," Edvar swept his arms round to point at both his own army and the army of the Namangans.

"You are not our kin!"

The Namangan King struck out with his mind, to gauge the claims of Edvar's overseer ability. The Traveran King held steadfast against the surging, energetic attack. Summerian was impressed. As Edvar fought against the attack with everything he had, his words stuttered. Summerian's mental assault never let up.

"This llland will only tolerate such an unbalance as yyyou for so long. Soon our saviour will rise. I once believed I was the one the prophesies foretold, but I now know I am no match for yyyou. The prophecy will be fulfilled. Our saviour will arrive wearing the skin of a cat, he will free all the people of all the lands from your eternal ppprison. When he is done, the sky will dance and the Gods will leave and the people will be free once more." Under the relentless pressure, Edvar fell to his knees, face twisted in pain, exhausted from the effort, crushed by the impossible power of the Namangan King's, overseer ability. Then the attack stopped and the pain dissipated.

"The folly of your ignorance. Everything is by my design. I am the one and only Immortal King. Now return and prepare your men for battle, I have commitments to keep,".

Edvar looked up, at the looming figure of Summerian and then towards his men across the battlefield, he could feel their minds. Their hope, their fear, their belief. Looking through their eyes looking back at him, on his knees before Summerian. He knew he had to stand once more. He could feel his soldiers, his kin willing their King to stand.

"You can do this," thought Edvar. "I may not be able to kill this bastard this day, but we can destroy his army." The minds of his men continued to ring out in his. Through their eyes he sees himself stand triumphantly; he sees himself walk back across the battlefield, confidence in every stride.

If only they knew how broke I am, thought Edvar.

Arriving back to his people, he smiled at his men before turning to look out over the battlefield again.

"The Namangans have raised the Black flag, sir," said one eager soldier out in front, stating out loud what every Traveran could see for themselves.

Edvar took one step back. As he turned to face his own army, he swept his hair from his face one last time, tying it up and securing it into a knot. Before him stood ten thousand warriors, the finest Traveras had to offer, all that Traveras had to offer. As he gazed out over the sea of blond-haired, pale skinned, green-eyed kin, he began to speak.

"Today we make a stand. Today we stand up for every Traveran, and for everyone South and West of our mighty borders. Today we fight for our lives and for the lives of those we love. To those amongst us here, thinking we should have surrendered to this bastard," Edvar points out across the battlefield towards the Namangans, his brothers and sisters before him hoop and cheer excitedly. Then as they settled, he began again.

"Hear this: I am the King, and heavy is my crown. I will not kneel to the Namangan bastard. If I fall this day, you may live to see if he is a better King than I. Now prepare yourself for death," his men sprawled out before him, and bashed their shields in unison, rhythmically.

"And if death calls you into her embrace... tell her to fuck off and swim hard towards The Nothing." As he turns back to face the Namangan Army, he whistles three quick bursts. Behind him, the Traveran's black flag rises.

He summoned every ounce of strength he had and pushed out from his mind directly into the minds of every Traveran soldier with his overseer ability. Within their minds, the great figure of Val Drack stood strong, unwavering and defiant, his long blonde locks and piercing blue eyes radiating with power.

"Be calm, my friend. I will fight by your side this day. Pick up your sword and let my power surge through you. I, Val Drack, radiate within you, today and always."

The Traveran mass stood in a trance as they received the message they believed was directly from God.

As the Traveran flag rose, the Namangan King broadcast directly into Edvar's mind.

"Know this, Traveran. Not even you, the most powerful overseer of your generation, can help your people. I have travelled across the known void. My people control an empire so vast; your feeble mind could not even comprehend it. Mark my words. These lands will flow red with congealing blood and the sky above will dance with rivers of soul energy by the time I am finished". As Edvar used every ounce of his abilities to push Summerian from his mind he raised his arm and pointed straight to the sky, before dropping his raised arm.

From behind him, the mass of his army charged. Thirty thousand strong. Edvar sprinted to the front, like the tip of a spear, as one, they surged forward into no man's land and into the front line of the Namangan attack.

It did not take long for the Namangan King to deliver on his promise. Within the hour, Edvar stood alone, the last Traveran. The ground beneath his feet now ran red with pungent, congealing blood. The harsh aroma of death engulfed everything, it's sharp, meaty, metallic notes, rose in the heat of the midday sun, enough to make the remaining hundred or so battle-hardened Namangan warrior's gag.

Across from Edvar, Summerian stood admiring his work. The last of the Namangan warriors behind him.

"Your job here is done. My clients have eaten well this day," laughed Summerian.

With no more effort to give, mentally or physically Edvar accepted what was his. In that instant he felt the woosh of air and saw a glimpse of the blade as it reflected momentarily in the sun, before his head left his body.

PROLOGUE 2

BEFORE HIM STOOD THE figure, long dark hair and olive skin, heavily scarred, as tall as any Gavod, radiating power with every fibre of his being. At his feet lay a thousand dead warriors, all white skinned, with red beards and pale green eyes, the likes of which Arran had never seen before. The blood, everywhere, looked even redder against their ivory skin. Again, his face was masked, blurred by some strange nuance of the dream. It was a dream, thought Arran, it must be a dream.

As he moved forward over the bodies of the fallen, it grew. Once again, he recognised it. He knew it was coming; the signs were so clear. The fear rising from his core, blind panic overwhelming his every thought. Again, it was upon him.

The powerful figure bathed in red mist, charged forward, faceless, emotion-less, ready for death. As he charged Arran shrunk, as he shrunk the Gavodeon nation sprawled out far behind him, began to disappear, then in an instant as the warrior from his dreams reached him, Arran awoke screaming.

"Shut up, you noisy wee shit," screamed Anderson.

"Sorry, Anderson," replied Arran, confused, still in shock from the dream.

"I canny take your screaming from nightmares, son, you're waking up the entire horde." Anderson scowled as he rubbed his eyes. "You'll have to bed with someone else tonight," he said with a little less harshness in his tone.

"Sorry, I don't know why I have these nightmares," said Arran as he looked up at Anderson, looking for answers he knew would not come.

"Ah, ok. Tell me about your fucking dreams lad," rumbled Anderson.

"I've seen this dream so many times this cycle, in so many guises, from so many perspectives. Sometimes he glows red, sometimes he glows white, sometimes he is torturing all that I know and love, sometimes he is killing strange foreign looking men and woman by the thousands. Sometimes it feels like I am observing historical events from a time long past, other times it feels like it's raw, happening right there and then in my dream. Other times it's like I am a bird looking down, observing his armies as they wreak havoc. I wish I could stop the dream; I wish I could stop them; I wish I could stop him. It feels like he is more, so much more. I wish I knew who he was. I just wish I knew what this was..." blurted Arran in a haze, so happy and relieved to be asked about his dreams.

"Sounds like you're living in the songs of old," said Anderson as he rose from his Yak hide cover for his morning piss. "My advice, you should focus more on the now. Like Mertak, standing up to the other boys, your trading supplies or balancing your books, for the end of the cycle is near. Forget your dreams," Anderson stumbled towards the exit, acknowledging the wisdom he was imparting. He moved towards the large flap of hide between the comfort of the yurt and the cold outside, as he pulled the door aside his beard was twisted by the winds. Looking back at Arran as he slipped behind the closing flap, he shouts. "And if these dreams persist, you need to speak to Rannoch. He will know what to do. Dreams like these are a Shaman's work,"

The sun was already above the horizon, beating hard against the outer skins of the yurt. Streams of sunlight poked and danced through the flapping door into the gloomy interior like fingers searching for those inside. The fire still smouldered and would need attention soon. Today was the last day for the hoard in Lower Asewar. They would do no trading this day, just packing, settling bills and setting off toward the mighty Aurd Mountains once more.

CHAPTER 1 - ARRAN

ARRAN WALKED IN SILENCE, one lonesome figure amongst many. The rain penetrating his furs, dampening his skin, but not his will. The path he walked was churned to mud by all those out in front, by his mothers and fathers, by his brothers and sisters.

Lightning shrieked across the sky. In that instant he seen the high mountain pass flicker into life, ominous mountain shadows converged and danced as the five thousand strong caravan of the Gavodeon nation continued forward. The thunder that came twenty paces later momentarily masked the roar of the pounding rain. Life as a nomad was hard, and soon the true winter of the Highlands would be upon them.

Arran's mind was built to cope, built by life's experience, built to endure the exhaustion, the pain, the need for sleep. The mind does what it can to deal with the true realities and hardships it faces yet no one knows what happens within the privacy of someone else's mind, no one really knows what others build in there, what barriers they create, what coping mechanisms they muster, to deal with unrelenting hardship.

The Gavodic horde walked in small interchanging groups. As a nomadic band, the Gavods were inherently social creatures. When the rain wasn't driving and sometimes even when it was, each group would be deep in the midst of an epic story of times gone past, or gossiping about the politics of recent cities they had traded with or arguing over the new prices of said goods or services bought or sold but mainly talk always turned to who was sleeping with whom that night. The only thing the Gavods liked more than gossip, sex, politics and business on the long walks between trading cities of the south was singing. Every day there was a rock-solid guarantee that the many clans that made up the Gavodic horde would join in song. Their voices were famous in most parts of the south, many of the settled people would hear the trading Gavods before they would see them, it must be a splendid sight and a sound, five thousand travellers spread out over many miles joined in strange overtone throat singing, the likes of which most cultures never practised and only experienced through contact with the Gavods.

Young Arran had a different coping mechanism. Gossip was not for him, he enjoyed listening to the business and political discussions, and he loved the stories of the ancient past when Nencom and Vantesera and other such Gavodic heroes roamed Lanasia but he doesn't participate. As one of the few loners in this sea of social animals, he would run from group to group, shunned by some, beaten by others, tolerated by few and taunted without exception by almost everyone. Over time he stopped trying, he was different, a solo traveller, a silence in the song.

The first hit snuck up on Arran like the light rain before the storm. And just like rain, the pain it brought was just an inconvenience, until the storm arrived, then it overwhelmed. It started with a kick to the back of the calf muscle that snapped him back to reality. A fist to the stomach and then the rain began to pour, blows rained into the side of his head, his ribs, his arms, his back. Like a hundred times before, Arran was bull rushed and taken to the ground. As he hit the ground, he did what he always did, rolled tightly into a ball. It'll be over soon, Arran comforted himself. Stay calm. It's good training for life.

"This is what weakness looks like," shouted Rum as the others cheered and jeered. The pressure of Rum's weight bore down hard against Arran's ribs as he used Arran as a pedestal to preach to his minions, encouraging the other youths to have a kick. The pressure and the building pain made Arran curl tighter. Then it stopped. The storm was fading. Rum jumped down from Arran to address his followers, before raising one foot up on his downed opponent for added effect.

"Mertak is almost upon us," shouted Rum as he stood proud amongst his peers. The hoard continued forward, unconcerned with the violence. "Arran will surely die up there in the mountains, for he is weak, weak of body, weak of mind and weak of spirit. He is not worthy of being a Gavod. He is not worthy of participating in Mertak. He is not worthy of being a contender to eat the flesh of the golden cap mushroom. When I return as Mertak, when I become our next leader. I will drive his kind of weakness out of the Gavodeon nation."

Arran remained motionless underneath the weight of Rum's yak hide boot, only moving slightly to swipe the mud and rain and stop it from entering his nose and mouth as the puddle now formed around him.

"To every other nation we are the outcast, but here amongst the Gavods," Rum turned from his small group of excited peers, bent down, lacing his strong fingers through Arrans matted, muddy hair and ripped his head up from the ground to face him.

Arran looked up directly into Rum's eyes. As he looked deep into those dark slits with everything he had, he let Rum know that he would not be broken, not today, not tomorrow, not the next day. With only his eyes, Arran conveyed defiance, and a bloody-minded refusal to be broken. Maybe this was indeed the thing that brought him back to me time and time again thought Arran.

Rum dismissed it and turned to his audience.

"We are a nation of outcasts. But here amongst our own people, you Arran, are the outcast, an outcast in a nation of outcasts. Soon, you will be glad to know, that your misery will be at an end. We are a sturdy people and the weak like you are meant to die," the other boys jeered. As Rum's grip released his hair, Arran entered the mud with a splash once more. Then they were off to regain the main mass of the horde. After some time, when the shivering had stopped, Arran looked up from the ground and seeing that there was no one nearby, he rose to his feet, wiped off the mud from his face and clothes and began to walk once more. Just another day, thought Arran as he looked towards the path trampled into the mud by his kin and smiled sardonically.

From the first step all those years ago of what would become his second full cycle, he'd put in place a coping mechanism to deal with the solitude, the stigma, the pain. He told himself that everyone had developed one. Deep down he knew this not to be true, but life on the trail was brutal. The changing environments, extremes of weather, the extra weight of newly acquired stock and the weight of poor business deals. Add to this the ever-present cultural stigmas that followed his people, he thought, they must have developed some sort of inner mechanism to deal with it. Surely they couldn't just talk and sing all the time as their only solution.

Up ahead of him, as the horde climbed out of the rolling lowlands and deep valleys of the outer Aurd mountains into the high mountain trails, the temperature dropped rapidly, adding yet another layer of hardship. His sodden, mud clogged furs, damp against his skin, done him no favours against the cold. His need to retreat overpowered him. Slowly, he dropped out and entered his inner world once again.

The young nomad's inner routine started with him finding his rhythm, concentrating on his steps, his pace, his breath, and once all was established and automated, he would begin retreating from the physical world and venture deep into the comfort of his imagination. An inner world where rich visual details came easily, each infused in ultra-vibrant colour, the other senses, however, requiring much more concentration. Touch, smell, taste and sound, for the most part, felt dull within his mind with rare moments of fleeting clarity.

In here, he could escape the punishing physicality of the relentless trail, the pain, the rain, the wind and the cold. In here, he could take shelter from the solitude, from the songs, the gossip, from his brothers and sisters, mothers and fathers. In here he was strong, in here he could entertain and amuse himself, in here he could prepare himself for his upcoming rite of passage. In here, he is welcome.

Travelling through his structured and compartmentalised memories of the last cycle, where labyrinth like pathways linked every conscious thought, an inner world shaped through trial and error. On this final day of the current cycle, his third cycle. He began his test, a self-imposed challenge that had become the sentinel to his inner world. He retraced the entire six-year cycle, day by day, checking and filing every nougat of information in its place. Once this task was so monumental, that as he recalled his initial thoughts of creating, of even attempting to create such a task, he laughed with joy at his progress, at his now effortless recall.

He remembered the ice and the snow of the south, the swamp and mangrove of the northwest. The majestic and mighty mountains of the Aurd, the endless heat and dryness of the deserts and life refreshing air of the forests. As he flew through his inner world where time has been locked in place at his bidding, he consciously invoked all his senses into his memories. Concentrating hard not to just visualise, he experienced fragments of the fragrances, flavours, sounds and textures. He delighted in the noise of the bazaars, the beauty of the music performed live, the heat of exotic chillies burning his tongue and lips for the first time, and on and on he ventured into his inner library of memories.

Once again, he began the never-ending refinement of his inner sanctum, his inner labyrinth, rearranging and creating new subcategories, to compartmentalise every memory and every connection between it and any that remotely associated with it; the meats, fruits, vegetables, nuts, grains and spices of each region, the customs and laws of each major city, and their associated cultures, politics, religions, gods, folklores and languages. Externally, the temperature dropped and the rain slowly turned to sleet as the trail gradually climbed. All were dull, distant sensations compared to his vibrant inner world.

He was born two years into his first great cycle. By the traditional Lanasian calendar, used by everyone but the Gavods, Arran was fifteen years of age. He marvelled at the ease in which he could now recall almost a complete cycle. This had been the first full cycle he had really paid attention to. His curiosity had been alive since they had left the majestic Aurd mountains, almost six years past. Every day on the trail heralding a fresh adventure, some positive, some negative. He took in new sights, smells, sounds, tastes and emotions. He met new people, learned new languages, arts, customs, laws and new forms of humour. He witnessed new acts of violence, new acts of magic, new hustles, scams and crimes. He felt new pains, fears and doubts. Everywhere he looked there was a new experience to shape his young mind.

"How had I missed so much of the trail?" he asked himself over and over as he reorganised and categorised the experiences.

"I was too young," he thought.

The end of the third cycle ushered in a rite of passage that every male Gavod must undertake. This for Arran was now just up ahead. The recent and intense rush of puberty had given him a newfound desire to prove himself to be a true Gavod, to show the other boys that he was not weak, that he belonged. All these factors had made this cycle so vivid, so memorable as he marched alone towards the end of the cycle and the test ahead.

"We make camp, the cycle has come full circle, we are home," declared Rannoch, the tribe's Shamans. Deep in the dark moonlit highland valley, as the rain continued its forward march, the horde sang loud. The song morphed as they took the message up and soon a new song emerged like a butterfly from its cocoon. The song of Nencom rose fast and loud and travelled like wildfire through the sprawled-out nation. As the lungs of the Gavodeon nation rose in joyful celebration, the automatic and skilful construction of a town began. A short time after the first syllable of the song, they had built the night's camp, the fires were roaring, and the beer had begun to flow. Tonight, would be a glorious night, well for most.

As the celebrations began, the great cycle was now officially complete and soon the clans would start the sacred rites of the special winter solstice, Mertak. This was what Arran had been waiting for this entire cycle. For a Gavodeon boy, the completion of the third cycle meant only one thing, Mertak! This was the winter Arran would become a man or die. Six years of focus, of preparation, and soon his trial would begin. Before Mertak, duties had to be done. Everyone pitched together to complete all aspects of the last cycle and all requirements for their longest settled camp of the new cycle. Arran's clan tasks were helping to prepare the animal shelters, storing trade goods, sorting certain business dealings, and as always, his personal task of making sure his books were balanced.

***

SEVEN DAYS LATER, ON the last night before his greatest test, Arran made his way to the yurt of his true mother and her partner. His true mother and her partner were the only ones of his many mothers and fathers that had really accepted him. Unlike the settled folks, the Gavodeon mothers had sex with as many clan males as they could, to secure a good mix for their offspring and to make sure that in the tough times ahead the males would look at each of the sons and daughters of the tribe as their own. Viki was his mother and although every male had shown him love, shared their yurts and the time honoured by a father, only Irvine had accepted him and attempted to get to know his inner world. On his arrival, they welcomed in the young Arran and offered him warm butter tea of which he graciously accepted, but he was asleep way before they served the tea.

"It's time to rise, my son," Irvine shouted again as his voice vaguely registered through Arran's morning haze. A warm buttery aroma wafted pleasantly in the air, the all too familiar smell of oats, yak butter, yak meat and salt. Oats were young Arran's favourite, yet so bland, but it was exactly this blandness that he could count on. Every morning he ate with the many members of his extended family and every morning they ate oats, simple yet fulfilling. The blandness of the oats, thought Arran, was one of the few constants in a nomad's life. He had often mused to himself on the enigma of the oat. Why did his people so covet the oat? Why did they trade their precious Reindeer and Yak for them? And how had they become such a staple amongst his people? They were not farmers, they had no land, no crop to grow. He had once asked Rannoch the hordes shaman and he had said that the oat was just one of the many signs of the interconnectedness of the whole, that the stories that build nations are all connected and deeply tied. It had baffled him then as it baffled him now. This morning though, just the thought of a warm bowl of oats gave Arran that extra incentive to rise, for he knew it would be his last ever, like it was his last night's sleep in the warmth of yak hide, the last of a long list of home comforts. "The next month would be tough," thought Arran.

Arran exited his yak hide and stretched; a strange routine based on his observations of the southern city's domesticated cats. His parents continued with their tasks, so accustomed to Arran's oddities.

"Nightmares again, son?" says Arran's mother gently as she swipes his dark matted hair from his hard, weather-beaten face.

"Yes, they have plagued me the last quarter of this cycle," said Arran.

"We heard you in the night, tossing and turning as you fought some invisible battle in your sleep. Hopefully, they will pass soon my son," says Viki. Her dark black eyes reflected his smile as she stroked Arran's thick shoulder length black hair from his shoulders once more.

"I hope so, but before they do, I would love to know what they are about. They feel so real, they feel like they are more than dreams, they feel important, as if I must do something. I can't explain it. And I can sense him, I can sense them, glimpses of them, when I am there, in the dreams," said Arran as he rose from kneeling before his mother.

"I feel their pain, their anguish, their hopelessness and sometimes their death," Arran's face grimaces slightly as he once more feels their pain.

"I've seen so many folk being slaughtered by this man, I can't fathom how he's managed it all in one lifetime. More than all the people of the great cities we trade with in an entire cycle. I've seen people with the creamiest skin, and eyes as green as the Lerr sea crushed by him. I have witnessed men built like bears, with skin as dark as night, with armies so large I could not count them, crushed by his might. I never see his face, but his people are as unique as the dark black and pale, light-skinned folks. They have olive skin, high cheekbones, where we are almost flat between our eyes. His people in contrast have a bridge to their noses, that divides the eyes, that is so large, pronounced and narrow."

Arran stopped and took a breath and a few seconds to reflect on his latest outburst before composing himself and bringing himself back to the moment.

"It's just a dream," said Arran.

"They are just dreams, son. We all have dreams and, well, that's that. They shall pass, anyway, your mind needs to be on Mertak. Today is the day of Mertak," smiled Viki as she nodded proudly and winked at her son.

"Mum, Irvine, soon I will become a man," said Arran as he looked towards Irvine, the large bearded face of his father smiled as Arran continued.

"I will come back from the mountains, a leader of men. I will conquer the peak. I will eat the Sun; I will be the next Mertak."

Arran stands strong, he stands convinced by what he has said, Irvine's smile loosely twitches as his eyes try not to destroy Arran's moment.

"Tell me about the Sun," says Arran.

Irvine's eyes light up, this time Arran could see he was not hiding his emotions. Irvine was an enormous man, a common site among the Gavods. Tall, barrel chested with powerful shoulders and arms. He stood tentatively stroking his long black beard.

"How will he answer me," thought Arran. "He knows that I am one of the physically weaker boys of the horde, a daydreamer, appearing absent minded to most and almost always lost in my own imagination. Yet he also knows that I am intelligent, with a mind that is unrivalled amongst my peers. He knows that when I focus my mind, I have the focus and determination of a Lerrian fighting dog. For all the social skills that I lack and I am shunned for, I hopefully make up for in my abilities to trade. I think I am one of the most highly regarded youths of all the horde in this respect," Arrans over thinking inner dialogue of hope and doubt came to a halt as Irvine crossed the yurt and stood before his son.

"They say it gives you direct contact with the great union of mother and father, that you develop special hearing and special sight. Like Rannoch, wisdom will flow..." Irvine's words are cut short by a pinch to his side. Arran watched on as his mother took control of the room.

"Remember, both of you," said Viki as she tapped hard against her own forehead; "Knowledge of the existence of a precious thing is a far cry from acquiring it." Irvine nods in agreement.

"Yes, yes, your wisdom never fails. Only a few men know the genuine power of the sun, that's why they get such respect. Only you Arran, it was not my journey to learn the lessons of the sun, to be a leader but you son have the qualities. Do you remember it all? All we have practised; all we have discussed about the mountain," Irvine begins to laugh and Arran and Viki join in as Arran nods and winks with confidence.

"Is there anything you don't remember?", the young man smiles contently, Irvines laughter tapers off as Arran moves to stand before him.

"Do you know why you are going into the mountains?" said Viki.

"I am going into the mountains to become a man," said Arran with confusion. He knew that his mother was asking him something else.

"But why?" said Viki, challenging Arran quickly to reply with something of substance.

"Why? Because if we want to become great leaders, if we want to become men, we must show our self to be worthy, we must participate in Mertak, we must pass our rite of passage," said Arran as he looked deep into his mother's dark eyes for confirmation.

"The boys who wish to become men must enter the forest to prove themselves worthy of becoming men. Worthy of becoming a father, becoming a leader to a child of the Gavodeon horde. To become a man is a great responsibility. In our society, only males who have participated in Mertak are equal to the women of the horde. Do you know why, son?" asked Viki.

"Because you give birth, because everything comes from the mother?" asked Arran.

"That's right, my son. We give birth. We need not prove ourselves. We are born leaders, we are chosen by life and when we transition to womanhood, when we give birth, we accept our rite of passage. Go forth into the mountains and accept yours and no matter what happens, accept it. And you will return a man worthy of becoming a father," said Viki with a nod.

Arran stepped forward to embrace his mother, her black hair, plump frame welcomed him into her embrace. As Arran left the embrace of his mother, Irvine spoke once more.

"Prepare, prepare, prepare looks like it has been your motto this last cycle. I have been watching you, silently and with pride! The hard work has been done and soon, if you want it bad enough, the secrets of the sun will be yours, my son," Irvine placed his arm on Arran's shoulder.

"I will return a man; I will make myself and yours proud, I will make every Gavodeon proud to have raised me as a son". They exchanged long comforting hugs before Arran left the yurt to meet the other initiates at the yurt of Mertak.

The stock rooms and the stables were right beside the yurt of Mertak. The young Gavod had been walking this path all week. This morning he walked through the rain. "Was it rain?" he thought, "it felt more like slow moving, wet air that clung to every inch of his outer surface". Arran realised it was a cloud, he was walking in the clouds; he smiled ear to ear, a cheeky, innocent, joyful smile at the revelations that he, a poor Gavod was walking in the cloud, like the songs of many a great Gavodeon tale, Arran was walking in a cloud. He continued through the cloud, his grin stayed put; he walked with purpose, with pride, with power, chin up, shoulders back, eyes open wide, greeting everyone he encountered. He heard Irvine and Viki weeping as he disappeared completely into the fog.

As Arran entered the Yurt of Mertak, he was welcomed and bestowed all the gratitude given to a potential leader of the horde. From this moment onwards until he returned from the mountains, they would treat him with the respect earned by a Mertak. After Arran's mind adapted to the strange gestures of total respect given to him by everyone in the community sized Yurt, he relaxed in the company of his peers for the first time in a long time. This unfamiliar sensation felt strange, felt good, felt natural, Arran smiled. The leaders then guided Arran to the first workshop of the day. The workshop was strange; it was aimed at those who had learnt none of the key survival skills. "Why would anyone take such a task as Mertak so lightly," thought Arran, "when the chances, when the numbers say you are more likely to fail or even die than succeed, why would you not prepare?" This boggled Arran's mind. After the many workshops had finished, the group moved on to listen to the advice of the elders, of what has worked previously and what has not.

The boys ready to become men sat together in a tight circle around the three elders and the central fire. Each of them had now completed two entire cycles and varying degrees of a third. Arran sat amongst the others, lost in a daydream of possibility. At fifteen, Arran sat comfortably in the middle age range represented by those who had completed two entire cycles. Amongst the thirteen ready for Mertak, some of his brothers looked like men, beards and all, whilst others... others looked like babies.

The sacred gong rung loudly. Arran jumped; his awareness was ripped from his thoughts. As the other boys began nudging each other and laughing at Arran's reaction, the first elder spoke.

"When the great sun shines through Theru Peaks, signalling the exact winter solstice before the light disappears, you will be stripped naked of all your clothing and possessions. From there, you will leave camp up by the northwest passage into the Aurd. Once there, you will have to survive for one cycle of the moon. As you will have nothing, you will gain everything, relying on your training and your instincts to find food, water, clothes, shelter, and fire,"

The clan chief, Leven passes the pipe to Lomond, he receives it with the proper thanks and retrieves a fire stick to relight the herb. As the flames meet the bowl, he takes a long hard and seemingly thoughtful draw of the 'One' pipe. For a long time, the room is silent and all that can be heard is breath, flame and the uneasy sounds of thirteen initiates waiting on the unknown. Finally, he exhales and the wisps of smoke envelope him. The thick plume takes on a strange ethereal form as it twists in the flickering light of the fire. Another long draw is followed by another long pause, then the draw is exhaled, strongly, sending the pungent moist smoke into the ether again, completing the connection of man and spirit. Arran felt it tickle his throat and held back the cough that it gave birth to. Then Lomond, full and anointed by the power of weed, addressed the initiates.

"In this winter, boys will become men and some will become leaders of men. To eat the sun, you must journey with courage in your heart to Mertak, for at the gate of light there is the medicine of the butterfly. There grows the orange caped mushrooms which will open the gates of transformation. "But, be warned, although the rewards are great beyond words, the journey to Theru Peak is a perilous trek. Remember, you must find water, food and make clothing and shelter to survive before you even consider climbing beyond the tree line to the summit. To build a great yurt, you must select an excellent piece of land and secure your foundations before you build the walls and roof. Only if your foundation is strong and secured will your Yurt weather the storm. On this journey, only the strong will survive, many will die."

"Fuck" thought Arran as he looked up, trying hard to distract himself as he suppressed the fear that he felt rising. "Death, I can't die, I have too much to live for". He knew that death was a possibility, but hearing Lomond's words out loud was a reality call like no other.

"One stick will snap easily, but when we bunch many together, they stay strong. Do not fear death, your soul will survive and be reborn to try again. To be a Gavodeon, you must be strong, there is no other option". The pipe held securely in Lomond's left hand crackled bright with the last glowing embers of the dying bowl. He took his time, completely untoward, the thirteen youths waited, reacted to his very breath. As he prepared the pipe for passing, the initiates sat in silence.

"Soon, some of you will become men," Lomond passed the pipe as he purposefully made eye contact with each and every one of the youths.

Rannoch, the clan shaman and senior Mertak accepted the pipe. A tall, flat-faced man, sporting the traditional full beard of the Gavods. On receiving the pipe from Lomond, he sucked down hard, dragging clean air through the burning leaf, the pipe glowed and crackled with delight. His eyes closed as he completed the long inhalation. As his eyes re-opened and his face all hard, hairy and flat relaxed, he spoke.

"Will you find and eat the sun? Will you be like the butterfly? Will you transform? Will your mind be opened to the true sight and sounds?"

A lengthy silence followed as the young initiates awaited more words from their Mertak, but none came.

Lomond broke the silence with an open gesture of his hand, which simply meant "Eat". As the initiates all simultaneously turned towards the food, the elders rose from their seated positions and left.

Never had Arran seen such a feast. Salivating uncontrollably and unconsciously, like a wild animal. As the leaders left the yurt, he pounced towards the mountain of food.

"Arran, why are you feeding? The weak die on the Aurd. You are wasting our food."

Rum smiled triumphantly, Arran's main obstacle in life stood in front of him, loud and proud and as always, supported by all the other boys. The twelve boys, most of them taller and stronger, routinely entertained themselves at Arran's expense. His aloof nature only encouraged their antics. Still sore from the last beating, Arran unconsciously stood his ground. This time, Arran would have to face and conquer his fears if he had any chance of surviving Mertak. He had made his decision, and he was ready to do what needed to be done.

"Soon we will be men and your attitudes will change. I might be weak of body, but my mind is strong and my will like iron. I will become a man, I will be a true Gavod...," Arran stood shocked at his own outburst and not alone in that, Rum and the boys were all equally shocked. Never had Arran spoken back, not even when he was being beaten, almost tortured. He always stayed silent, but this offbeat state of tranquillity was abruptly cut short.

"You might be clever Arran, but it is the strong that live and we will outcast you from the group, you will die on the Aurd." Even now, with this newly added pressure, Arran did not doubt his preparations, his commitment to success.

At this, Arran dismissed them and turned to the food, to their shock and amazement.

The feast of Mertak was savaged by the thirteen youths, knowing it would be their last meal for days, weeks or maybe even ever. After a time, Rannoch and the other clan chiefs re-entered. As the clan leaders formed their traditional circle, Arran and the others knew the time was near. Leven spoke;

"Dusk is arriving, strip naked of all your clothes and possessions. This will be your final time, do not fear, be at one with nature. Trust mother earth and she will provide."

Rannoch, face masked in green smoke, added. "When in trouble, turn off your mind and float downstream, let all your troubles wash away." He paused and then with conviction and with all the authority of the current Mertak he bellowed, "Now, the time is now."

His arms swept up and pointed to the exit, physically moving the thirteen initiates up onto their feet. In a wave of panic, excitement, anticipation and fear, the naked boys made for the door. Just beyond the flapping Yak hide that covered the exit, as they left the warmth, comfort and protection of the Yurt, the rain pounded their naked flesh. Arran's eyes strained hard to catch the last shimmers of sunlight as dusk passed beyond twilight into darkness. Arran and his naked companions are struck by the harsh reality, surviving Mertak would not be easy. Thirteen boys trying to become men, naked, with no food, water, clothes or tools and now in desperate need of shelter, run frantically deeper and steeper into the darkness.

CHAPTER 2 - ARRAN

"MERTAK, HERE I COME," shouted a naked Arran as he ran out into the darkness.

Arran's strategy was simple, he knew from his few years of trading that, for a plan to succeed it must be simple, actionable and realistic. As he ran, he prepared his mind to accept the uncomfortable reality that, not one of his brothers would help him. With this as his foundation, he planned. He knew he must find and secure food, water, clothing and shelter before climbing higher and higher into the Aurd. He had one month in the mountains; he concluded that he would need to reach the summit of Ben Theru no later than the third week.

Arran was used to having conversations with himself; unlike the other initiates he was always alone, it seemed. He was looking forward to the rewards of Mertak--not the respect, the gold or the yaks that were promised to each new Mertak, but the more satisfying life lessons from challenging himself. It was a once in a lifetime opportunity to confront and understand his own fears, to learn what drives him, to test his will in an extreme life or death situation. Situations like the Mertak, he'd been told, tested the potential of the tribe's males, to find out exactly what they were made of. They'd designed the whole situation to generate great stress and near impossible challenges that made the participants confront themselves face on, crack and fail. If Mertak was to be survived, Arran knew he would have to confront himself head on, his fears, his emotions, his weaknesses, he wasn't against the other boys; he was against himself, a familiar foe, thought Arran.

Questions of every kind flooded his mind. "Hopefully I'll have some answers soon", thought Arran. Rum and the boys scrambled forward into the darkness, leaving Arran behind, alone. Their laughter, laced with taunts, slowly faded and merged into the background noise of the majestic mountain scape, unregistered. Arran was glad. This may prove to be the first month in years with no daily beatings. He was looking forward to his first full day without the stress of his normal life.

He jogged forward, following the contours of the land as best as he could, the darkness engulfing his every step, slowing his pace considerably. The light of the moon was dim as it hid from him behind the mighty Aurd. The solitude that the surrounding darkness brought was embraced and welcomed. In the darkness, alone and struggling with his footing, Arran fine tuned his plans.

"It's cold, It's bloody freezing more like! I'll head for the trees; I'll find a pig or a goat and I'll eat it". Arran's imagination filled with comforting visions of spit roast pig, fur skins and a ridiculously lush multi-level tree house. Arran's delusions masked the here and now.

"Right, let's think straight a while, I'm naked, it's dark, it's wet and I'm cold. I can't travel too far in this darkness. Priorities, priorities. I've eaten. Necessities first, clothing, shelter, fire. For clothes I need to find and kill an animal, so I need a weapon. Shelter, I'll make camp under a tree tonight, a simple, fast lean-to structure. I'll mix some leaves and grass and use it to insulate me. Fire, I'll need dry grass, wood, bark and some staden flower buds to get it going. How am I going to find all of this, it's pitch dark? Think, Arran, think. The key things are the leaves, grass and a decent tree and I'll sleep until sunrise then I'll really get going," said Arran aloud to himself, the darkness swallowing his words whole.

Arran's brainstorming had sent him a short trek towards the very heart of darkness, out in front was a dense, lightless forest that he knew bordered the vast mud shores of the River Olenak and the entrance point from where he would need to ascend into the Aurd. On the other side of the forest was the perfect location to set camp for the night and plan his journey ahead. Now he just had to navigate this small forest. In the pitch dark. Alone.

And beyond the darkness, he realised after entering, beyond the absence of light, there was the noise. Surrounded by the grotesque sounds of the forest at night, Arran had never felt so vulnerable as he did then, just metres from the tree line, and just miles from his family. Doubts pried their way into his mind, until it raced with scenarios and what ifs, possibilities and permutations, slowing his pace once more, forcing him to focus on every noise, every shadow, as if each one was a mortal threat. His imagination had made the forest come alive: in his mind it was angry, it was hungry, and he was the food it needed to quell it's growing appetite. His heart jumped as each new sounds and sensation grabbed his attention and compounded the fear within him, growing until he retreated from the forest, backtracking on the paltry progress he'd made.

"Pathetic" he taunted himself. All of his preparations would not help him. Arran knew, if he couldn't get his mind in order, walking through a forest less than three miles from the Gavodeon camp, he would have no chance of surviving the full moon cycle.

From deep within Arran's own mind, he heard his himself saying 'return home, there is no shame in it. Mertak is not for everyone, you took part, that's what counts most. Many fathers of the horde returned before the entire cycle of the moon', but as it rose in his panicked mind, he dismissed it. He would last at least one night! Then he heard another voice rise 'you need to release the fear.' But saying that from the comfort of his own mind whilst his body, his unconscious mind, his heart and every other fibre in his body is reacting uncontrollably, to some unknown factor, some factor that cannot and will not be rationalised with, some emotional response that is so deeply ingrained within his being that he can't even pinpoint its being. Yet it is there, growing, feeding, mocking, expecting.

In that moment as Arran's mind was now completely distracted by fear, by the darkness, by the what ifs, his quickening heartbeat, the terrible unending dread and the uncontrollable sense of doom that now encompassed him from every angle. As he retreated, he missed his footing and tumbled head over heels to the ground. Uncontrollably and instantly, Arran began to sob. Simultaneously, he curled up his cold naked torso into the tightest foetal position he could muster and attempted to hide from the darkness, the noise and the fear that now engulfed him. After the uncontrollable fear, panic and shaking, Arran's body relaxed, it began to be. As the calm regained footing, Arran opened his eyes and with no more energy to give to fear, he released it. Curiosity slowly took over, a new desire overwhelmed him, he found the courage to explore the beauty, to explore the rhythm, to explore the wholeness and all the individual parts of the noise that now enveloped him. As his senses merged, a song of beauty could be heard. Nature's orchestra. In the chaos, there was rhythm, there was beauty, there was an absence of fear. Arran's mind, now calm and relaxed fluxed between the warmth and comfort of his inner sanctum and the cold moist air penetrating his naked flesh. Arran rose to his feet and began moving forward again. "A minor set back on the trail to success," thought the young nomad as he re-focused on his mission.

As he approached the other side of the forest, the light from the moon was now visible, shining through a deep valley high in the Aurd, reflecting majestically off the calm waters of the Olenak.

"Who's there?" shouted Arran into the moonlit darkness before him.

"I am a friend. Who goes there?" the stranger replied.

"I am Arran son of Viki. And you?"

"It is I, Mull,"

"Well, make yourself known you are no stranger." Arran scanned the scene in front of him, but still couldn't pinpoint where the voice was coming from, "I am heading towards the river. Join me, we can exchange ideas on survival," said Arran.

"Aye, but why are you heading towards the river?" shouted Mull.

"It is as good a place as any, don't you think?" replied Arran as Mull sheepishly came into view, his hairless face twisted in discomfort. As he walked forward, Arran noticed how short and skinny Mull was, his ribs protruding hard just above his belly. Mulls dark red hair was unique within the tribe.

"Do you think we'll survive Arran? I'm so scared. An entire moon cycle. I just hope I'm tough enough."

"I hope so too, Mull, why are you alone? Where's Rum and the others?" asked Arran.

"I was falling behind. They were going too fast, I couldn't keep up," said Mull.

"So, they just left you," Arran's voice shook with anger. "Do you ever think for yourself? Always following Rum's command, obedient like dogs. Makes me sick and yet you guys taunt me and call me weak," Arran realising that he was now shouting like a maniac, took a long steady breath and exhaled before continuing, "At least I accept myself," Arran paused to catch another breath.

"Anyway, we will survive. Let's make a quick shelter and make it through our first night. We can talk in the morning," said Arran in a very commanding tone.

The two naked youths, covered in a mixture of dry and damp foliage, huddled tightly together under the canopy of loose, broken branches. Unable to sleep through the cold, Arran distracted his mind and stared up at the great void through the gaps in their shelter. Just beyond the fast-moving clouds he could see the many lights, each under its own will, shining and dancing across the night's sky before disappearing again and again behind the clouds high above. Unconsciously he began to sing the song of The Void, a tale of ancient nomadic Void men, who had once travelled across the stars in boats the size of cities, trading goods to the gods and then before he was aware of it, he was asleep.

***

THE NEXT MORNING, THEY awoke to a majestic landscape, a frozen expanse extending out towards the horizon. The Olenak Valley beneath them flowed like the river with endless morning mist. Cold, stiff, shivering and covered from head to toe in damp foliage, Arran rose triumphantly to his feet.

"Mull, rise!, it's a glorious morning," shouted Arran, as the moisture from his mouth formed vapour clouds in the crisp air.

"Morning, glorious, those two words no longer go together. It's cold, I'm cold. I didn't sleep, I'm naked," moaned Mull in response.

"Listen here, Mull; let's get into the right frame of mind. Stop your moaning. We need a weapon for hunting and dry grass and fuel for fire and some materials for a shelter". Mull did not look impressed, yet Arran knew that Mull had to participate, for there were only two options in Mertak.

"For a moment there, all I heard was my mother's nagging voice echoing in my mind," Mull prised himself from the ground, grudgingly. Before continuing. "Survive or die son, survive or die, no son of mine returns home early," shouted Mull as he rose from the ground. As he did, the shivering intensified.

"I will find a weapon; I'll be back soon," said Mull with as little enthusiasm as Arran had ever heard.

Within one step of the now faintly steaming foetal imprint left by Mulls body, Mull shouted with the slightest hint of triumphant success.

"Here," Mull picked up and then passed over to Arran a fairly substantial branch with a heavy knuckle.

"That was quick. See what you can do when you put your mind to it!" Arran winked as he finished the sentence. "Ok, we have one weapon sorted, now we need to make a real shelter,".

As they set out to build their first proper shelter, their eyes made contact as they stood naked, dirty and shaking. For the briefest of moments, Arran experienced Mull's mind. An external vision of himself, from Mull's perspective flashed in his mind and he smiled. "Fuck. That was strange, it was if our minds connected," said Mull uneasily. "I experienced that too," said Arran. As Arran attempted to rationalise the strange experience, Mull burst into action. Before long, the foundations, structure and insulation had been sourced, and the shelter took shape. This had been the first time Arran had had to recreate the standard forest hunting shelter without his mother and Irvine. As the two young men stood marvelling at their accomplishment, Mull broke the silence.

"I'm so hungry," moaned Mull.

"Don't start your moaning again.... Come on we can look for edibles on the hunt,". For most of the day they hunted and scavenged, while their hunger grew uncontrollably. They pushed themselves through thick frozen under-growth, through tributaries to the River Olenak, over hills, through dark living forests and well-lit dead woods. Time and time again, they pushed their naked bodies on, through the pain, through the cold, through the hunger. As they travelled, they sang, they laughed and they bonded. The two outcasts had found friendship through adversity. After some time, the young hunters rested. With the failing light, they returned to camp for their second night, with their tail between their legs. Huddled together once more, hungry and defeated, they went to sleep.

Before him stood an army, thousands of battle-hardened men formed rows as far as the eye could see. Arran stood motionless, readying himself for the inevitable, then out beyond the front-line, Mull appeared. He was dressed head to toe in fur, Arran instinctively called out, 'Get out of there Mull', then the army charged. At that moment Mull began to scream, instantly waking both of them.

"What the fuck was that," shouted Mull, still recoiling in shock as if the army was still charging.

"What the fuck was what?" said Arran.

"The army, the fucking big fucking army," shouted Mull, still moving backwards.

"The army?" It was at that moment that Arran realised that Mull had somehow experienced his nightmare with him, that the Mull in his dream was actually Mull and not just a representation of him.

"It's his army, the warrior that plagues my dreams. How did you enter my dreams?" asked Arran.

"I don't fucking know, they're your dreams," retorted Mull.

As the two emerged from their shelter, naked and cold Arran replied,

"Look, I don't know what the dreams are or why you could enter them, all I know is it is weird."

"Weird, yes, it is, very weird," laughed Mull, not knowing where to look. "But I did not enter your dream, I never entered your dream, you fucking kidnapped me and held me hostage," screamed Mull as he moved frantically backwards.

"I was sleeping..." said Arran confused.

"Is that what you call that. Sleeping? I have never seen such a strange performance, nor someone so unresponsive to communication. It was as if the dreams had gripped your mind and your body was fighting to regain it," Mull mimicked the strange convulsing movements.

"I couldn't take anymore. You woke me up so many fucking times. As I leaned in to shake you awake and give you a piece of my mind, you kidnapped me. I found myself instantly transported from the morning light-filled interior of the shelter to what I assume was your fucking nightmare scape of a dream."

"It doesn't make sense you can't be in my dream and be conscious of the fact that you are in my dream. That is not possible," said Arran.

"It is, I was just there," retorted Mull sarcastically.

"Well, it is what it is. I have no explanations for you. My strange dreams aside, we need food," said Arran as Mull nodded in agreement.

The two young Gavods put the strange experience behind them and marched themselves deep into the wooded valley they had discovered the day before. After some time, they found themselves in an area that stood apart from all the other parts of the forest they had previously explored. This area almost looked as if something had shaped it. Arran's curiosity grew and as it did, doubt rose in his mind.

"We have followed the sounds of the forest to this location, tracking the animals of the forest with no avail. I have a gut feeling that we are not the hunter," said Arran.

"What are you talking about, Arran?" squawked mull.

"There," Arran raised his knuckled branch pointing it out ahead of him, Arran found himself squinting, attempting to see through the thick bush in front "there, it's moving," shouted Arran.

"And it's moving fast. Arran, what is it? They never told us about this. I think they're surrounding us. What we going to do? What are we going to do, Arran?" screamed Mull.

"We are going to fucking kill it, that is what we are going to fucking do. We are going to wear its dead carcass as we feast on its heart." Arran let out a battle cry of sorts before thumping his naked chest. "We are the hunters, we are Gavod. It is time to become men," proclaimed Arran with a cool certainty and undertones of ferociousness.

"I think it's surrounding us," mumbled Mull as Arran nudged him to fall in behind him.

Arran shouted out as loud as he could, "Come out, reveal yourself," as he did, he puffed out his chest, making himself as big as he could, his senses now on full alert. The beasts circle, Mulls imagination did him no favours. The two naked teens battled their fear, as they stood their ground ready for battle.

"What is it, what is it, what..." screamed Mull

"Whatever the fuck they are, two naked young men are probably a rare and delicious treat. A treat it would seem, that they are fucking keen on. But not on my watch, not on my Mertak," shouted Arran.

From behind them, an almighty roar made them whip their heads in that direction. Arran sees it for what it was, a distraction and instantly returned his gaze to the creatures out in front.

"It's coming, and it's fucking huge," shouted Mull. From the dense frozen undergrowth, a hairy cat-like creature emerged, a Cassartan charging, eager for a meal. The hunters had become the hunted, and Mull had become the target of its attack.

"Ahhh, stay back, stay back, ahaaa, it's got me, help meee...," shrieks of pain mixed with the grunts of a predator in kill mode consumed Arran's attention as he attacked the beast with his knuckled branch, hitting hard at its head, but the Cassartan was in it for the prize and would not release its grip on Mull's throat. Arran's naked body twisted and turned as he lashed out again and again. A last ferocious shaking ritual by the massive cat like beast confirmed Mull's death. As his soul left, the Cassartan urgently dragged his carcass from Arran, dumping his body aside to tend to its wounds, its attention still firmly on Arran. He watched his first and only friend's blood drain from his lifeless body.

Cannibalism had never entered Arran's mind, but these were trying times. Survival was at the top of his list and Mull's body was now a valuable commodity, which he was not willing to surrender to the Cassartan. Arran charged, swinging his club. Three steps in, he raised it high to strike down at the beast as it protected its kill but before he could bring the club down, the Cassartan lashed out, its claw ripping through the flesh of Arran's cheek.

"Ahhh," screamed Arran as the pain surged through his skull, instantly he felt his eye begin to shut. Heat and pain merged as blood leaked from his face.

"Is that all you've got, you bastard," roared Arran in defiance. The first drops of blood from his cheek wet his lips, he fought hard against the urge to flee.

'You can flee or you can fight, make your choice son,' remembering his mother's words brought him clarity, he was here to become a man, to become Mertak and like that, he was charging once more. This time his strike landed flush on the already exposed bone from his earlier attack dazing the beast momentarily. Targeting the exposed cut on its head, he continued until the flesh wound shone white with skull and dripped red with blood. His weak and weary body that had been on the brink of total exhaustion was rescued by the Cassartan's reluctant retreat.

"I was finished, but you will not have me," Arran shouted as he sank to his knees, stick raised in protest.

In the aftermath's silence, a few yards away, Mull lay dead. Arran had seen men die, and he had seen many dead men butchered, but nothing like this. The hunt, the violence, the emotion, the effort, this entire experience had been overwhelming and deeply personal. It had left Arran emotionally drained, full of adrenaline and shaking from exhaustion, but he now knew that Mull had to be gutted. Arran began prepping Mull immediately. To Arran, a Gavod, preparing a recently departed friend was a great honour. Gavods hacked their dead to pieces as soon after their death as possible, to force the soul out of the physical carcass, force it to reincarnate quickly. Being buried was expressly forbidden. As soon as they dismembered the body, they would feed chunks of their loved ones to the birds, cats, dogs, rats and anything else that would eat them. Nothing went to waste.

Arran's hands were wrist deep in the pungent dark blood now, its warmth was a gift. As the blood flowed to the ground, it congealed. The intense and meticulous ripping and poking set free the tender meat.

As Arran freed Mull's heart from his lifeless chest, he sang the Gavodic ritual song of rebirth for Mull, calling his friend back from beyond and guiding him once more to the Gavodic horde.

By the time Arran had finished, midday had been and gone. When everything had been salvaged from Mull's body, and the song of rebirth had been sang aloud. Arran wrapped as much of the meat as he could into Mull's dead wet skin and carried it back to his shelter, leaving Mull's head and much of the carcass for the Cassartans.

Naked and covered in blood, he returned cautiously to his shelter, fully expecting another encounter with the Cassartan. The natural choir of the forest sang loud, strange noises flowed around Arran, shadows danced, Arran's heart filled with a fear that bordered on his previous experience.

This familiar sensation amplified the chaos in his head. Arran made camp, prepared a fire from some dry foliage he and Mull had collected the day before. Arran had, what can only be described as a feast that night. The third night in his new home lasted forever. Guilt moved Arran to tears as he replayed the events of the fight over and over, until exhaustion took over his thin shaking body and he collapsed into sleep.

***

ARRAN AWOKE, STILL TIRED. He felt strange wearing Mull's raw skin as he huddled into the raw meat of Mull's carcass, but survival was the name of the game and Arran would prove he was a master.

Anxious and wary as to the whereabouts of the Cassartan. Arran stretched as he scanned the area surrounding his shelter for the beasts. After a breakfast of dead friend, Arran retrieved some flint he had seen close by his camp. On returning, Arran got to work preparing what he had salvaged from Mull's body. Manipulation of the stomach provided a flask to store water. Arran then moved onto making his spearhead. His meticulous flint knapping had turned a large piece of prime stone into a serrated spear head, before he mounted it onto a long straight-ish shaft with ligaments and sinew. Before sitting them by the fire to dry and bond. Mull's forearm bones were next, they were sharpened, manipulated against a rock, one end rubbed down to create a handle, the other a lethal weapon. One of his thigh bones was manipulated and bound with flakes of the razor-sharp rock left from the spear head production. A spear, a simple axe of sorts and sharp bone for poking added three lethal weapons to his arsenal. With his axe in hand, Arran chopped down some nearby saplings and fashioned a frame to stretch and dry Mull's skin. The raw hide, though not as good as tanned leather was all he could prepare in the time he had. Soon, he would have what he needed to travel higher into the Aurd, but before that could happen, he knew fear had to be overcome.

As night after night passed, Arran struggled with the basics of survival. For the first time in his life, he could not focus, his mind was lost, broken by the experience of Mull's death, of the reality that if he continued onwards to the summit, onwards to become a Mertak he would have to, at some point encounter one of those beasts again, alone. Arran knew that it's thick fur would be the key to surviving the cold as he climbed higher into the mountains. Then Arran stopped walking. He stood motionless, semi-naked, alone in the open wilderness, the Aurd high above him looking down on him, he snapped.

"I am coming for you," Arran shouted as he raised his axe high, puffing out his chest, closing his eyes and sniffing at the air around him.

Scared and cautious of every move he made since his fight with the Cassartan, fear pushed Arran to confrontation. Arran, for the first time in his life, actively sought his fear. He would eliminate this cloud from his mind. Arran returned to the scene of the fight, sharpened thigh and spear in hand, he scanned the area, trying to remember in which direction the Cassartan fled.

"I am coming for you," again, Arran shouted as he ran through the bushes in the general direction that the beast had fled. As he searched, his anger grew, a newfound confidence replaced the fear. Realisation that he was the hunter struck him. "Power feels good", thought Arran. This is what had fed Rum, this feeling had fed his bullies, and it felt good. As Arran contemplated his new state of wellbeing, the strange yet familiar smell of the Cassartan wet the back of his throat. Instantly Arran's wellbeing changed, anger fought fear, fight or flight was now upon the young warrior.

The beast entered his view and before his mind could rationalise the fear, his legs were moving. He charged the Cassartan. Within the first two strides he had released his spear, it flew straight and hammered home deep in to the right shoulder of the massive beast. The distance between himself and the Cassartan disappeared quickly, Arran's naked torso rammed hard into its huge muscled torso, as he bounced back from the impact, he realised it had cut him. Pain seared just below his right eye, his previous cut burst open once more. As he brought his hand up to assess the wound, the Cassartan attacked. Arran met its attack with his own. Striking hard with his weapons of bone and stone. In the frenzy of the first few strikes, Arran realised that this was not the Cassartan he had previously battled, this was another. Where then was the one he was here to kill? In that instant, Arran glimpsed another, and realised he was now up against two, possibly three of the colossal cat like beasts. Arran's patience, his quest for perfection had paid off, the hand-crafted bone axe, hacked and slashed through the Cassartan's thick hairy hide before finding a home in the major artery of the beast's neck. This time there would be no escape for the strange creature of the forest. With his weapons in hand and blind determination, he had no problem dealing death to the first Cassartan, the others swiftly retreating. Their fur, thick and luxurious, would do wonders for Arran as he climbed higher into the cold peaks of the Aurd. From the dead Cassartan he would salvage much meat and fur. Exhausted from the exchange and now bleeding heavily, all Arran had to do was survive getting it back to his camp.

CHAPTER 3 - ARRAN

JUST OVER A QUARTER of a moon cycle had passed since Arran entered the Aurd, naked and determined to become the Mertak. On this day, the evening arrived quickly, its darkness sucked out the last light from Arran's shelter, it now left him with the dull multi-faceted dancing shadows produced by his small smouldering fire. Arran kept the fire small on purpose, feeding it just enough. The roar of a full fire was too intense, too loud, too distracting. He sat quietly in the hope he would hear the songs of the other boys, a signal that they were still alive, since his experience with the Cassartans, he had hoped that his fellow Gavods would somehow slip past them, yet he knew this was wishful thinking.

After not hearing anything of note, Arran again left his physical surroundings and entered deep into his mind. As the fire smouldered, Arran sat upright in his small survival shelter, wrapped in Cassartan fur. It was soft against his skin, the outer layer still moist and decaying, and with every passing day the smell grew worse. However, he was not there, he was deep in his mind and as always, he was preparing, categorising all the items, all the knowledge, the songs and the stories of the Gavods, before moving onto and examining everything Mertak had taught him so far. He knew that he would need more than a list; he knew that he would have to push himself to his limits in order to reach the summit and claim Mertak. As he went through his checklist, he sat smiling. He was now as prepared as he believed he could be. A strong, insulated shelter, thick fur clothing, food stockpiled and buried in the snow nearby, weapons and a flask.

The next morning Arran awoke to see the sun's rays dance through the last weak trails of smoke from his fire. They had transformed his small, dark shelter with long golden rays of morning sunshine. Arran knew that this would be a good day to walk up beyond the tree line, test out his kit, inspect Theru Peaks and scout out a viable route to the top.

"Mertak will be mine," said Arran as he exited his shelter. As he set off, packed like a trading yak, he began to sing.

"Nencom The Great, Nencom The First. He entered the darkness, he faced them alone, he freed us all by freeing himself....... Nencom The Great, Nencom The First...."

As Arran approached the tree line, he looked up to the peaks of the Aurd. Deep snow covered the majestic mountain tops. It was here that the true scale of the mountains before him hit him like yak kick to the head. Arran, for the first time understood the true magnitude of the challenge that now lay before him. The stark reality of at least four days' continuous, vertical trekking, with some scrambling and climbing to reach the peaks of Theru and a round trip of anything up to ten days, Arran thought to himself, "Only the strong survive. Only the strong can become Mertak, so I will be strong and I will be Mertak".

As Arran noted the routes, he felt his skin skirt slip and then fall to his ankles again; the reminder that Mull was dead saddened him, but he knew that the resources Mull's body had supplied him with, was, and would be, instrumental in his continued survival. The skin skirt slipping brought it to his attention, and Arran once again made a list.

I need to better tailor my clothing for it to be effective whilst I am trekking and climbing. I need to make some warm socks from the fur, my feet are numb and this is just a short scouting trek. I need a belt to hold my flask and weapons securely. Arran's list continued as he turned and began his descent. Arran knew what needed to be done, so he returned to his camp, where he made simple shoes of double-lined fur before working through the rest of his list. He cooked enough meat for ten days, filled his flask with sweet, cold, water and moved on to the next task as dictated by his inner list. After an industrious day the young nomad set his fire and lay down exhausted to enjoy his last night's sleep in his new home from home.

As the morning light arrived, Arran awoke, fresh and ready. He wasted no time that morning and set off on his mission to find the elusive Mertak and eat the sun. Pausing on the edge of the woods, his final goal in sight, Arran took a deep breath to reflect. As he stared blankly upwards at the majestic peaks, he gave a simple saying of thanks, of gratitude, of acknowledgement. If it were not for the deaths of Mull and the Cassartan, he would not be here, about to make an attempt at the peak. Grateful, Arran sang praise to the wind. Rising to his feet, Arran could feel the moist rotting flesh against his skin and the rough, stuffed interior of his makeshift clothes, packed down with grass and foliage, scratching at places against his skin. Arran took up his walking stick, his bone weapons, food and water, and with one last breath he left the shelter of the trees.

For many days Arran trekked, forcing himself onwards, the peaks in sight, his mind's singular focus passed in and out of his visual reference time and time again. The clouds, the snow and the rain would take turns to obscure the peaks and when the weather stopped hiding the goal, a large rocky out-crop or competing mountain took up the mantle. But Arran kept the sight of Theru Peaks clear in his mind's eye. The focus helped him push beyond his physical limits, it literally kept him from falling, from admitting defeat. The wind lashed and whipped at Arran's unprotected face. Sleet, snow and rain pounded his weakening body relentlessly. The higher he climbed, the worse the weather seemed to get, but he kept on pushing forward. After many days of slow progress, tired and in pain, he reached the peaks. The break in the weather went unnoticed as it welcomed his exhausted body. The magnificent location greeted his battered senses. Its power to inspire, to generate awe, soon refreshed the tired traveller. Arran bore witness to one of the mightiest views in all of Lanasia. Basking at the moment's glory, Arran observed that there seemed to be no rain or wind and limited snow here at the top of the world.

The golden mushrooms grew wild across Arran's full field of vision. Elation swept over him. He was here, he had made it, he was at the roof of the world and before him, fields of golden mushrooms grew. The most precious item in all of Gavodia grew freely across his entire field of view. The great mother's gift, glistened under the sun's rays, their golden caps were his for the harvest. Arran wasted no time in picking and preparing the mushrooms, dancing slowly, he ate until one full fist was gone. The rhythm of the dance engrossed the young voyager as he spun faster and faster. Suddenly, his attention was ripped from the ambient warmth of achievement, for between the centre of the peaks Arrans eyes now rested on a sight that surely could not be.

A magnificent temple, the grandest he had ever seen, greater than any other. Even the magnificent Lagoasian structures he had passed on the trail did not match this on any scale. Three magnificent stone towers, interconnected by a wall at the bottom and a bridge at the top. Each tower had a door at its base, with the central tower having the largest of the doors. There was symmetry, artistry and engineering in its exquisite stone construction, Arran was in awe. There had been no word of any temple at the peaks, only of the golden mushrooms of the sun. Tired and confused, Arran felt an instinct to approach the temple, as if his senses had united, performing beyond what he knew possible, yet not an unfamiliar experience. As his senses merged into one they led him to the doors of the temple, Arran could not explain why, but he was expecting the great shaman that greeted him as he approached. The shaman's eyes were alive and untamed, his hair long and unkempt with a beard to match. His clothing was black and simple. As the eye contact broke, Arran's senses returned and a great emptiness filled him.

"Don't worry Arran, you will feel it again, but then it will be under your control."

"Who are you? Why was I not told about you and what just happened to me?"

"I will answer all your questions, for an exchange," said the shaman.

"What sort of exchange?" replied Arran

"All I ask is that you stay here by the doors of the temple for four days and nights, two standing and two seated. If you Arran, son of Irvine and Viki can do this for yourself, we will grant you the answers to the golden mushroom."

At this, the shaman disappeared, Arran's mind was spun rapidly, unsure of what he was experiencing. Everything now felt strange, just out of touch. However, Arran did as he was asked. On the first day, the sun appeared and disappeared, as if it was not even time for breakfast and yet when the second day arrived, it, in contrast was as long as a cycle. Continuously, Arran slipped into daydreams, as real as the reality he had entered, but time after time his will pulled him back. He found it strange that he did not need sleep or to eat food or to excrete during this vast time. On the third day Arran rose to his feet, as he did, he noticed that there was no night, no sleep, no discernible gap between the day before and the new day of the present. This curiosity subdued quickly because the third day was warmer than the infernos of the north eastern deserts. Thirst ravaged Arran's mind, dehydration gripped his body and again he kept steadfast and then it was the fourth day. Again, Arran registered no sleep, no sun rising or falling, just the unmistakable emergence of a fresh day. This day was empty, void of all things which characterised reality. As he concentrated on nothing, the shaman arrived and like before, the normal sensations of the day returned.

"You have done well, young Arran, very well indeed," proclaimed the shaman.

"Thank you, what is your name?" replied Arran.

"I am the black shaman and I am your shaman, I am Mertak, we are Mertak, you are Mertak. We, my young apprentice are about to embark on a journey, far beyond the Aurd but first you must, we must..." The strange, black bearded figure paused, took in a deep breath, similar to Rannoch's long draws on the pipe and then began again. "Educate you into the manner of things."

Arran knew this was the way, it felt right that the man talked truth, but he knew some things, were just out of touch.

"Yes, that's a splendid place to start," said the shaman.

"Where is a splendid place to start," replied Arran.

"The feeling that something's... just not right. Well, start from there. You ingested the golden mushroom. The power of the mushroom allows you to

--for lack of a better expression- - it allows you to actively dream in the highest level of your being, deepest level of your being, most hidden part of your being. All that you are experiencing here is a figment of your imagination, me included, but I am you. I am the higher part or hidden part of you. You see, you have a physical body, but it is not the only body you have Arran." Before Arran's field of view he sees his body lying motionless by the field of mushrooms.

"This is the physical body, but this is just a fancy machine, which for a very brief time allows you to experience a physical dimension, in our case this physical dimension, but this is not all of you. You, Arran are not just the machine, you are this which we are now, the reincarnated soul that has lived a thousand lives and you are also the meat sack over there, living this one. Do you understand?

"So, what you are saying is that I am dreaming?" exclaimed Arran.

"No, I am you, your essence, the 'I' you refer to. I am you, activated by the mushrooms, an alarm call to self-realisation, to your whole self," said the black shaman.

"So, I am you and you are a part of me," replied Arran.

"Yes," laughed the shaman.

"But how can that be?" asked Arran.

"I am what you have heard, your shaman's call, the Mertak self. The sun mushrooms have temporarily given you the power to actively use this resource. The mushrooms act like a bridge that allows for a short time, the different parts of your mind to be linked together, parts that are usually hidden behind the great door. The bridge created by the golden mushrooms allows us, that is you and me, two invisibly linked aspects of the whole to join in plain sight, temporarily. I am the higher, hidden, always working intelligence and today you will experience a glimpse of our full potential. To use your full resource, you will need to tap into areas that are usually reserved for all the things you take for granted; like walking, breathing, balance, digestion, language, dreaming, reincarnating, connecting with the Bar En Dough and more," says the Shaman.

Arran looked up at the black bearded Shaman, trying to observe his features, trying to observe the man behind the eyes, but in this strange lucid, psychedelic realm of his inner mind, he could not pinpoint any features, yet they are there. A similar nuance that my mind applies to: the bastard that plagues my dreams, thought Arran. The veil masking the face danced illusively, always moving, flickering, shifting. The shaman continued.

"Whilst conscious in the waking realm, most Lanasians will never experience this awareness, this understanding, this Mertak consciousness. Few ever awake to the true reality that surrounds them. I am usually safe guarded behind a barrier, a barrier the great maker created when our time began. I am the spirit that flies beyond the body, the intelligence that makes the meat sack work, so your conscious mind does not have to. Acts like breathing, or your next step, or the complicated dance of digestion or dreaming. It is me who makes these things happen. But I am so much more, we are so much more than the meat sack."

Arran once again looked down at himself from this strange third person perspective, seemingly unconscious, wrapped head to toe in cassartan fur, immobile amongst a small field of mushrooms. He was motionless, straddling the roof of the world.

"The golden mushroom creates a bridge and a glimpse which you have seen before, deep in your mind behind the grand door at the end of the darkest corridor in your mind's memory vaults. After you entered that first and only time, I locked the door for your safety. But it is possible for us to be one in the conscious realm," explained the shaman.

Arran shuddered, piecing memories together, attempting to experience clear rational thought in this strange lucid environment of the mushroom fuelled mind he now inhabited.

"I know the door you talk about, I have seen it, I have entered it once, but it was so strange, I retreated, I have since tried to enter it many times but I could not re-open it," said Arran.

"One day you will possess the key..." the black-bearded apparition was waved aside as Arran's conscious mind fought to gain control of the unfamiliar environment he now experienced. And as he did, many questions erupted into his conscious mind, one after the other.

"What was the significance of the four days outside the temple? ... You said the mushroom was a bridge, do I need more mushrooms to make the bridge again or now that I know of the bridge, does this mean I can make it myself...... The door and the bridge are connected, is the bridge the key to the door?... Why a bridge? Is it linked to the physical properties of a bridge, the idea that it links different areas of my mind together. Metaphysically the bridge is the thing which shows the grand door, but I have seen the grand door before. So, have I made the bridge before, without the mushroom, or does the mushroom just allow the bridge to be more accessible? If I am you and you are me, then the knowledge that you have imparted to me, I already know at some level, what else do I know? Does everyone know everything?"

Arran's conscious mind was firmly cut off by his Mertak self -represented by the black shaman standing upon the vision of a bridge that was now crumbling.

"Your journey of the sun is nearing its end, young Arran, but before you go, we will journey to a distant land. Your body is still on the mountain, we will travel, spirit flight and you will see before you return, one possible reason for why you are here, for why you returned. You are more than a meat sack, we are more than the meat sack, we are unbound conscious energy," proclaimed the shaman.

Arran flew at tremendous speed. The sensation was strange in its clarity; it recalled every flying dream he could remember. "This is the here and now," he caught himself thinking, "will I remember this one?" He flew high above the Aurd mountains and then descended across a golden red desert. His flight path continued north beyond the desert to a magnificent living forest, moist with life, abundant with rivers and noise. The fog from the vast swathe of trees merged into clouds as the trees climbed up into mountains once again. These mountains differed from the Aurd. "If the Aurd is one land mass that melded into many mountains with little peaks beyond its mass, these are sharp teeth like peaks, that jutted up independently of the mass below. Way below," thought Arran.

As his spirit reached the furthest lands to the north, the area just before the great oceans began, he approached a land that was almost invisible, hidden deep under a layer of thick fog. From this rare vantage point, it was as if a single dark red veil covered the entire country. Then suddenly and dramatically, his spirit flight halted before being sucked down, pulled by a magnificent force. Downward through the fog, he flew low and fast into this land of monumental architecture and wealth. In that instant, he realised that there were people everywhere, that this was the most densely populated city he had ever seen, and he had seen a lot of cities. Then he saw them.

"These are the people from my dreams, these are the murderous bastards, they are real!" he shouted out loud in his mind, to no avail. Arran panicked. He consciously gave everything he had to flee this place, but he had no control in this strange experience, just like his encounters with these people in his dreams.

As he fought to regain his composure, he looked around. To his astonishment, he saw them everywhere, the dark olive skin, the high cheekbones, sunken eyes, dark red hair and large hooked noses. He now knew that this strange land to the very North of Lanasia is where the people that plagued his dreams came from. "But how is that even possible?" thought Arran. After the shock of his dreams having substance, Arran noticed that the people here, unlike his dreams, shone red, as if each were engulfed within a giant bubble that shone with a dull red flame. "Strange" thought Arran.

Then his flight picked up speed once more. Across the land, Arran flew fast and unhindered until he reached a mighty castle which stood tall on a mountain, one of the most dramatic buildings Arran had ever seen. Then, just as the flight started, it stopped. Arran now hovered over a small hut, architecturally out of touch with the rest of the castle and surrounding buildings. At about thirty feet from the ground, Arran hovered as a man and woman walked out from the hut. They then walked across the moat in thin air. There was no bridge. Arran pushed closer towards them, and then his flight came to a complete stop. Now he hovered directly over the two radiant figures as they talked.

"Do you accept my offer?" said the man.

"No, your majesty," spat the woman defiantly. Arran was shocked. Was he really staring down at the King of the north? He did not resemble the impressions Arran had of the man, but with absolute certainty, Arran recognised him. He was the faceless figure that tormented his dreams with violence and bloodshed. He would recognise that physique, that stride, that voice, that arrogance anywhere. Arran now had a face to go with the body that plagued his dreams. He was hovering above the Namangan King, he was the stranger, the illusive butcher, the destroyer of nations, the conqueror of so many peoples. Arran felt sick to his stomach, his non-real stomach.

"You are here, because you are Mertak, because the mushrooms willed it, because you willed it. Listen closely," he heard the black shaman whisper.

Arran calmed himself and concentrated hard on eavesdropping on their conversation.

It was apparent from the offset that the King was not pleased, the powerful woman talked fast and loud, she would not accept what had just happened, she was not pleased and the King patiently listened as she talked. As the two walked through the gardens and further into the crowded section of the castle, a small group of men gathered in behind the two. The group composed of five men, each wearing different uniforms, each of different shapes and sizes, each walked in perfect symmetry and to the same rhythm. The debate between the woman and the King intensified. Arran could now see tendrils of energy being released by the woman, pulsing out to the five men. The silver light connected the six of them in a strange glowing web that pulsed from the centre of her head. Then with no warning, the five men, attached by energetic tendrils, attacked the King in one perfect synchronised movement that mirrored the attacking movements of the woman. The King's sword came up from its mount in a flash, decapitating the first attacking man. He then kicked the headless corpse out of the way before his head hit the ground. The King then slipped through the gap in the attacking circle of assassins. Clearing the line of attack, the king dived forward, rolling against the ground as he turned back to face them in one smooth movement. Then he began to laugh.

The four remaining pawns fell in around the woman. As she moved to her right, circling the King, her pawns moved fluently, in perfect harmony, mirroring her every step. All five attacked, she with her sword, the men with their hands. These were not warriors, these were the castle's servants, thought Arran, as he watched the strange battle unfold from his floating vantage point. The King freed a few hands from their arms but the men did not seem to notice, nor react, whilst the King attacked. He also began to glow, the bubble that encompassed him grew bigger and bigger, like a giant transparent soap bubble with mini lightning storms, flashing across the surface of a stormy sea. The woman, still attacking with her pawns also began to glow. The King then pushed out an energetic bubble, the glowing, energetic field slammed against the women's smaller field, sending her back a few yards. The king manipulated the force of the two fields clashing to push off of hers and fly back through the air away from her. The King easily jumped back twenty feet, as if an invisible giant had thrown him. Arran hovered, amazed at the impossible spectacle.

"This is your last chance to accept my offer. Accept or die," shouted the King.

"Never," shouted the woman as she charged with her remaining pawns.

Then the tendrils flew out from the king's glowing sphere to the woman and her four pawns. As they connected, the charge stopped. The five attackers changed instantly, their postures, their facial expressions. The once powerful woman's head now hung slightly as she stood frozen in time. Then, in perfect synchronisation, they all moved forward towards the king, slowly forming a tight circle around him. As his sword came up, the first head came off. The soul energy of the man kept its physical form as it left his slumped carcass and ascended upwards. The King's gaze followed it and laughed as he shouted. "There is no escape for you, even in death". In that instance, many of the subtle red energy sacks zoned in and latched onto the ascending soul. As they did, they began to pulse and grow, until it left nothing of the man's soul. "Did you enjoy?" asked the King. The red mist coalesced in and around him, and then the buzzing noise grew. "More" came the noise as if it were generated by the buzz. "You will get what I give you." laughed the King.

The remaining four attackers stood like statues, frozen in place by the King's strange energetic tendrils. The next head in the circle hit the ground, "More" came the buzzing voice again. Then, one by one, the final two heads came off. The King returned his attention to the once powerful woman and spoke.

"You could have been great; you could have fought by my side. I would have shown you how to use your talents. There are few energetic overseers left, even fewer now," laughed the King.

"More" came the buzzing as the Kings sword cut through the woman's neck, before her head bounced loudly off the ground, as her body slumped over, hundreds of red energetic sacks from far and wide descended upon the vibrant pulsing soul of the ascending woman. The king looked up to the red energy beings now latching onto and devouring her soul.

"Be ready with your payment, I have only a few more wars to win in this rotation, before I expand beyond the Aurd once more, to the fresh fields there," said the King. The buzz sounded again. "More,".

What was Arran witnessing? What were those strange tentacles, and how did the King and that woman control those others at will to give up their lives? Did the King just unveil a plan for conquest and expansion of his people? Was he engineering wars to release the souls of his enemies just to feed the thirst of these strange red beings? Feeding them on the abundant mortal men and women of Lanasia. It was instantly clear that this excuse for a King had sold his very soul in exchange for power, instead of protecting his people as a glorious leader should, he had condemned them to death; "he is the anti-Mertak," thought Arran. Arran knew that his direction, his mission from now on was to stop this man from the north from conquering the Gavodeon, from enslaving his people and steeling their souls.

"You will not have my brothers and sisters," shouted Arran.

Information surged through Arran's etheric mind, ideas and images of a quest as great as any Gavodeon legend, of any song he had ever heard. As Arran contemplated returning to the Aurd, to begin his great work, the great fear from his nightmares engulfed and overwhelmed him. The apparition of the man in black that had just been in peripheral vision this whole time, disappeared from sight. His senses faded, his mind quickly became dull and heavy. The King looked up and seemed to make eye contact with Arran's spirit body, Arran reeled in panic. The dark cloud that seemed to cover the city glowed intensely red as it collected around him, becoming denser and denser. As Arran faded in and out of consciousness, the sky above him opened, a brilliant light exploding before the red glow separated into millions of individual lights and flew upwards. Arran experienced a moment of lucid clarity, before being tugged hard by a silver umbilical cord with such force, that the lands below moved so fast, they blurred into greys. Arran, returning to his full conscious awareness was now hovering above the Aurd. In a flash, it had transported him instantly across the known world.

Arran opened his eyes and screamed at the top of his lungs. "Whooooooooooooooooooooohaaaaaaaaaaaaa," as the icy air permeated his awareness, he stumbled to his feet and looked out over the south of Lanasia.

"I have been chosen by a shaman, that is in fact me, so he says, or so I say, or so some unlocked higher version of myself, masquerading as the black shaman says. It looks like I have been chosen by myself to save myself and my people from the most powerful being alive, a magician who has conquered untold armies and peoples." Arran shook his head and laughed.

"Mertak, you have put a mountain on my shoulders, but I will not fail my people, I do not want war, and I am not the man to save the South but I will not fail my people."

Arran took a breath as he realised the true weight of what he had just experienced, the power of the sun unleashed, mind and body separation, Mertak consciousness and the layers of consciousness beyond the conscious, fast as thought travel, magic, shining beings, red glowing Northerners, a powerful, magical king and a possible future.

A multitude of thoughts flooded the young Gavod's mind, 'I must prepare, I must learn, I must not fail my people.'

The thin mountain air and cold winds began to slowly reassert their self on Arran's experience, but they would have to wait a little longer, to reintroduce themselves. Arran was still deep in the thralls of unravelling the experience.

'If our spirit or soul is the real us, and survives beyond death, and we lose this war of wars, the powerful figure in the north and the soul devouring demon gods he worships, will feed upon the souls of all Lanasia. How do I free those who have been eaten? How do I strengthen those who are already being fed upon? I will need help, no man can do this alone, I will find the best of the best, I will risk it all, I will win, I must, for I am Mertak.'

Arran took it all in his stride, as only a youth's optimism can. He realised that he, a simple nomad from a simple people must play an instrumental role in stopping an invading empire, for the peoples that lose in war to the Namangans may not be freed by death, they may not be born again to walk the great trail once more, this thought made Arran very sad.

Arran drew a long, slow, deep, powerful breath. The air up in the Aurd peaks was crisp and clean. He was truly back in the physical. Arran's eyes fixed to the grand views of the forest's far below as he stumbled, still unsteady on his feet. His first steps were uneven. Once again, food was on the forefront of his mind, his belly empty and his thirst needing quenched, he looked to the sky to re-affirm his bearings. The position of the moon showed that only half a day had passed. Arran's senses told him differently. His initial task remained the same, to survive until the end of the cycle. Arran drank deeply from his flask, ate his day's rations before beginning the return leg back to his camp. Arran packed away some mushrooms for himself and Rannoch, then filled the rest of his flask with snow. A new strength encapsulated Arran as he descended through the Aurd. Over three days pass before he entered back into the forests of the lower Aurd.

Returning to his camp, his laughter bellowed through the forest. Catching his reflection in a puddle of melted snow took Arran by surprise, what looked back was almost unrecognisable. The eyes he looked into were strong and infinite, the face now covered lightly in hair and caked with dirt was rugged and strong, the shoulders wide because of the furs. The shock of his appearance passed quickly but not before he acknowledged the change. The excitement of achievement registered. Arran was now a man, and soon he would be expected to be a leader of men. He returned to his shelter and prepared himself a meal fit for a leader of men.

Over two weeks had now passed, Arran had achieved the highest status one could achieve at Mertak. Now he just had to stay alive. Arran surveyed his food supplies. He had half of Mull left and a quarter of the meat from the Cassartan. The food supplies were good, snow was within easy reach for preserving the meat and melting for drinking water. Days passed as Arran conserved energy by meditating and contemplating all he had seen and experienced. As the days passed, Arran found himself meditating for longer and longer periods of time, each time becoming absolutely absorbed, lost in the moment. As Arran meditated for longer and longer periods, the new but familiar experience of his senses uniting came over him as random images plagued his inner vision. Not as intense as the sun, the images were random and confusing, and Arran's mind struggled to compile the information he was receiving. As the purpose of the images eluded the young voyager, as frustration grew and the images became less and less, Arran forced himself back into the calm head space of the initial meditation. As he re-entered this space, the noise and the randomness became clear. In his inner vision, Arran saw Rum being hunted by the Cassartan, through the eyes of a third, through the eyes of Cob. As the information revealed itself, Arran's physical senses returned.

He knew the area of the forest; he had passed it; it was only a short brisk walk from his camp; he could run it in no time. At this, Arran wrapped his fur tight, took up his weapons, two rations of meat and the flask. As Arran ran to help Rum and Cob on the tip of yet another vision, he struggled to determine why he was doing this. He just knew that as Mertak, it was his duty.

The Cassartan smelt the fur that Arran wore before it saw him, unsettling it. Arrans first advantage point was manipulated skilfully, as the beast's savage instincts reacted to the strange, familiar smells, Arran attacked with a newfound speed and focus but this Cassartan was strong, far stronger and faster than the other two that Arran had dispatched. Arran's second attack was too wide, the Cassartan entered his space clawing hard at his left shoulder. Arran's body flew through the air. This Cassartan was not like the others. Rum, covered in one insignificant piece of rotting skin, helped Arran up.

"Rum, distract it while I attack," commanded Arran.

Rum let go of Arran, turned towards the Cassartan and ran headfirst into the beast. Arran attacked the Cassartan from the side as it focused on Rum. Three large, stabbing movements saved Rum's life, the Cassartan slumped, the warm blood steamed as it enveloped Rum. The sheer weight of the beast overwhelmed Arran, Rum and Cob. The three young men sat panting in silence. Then Rum spoke.

"We didn't need your help Arran, we had it trapped"

"You're welcome," replied Arran

"You're different, stronger......... strange," Rum looked Arran up and down, Rum's face expressed genuine confusion.

"Yes, I have changed, you haven't, but we will talk later, now we've got to get out of here before any more of the beasts come," said Arran.

"Go where," asked Cob.

"My shelter's a short walk from here," replied Arran.

Arran released his food and water from his belt and passed it to Rum and Cob. The speed at which they guzzled the meat showed that they had not been surviving as well as Arran. The three youngsters dragged the massive Cassartan carcass to Arran's camp. Without rest, Arran prepared to salvage all he could from the Cassartan. Cobs expertise shone when he used Arran's stone spear head as a knife and skinned the Cassartan with ease. Rum and Arran hacked and twisted the meat from the bones.

"You are Mertak?" spat Rum, he confirmed what he already knew.

"Yes, I am Mertak," replied Arran.

"Congratulations," replied Rum.

"What a surreal conversation, I never thought this would ever happen," said Arran.

"Yes, that's true. I still think you're a dick," said Rum softly with a scowl as he looks away from Arran.

"A dick, I will take name calling over a beating any day," laughed Arran.

"Yeah, I have been a dick to you for years. You can get your revenge on me, once you claim Mertak. I suppose I owe you an apology," said Rum, still unable to look in Arran's direction.

"No apology needed, we just need to survive, that is all that is needed of us," replied Arran, with no sarcasm in his tone this time.

"Well Arran, I am sorry. I am sorry for everything that I have done to you and all that I have encouraged others to do to you," Rum's head fell, as he returned his gaze to Arran.

"All of that is behind us now; all we have to do is survive until the end," replied Arran.

That night, three young men sat around the fire wrapped in wet, damp Cassartan fur, eating meat fresh from the fire.

Demonstrating his mastery of survival, Arran, with Rum and Cob in toe, spent the rest of the month moving gradually closer and closer to the Gavodeon hoard. As the first light of morning broke the dark veil of night on the dawning of the final day of Mertak, the three weary travellers ran desperately, excitedly, back to their homes, to their families and the Gavodeon hoard.

CHAPTER 4 - ARRAN

THE DAY OF RETURN was long, from first light to last light. Families awaited the return of their brothers, sons and grandsons. The day of return was a grand celebration of life for all Gavods. The Mertak participants camped just beyond the borders of the main camp. On hearing the 'day of return' songs and festivities, they knew that the day had arrived and it was time for them to return to camp. As the initiates returned, the horde embraced them, kissed them, serenaded them in song and for those who did not return, they sang songs to remember them and draw their spirits back to the horde, ready for reincarnation.

Only six men had returned this day to take up the seats around the fire. These were Arran, Rum, Cob as well as three others. All but Arran and Rum looked as naked as the day they had left. These six were accompanied by the three men who had returned early, totalling nine survivors. All who returned this day were welcomed like heroes by the vigilant tribe, all had gathered, all were waiting, and all showed their respect to those who returned. After re-entering the winter camp, each Mertak initiate was cheered, their name sung aloud and proud before being given direction to re-enter the hut of Mertak, which symbolised the completion of the transformation. There they were fed and watered until last light.

***

AS THE LAST LIGHT of day disappeared, the small leather yurt door flapped closed and Rannoch rose to his feet.

"My brothers, my friends, my leaders, my past, my future, may the Mertaks approach with the gift of the sun."

Two of the six stood. Arran looked over to his left, confused, dumbfounded and somewhat enraged as his eyes met Rums.

"No Mertaks in six long cycles and now we are blessed with two," Rannoch beamed with happiness.

Arran unfolded the small flap of fur containing his mushrooms. All that lay before him was moss. There were no mushrooms. A momentary sense of dread, like his initial encounter with the Cassartan, washed over him. Rum's eyes glanced back towards Arran as he handed a small quantity of golden mushrooms to Rannoch.

"Arran, do you have the Golden mushrooms?" said Rannoch.

"I have not," Arran was not the weak boy that Rum had once bullied, a timid boy to keep his tongue in check. Arran called Rum's name as Rum turned. As all the young men turned, Rannoch relaxed and Arran addressed the hut.

"In my quest for survival, I must have misplaced the mushrooms!" Arran bowed slightly, then took the floor once more. "I harvested the mushrooms I misplaced from the tranquil grounds of the largest temple I have ever seen, a temple so vast it obscured the great mountain's peak. I might have misplaced the mushrooms when I returned from my spirit journey to the north, or when I was tested by the black shaman over and over. It was a strange few days. Or possibly I misplaced the Sun mushrooms when the black shaman distracted me with tales of a heroic journey, of a quest to save the souls of every living Gavod from an evil King who lives in the far north of this great land. I may have lost the mushrooms when my Mertak consciousness revealed itself to me. However, the most likely scenario of how and when I lost the mushrooms is in the carnage that ensued when I left my camp to assist Rum in securing his life against the great cat beast," Arran paused, looked towards Rannoch, then casually re-took his seat.

Rannoch looked at Rum, his hand still stretched out with the golden mushroom's clasped tightly within.

"Rum, did you also collect these Golden Caps from the same tranquil grounds? The ones near the vast temple that stands so magnificently at the top of Theru Peak?" asked Rannoch as he filled his pipe with leaf.

"I did...," his voice wavered and stopped as he stood there motionless, unable to look up, or down, left or right.

"Rum, you have produced the Sun yet you have not consumed it, you have not transformed. You are standing in front of me playing the same game, by the same rules that you have always played," said Rannoch.

Arran knew that Rannoch knew, without a shadow of a doubt that he had journeyed to the peak and that Rum had not. Arran looked on as Rum's posture, his expression, his confidence slowly leaked from him. In a last desperate attempt Rum retracted his hand and before anyone could react, he forced the mushrooms into his mouth, consuming them all.

Rannoch stood up quickly, forcing the moist air that still clung to him to interact with the warm air of the fire. As the rising smoke danced with the moist air it threw dark shadows across his face.

"Everyone leave, go and enjoy your Mertak festivities. Arran, Rum, stay," said Rannoch. Then turning to Arran, as Rum slumped to the floor.

"Arran, we must stay with Rum and guide him on this journey, he may not be strong enough for what he is about to encounter. His mind is in the wrong space to be eating the Sun, it will just amplify his fear and loss, his guilt and failure. Go now and return with food, fresh water and firewood, we will be here a while," said Rannoch.

With passion, lucidity and animation, Rum presented his inner world, completely unaware that Arran and Rannoch where present. As the hours passed by, Arran and Rannoch gave words of guidance to the inner explorer as his mind erupted, caught in a drug fuelled voyage of no return. Then, the silence gripped him and he fell asleep.

"I think it's time for you to tell me what you saw," said Rannoch, turning to Arran. As Rum slept, Arran recalled every detail of his vision to Rannoch. When he was finished, Rannoch simply smiled, and the three sat in silence. Before long the sun emerged and with it, so did Rum. Slowly but surely, he awoke from the inner world that had gripped him so tightly all night long. As he rose to his feet, Arran and Rannoch looked over. Rum returned their gaze.

"How are you feeling, Rum?" asked Rannoch as he stroked his long dark beard.

"I know that I have violated some of the most sacred rules of our people, but I now know deep inside, that these sacred rules are wrong," said Rum with conviction.

"Ah, they are wrong, are they?" said Rannoch calmly, as he continued to rub his long fingers through his coarse black beard. His lack of reaction invited Rum to elaborate more.

"I am awake, I am an echo of many colliding realities. I am one, one that is connected to all. I am curiosity reborn. Last night, I had the answer to everything... I think I will need some time to understand what exactly happened here," said Rum.

"It sounds like you had a very different experience from me. Yet everything you said sounds familiar somehow," said Arran as he looked deep into Rums eyes, as he placed his left hand over his heart to show the common ground they both now shared. Rannoch laughed, deep and infectious was his rumble, "You will need a lifetime. Trust me, both of you will need a lifetime to understand what exactly has happened here," he pointed to his head and to theirs.

Rum points to his head, "I am glad that I broke the rules, for every one of the horde should have to experience that. If they did, it would unite us, we would all benefit." Rum fell to his knees, struggling to encompass all that he had experienced. Arran and Rannoch both agreed with everything Rum had said as they moved forward to physically support their brother.

"I agree in sorts with you, young Rum, but the Mertak has another purpose," said Rannoch in a low hushed tone.

"The physical survival test of Mertak is to determine who is ready for the Sun. This tradition has evolved over many hundreds, if not thousands of cycles, it is a product of generations of Mertak wisdom. It is this way for a reason, If one cannot deal with the hardships that a month's survival can bring, if one cannot deal with the hardship that climbing a mere peak can bring, then they will not be equipped for the ultimate trial," Rum looked up from his sunken position.

"Ultimate trial?" blurted Rum as he looked up at Rannoch in confusion.

"To meet your inner world face to face, to start the domino effect on the Illusion of all reality, to start the final journey of life, the journey that comes in many names and many forms, yet underpins every religion, spiritual path, great messiah and broken individual who has tasted even the faintest sliver of its truth. Today you, like Arran, took your first steps on the true path, the path to the inner realms, layer by layer, like an onion you will peal them away until you realise that there was no onion there in the first place, that you are the onion and you are not the onion. I have been on this journey into the illusion for almost ten cycles now, and it is a lonesome journey. The spiritual warrior's battles, victories and defeats are rarely seen and their lessons and insights are rarely understood by others but none the less, you two are Mertaks, one earned and one in earning," said Rannoch.

The three stood and hugged. Tears of joy, tears of fear, tears for the sake of tears. Then the leather door flung open and the elders, all survivors of Mertak in their own right, entered.

The day began as the clans and many peoples of the horde met up to reward the new Mertak but before Arran's rewards and rights were given, before the ceremony could even begin, Arran announced his plans to leave the horde. Arran, the silence in the song, a loner in the sea of social interactions and the new potential heir to all Gavodeons, stood in front of the council of elders and told them of his plans.

"I am sorry to abandon my duties as Mertak in training but up there on the mountain I had a vision. Many of you know I have been plagued by night terrors for at least a quarter of a cycle now. These dreams, all this time, were in fact connected to the visions that the golden cap presented to me. I now understand what I must do and as a man free to make my own choices, I am going to follow that vision as I believe it is more important for me, for us, than me staying here." The gathered crowd stood in silence, unsure of how to react.

Arran continued, "I plan to leave Gavodeon territory and travel back into and then over the Aurd and beyond, deep into the north to seek new experiences, to gain new knowledge and follow my vision. The task before me is incomprehensible but I must try."

The ceremony that took place after a new Mertak returned was usually joyous, a time of celebration. This was not and Arran could feel it. The Gavodic elders were outraged at such a suggestion, for Arran was now the heir to Rannoch's position, as spiritual leader. No one, except Arran had reached the peaks and ate the sun, in six long cycles. Arran knew he was Mertak in their eyes. The odd young man had no choice but to bend to their will and the collective will of Gavodeon tradition. There were no other options, Rannoch was old, and Arran knew that prior to him, no one had summitted Theru in the last six cycles. Rannoch needed a new apprentice and may not live long enough to see another suitable candidate arise. Every elder rejected Arran's plans, believing that he had no choice; he was to stay; he was to be Mertak in training. Even Arran's mother and his favourite father, Irvine, joined the side of the council against his wishes. Arran's mind was set against all the odds and at the cost of being exiled from his people and his only friends, his mother and Irvine. He stood, defiant against all, clinging to the prophetic vision that now motivated his every breath.

The great yurt came to a silence as Rannoch rose to his feet, pipe in hand, smoke still billowing from his nose. "Have we forgotten what it is to be Gavodeon and how we as Gavods came to be? Remember, we were once like the settled Lagosians and the Lerrians, Tanni Ma Bar and even the Namangans, before Nencom the great set out on an adventure. A slave from the pyramid cities far beyond the Aurd, he dared to believe that there was more to life. This is the urge that spawned our nation, this urge powered by the Sun that led him to the great Sun, to the Aurd, to the original path. The path which then led him to the knowledge. Arran is pursuing one of the truest and purist of all Gavodeon lore, a vision quest and a quest for knowledge. This is a great beginning for all of us, for Arran's Mertak will transform us all and possibly every generation of Gavodeon to come. The spirit of Nencom has returned," declared Rannoch.

Arran noted that the fear of change had entered the heart of every Gavodeon. His people were now set in their ways, set for generations. Lanasian fears had cemented themselves into Gavodeon culture so subtly that they were not even aware of his freedom, of the gift he had unleashed. The simple freedom of being able to choose one's own path, outwith what was expected of him by duty and tradition. Arran looked at the crowd, trying to make eye contact with as many of his brothers and sisters as he could. Trying to communicate to them his necessity, his purpose. The silence of the moment was broken as Rannoch broke into joyous song.

"They will not feed upon my labour any longer, I reclaim my right to my sovereignty. I will experience all that Lanasia offers and I will share my well-earned freedom with everyone freely."

Arran watched and witnessed Rannoch's power as he brought the great Nencom's words to life, recalling the traveller's spirit back into the heart of every Gavod in the great yurt.

Within his mind, Arran experienced the songs of old come to life, as the vibrant visions danced in sync with Rannoch's voice. Arran looked up to see everyone had been touched by Rannoch's singing.

"Most of you have acknowledged a deep-rooted, unconscious fear of change. This night, we the Gavodeon's will take a collective step towards freedom. Nencom the great built our ideology on the principle that the only thing that never changes is the fact that everything always changes. I hope that things are now clicking into place, phrases, quotes and songs of old should be ringing true in the ear of everyone present. Arran has lifted a great veil. Arran's defiance and thirst for adventure and knowledge has unknowingly to him, forced the Gavodeon nation's first steps in entering a new group Mertak, a new transformation. Deep down, you know that Arran has brought the power of Mertak to us all, he has rejected and reclaimed Mertak for all, allowing us to once more, transform and grow."

All of the leaders, one by one rose to their feet, silencing the chatter in the room as all eyes turned to the one and only spiritual leader of the Gavods.

"Arran, listen, my son. The task you have taken upon yourself is too large for one man. The weight of the world is not yours to bear, you are but one man. Remember that. But beyond the Aurd, I am sure there will be many people who will come to your aid, just as many came to the aid of Nencom. Be kind, be just and open, and the many people you meet will treat you similarly. There is much good in this world, as there is much evil.

Just like the great cycle has many distinct peoples, the north has just as many, maybe more. I think you have seen some of these tribes in your dreams? Every culture and every soul within that culture has the potential to teach you something profound about your journey in this life and of the illusion. Every culture has a different understanding of the mystery of life and of what happens at death. As Mertak, you must learn to make wise choices. Unfortunately before wisdom comes, you will make many bad choices. You must cut through the yak shit without dismissing the truth.

Our journey as Mertaks is always about truth. But there are many truths. Every culture, every person, every friend, every foe will have their own truths. Always seek your truth, for the seeker of truth there are no limitations. Where one truth ends, know that another truth is just beginning. And when one finally grasps one lesson in life, another lesson is already waiting to begin. Just like travelling high in the Aurd, there are many false summits before one reaches the summit. You have begun your transformation; you have begun all our transformations, and one day you will take my place and be the senior Mertak to all. When you merge with all of creation, seen and unseen, whilst it still houses you in this illusionary body. Then you will truly understand what it is to be Mertak.

Only you can do this, only you. The sun chose you. I will always be near, I cannot hold your hand, nor would you want me to. But I will always be with you in spirit, for you are still transforming Arran. Unlike Rum, the sun has unleashed a tremendous power within you. When it comes, embrace it."

Arran took five steps forward and embraced Rannoch, then his mother Viki and Irvine.

"Don't go my son. You are not some Nencom reborn, some hero. You are my son, a natural trader, born for the trail. Give up this folly, of dreams and visions, the north will kill you. Your place is here as Mertak in training. Why would you abandon your mother like this? The Namangans are the north beyond the Aurd and they are born evil. You are not ready to travel solo. Stay...," Arran fought back the tears as he turned his back on his crying mother before exiting the impressive community yurt to retrieve his belongings from his mother's Yurt.

Arran knew that not everyone pitched camp for the winter at the base of the Aurd. A few of the hoard chose more trade instead of settling at cycle's end. These hardcore Gavodeons entered the highlands for its winter trade, a lifeline to some of the mountain folk of the Aurd taking key medicines, tools, fabrics and more. Arran Joined them. After packing his few belongings; Arran left a stranger in his only known home.

CHAPTER 5 - NANOC

"Thoughts, ideas and assumptions are always carried in the mind of the solo traveller," thought Nanoc. And some of these thoughts prove to be true, dangerous roads were in fact often lonely". For example, this lonely road he now walked was long and infamous, known formally as 'Messers Pass', and locally as 'The path of pain', the 'The pirate strip', and even 'The road to death.' For Nanoc, it had been the shortest, most direct route to his destination. For him it had just been another road with a ludicrous name, straight through the heart of bandit country. As his father had always said, "For the adventure, always take the road less travelled and if you're lucky son, for the glory." This road was undoubtedly less travelled and definitely not worthy of its reputation, for no other soul had he encountered, he found no Glory nor adventure here, just a shorter route to Asewar. He recalled another one of his father's phrases, "All talk, no action." Five weeks to get to Asewar was perfect for his schedule, 'life is about risk', this was Nanoc's father's favourite saying. The hot, wet days and the cool cloud covered nights would continue and so would he.

Four weeks in and the road ahead finally branched out, the fork in the road was a very welcome sight, the coward's route had finally met with the dangerous Messer's pass.

Nanoc knew that now that he was back on the trade route there should be a good chance of coming across a small village, a trader, maybe even a convoy. As he walked, he dreamed of a large passenger waggon, with comfy seats and a good supply of meats and wine, some salted nuts and oh, fruit! Nanoc smiled as the fantasy took hold, smiling ear to ear. The huge warrior turned and looked back down the route he had not travelled, his eye tracing the path far into the lowland forests, eager to glimpse a luxury passenger waggon, and then he turned back to face the path in front. No waggons anywhere! "Oh, well," shouted Nanoc aloud.

"Sitting back, relaxing on a waggon for a few days would have been good, sitting on that same waggon eating and drinking would've been even better," Nanoc smiled. "Give these legs some needed rest," Nanoc shouted out loud and proud, smiling as he slapped his thighs.

'Lucky these legs are strong as fuck, with the stamina of fifty mating Elks,' Nanoc laughed at the nonsense he was gibbering to himself and then once again he picked up the pace and headed forward on the not so dangerous road to Asewar.

As the day passed, his legs began to feel rejuvenated from the idea of rest and recovery. The rain abated, well maybe not abated, it stopped raining as much, the sun still clung high to the sky and its heat intensified without the constant rain. The heat reminded Nanoc of his home, of a time long ago, a time filled with lessons, passed from warrior to son, battle tested knowledge acquired over a thousand years. Physical and mental tests fashioned to mould an iron body and mind. Hardships to endure that forged and materialised the reality of the words taught. Nanoc continued onwards, lost in the memories of his family and late youth. Roads met and disappeared, time and time again, yet no fellow travellers appeared. On the third day since he exited the boundary of Messers pass, the weather turned. As the rumbles of thunder began and the wisps of wind developed into the storm they were born for, Nanoc looked back over the road to see the majestic storm clouds rise and swell, roll and tumble. The lightning gods showed their approval. As the warrior clouds danced beneath the titan's battle, Nanoc realised a waggon was coming.

It looked like his luck was in. A few miles back along the trail, a trader's waggon stirred. "Perfect," thought Nanoc. "I'll wait and barter passage." Nanoc's legs, as strong as they were, were relieved when his mind said stop. To his right was a wet rocky outcrop, multiple streams of water that no doubt became a fast-flowing torrent when the rain gods got serious. In the middle of them was a single tree, all of its roots above ground, as it clung to the barren rock. A survivor against all odds, this tree had warrior spirit, thought Nanoc. He slowly climbed seven or eight feet up the wet slab to perch on a rock by the tree of his own nature.

He looked back along the route, his gaze stared out past the waggon, to the not-so-distant skyline where the gods were now in full battle. The storm was angry as it moved high above the distant mountains; the weather was worsening as the day moved into late evening. "Soon I may be sitting in the middle of a stream," laughed Nanoc, "If you can do it my friend, then so can I," he said to the tree, which seemed to rustle in agreement. Nanoc reciprocated with a big toothy smile, happy with his choice of seat as he waited on the distant trader. It seemed to take the trader an unusually long time to cover the relatively short distance between him and Nanoc's rock. As the waggon arrived, a small round man with giant whiskers and pedantic eyes drilled down from atop of a fairly decent sized waggon.

"Hello," bellowed Nanoc. The trader attempted not to look, attempted not to notice, attempted to roll on past.

"Hello, I mean you no harm trader, in fact I wish to trade," shouted Nanoc from atop his wet perch. The small man, visibly on edge, slowed his waggon ever so slightly with a gentle yet precise tug of his reins, a gesture that communication was now open, that he was listening. In one seamless movement, Nanoc bowed to his kin, the tree, and slid down the wet rocky embankment with perfect balance.

Nanoc left the trader no choice but to listen to him, for within two heart beats Nanoc had descended the slab and covered the distance between the embankment and the road and was now moving gracefully, parallel to the trader's waggon.

As he bounded alongside, through the noise of the horse, the wooden wheels churning the wet road and wind rustling through the forest, Nanoc heard the faintest whisper. "The barbarian's movement is unnaturally smooth and balanced for a man of his size. Any man that travels with weapons in full display is a madman or a warrior and both need to be handled with care. To ignore him would most likely mean death. Engage him father, we are ready," came the female voice.

"Ah there is more to this wagon than meets the eye," thought Nanoc as he opened up dialogue once more. "You look like an experienced trader, like a Gavod but you're not, you have no hoard! But this is some wagon," shouted Nanoc as he continued parallel to it on the road.

"Yes, my friend, sorry I was .... eh day dreaming, caught up in my own little world ... you know how long days on the...," the trader's response was cut short by Nanoc.

"I will trade, a seat on your waggon until Asewar for the protection of you, your goods and your women!" shouts Nanoc.

"My women, I think you are mistaken sir...," said the trader.

"Yes, your Women, I can hear them lad, I can smell them as well," Nanoc winked at the trader and gestured with his hand, as if wafting the scent of freshly cooked meat across his nose.

The rain was fast approaching; the gods were almost overhead. Nanoc moved swiftly towards the waggon and as he made the step up, the trader attacked.

"As expected," Nanoc parried the short stab, taking the blade off the trader like he was some child that had misbehaved and quickly handed the blade back to him.

"Now that we have established that I am your protector and guest, I am Nanoc. You're the first person I've seen in almost five weeks, break out the meat and the wine, this calls for a celebration! The storm gods have blessed me with your presence," shouted an overly enthusiastic Nanoc, to the bewilderment of the trader. The trader was in utter shock at what he was experiencing, both physically and verbally, Nanoc continued.

"The storm is going to be slow travelling my friend, oh and you can tell your daughters, wives or whoever is back there that they can breathe, I mean you no harm, I am Nanoc, I am your protector." Nanoc took a long breath and looked down into the eyes of his new travelling companion, "Well until Asewar."

The trader moved uneasily on his seat, then suddenly and with no warning the waggon stuttered and swayed, the horses rose in tandem, as they snorted and bucked uncontrollably. The waggon banked hard from left to right. 'Did we hit a rock or a rut? Have they smelt a wolf? Have we been ambushed?" thought Nanoc. The trader's eyes broke from Nanoc's as they both swayed in perfect balance atop the front seat of the waggon. Without missing a heart beat the trader simultaneously scanned the road out in front, quickly taking in the sides and rear and shouted aloud, powerful command to reassure his horses, whilst his seasoned and trained reflexes retook full control of the rains with a powerful tug. Again, his eyes quickly re-scanned the road and trees to the right. Before the chaos took grip, the trader had regained control and brought order to the chaos.

"Outstanding work, outstanding work indeed," Nanoc laughed, as he often does. He raised a hand and slapped the trader on the shoulder. It was a hard slap but the affection was carried through. "Never judge a book by its cover", Nanoc paused for a few seconds to acknowledge earlier ill-informed judgement, "poor character judgements like that will get a man killed" thought Nanoc. "You are a skilful driver, at one with his waggon and horses. Experience, skill and autonomous reactions built from years of repetition. I see you clearly now." Nanoc looked deep into the trader's pedantic eyes, time stood still as their individual thoughts danced behind their mirrored shield. "Tell me, Master of the waggon, what do I call you?" Nanoc's gesture and tone conveyed nothing but respect.

"You may call me Jarred," stated the waggon master, as he once again looked over his shoulder at the trees just beyond. "Now is your time to earn your passage, the wolves are coming," Jarred pulled hard on the reins and pulled the waggon to a complete stop. "Merrseayaia, bring your sisters and crossbows, here, at once".

From the hemp canvas doors, three beautiful young women emerged, strapped with bolts and crossbows ready for war. Nanoc was instantly impressed.

"Wolves, are you sure Master Jarred? I haven't seen them, nor smelt them," stated a calm Nanoc in the unfolding chaos.

"The horses have senses way beyond ours, they have heard, seen or smelt a predator. When I scanned the road looking back, something caught my eye on the left. I can't tell you what, but my gut sensed something," said Jarred.

Nanoc rose to his feet and in one smooth continuous step, he jumped down from the now stationary waggon. The three women took up high positions atop the waggon, crossbows racked and ready. Nanoc took some steps out from the waggon, approaching its rear with his senses focused." This is more like it," he thought. Sure enough, the horses were right, 'primal instincts trump trained senses every time' thought Nanoc. About four hundred paces back, Nanoc caught his first glimpse of the eyes deep in the forest's underbrush. Behind it, he noticed many more.

Suddenly the tense, focused connection with the distant eyes was ripped from its premature moorings, by three whooshes, followed by two thuds and a whimpering high-pitched scream. The bolts were unleashed from the sisters' crossbows. In complete synchronisation, they had left their strings and travelled deep into the forest to the right.

Four hundred paces from the waggon, the lead wolf had moved out from the bush to the centre of the road, his magnificence in full view in the open road. He looked at Nanoc, again their eyes connected, without breaking contact he began to howl, his song was loud and confident and instantly sent some sort of primeval shiver down Nanoc's spine. "Hold your fire," commanded Nanoc, "they are retreating, their commander has decided". The lead wolf turned slowly and re-entered the woods.

Jarred listened as he walked the waggon, reassuring each of his horses personally, before stepping up and setting the waggon once again in motion. Within a heartbeat of the wolves' retreat. Jarred had the waggon moving and moving fast. Nanoc climbed up and over the back end of the waggon, to the now crowded front seats.

"You slowed down, after you saw me! The wolves were probably following you for a fair time beforehand. The slower pace and complete stop were an invitation to them. They won't be back."

The gods had finally arrived overhead. The rain was always welcomed by Nanoc, not so much by his new companions.

Nanoc turned to Jarred and his daughters, "How long have you been on the road? You never came via Messers Pass, where exactly have you come from?"

"Correct, the locals call it 'the road of pain', I always avoid roads and passageways controlled by pirates and thieves, especially ones with such ominous and uninviting titles. Call it, 'lesson one in being a trader," Jarred's whiskers moved as he laughed and the rain bounced down atop his bald head as the air filled with his infectious high-pitched laughter.

"Talk about bad promotions, they should change its name, the road should be called paradise way, or the shortest route to... Their sales pitch is weak, absurd even!! No one travels the pass because they believe they will get robbed. True?" Nanoc looked to Jarred for confirmation, "If they really wanted to do some robbing, then they need to change the rumours. You hear what I am saying?" Jarred nodded, he couldn't hold back his laughter and neither could his daughters. "You're a funny man Nanoc, strange, but funny, Merrseayaia bring some wine, we have a guest".

After a while, Nanoc asked Jarred if he could retire to the back of the waggon for a quick sleep. It was the first comfort Nanoc had experienced in weeks, a deep luxurious mat, mixed with the scent of Jarred's daughter's perfume. The giant warrior was snoring soon after his head hit the pillow.

The sleep and the dreams were pleasant and rejuvenating until it all turned strange. Nanoc began to fall forward, he was no longer in bliss. The peace and tranquillity that occupied the utopia he was in began to scream his name. His name rang out via a multifaceted, multi-layered female voice, from the sky, from the trees, from the very road he stood upon and from the wolves behind him. It encompassed him. Behind the female voice, the dream filled with loud, aggressive male tones.

Nanoc, realising the truth of the dream, awoke ready for action. Within a heartbeat of his eyes opening, he had burst from the rear of the waggon, sword in hand. Within two more heartbeats, he had taken measure of the scene and was leaping through the air like a god of war, as the highway men plied their trade, blocking in the waggon up front and behind, before moving in to loot Jarred's waggon. This was not a good day to be a pirate thought Nanoc as he flew through the air. The sickening sound of his sword connecting with the first highwayman's collar bone before it exited just below the nipple, got the attention of all around. As the robbers moved their attack from Jarred and his daughters to Nanoc, one by one they fell. By the side of the waggon, Nanoc dealt death to everything that moved. Within moments of his first cut, all the highway men now lay dead. A feast for the wolves. Those out behind the rear blockade, realising what had happened, were now charging forward to secure

the waggon. Nanoc turned and ran forward towards the waggon-come-barri-
cade. Slapping the horses hard, they jumped into action opening the road.

"The road is clear, ride Jarred, ride," shouted Nanoc with urgency.

Jarred took no time in getting his horses up to speed.

"Well, that was exciting. One moment I am dreaming and the next my sword
is deep in some poor bastard's soul," shouted Nanoc as he casually jumped
onto the side of the waggon as it rushed forward to distance itself from the
rear blockade.

"I have never seen anything like that! And I have seen a lot of things," said
Jarred, still in shock at the scenes he had just witnessed.

"Yeah, it can be harrowing the first time you cut a man in half. I was twelve.
But as they say, if you're going to live by the sword, you're going to die by the
sword. So, you best practise. Well, that's what my dad used to always say to me
and my brothers," laughed Nanoc as he smiled at Jarred before turning to make
eye contact and reassure the daughters with a wink and a smile.

Jarred smiled, not knowing how to react to the large barbarian. For the first
time in a long time, he thanked the gods out loud. Nanoc could see he was
grateful for the protection he offered to his daughters. The new companions
travelled the wet road to Asewar for two days, before they parted company.

***

THE STORM GODS HAD followed the waggon all the way here and again they
had blessed him with relentless rain, heat and humidity. Nanoc stood in the
middle of the latest down pour as the town folk ran and scuttled for shelter.
His hempen poncho was now so drenched that it formed streams across its
surface. The barbarian stood content; his gaze focused towards the door of the
building in front of him. The model above the door was two hands interlocked,
gripped at the wrists, which identified it as The Firm Hand Inn.

Almost a year Nanoc had searched for the last part to the puzzle and now
he was sure that he had found it. It had not been hard to find, once he had
arrived. All of the clues and their answers had led him here. The two hands
interlocked above the door had been the confirmation, an invitation of unity
even in troubled times, a symbol to unite for the greater good.

Nanoc made a beeline for the inn. This was it. The year of hard work had
been done, it was now time to collect, and his prize lay just beyond this last test.
One hundred yards of thick, slippy mud. Nanoc looked at life as one continuous
test, this was just one more to conquer and overcome.

The small door unceremoniously twisted inwards, giving out a large creak as Nanoc threw it open. His upper torso dwarfed the door frame of the ancient inn, a rare sight in these parts. As Nanoc entered the crowded inn, every eye in the place momentarily glanced in his direction. The warm aroma of roast meat and beer enveloped him as it battled with the wet musk of the midday rain that now clung to Nanoc.

"Inn keeper, some meat, bread and water. A feast, I am famished," shouted Nanoc. His presence, his entrance, his manner, or lack of it as it may have been, were as effective as usual. It had silenced the room. Nanoc stood by the door and slowly peeled off his poncho, with three quick whipping motions he had wrung out most of the water from his garment. He now stood, half naked in the doorway. Nanoc looked over and admired himself in the large entrance mirror of the inn, a strange yet welcome sight. His muscular physique was covered only by a thin vest and loin cloth that hung tight and damp to his groin and upper torso. He wore a lifetimes collection of scars and traditional tattoos and his leather wrap concealing his weapons that now hung over a shoulder and a small waist bag with various pouches. For a moment Nanoc was lost in admiration of his own reflection, then he remembered yet another of his father's sayings. "True warriors don't do vanity. Vanity leads to arrogance and arrogance leads to a lack of discipline and a lack of discipline in training leads to death on the battlefield."

"Yes sir" replied the innkeeper, who was old but quick to clear some punters from the head table. The regulars scowled in disapproval as they were removed from the table, but this was not for Nanoc's concern If they had an opinion, they would have to voice it to be heard. Scowling instead of talking, and talking instead of acting always made Nanoc chuckle.

'Common folk' thought Nanoc, 'Each and every one has the potential to be a warrior of unimaginable power, yet they hide behind a wall of invisible non-existent fear'.

The innkeeper signalled to Nanoc that his table was ready. With a final shake to remove the last vestiges of water from his skin, he slowly but firmly took the fifteen or so steps to his table, passing the evicted locals with a smile. "Have a seat sire, please have a seat. Let me take your outer garment, I will hang it by the fire, it will be dry in no time," Nanoc passed his poncho and then slid down onto the bench before sliding along until his back was against the wall. 'Perfect' thought Nanoc. Like all great warriors, he had made many strategic decisions within the limitations he was given. He now found himself directly left of the main entrance, with his back against the wall, the bar directly in front and the sprawling tavern laid out directly before him. The tavern's atmosphere slowly regained its jovial, drunken volume as its patrons' attentions reverted to their own personal spheres. Nanoc relaxed into the chair and began to observe everything. It was here. He knew it.

The old inn keeper moved towards the fire with Nanoc's poncho. With a look and a point, the inn keeper summoned one of his serving staff to him.

As she approached the innkeeper, as she brushed past a few of the pub's patrons with a smile. The smile seemed genuine, it seemed to be a key part of her character, observed Nanoc. An always sunny kind of person. Her curvaceous hips, ample bust, warm smile and tactile approach was always welcomed at an inn.

"Take this order to the kitchen Daisy," the inn keeper relayed Nanoc's order, pointing over at the huge barbarian. Nanoc looked past him, trying to portray the idea that he was lost in his thoughts, not trying to draw attention that he was now observing every action. Daisy looked over in Nanoc's direction and smiled. The inn keeper then passed Daisy a silver item of some description, possibly a coin, securing it firmly in her palm, before whispering in her ear "relay his order to the kitchen and then post this in the box at the entrance to the cellar". Daisy tried not to react to the command he gave her, but Nanoc seen it, clear as day. He was asking her something out of the norm. Then the innkeeper continued, "When you return from the kitchen, I need you to ask around, see if anyone has any information on this barbarian. Please be as subtle as you can and act just as if you're going about your tasks, taking orders and the like. Only regulars, no traders, journeymen or folk you don't know. Then report back to me," Daisy nodded and swiftly moved towards the kitchen. As she pushed through the swinging doors, a great waft of the most exciting aroma flooded the tavern. Nanoc smiled at the smell, he was famished.

Thirty minutes had passed and still no sign of his food. Nanoc sat patiently observing the room, following Daisy's every movement, soaking up the heat, the conversations, the smells, the colours, the architecture. The rain outside was still at full pelt, its warm, wet embrace making a single push into the Inn behind the only fresh face to enter since Nanoc's order. He scanned the room again and again, honing in on anything of interest, his mind again and again filled with questions. Nanoc was certain this was the place. But food first.

"All right sir, will that be all," the innkeeper set down a mighty feast. A tray full of meats, bread, cheese, fruit and a flagon of ice-cold water.

Nanoc thumped the table hard and yelled aggressively in the Innkeeper's face. "Yes, that's all-old man". The inn keeper didn't jump, or react in any meaningful way to Nanoc's intimidating display, he simply pivoted on his heels and returned to the bar. Nanoc's hunger turned to delight and pleasure as the first morsel of moist meat touched his lips, his mind quickly focused on the sumptuously tender meat and the excellent flavours they possessed. Instantly, he identified the herbs and spices used. He could taste cinnamon, orange zest and cloves but the last flavour hid deep behind its pungent brothers and sisters. This seasoning is amazing', thought Nanoc.

At the other side of the room, the innkeeper's quest for a tale of the newly arrived stranger began to bare some fruits. In these parts and in these times, rumours often spread fast and grew arms and legs at the same rate. However, good, reliable information could always be sold high or held as a valuable commodity for leverage.

Daisy had done her job well, she had danced and laughed between her punters as she always did, whispering into their ears and noting down anything of interest. No one had even glanced in Nanoc's direction. This was probably not the first time this month that The Firm Hand Inn's regulars had had a strange guest beyond their regular traders and journey men.

As Nanoc tucked into his food, intentionally showing all that observed him that he was oblivious to anything beyond his plate. In reality, he was now more than ever, tuned in on the Innkeeper and his accomplice, the beautiful Daisy.

The Inn keeper took a step back from his bar to face in Nanoc's direction as he sifted through the various notes that Daisy had passed to him.

"Good job Daisy. Do you know why he is here? Why they have been coming here?" whispered the inn keeper. Nanoc smiled as he took yet another bite. He could see the older man was eager to impress Daisy. As the innkeeper began his tale, Nanoc continued attacking the plate of food before him, continuing his illusion of ignorance for all to see.

"No one but I know why the warriors are coming here. I tell the punters half-truths to cover the truth of what is happening, but you have been my eyes and ears many times, Daisy. You have probably added two and two and got four. So let me tell you straight." The inn keeper broke gaze with Daisy and once more looked towards Nanoc before continuing, but before his gaze returned to her, an angry, sarcastic Daisy replied. "You mean to say that it is not just a fad? That the travellers are not coming all this way for Mam's cooking?" Nanoc smiled as he listened into the exchange. "Or that they are just warriors looking for a bounty, you know you have seen it many times over the years. Or the last one you spun, oh, it was the best, that you believed they were here to enter the great darkness, to seek advice from the spirit of the late great Valdahar, the blind mystic that once lived deep below the tavern and as legend goes will speak a truth and give great insight to anyone brave enough to visit his tomb. Knowing that we locals put so much faith in the legends of the deep cellars beyond the taverns' storerooms, knowing as well that everyone, even us staff, stay away from the deepest cellars." Stated Daisy as she whipped back her hair, unimpressed. 'She is fiery, this one' thought Nanoc, before looking back down at his plate.

The Inn keeper took a step back from the bar, accepting the sarcasm and scathing of Daisy. As he turned to face in Nanoc's direction, he seen Nanoc relaxing, kicked back and observing the room. Nanoc watched as he sifted through the various notes that Daisy had passed to him. As he began sifting, reading and gathering the information, he kept a tight eye on Nanoc, content that he was oblivious to all, as he feasted in the corner.

He passed the first note to Daisy and she began to read.

"Rayer seen him arrive with Jarred the fabric merchant and his daughters earlier today."

Then the second note.

"Stev observed that the barbarian was reading a map or something as he walked around town earlier, odd behaviour. This was when the rain began and he took shelter in here. The barbarian just continued with whatever he was doing in the rain."

Then the third, this time Daisy gave some context, for which Nanoc was happy to hear. "Thomas's note is next, he is not a local but as he is now settled here at the end of the track, I asked him, I see him as one of us", "Yes, yes but what did he say", quipped the Inn keeper.

"He said that he fits the bill of the legendary travelling warrior", the inn keeper chuckled as he gasped the words "Travelling Warrior, aka the King slayer", before nodding for Daisy to continue. "The story describes him as heavily built and heavily tattooed, specifically the three interlocking rings of Berg, loin cloth, vest, and weapons on full display..." Daisy was cut short by the Inn keeper's swipe, she was not best pleased. "Not this fucking tale again?... And yes, he fits the description but there are lots of warriors that fit the description. In fact, everyone from fucking Berg, would fit that description, they're all massive warrior types, swinging their dicks everywhere they go. This is why this one probably dresses like this. Just a big dick-swinging attention seeker", Daisy laughed. Nanoc did not.

"Thomas's note continues with his version of the traveling warrior story. Do you want me to read it?" asked Daisy, as she looked across at the inn keeper then over to Nanoc, who coolly responded to her gaze with a flirty smile and a wink. "That was strange, I just glanced over at the barbarian, I caught his eye and he winked and smiled at me. As if he acknowledged what I, what we were saying. I'm sure he was listening. You want me to continue?" Nanoc stayed calm observing the open room as he heard Daisy acknowledge that she thought he could hear her, but the inn keeper thought otherwise. "Yes, continue there's no way that bastard can hear us, he's sitting over there eating like a fucking animal.

He winked because you're a beautiful woman, nothing more, nothing less." The inn keeper waved over to Nanoc and in return, Nanoc gave the universal sign of his right hand over his heart to acknowledge he was good and then pointed at the food with his left hand to acknowledge the food was good. Daisy let out a breath of air in relief and continued. "The story is at least ten years old and has passed many a mouth. The travelling warrior comes from the deserts of the north east, where the Namangans killed his parents. He now wanders like the Gavod but with no routine. They say he is training, preparing himself before he enters Namanga to kill the king."

The innkeeper raised an eyebrow in disbelief at what he was hearing; he struggled to control the deep urge to laugh; he glanced up to check Nanoc, but Nanoc was two steps ahead and appeared to be looking out at the rain once more. As he returned his gaze to Daisy, a loud creaking floor board alerted the innkeeper and his men.

"I guess it is time," stated Nanoc out loud to no one in particular. From the carcass of the feast, Nanoc rose.

Nanoc observed the Innkeeper looking towards his right-hand man, a fairly average sized fellow with a real mean look, who sat by the door opposite Nanoc. With a quick flick of the wrist, his man is up on his feet and ready for action. As his right-hand man stepped towards the bar, a signal clear enough for the inn keeper's other men to approach the bar.

"Don't look now, but old Thomas thinks this one, is the fabled travelling warrior hell bent on killing the Namangan king," His men, noted Nanoc had some discipline, each internalised their laughter but let their eyes danced with the absurdity of Thomas's Story.

Deep laughter filled Nanoc's belly, "I go by many names in many lands. I have heard many a version of my past, all bastardised. One day, I might pay for the truth to be recorded!" shouted Nanoc.

The innkeeper controled his momentary shock as he turned towards Nanoc. "You have impressive hearing".

"Well, the next time you seek information on a patron, do not be so obvious. You have no written sign above your door, just a model, signifying that most of your patrons are illiterate. Much to be expected out here at the ass end of nowhere. Just look at them."

The men gathered by the inn keeper looked to the old man for direction. Anger shone on every one of their faces.

"So, when the pretty one with the big tits started dancing between and writing notes from every god forsaken, ugly mongrel looking mother fucker in here. I tuned in with my 'impressive hearing' and I have some more information for you old man," mocked Nanoc.

The inn keeper held out his arm to ceremoniously hold back his men.

"For it is true, my father died at the hand of the Namangan's, but he died in battle, he died honourably. He is the reason the Namangan bastard has never again attempted to enter Lagosia through the north-eastern deserts. You and every other weak bastard owe him thanks for his dedication and sacrifice. As for my mother, she still grieves my father's passing and will do for another twelve years at least. It is true, I am training, preparing myself for combat against the king and yes, it is a fact that the king and his soldiers killed my father but I train to be the best combatant in all of Lanasia and the Namangan king is not the king for no reason, his skills are legendary."

Silence swept the tavern, tension filled every space, and every man of age now ambled to stand behind the innkeeper. From behind the bar, the innkeeper finally addressed Nanoc directly.

"Your might is much, your hearing is evidently exceptional, your will is strong, you're intelligent and capable but your magic is weak, I fear that it may be practically non-existent. You stand not a chance against the King in the north, not a chance," the innkeeper openly mocked Nanoc.

"If you have the information I seek, you will survive that comment," said Nanoc, his anger showing for the first time, deep behind his eyes.

"What do you seek, barbarian? We are but simple people, we have little...," The innkeeper raised his hatch and moved out from behind the bar, turning swiftly, he signalled to all the men of the tavern with a palm down gesture, meaning that everything was OK and they should return to their duties, return to their drinks. The men scowled at Nanoc as the inn keep moved quickly towards the barbarian.

"Don't waste my time, I have searched for years for the location of a particular thing, a thing which is very precious to me, do you understand?" Nanoc stepped back, waving his golden trinity coin and a bag of northern spiced salt, like he would wave a carrot at a donkey. "They have led me to you. Now tell me when and where the Valdahar will take part..."

"HUSH," the inn keeper shouted over and cut Nanoc short as he announced his true intent.

"Put them away, as impressive as they are, that you collected the correct exchange, but collecting them was just a task, one of many. The genuine challenge of the third gate awaits you, barbarian follow me," said the innkeeper, with a voice of newfound authority. Nanoc did not like this change in dynamic, but he liked that the strange old innkeeper had confirmed that, he was in fact where he should be. 'Business is business' thought Nanoc.

In a hushed tone, the innkeeper continued "We may talk openly through here," Nanoc is shuffled through a small corridor, past the kitchen and down a first set of narrow stairs. "I am the token keeper of the third gate of The Firm Hand Inn".

Nanoc nodded and smiled in acknowledgement.

"Beyond this door, lies your test, pass it and you will receive your final trinity token. Leave your weapons here, they will be with your poncho, ready for your collection after your test. Barbarian, you do know what a spy is?"

"Yes, of course," mocked Nanoc.

"Then in future you may wish to blend in more," retorted the innkeeper.

"I am the warrior laying everything on the line to save a nation. You are an innkeeper and token master. A spy should blend in," Nanoc lets out a full belly laugh. "When I pass the tests and am rewarded with the Valdahar, I will go north, a man like me has no chance of blending in, so why start now? In life, one must be bold," Nanoc passed his leather wrap of weapons to the innkeeper, "Now open the door spy master".

Through the small, wet iron door Nanoc stepped, the door closed behind him fast and hard, right on the heels of the now hunched barbarian, then one by one, the bolts were levered shut.

"Well, that simplifies things, forward it is," laughed Nanoc.

With the door, went the light, Nanoc, now blind to the world, progressed forward, slowly. His eyes failed to adjust to the new environment. Everywhere he looked, all he saw was a single depthless black. Depth perception disappeared and with it, the first fragments of doubt attempted to hammer themselves into Nanoc's mind. The narrow corridor Nanoc now found himself in was so narrow, that with the slightest rise of his arms, his elbows touched the sides, both left and right. Behind him was the door, left and right were the walls, below was the floor, all verified with touch. The eyes registered nothing, not even the faintest glimmer of light. A strange, unfamiliar sensation washed over Nanoc; without movement on his own part, the infinite darkness began to spin, disorientation gripped him, just one step from the closed door.

'Hold yourself together warrior, breathe, relax, fight it, fight it' shouted and screamed Nanoc's inner voice as it forced itself to be heard over the disorientation of his now rapidly crumbling and disharmonious inner world. Nanoc took a long powerful breath and centred himself using a kata from his family's own traditional hand to hand martial art, techniques that had been passed from warrior to son for a thousand years. Harmony was restored as he stretched out his arms and anchored himself in the infinite darkness before him.

'My eyes are useless, they are tricking me, playing with my mind. I must ignore them and feel my way through this test, everything I need is before me. Map it out in here, in your mind' thought Nanoc. With no further hesitation, the barbarian pressed forward, one foot at a time. Keeping all of his weight on the back foot as the front foot probed forward, his arms and hands wedged against the tight walls of the corridor, until his front foot settled. The slow, steady pace sped up as Nanoc found his rhythm, as his mind concentrated on touch and sound as his primary senses. Then, the corridor turned and a sharp descent began. The steps were slight and curved down to the left. Nanoc kept his right shoulder and back to the wall as he navigated the unknowable depths of this descending, spiral stairwell. His next step was different. As his front foot, free from weight probed for the next step, it found it, as sure as it had the last fifty, however this time something was different. His foot, when probing somehow moved differently. As he brought his foot up, removing it from the step in front, the sound gave it away. In front of him, the stairs were flooded.

"Fear," shouted Nanoc, "you test my resolve." Nanoc took three full breaths and descended rapidly into the dark water. Within seconds, he was weightless and with nothing to grab, no banister to help pull him down, he quickly realised that he would need to turn in the infinite darkness and descend head first.

Nanoc began to turn in the water. He began by moving his head down towards his toes, crouching lower until he formed a foetus like position, then once he was as small as he could make himself, he slowly pushed off from the step. As he began to dive down deeper into the infinite darkness of the airless stairwell, his shoulder hit something hard and within seconds, he had spiralled out of control, up was down, down was up, as his mass hit off a wall or ceiling. Again, the fear created chaos in his mind, however, he slowly but surely re-took command, probing in this weightless darkness for the defined ridges of the steps. On correcting his orientation, Nanoc climbed the stairs out of the water. With moments to spare, he emerged gasping, his lungs desparate for fresh air. Pushing hard against the walls of the spiral staircase, left and right, Nanoc anchored himself in the warm air of the void he was now trapped in.

"I will not be defeated," Nanoc reassured himself but unfortunately, the spiral staircase was too tight for Nanoc's colossal frame, for him to take the chance of attempting to reverse under water again.

Invisible in the darkness, his chest expanded and contracted, his heart rang loud as it pumped adrenaline and berserker like rage through his barbarian veins, then with the most primal of screams, Nanoc took one huge breath and once again, moved from the warm dark air into the wetter, scarier nightmare, head first.

Within seconds, he was descending rapidly, using the stairs as a touch guide as he swam, he kicked and pushed his way deeper and deeper and deeper. Then his momentum was snatched away as his head rammed hard into the floor of the stairwell. The shock of an unexpected blow was something he had trained for his entire life. The first time it had happened, here in the underwater, darkened hell was all Nanoc needed to adjust to it. He quickly brought himself to his feet and began feeling around, while thinking, 'There must be an exit, there must be a door'.

As Nanoc frantically fumbled in vain for an exit, now desperate for air, he noticed the faintest shimmer of light. With no hesitation, the barbarian swam towards the minuscule shimmer, fast and hard he pushed and as he moved towards it, it became brighter and brighter. Quickly, it became too bright for him to look at. Nanoc closed his eyes and continued kicking hard towards the light. Time slowed, and the light faded. As soon as it came, it was gone. The darkness engulfed Nanoc again, then with all the emergence of a new life, he surfaced, breaking the barrier between life and death, where he emerged into the cool air of an open room. Unconsciously and uncontrollably, he grasped the air to breathe. Instantly his wits returned, and within one heartbeat, his warrior-trained brain scanned his new environment. He was in a well-lit, natural pool of sorts.

"Welcome warrior, you have successfully passed the first challenge. Your second challenge now awaits. Follow me," stated a tall, cloaked figure. The last set of doors at the end of the cramped, damp, poorly lit corridor opened up into an equally dark, earthy, airless room. As the candles were ceremoniously lit, they sent their dancing fingers across the darkness, bringing the room to life in no time, Nanoc smiled. As his eyes adjusted to the dimness, a sense of joy and relaxation enveloped him as he realised, he would have to fight for his token.

"As a guardian of the token, I must verify you are worthy of its receipt. Every guardian has a previous Valdaharian entrant to test any future prospect. Our warrior, Elgato will be here within the hour, take this time to prepare. The bout will be unarmed combat. If you pass, we will begin the memory and recall tests,"

Nanoc smiled, his thighs quaked with excitement, his heart beat faster with anticipation. He did not need to prepare; he was always ready for combat, even moments after his first near death experience.

The cloaked figure retreated, leaving Nanoc alone to prepare in this underground arena, this home from home. The warrior took a deep breath and stretched, the thorough stretching routine was followed by a quick paced bodyweight routine of push ups, squats and more. As Nanoc concentrated on his preparation, he began to think he may not be the only person in the room. Time and time again, his senses alerted him and time and time again, as he reacted, he found no one in sight. His ears, still heightened from the darkness, heard movement. The impression of someone else's mind seemed to burrow into his, a strange and unsettling idea that someone was watching him, not just from the shadows but from inside his own mind, an invasion of his inner world. Up until this moment, Nanoc did not think that it was or would be possible to enter another man's mind, however the reality of the here and now was challenging this long-held belief. No one was entering Nanoc's mind uninvited, so with everything he had, with every ounce of willpower he could summon, he emptied his mind, 'it's harder to hide in an empty room' thought Nanoc. The intense concentration brought everything back to his breath. He breathed the square. Slow, in for five, hold for five, out for five and hold for five. As he regained his composure, the mental intruders faded away, a flutter of a robe and footsteps were heard. As Nanoc spun fast on his heels, from deep in the shadows, three sets of eyes peered back.

This Valdahar business is a strange one, thought Nanoc. "Show yourselves," shouted Nanoc. In a hushed tone that somehow carried as if it were shouted across the room, "We are priests of the order, we are simply observing as part of the tests, please continue your warm up. Your next test will begin shortly".

"You think the *we are just priests of the order*, yakshit! Cuts it here. Enter my mind again, magicians and I will cut your fucking heads off. Are we clear," shouted Nanoc. This time it reverberated across the room with all the intensity it was projected with.

The priests, in unison said "We understand," and retreated even further into the shadows. A while later, an older warrior arrived into the now well-lit room, a veteran of many a battle, that was for sure. Nanoc could see the classic signs of a man from outstanding warrior stock, broad shoulders, head held high, chin down, powerful calves and confidence in his stride. Nanoc paid special attention to the warrior's face, noting his flat bridge and buckled nose, his scarred lower jaw and cauliflower ears. To Nanoc, this was the accurate measure of handsomeness.

As both warriors entered the centre of the fighting pit, Nanoc knew he had to dispatch him quickly but not brutally, to cement his claim for the Valdaharian token. In the time that Nanoc sat waiting, he thought about his own future; he contemplated the idea that if he doesn't die at the hands of the King or deep in the heat of battle in some foreign land, then this may be the only battle that awaits him. Like this Elgato, he may be forced to become a mere gate keeper to the next generation of warriors, just to earn a crust. The thought; however, was fleeting as Nanoc recalled his lifelong affirmation, that he is the best. Just the thought of becoming a gatekeeper angered Nanoc, a part of his subconscious mind spreading doubt. Nanoc seized it and crushed it.

As the bell chimed, Nanoc moved to the left, circling away from the south paw's power hand, consciously keeping his foot on the outside of his opponent's, as he circled. Nanoc parried the first Jab, slipped the second and thundered a left body, right uppercut, left hook combination that seen the aged warrior slump unceremoniously to the earthen floor. Nanoc moved back and paid his respects.

After some water and a little help to get back to his feet, the elderly Elgato recovered fast. He stepped towards Nanoc and embraced the young warrior. Nanoc took time to speak with the vet, probing question after question about his Valdaharian experience, fighting techniques and more. Finally, Nanoc paid his respects to the old warrior and gave him some gold. Elgato thumped Nanoc's back, his face a mixture of happiness, shame and pity. "Brother, I wish you success and stamina in all your future battles." Nanoc replied "I wish you many more years of health," before turning from Elgato and shouting;

"Inn Keeper, no more delays, get me my token".

CHAPTER 6 - LATHORAN

LATHORAN LOOKED DOWN AT the paper curling in his youthful looking hand; the next two names were the finals in this bracket. This made him smile. Lathoran's skin was pulled tight to his skull as his lips curled into a cheeky grin. Now he was certain that he knew who one of the Valdahars would be. For a few weeks now, he had watched as warriors from all over Lagosia arrived in Partu, each clutching their hard-earned token in hand, ready to exchange it for access to the Valdahar.

Partu was a relatively unimportant city that clung heavily to its important historical past, but it was Lathoran's home, and the brotherhood's home. The city was just over one hundred miles to the west of the Lagosian capital.

The warriors gathered to prove their skill, to win a place, to be one of the two who would lead Valdahar. In reality, Lathoran knew that most were here to bolster their ego, to expand their brand and had no genuine desire to become an undercover warrior spy. But instead grow their name and fame for the year ahead in the arenas.

Valdahar, after all was a word synonymous with the ceremonial beginning of war. The brotherhood had made sure that only those who had invested the time and patience to decipher the clues, combined with the skills to pass the tests, were here with their token. Unlike the arena, where men and women fought for wealth or for personal ideological concepts of honour and respect, the prize here was less tangible. To be victorious here, potentially, would see the warriors becoming responsible for war. A win here would see the warriors leaving their homelands to enter voluntary exile, no roars from the crowd, no adulation, no money. Only the responsibility and fate of a federation of nations being firmly placed upon their shoulders. The warriors selected would have to walk a thin line. Would they become a bringer of war or a bringer of peace?

Lathoran knew this, and had thought long and hard upon it. He knew that unlike the many generations of Valdaharian officials before him, it was his responsibility to really drive home the fact that this was no longer a ceremonial position that increased ones ranking in the arenas. Valdahar was now real.

As a final test, a final entrance to the competition, each warrior on presenting their tokens, was ushered into the history room, to receive a short lecture in the history and tradition of Valdahar. Before advancing beyond the room, they had to accept the position if they were triumphant in competition. Lathoran recalled the words he spoke to the first such group of potential competitors.

"Valdahar is now, no longer ceremonial. Let that sink in," Lathoran recalled the excitement and the disappointment that filled the room with that first group of entrants.

"So, as the potential winner of Valdhar you must know our history. As you know, Valdahar is a strange bastardised tradition that stretches back over a thousand years, a tradition that seen the north eastern states of the southern quadrant of Lanasia unite and become the place it is today. Years of inter-changing national boundaries, of extreme political states, bickering parasitic royals, ethnic cleansing and religious intolerance led to the creation of the Valdahars. Intelligent warriors" Lathoran recalled looking out into the crowd and seeing a few curious eyes looking back, but most were already bored by his history lesson. However, he knew the importance, so he carried on. "Those warriors were sent into their neighbours' territories to seek advantage, to spread propaganda and dissent, to collate, spy and assassinate. But after a time, all the volatile peoples of the south, we have become one, a federation of sorts, we have become the south; we have become the Lagosians. We are the many peoples south and east of the Aurd mountains. Valdahar is the system we created for keeping tabs on neighbouring lands, in those troubled times. Today, Valdahar has become a distant notion of its real purpose, a ritual that awards great honour, with no responsibility. This is no longer. Today, before you fight, before you compete, you must decide. For through that door, only potential Vadaharians may walk," Lathoran pointed at the entrance to the main hall, as he scanned the faces of the warriors before him.

"The truth is, the King in the north has expanded further south. His slow, unyielding advance creeps ever closer, inch by inch, border by border, nation by nation. And now, Valdahar is returning to its true purpose, a system created to protect the south from its neighbours, by training two elite spies worthy of the job."

"The Namangan empire? Are you bloody fucking serious you old bastard? How about you just shut the fuck up and let me get on with defeating all those that think they are worthy of my axe." Scowled, the large bearded warrior evidently not happy with the notion that he must concern himself with, the Namangan empire. There were a few other heckles from the crowd in that first group but Lathoran remembered the quiet, the seriousness and the nods of those warriors who were keen to embrace such a task.

"Yes, the Namangan empire of the north has been expanding, but expanding slowly, progressively over centuries. So slow is their advance and consumption of northern lands beyond the Aurd that most in the south struggle to grasp its relevance. We are ultimately blinded by our own short life cycle. But nothing escapes the gaze of The Brotherhood. It is our job to record all things. Yet, in fairness, most peoples of the south struggled day to day, caught up in their own lives, unaware and uninterested in the north's affairs. Oblivious to the slow creep of death. As the final free empire of the north, the once great Tanni Ma Barian empire, incurred its first invasion by the Namangan empire, we as the south behind the Aurd must awaken to the genuine threat of the Namanagan north. This year's Valdaharians are not fighting for empty, long forgotten ritual and pomp. The winners would have the actual weight of the south firmly on their shoulders. So, decide now, this is the final test. By walking through the door to the hall, you accept the mission, but if that is not for you, please leave by the door you entered," Lathoran recalls the eruption, the bravado, but as he foretold, only a few warriors progressed into the great hall.

On the first morning of Valdahar, as the sun rose clear of the majestic Aurd, its golden rays generated a much-needed warmth as it penetrated the cold icy atmosphere. The warriors who past the final test entered the greatest hall of Juy, an arena that had seen more blood, more action than almost any other, its grand design was not of this era but a lone survivor and a great reminder of a once mighty empire, long fallen to the sands of time. The warriors, as was the custom, were allotted one hour of privacy for preparation before they were summoned to fight. As they entered the inner combative area, many of the warriors continued their preparations, some performing exercises to limber and stretch their muscles, others waved strange talismans in bizarre rituals, others sat deep in meditation preparing their mind for the battles ahead. All day, the Brotherhood called strange names, in their native languages and as they were called, the bearer, be they man or woman, slim or fat, tall or short, entered the pit and fought for their life. The Brotherhood marked and judged each warrior's skill; they recorded notes on every aspect of their abilities, only keeping the notes if they survived. As the day passed, much blood had been spilled, much sweat and saliva hung and moistened the air. As the day came towards a close, only the finest warriors remained.

Lathoran, the leader of the Brotherhood, keeper of the tradition and event organiser, watched with great intensity, watching every fight with the attention, and importance that it deserved, for the weight of the ultimate decision was his. Lathoran knew that two of the finest warriors in all of Lagosia must be amongst the pack, because they were now the only ones left.

Lathoran scanned the crowd, looking for the small, petite figure of Loo, whose skills had captivated him so thoroughly earlier on in the day.

"You there," Miss Loo reacted to the finger pointing right at her by smiling and moving towards Lathoran, her small frame dwarfed by the giants around her.

Lathoran continued. "Mary Loo, please take your place in the pit," his voice was warm and inviting.

As the small woman of slight build entered the fighting arena, Lathoran keeping with tradition shouted "We need a challenger," even though it was an eliminator and they had confirmed Loo's opponent, traditions had to be up-held. Out from the crowd, many figures walked forward, confident in destroying the tiny figure presented. Lothoran gave a quick glance down to the parchment to confirm the competitor's name and reminded himself of their skill set.

"Nanoc Ranoh," Lathoran pointed directly to the huge tattooed barbarian, a colossal figure, a man mountain with the ultimate physical form. This model of warrior perfection walked forward to the centre of the combat area, dwarfing his petite opponent, his weapon of choice in hand. Wet blood still dripped from its edge.

"High one, get this fool a weapon," snarled Nanoc directly into Loo's face. Her calm, stoic like exterior did not flinch.

In the crowd, the banter and betting had started, but one or two had realised that there was no match in this fight. These were two different warriors and one did not fight with muscle and steel. Lathoran observed as the small warrior replied to the cry of Nanoc. Her stoic exterior barely flickering.

"I do not need a weapon, for you have already lost. Start the count," said Mistress Loo as she took one step forward.

Laughter filled the arena as the countdown began, ten, nine, ... one fight. As Lathoran gave the word, Nanoc charged, fast and coordinated, he moved exceptionally well, for a man of his size. But as he charged, he dropped, the initial momentum of his charge seen him skid forward unconsciously across the floor, coming to a full stop at the feet of Mistress Loo. Mary Loo bowed, as was her custom, stepped back from the slumped form of Nanoc Ranoh and waited quietly for Latharon's signal.

"Ah, a fine display." Lathoran was right, an energy dancer, possibly a hybrid? How rare, how unusual. Lathoran, realising the gem that had just been granted to him and Valdahar, smiled widely. The wisdom and experience that Mary

Loo would bring to the Valdahar excited Lathoran. He announced to the eager crowd.

"Brothers and sisters, we now have our first member," Lathoran then shouted "We need a challenger." He then looked at his parchment, announced their names and pointed them out, "please enter the pit." The first man, a large man of Lerr, made the sign to stand down due to injuries incurred in previous fights.

"Okay, we need a competitor from the remaining three qualifiers," said Lathoran.

Now with only one place remaining, all three warriors, keen to display their hard-earned skills, step forward.

"I have been dishonoured," the room deep in speculation about the mysterious and magical powers of Mistress Loo stopped. Every warrior quickly turned in silence to face Nanoc, as the barbarian climbed to his feet.

"I have been dishonoured," this time addressing Lathoran directly. As their eyes met across the now silent room, Nanoc raised his sword and poised ready for action.

"Magic," Nanoc looked towards Mistress Loo and spat.

"No man or woman standing in this hall can outmatch me in physical combat, not even the men of Lerr. If I am not mistaken, I am the only warrior to defeat any man of Lerr this day? And I have silenced three of the bastards. I will not make the same mistake again, sorcerer." Nanoc kept his gaze on Mistress Loo as he continued "physical combat, not trickery or magic," spitting the last words with the venom magic deserved.

"Warrior...," shouted Lathoran, with every ounce of confidence and authority he could muster. He knew he had to retake control of the room, but before he could, Nanoc cut him off.

"My name is Nanoc Ranoh," the large barbarian darted his gaze from Lathoran and Loo, to the crowd before him.

"In all my years in combat, I have rarely been defeated and never like this, by magic. I have only ever seen magic, real magic, once or twice. Until now, I admit, I have been ignorant towards it, passed it off as only working on the weak of mind. Today I learned the truth. I am a warrior, unmatched in physical combat. Most of you in this room know of me, we are not strangers. This room is filled with the finest warriors of the south and I am proud to say that I am also a warrior of the south, however there are many that stand among us today who disgrace themselves and disgrace Lagosia by claiming to have won a token," shouted Nanoc. The crowd erupted, some cheered in praise of Nanoc's words, others jeered and shouted slurs, unpleased with Nanoc's speech, yet none who disagreed were brave enough to remove him from the combat pit.

"Some amongst us did not go through tests or endure years of hardships to achieve their token. Some relied on privilege, others relied on bribes and family connections. I do not stand here and judge a man who is not a warrior. We all have unique roles to play. I stand here and judge men who on no merit of their own, think they will take my position of Valdahar away from me." Nanoc stopped, Lathoran started.

"Your bout is over; your skills were not sufficient," shouted Lathoran, as he attempted to retake the authority from Nanoc.

As he did, Mistress Loo moved closer to Lathoran and whispered in his ear. "I have been watching my competitors all day. He has no energetic defence but his martial skill is unrivalled here in this hall, he knows it, I know it and you know it. The Biergyen warrior is the greatest other in this hall and my choice of those remaining to partner with me in Valdahar," as Lathoran listened intently to Mistress Loo, he simultaneously scanned the room keeping Nanoc in his site. Nanoc looked away from the whispering Loo and continued.

"This is not some game, some empty trophy or accolade. You took the oath to enter this hall. You think you're fighting for some redundant title to flaunt around to your friends, to give you political gain. The immortal king is almost on our doorstep. The Valdahars, from this day forth, unlike the thousands that have come before us, will actually have to go north, beyond the Aurd to kill the King and protect all of our people from the plague that is his never ending, ever-expanding empire," shouted Nanoc.

The crowd burst into roars of laughter, they had all given their oath, but Lathoran could see clearly now that its importance had not registered. To most, becoming Valdahar was still a badge of honour and nothing more. He was glad that those laughing had already been defeated.

"No one here but me wants to go north. No one here but me wants to fight the King. No one here but me has the skills to succeed," shouted Nanoc, even louder this time.

Lathoran now knew that Nanoc was the man for the job, but tradition was tradition and just like Loo, the last place would have to be won. Valdaharian spots were not given. His attention was drawn towards the two warriors who were eagerly waiting and keen to show their ability. The other eligible warriors having weighed up the odds and the real threat of having to uphold Valdahar and decided to fade back to being just another face in the bustling crowd, amongst the other failed warriors.

"Nanoc Ranoh, Cannist of Lerr and Berat the Sarn. Please come forward," commanded Lathoran.

Each of the warriors walked into the combat space, still filled by Nanoc.

"Whoever succeeds against Nanoc will be part of Valdahar. Who will go first?" said Lathoran to the now silent room.

Lathoran watched as the first determined warrior strode forward with glory in his heart. Lathoran knew that Cannist of Lerr was a truly exceptional warrior, well renowned throughout southern Lagosia. The most skilled warrior in a nation of skilled warriors. Lathoran had been observing him all day and knew his only true weakness, and surely all great warrior's weakness was his overconfidence. Cannist was sure, of his lightning-fast sword skills, trained from youth by the finest sword masters, from all over Lagosia and his first-class education and superior intelligence. With this, he proceeded to mock Nanoc Ranoh. Lathoran observed the fatal mistake.

"This oversized child will not get by me; this I can assure you. The child defeated him with her bad breath. Therefore, he is of no match for a warrior of my calibre. I, Cannist of Lerr will be the second member."

Nanoc's rage flared for all to see. "No man has ever insulted me to my face and lived, and I will not make an exception for you, Knight of Lerr," spat Nanoc. The insult and following smirk from Cannist fuelled Nanoc into a berserker-like rage. Nanoc began to scream. Then, with no warning and no respect for Lathoran's signal, Cannist attacked, his sword lunging forward. Nanoc's reaction to the attack was seamless, as the sword looked like it would land. His upper torso rotated, just enough for the blade to woosh past him, just a hair's width from his neck. Cannist did not look amused. Nanoc unleashed his axe as he rolled back from avoiding Cannist's sword. Now with berserk fury firing his soul, Nanoc attacked. Cannist was no slouch, he was a seasoned high-born warrior who had been trained by the best swordsmen his entire life. However, he had not wagered that he would have to use every bit of skill and strength just to survive Nanoc's first attack. As he regained his composure from Nanoc's blitz, the two warriors danced, feeling the distance and watching the fakes and bluffs of their opponent. Then Cannist broke the deadlock and attacked. Again, Nanoc moved just enough to evade the thrust before returning with a counter move of his own. As Cannist parried Nanoc's thrust, the force was so intense, it made him stumble and spin. Experience took over as he used the momentum to spin on his heels and thrust his mighty claymore high. The tip of his sword traced out an arc of light with the sheer speed of its movement. In the lost time between Cannist's spinning attack and his blade attempting to find its home, Nanoc had responded. Nanoc's feline-like defence was almost godlike, his hard-wired reactions instantly countered Cannist's spinning attack by charging forward. Cannist's lightning-fast reflexes and cowardly actions were not enough to save him that day. The crowd, eager for blood did not wait long. By the time he had stopped rotating, Cannist's leading leg had been severed clean from his body. He shrieked in pain; his body shattered. His shrieks were pushed aside by his own frustration and amazement at defeat.

"If only my fate was as certain as yours Cannist of Lerr". As Nanoc's axe left Cannist's body lifeless, the other warrior entered the periphery of Nanoc's vision. Nanoc spun to meet him straight on, he was now eye to eye with the Sarn. At least the Sarn was noble enough to wait for the start of the contest, unlike that coward of Lerr, thought Lathoran, as he began the count. Ten, nine, as he continued the crowd calmed slightly, ready for the next contest to begin. In true barbarian style, as Lathoran finished counting, Nanoc cried "Your destiny is set" and in that instant, Berat the Sarn's battle axe swung towards Nanoc. Full of rage and adrenalin, hungry for another victory, Nanoc's colossal frame launched at the Sarn, to be met with a kick to the face. As Nanoc ate the foot to the face, the Sarn's battle axe swung for his head. Nanoc's own axe met it with a mighty thud inches from his right shoulder. As the two warriors jostled for position, Barat mis-stepped and stumbled slightly, Nanoc took the advantage he was given and with terrifying speed, strength and intensity, overpowered the Sarn before he could reclaim his balance. Without haste, he clubbed the equally large man with the butt of his axe, landing it hard behind the ear, leaving him slumped unconscious but alive on the ground. Out of the silence, Nanoc rose to the centre of the combat area and claimed his victory.

"It looks like we have our two members. I thank you all for participating. Even though you failed, your belief in Valdahar was strong, your will to give up all for the quest, for your country's freedom is respected. I am honoured by all present, and by all who lost their life here today. Thank you. And as you have vowed, remember that at any time our Valdaharians," Lathoran points to Loo and Nanoc, then back to the crowd, "may call upon you at any time to assist them. So please stay vigilant. Come Nanoc, Loo," said a very calm Lathoran as he turns from the crowd.

As Loo and Nanoc followed Lathoran, their chins held high, he could sense their anxiousness, he wondered if they were anxious about the mammoth task that lay ahead of them. As Lathoran walked, he pondered on their predicament once more, he knew that both of them had fought in the big arenas at one point or another to finance themselves. Everyone knew that men and women of the arena were some of the best paid in all of Lanasia. Both of them could have pursued long and illustrious careers but neither did. He knew that both of these warriors used the arena as a bank, their skills so beyond the average arena warrior's skillset that money was of easy access. Yet both were here, following him, ready to give everything to protect the south. As both Valdahrians walked away from their victories in the unfamiliar silence, Nanoc began to speak.

"Well, this is fucking strange," his hand raised to his ear. "All I can hear are those losers leaving. Fights in an arena should always finish with the victor's name being chanted by the crowd. Today we won the ultimate prize, and we are walking away in silence instead of revelling in the limelight of victory," laughed Nanoc.

"I have never liked the limelight of victory," said Loo in a low, hushed tone.

"Well, I fucking love it. Yes, it is a strange one, after a day of continuous fighting, of continuously testing our skill against the best. We are given silence, the ultimate prize this day is silence. Silence should be reserved for the dead," said Nanoc with a smile.

As Lathoran led them through the closest door into a well-lit, well-furnished room, he turned and addressed the two competitors directly.

"As you are in no doubt aware, the holding of Valdahar was synonymous with the beginning of war. Now it is up to both of you to determine if we go to war or not. You will travel deep into the northern territories to gather information, then when you return, if your intelligence warrants it, we will go to war, we will defend our nations. As rare as this event is, our hand has been forced by the southern expansion of the Namangan empire, warriors are now required to implement Valdahar for our people's survival. Our future now rests with you," said Lathoran.

"And if we have an opportunity to kill the king?" asked Nanoc,

Lathoran replied instantly. "Then take it!"

CHAPTER 7 - GIAT

GIAT STOOD IN A somewhat fearful silence, as his father passed him the envelope. It was exquisite. It was made from the highest quality paper he had ever felt, with intricate hand drawn Namangan motifs mixed with inlaid gold leaf patterns and sealed with the Namangan king's very own personal seal.

"It came yesterday son. Hand delivered by the local Namangan official," said Giat's Father.

After opening the letter delicately, Giat read it out loud. "Giat of Hetier is formally invited to The Royal Palace of Summerian The First. I bestow this honour upon you in recognition of your status as the greatest unarmed combatant in the Namangan territory of Hetier". The King's reputation proceeded him. He was, after all, the immortal King and Giat could feel the weight of this expectation and the unknowing of what lay ahead leaning heavily on him as he looked across at his father, as he walked back towards his horse.

"Well, there is no time like the present," said Giat. As he mounted his horse, he looked across as his father rose from his rocking chair and walked towards him.

"Son, we knew this day would come, be careful. You are the best our nation has ever produced. But the Namangan bastard is something else."

"I will, make sure my daughters are looked after, Mia and Anne will be fine but the other two...," Giat laughed and gently shook his head.

"Fareie and Maisy will need your wisdom and strength, they're both so sensitive. I will be away for longer than usual," said Giat, as he looked down at his father from his horse. In those sunken eyes, the deep ridges and wrinkles that now made up his face, he was old but sharp and Giat knew that his daughters would be safe.

"I will my son, the girls will be fine. Jeander will have returned by tonight, you should wait for her, you haven't seen her in weeks," said Giat's father.

"When the King summons you, you don't wait around to say goodbye to your wife, to your loved ones, you leave. He has spies everywhere. She will be fine, she will understand," said Giat.

"True, we will be good here until you return, just as we always have been. You just keep your attention on the King. Remember everything the wisdom has said, it is about the best information we have on him and his true story. Remember everything I have said. The application of knowledge is power, knowing your enemy is true power. But never underestimate them, ever!" said Giat's father, as Giat acknowledged his words, he saw, for the first time, the ravages of time upon his father.

"You have taught me well; I will not underestimate the Namangans. Fret not, I will be home soon enough. They will just want to see for themselves, in the flesh, the legendary Giat of Hetier," Giat winked as he spurred his horse and pulled gently on the reins.

"As I ride north, I will re-live your lessons and the wisdoms in my mind. Your insights have kept me alive all these years. I will see you soon. Keep my daughters and my wife safe," and with that, Giat was off.

As Giat rode north, he recounted all he had learnt about the Namangan King.

The King was both an enigma and an axiom to his people. On one hand, the people knew exactly who he was, they knew his history, after all it was their history and they were proud. On the other hand, they knew nothing of the real man beyond the propaganda of the man they knew and loved.

Everyone knew that before he was the King, before he was a conqueror, before he was a commander even, before all that, he had been an arena fighter. From humble beginnings, he'd conquered the north and taken his crown... or so his propaganda said.

Everyone knew that the King liked nothing more than training in his own gymnasium, that he was handsome, tall, wide shouldered, muscular and still in prime physical condition, strange for a man who had been ruling for at least three generations. Everyone knew that he spent most of his days exercising, honing his potential, isolated from his people.

His passion for power, for perfection and for the fighting arts was well known and celebrated as a sign of Namangan strength, for the immortal King ruled them.

The Namangan territories hosted the largest and most profitable arenas, with most of the others beyond the ever-expanding Namangan borders being managed by Namangans. The King's people held events that catered for all, from novice fighters entering the business as he once did, to the grandest of grand events, held in the royal arenas where international contenders at the peak of their game, fought with a lifetime of hard-earned skill. Here, it was a regular occurrence to see magnificent displays of combative genius.

The King understood the arena; he understood its drama; he understood the theatre, and he knew how to mass produce it. Low quality shows entertained the masses daily, throughout the length and breadth of the Namangan empire. The King's philosophy on control was simple; at all times, the people must be distracted. He firmly believed in an individual's potential for greatness, he had seen it flower so many times in the arenas. He promoted his story as the ultimate example of what a 'nobody' could achieve.

The royal arenas were the most lucrative, attracting the best of the best from far and wide, fighters from all across Lanasia. Most saw the royal arenas to be the only true proving ground of martial skill. This is why so many international fighters, tribesmen, barbarians and noble lords came from far and wide to fight. They came for fame; they came for riches; they came to be treated like gods. The arenas had served many functions for the King: they'd enabled the fulfilment of a warrior's dreams; when his potential for personal excellence was realised, they'd become a place for him to recruit the best warriors for his growing empire; then they'd become a franchise, through which he spread his propaganda; and finally, they became his eyes and ears, the stability for the entire system he had created.

His arenas were, for all Namangans both natives and conquered. Entertainment was for the poor and the elite. All were considered subjects and they entertained all with equality in Namanga. All who crushed and conquered in the royal arenas were summoned to travel to the Namangan capital to meet the King and today was the day for Giat to meet the king.

As Giat arrived at the gates to the Royal palace, he took a few moments to drink it all in. For him, it all happened as if in a blink of an eye. As he stood amongst the tourists at the gates of the palace, he recalled his life's journey to this point. He recalled his first day of training. Training could be a word to describe it, taking a beating may be a better way of describing it. It was at his cousin's wedding; he was ten years old, and as with most Hetier weddings, the single men would wrestle to show off to the prospective women. Giat was transfixed. As the drums and guitars played, the men in turn entered the centre of the dance floor, clinched up, one hand on the waist belt, the other hand grasping tight behind the tricep and wrestled. He was only ten, but he was hooked. From that instance, he knew his destiny, he knew what his life's path would be.

After a few rounds and no new challengers stepping forward, Giat the bold stepped forward. He recalled the laughter, he recalled the look on his cousin's face as he stated "If young, bold Giat wishes to wrestle, then we should wrestle".

His first time had not lasted long, but from the very next day his training had started. Every waking minute would be consumed by it, the movements, the techniques, the mechanics, the strategy. When he had mastered the standing game of his region, he travelled, seeking any and every other form of wrestling. In time, he had mastered them all, from the sheep farmer's back hold to the miner's catch as catch can. Then young Giat entered the arenas. He loved the arena, he thrived in the arenas. New puzzles presented themselves weekly, new systems and problems to master. He no longer had to travel far and wide to find new fighting styles. He just went to work and the challengers queued up to test him. Giat still vividly remembered the opening of the first Namangan arena, it was grand, like nothing they had ever seen in Hetier. They paid three times the money per fight, but everyone knew the drawback. For the Namangan empire would soon be at their borders, to swallow them whole into their empire.

As much as the Hetierians were a fighting people, that was steeped in legend and songs about combat, warfare and the glorious battles of the past. As much as they beat their chests and wrestled at weddings and towns fares. When it came to war, his countrymen bowed their heads and signed on the dotted line. Giat as well, he always thought he should have joined a resistance, or at least listened to their words, but all he ever thought about back then, just as now, was single combat. And with the Namangans, came arenas, warriors, money and the chance for Giat to travel throughout the empire, as a Namangan citizen, as a champion gladiator. He had always been rather selfish in that respect.

As the years went past, the Namangans consumed Hetier, they brought their sophisticated engineering, magnificent contemporary structures to house the arenas, roads, sanitation, waterways, farming techniques, medicine and more. The bad was just as obvious, Namangans brought their culture, their religion, their customs, their rules, the salts also known in Hetier as 'the great white depression' and finally their arrogance.

With his work in the arenas, he had done his best to kill their arrogance, and give his people one last sense of pride by beating their best unarmed combatants, time and time again. To be fair, Giat had always remarked that the Namangan warriors were the very best non-Hetierian wrestlers to be found, but in Hetier, Giat was King, King of the arena. And now, a true King had summoned him here. He had travelled for six months over land, through territories once held by warring tribes and strange cultures, alien to Hetier, all now under the Namangan banner, and when he finally arrived at the centre of the empire, he wasn't expecting the grandness, the splendour, the craftsmanship of the capital. However, here it was and here he was and nothing he had ever seen before had prepared him for the wealth of Namange. Standing with a sign, awaiting his arrival at the other end of the crowd was a member of the royal staff. She was tall, her face was hard and cold. Within minutes, they were off. As they ascended the wide, winding streets, Giat caught glimpses of the palace steeples. Then, as they climbed the last set of steps, they emerged onto an unbelievably spectacular vista that, for Giat, blew everything else away.

From this vantage point, he embraced what can only be described as the grandest castle- grand on a scale he had never seen or even imagined before, but here it was and here he was. As he was ushered through the first gate, onto the bridge entrance to the main castle, Giat instantly realised that the bridge had no barriers. Out of place to the grandness of everything that surrounded it, lay a simple cobbled road that paved the surface of the bridge, right to its very edge. No wall, no fence, no anything between the edge and the ravine below, just the very new and very real feeling of vertigo that made Giat's heart pump faster, his eyes dilate and his feet unconsciously move backwards. It was an unsteady step back; the Namangan escorting Giat found Giat's reaction to be hilarious. Without missing a heartbeat, she ushered Giat on. The escort herself, moved to the extreme edge, as close to the abyss as was physically possible. As she moved forward with pace, she looked back, as if mocking Giat. Giat felt his inner warrior rise. As Giat walked on across the bridge, sticking to the centre as any sane man would, he could not help but shake his head in disbelief, as he observed everyone else traversing the bridge, walking as close to the edge as they could. It was as if they were all insane or on a death wish. Why would you not take the infinitely safer path through the centre of the bridge? What were they trying to prove? As they passed Giat, their faces contorted in disgust, looking at him as if he was below them, weak or feeble. 'Strange these Northerners thought,' Giat.

The castle walls were tall but its moats were deeper, fortified high on an outcrop. Everywhere one looked inspired awe and wonderment of how it was constructed. As she ushered Giat through the second gate, she stopped and pointed at four young women standing high above the ravine on a wooden platform. The clapping of her hands snapped Giat's attention back. She then gestured to Giat, vividly waving her hands, as if Giat had stopped for a break that was not allowed. Again, Giat was walking forward, more gates leading them to the inner sanctums. They continued in the direction of the main castle, as they passed under the last set of gates, they emerged into a beautifully maintained garden. In the centre of the wide-open walled enclosure, beyond the vibrant red and yellow flowers and smooth, perfectly manicured grass spaces, lay a relatively small, heavily weathered building, its walls faded and eroded. It had none of the intricate detail that seemed to adorn every other wall here, 'crude and completely out-of-place' thought Giat but somehow, the more he observed it, the more he thought it belonged here. The hut stood within the castle grounds, surrounded by its own deep moat, filled with spikes, not like the ravines outside but nonetheless they looked fatally deep and treacherous to navigate. 'For any would be attackers, the access bridge must be just out of sight, behind the hut,' thought Giat.

His escort had not stopped. As Giat's attention flooded back from his curious inspections, he noticed his guide was over a hundred yards away, and fast approaching the outer moat to the assumed groundsman's hut, which prompted Giat to leap into a quick jog. As he arrived at the moat, the Namangan was again, strangely standing as close to the moat's edge as one could get. She signalled to Giat to stop and wait. She then began a strange breathing, chanting and arm waving ritual. It looked very strange and laboured. Whilst she laboured over her strange dance, Giat took time to observe her for the first time, noticing the red dot tattooed in the middle of her forehead, her overall calmness and the strange feeling of awe that surrounded her. He also noted, for the first time that she was in tremendous physical shape. Then before Giat knew it, his instinct had taken over, he was leaping forward as his escort stepped forward, as if to catch her from stepping off into the abyss of the moat. Giat dived forward and as he failed to rescue her, his body clenched, as he anticipated the fall. But it never came. He now lay belly down, hovering above the moat, suspended in thin air, high above the spikes, he panicked.

"What are you doing, you fool?" shouted the escort, "I told you to stay still". Giat's heart beat faster, sweat lashed from his brow, adrenaline pumped through his veins as the escort pulled him to his feet with absolute ease.

"Follow me," shouted the escort. At this, Giat stuck to the escort's heels, they moved fast across the invisible bridge towards the strange building, Giat held his breath as he charged across.

"What the fuck was that," blurted Giat.

"It is the invisible bridge, was that not clear?" mocked the escort.

"I gathered that, some sort of magic?" blurted Giat in quick response.

"Not that I am aware of, all I know is it has always been there. I have walked across the bridge every day of my adult life. I have never really questioned it. I just know it is the path to the King's training room, to my training room," said the escort calmly as she gestured for Giat to continue moving.

The escort ushered him with an open hand into the building and promptly left. As Giat passed the threshold of the door, still shaking from the bridge, he knew instantly that he was entering a combat training room. By the look of it, a peasant's training room. The room was sparsely populated with worn mats, threadbare leather bags, desperately in need of repair, no ventilation, no heating, in fact not much of anything. Some old rusted heavy bells and angular clubs, for physical conditioning were stacked in the corner. It was a humble but evidently well-used gym. An unusual sensation of inferiority overwhelmed Giat as he stood, waiting in silence. He did not know for sure what became of the elite warriors who were summoned by the King. He knew some were commissioned into the Namanga elite guard but others, so the rumours said, never returned. 'What became of them?' thought Giat. After a few moments, Giat stretched out, trying to relax, although his heart was still on edge from the magical bridge. As a faint creaking grabbed his attention, the room's door opened.

"Hello Giat, welcome to my training room," the King smiled as he entered the room, relaxed and happy, he gestured with pride at his humble surroundings.

"You met Vertomina; I hope she was courteous? She has been known to be very rude to Royal Arena warriors that she thinks are not worthy of my attention. After me, she is the single greatest warrior in Namanga and therefore the world," said Summerian.

'The second best? You haven't fought me yet' thought Giat.

The relaxed nature of the king totally overwhelmed Giat, this was the immortal King! And there were no introductions, there were no guards, there was no ceremony, there were no title announcements, even an arena champion, such as him had someone announce his entrance into his own training room. Just casual conversation. Informality was the least of Giat's worries. As soon as the king entered, his power was clear, it radiated like he was a god. What Giat was experiencing was how he had imagined the great Hetierian warriors of the past, like Hedered, the half God, as described in the marvellous stories of the origins of his people and recorded in the Peracan scriptures. Giat sat up, easing out of his stretch and moved seamlessly to a knelt position of subordination.

"I thank you, my Lord for bestowing this great honour upon me. Vertomina was not rude," said Giat.

"A good sign, for sure. Now, please rise from your knees, it does not suit a warrior of your reputation," the King paused then looked down at Giat, "or does it? Soon we will find out Giat of Hetier," said the King, Giat looked up and as he did, he felt the fire in his belly rise in anger. The King continued.

"Please take ten minutes to change and prepare yourself for unarmed combat, is there anything you require?" asked the King.

"Yes, thank you Lord," replied Giat as he rose to his feet to make direct eye contact with the king, with his competitor. Then Giat quickly removed his shoes and socks and then just as quickly, he stripped off his outer garments, he now stood in front of the King in just his pants. Giat looked at the king and smiled.

"I am ready!".

The King removed his outer garments and stripped naked. "Traditionally, there are no rules in unarmed combat, this shall stand," said the King, then sounded the gong, signalling the beginning of the bout.

The two men circled the threadbare mats. The King was almost two foot taller than Giat but Giat was wider, and more muscular, especially around his chest, arms and back. Giat had been an arena fighter all his adult life, he had been winning now for eight years straight, with over four hundred victories to his name; he was undoubtedly the best Hetier had to offer. His speciality was grappling, taking his opponent to the ground. Once there, he would aggressively attack the neck, limbs and joints until his opponents either submitted, their limbs or joints gave way to breaking or they died. On those rare occasions, when his opponent had a sufficiently good ground game, he would use his superior grappling to make them work hard. He would wait them out whilst making them carry his whole weight, he would make the fight as entertaining as he could, he loved providing great value for money. 'Great entertainment always brought the fans back,' thought Giat. He would systematically block their punches to make it look like he was taking their punches. Over time, this would force his opponent to use up their energy, then at a time of his choosing, he would choke them out or break them. But often he never had to use his ground skills, he could just punch and kick his way to a victory.

It was Giat who was first to test the water. He lunged forward with a low right, trying to deceive the King as he decoyed with the right, his left came up for the King's chin but the King saw what was happening, efficiently stepped to the side and parried the left uppercut. He then thundered his own huge right fist into the solar plexus of Giat. Giat buckled, took two steps back, composed himself, then attacked again. After about three or four minutes of taking severe counter strikes, Giat decided to take the King to the floor and show him some southern hospitality. Giat pressed forward and released a sharp, fast flurry of punches as the King's hands rose in defence. Giat faked high and then shot low, plunging head down into the King's groin. His powerful arms hooking around and wrenching the King's feet from beneath him, Giat drove forward and turned to the right, countering the King's attempt to sprawl his weight back, making his hips heavy in defence. The King rained down blows to Giat's head, but Giat took no notice as he continued with his manoeuvre and as surely as he had started, he would finish. Giat was now on top of the King, finishing his take down, body to body, head to head, the King on the floor with his back to the ground. To finish the position, Giat hooked his hand behind the King's head to control his posture and anchor himself in the position. Giat relaxed his massive torso. To Giats amazement, the King also relaxed. Then in an instance, the King swept Giat, reversing the position. Now the King was on top.

'He knows this style of fighting, possibly even better than me.' Giat thought as a wave of panic unsettled his short lived confidence. For every move Giat made, the King made subtle counter moves. The King continuously out witted and out grappled him at every turn. Giat knew the strategy that the King employed, it was Giat's strategy and here was the King playing it better than Giat ever could. Giat knew it was just a matter of time before he slipped and the King seized victory. Knowing the odds were firmly against him, Giat exploded with everything he had, trapping the King's tricep, bridging his hips and giving maximum effort to bridge and roll from his bottom position. The effort was in vain. As Giat bridged, the King rode him like a wild stallion, his balance and counter movement perfect in every regard. Then the punches began. Giat had no option but to accept the King's punches, taking them in vain in an attempt to either tire the King out, or by some all-mighty intervention, seize a moment in the flurry, a gap to exploit and improve his position. However, nothing came but flesh and pain.

Giat realised that the King had drilled these techniques countless thousands of times before, possibly with that escort. Giat could feel him waiting, like a predator in kill mode, waiting for him to make the slightest of positional mistakes. It was strange thought Giat, to be the fly in the spider's trap. As the fight continued, Giat knew he wasn't even aware of the mistakes he was now making, all he knew was that he was making them.

In a last desperate measure, Giat pushed hard, as he bridged and rolled one last time. This time it worked, this time he caught the King in his sweep and he moved towards mount, a heavy position on top where he would ride the torso of the King and rain down blows of his own. In the chaos of the moment, Giat felt the excitement of victory, his confidence fed his movement and as sure as he started, he was rolling up on top of the King. Giat's strikes were fierce, he rained down elbows, fists and headbutts with fury he never knew he had. Suddenly, Giat's strength faded and fear engulfed him, his conscious, rational mind could not comprehend the irrational emotion of fear as it ravaged through his very being. Paralysing his body instantly! As his mind lost focus of the fight, as the fear gripped his mind, the king pulled down on a small positional error that Giat had left open as he slumped in his mounted position. A lone high elbow, a weak position that the King liked to call chicken wings. Giat's mind was reeling in fear and the King now had one of his arms. Without hesitation, he switched out his hips and applied his favourite double wrist lock by manipulating the joint back on itself. The fear quickly vanished, bringing Giat back to physical awareness, on the brink of a double wrist lock. As Giat moved his leg up to grab his inner knee and counter, he realised it was too late. The fear that encompassed all of Giat had removed time from his game and gave the King the upper hand. Giat resisted momentarily, just enough to say, I tried, his mind was unusually weak, he acknowledged this and tapped the mat in submission.

The king rose to his feet, pulling Giat to his.

"Fine display, young Giat, interesting take down technique. You might be wondering why I bring the arena fighters to my training room? It's simple, I need to be the best warrior, after all, that is why I am the King. Today, another champion was defeated easily..."

Before the King could continue, he paused and smiled. He could evidently see the anger rise on the face of Giat. Giat knew when he heard the words 'defeated easily' his face had lost all composure.

"Giat, I apologise if the truth offends, but the truth often hurts, allow this truth to let you grow," said the King.

Giat could not believe his ears, yes, he had been defeated, but not easily.

"Giat, we shall have a second bout, this is not to show you my total superiority but to allow you the chance to grow, for I see great potential in you and to inspire you to work to your very best. If I take longer than ten seconds to defeat you, the four young girl's representative of your daughters will survive, if not, they will die! Now ring the gong," said the King.

"What four women?" asks a confused Giat.

"On the platform above Eskers gate, I had Vertomina point them out on the way in, the women dressed as your daughters," the King's voice had sadistic and sarcastic qualities that Giat did not like. In that instant, Giat was transported beyond the gymnasium into his most treasured memories. Across from him, his daughters smiled and laughed as they ate and enjoyed a family meal. Their sweet voices, the scent of their hair, the familiarity of home and his father sitting proudly watching over them all. The memories were real, they were his, but the intensity in which he was now experiencing them was unimaginable. He was there, he was home and his daughters Mia, Anne, Fareie and Maisy sat across the table. They are here with me. Giat stood from the table, calling on his daughters to come closer to embrace him. As the reality of the dream overtook the here and now, as Giat entered further into the mental landscape, unconcerned with the King and combat, the King's voice thundered in from the heavens, shaking the very fabric of reality, and then he was pulled back to the presence of the King instantly.

"What was that?"

"What was what?" asked Summerian.

"My daughters, the dream, I was home," shouted Giat.

"Concentrate Giat, take control of your mind," said the King. Giat took a second. Whatever had just happened, he would deal with it later. Now he had to be present, now was time for combat.

"If I can hold you back for ten seconds..."

"Yes, it is that simple, now ring that GONG," shouted the King.

***

THE KING DEFEATED GIAT instantly, the ring of the gong still vibrating in the air as Giat's body hit the floor hard, unconscious. The room fell silent as the King entered a kind of standing meditation, while Giat's body fitted on the mat next to his feet.

***

AFTER A FEW MOMENTS, Giat sat up slowly, his mind was all over the place, it felt like he was attempting to swim, to tread water, to stay buoyant in the violent churning waters of his own mind. White noise engulfed him as he dragged himself to his feet. As Giat returned to consciousness, the King began to talk.

"I am especially interested in you because of the way you think and how you have been using this to make winning your bouts easier. This is the actual reason you have been undefeated in your land, and this is the reason you're here, Giat. It's the same reason I conquered your people so easily, but.... I forget myself," said the King.

Giat now stands in front of the King, the white noise that had provided the thumping background to the King's words slowly began to subside.

"Yes, your skills of unarmed combat are good by mortal man's standards, maybe even exceptional. You, Giat, were defeated easily by, for use of a better term, magic. I know that may come as a surprise, as no one believes in magic. After all, it is only for outsiders, witches, blacksmiths, lawbreakers and religious cults. But that, my friend is by my design," the king winked at Giat.

"A magician?" spat Giat.

"Remember where you are and of whom you are addressing, young Giat. I am not just a magician," mocked the King.

"I am the magician, the master behind the curtain, misdirection incarnate, master of energy, mind and body," laughed the King as Giat reacted in the most predictable of ways.

"Have you never given it a few moments to think on how or why I am immortal? Or why magic is outlawed? Like most deep, cultural quandaries that have the potential to create uncertainty in the questioner, we ignore them. Most people just accept the lies I feed them. If they gave it two moments to think about it, they would conclude..."

The King takes a few steps forward and hunches over, as if imitating his subjects, in a slow mocking tone, the King whispers.

"The King has outlawed and tabooed magic, yet he must use magic to prolong his life," laughed the King.

Giat sees the King, sees the truth, or was this just another layer of the truth that the King wants Giat to see?

"But enough about me, we are here to talk about you," said the King, in a friendly, warm tone.

Giat brought his hand to his chin as he shook his head in confusion.

The King continued.

"You promote yourself as a living legend, pumping fear into your competitors. I especially liked the way you promoted your last campaign at the great wester arena, your slogan: *'Can anyone defeat a man who's been winning for eight years straight'*. You, Giat, are a master of propaganda and I will use you. You have the blood of the Overseer. I will teach you, train you, and then I want you to lead one of my armies and push our propaganda into the Tanni Ma Barian empire to the south."

***

THE KING LOOKED DEEP into Giat's energetic vibrations for a true, unfettered response and as Giat seemed pleased, the King smiled.

***

THE KING WALKED FROM the training room, with Giat in tow, as the King exited, he looked towards the girls, high on their platform and gave the simplest of nods. In that instance, the four young women were thrown off the platform they once stood on and all at once, they screamed. As the momentum of gravity took over, their bodies fell from sight, beyond the walled gate, destined for the ravine bottom, far below. Slowly, their screams faded.

The King turned to Giat "Did you like my training room? It, as you may have guessed, was the first building up here on Gragersetiums Rock, everything else came later... including me," the King laughed "... Oh poor Giat, you are a sensitive soul.".

Giat's eyes are filled with tears, yet his composure and etiquette are in place. "Yes, my lord I am, I have four daughters myself," said Giat.

"I am aware of this, but in the campaigns ahead, many tens of thousands, hopefully many hundreds of thousands will die," said the King, as if he knew something that Giat was not privy to.

Giat's mind raced. The King was a maniac; it seemed like all he wanted was death. Despite his mind racing, Giat managed to keep his exterior calm.

"I can see the turmoil in your energetic pathways Giat. I see your unsettled by the deaths. Let me tell you that, like you, I also have masters..." The King, swiftly looked up and laughed before continuing.

"Master is maybe the wrong word, colleagues, business partners is possibly better," laughed the King, again unsettling Giat.

"And like all of you, they are demanding. Over the many, many years that our relationship has grown, I have had to sacrifice more and more to continue as I am. Immortality comes at a price! Death is the coin in which I pay, in which my people pay. Decide now, if you wish to be the coin or the tax man?"

CHAPTER 8 - THE KING

THE KING TURNED IN his bed, the luxurious silk sheets gently folded and moved across his frame. The morning sun still hid behind the night sky, the King, after three hours' sleep, was ready for another day. The King slept alone, as he did most nights, no Queen, no mistresses to keep him company, just his trusted aid, Vertomina, she was always close by, day and night, home or away, on the battlefield or in the training room, Vertomina would be within earshot. A brilliant woman. The King did not surround himself in any kind of weakness.

"Vertomina, what are the plans for today?" asked the king.

A brief moment passed before the King's chamber doors swung open, large ornate doors, delicately inlaid with precious metals, symbols and texts.

"My King, good morning, your power radiates today," said Vertomina as she entered.

"Yes, yes, Vertomina, what's the schedule?" said the king

"Today after training, you have a meeting with the major salt manufacturers and distributors, then breakfast, military strategy with Major Tenneah and his people, then a meeting with Jarineef for today's news from the Empire. Lunch today is being provided at the house of the sun. After lunch, you have time in the house of the sun. I will collect you from there at supper time for sword training, then we will eat supper together. A short government meeting after supper, then an appearance at His Majesty's square tonight, for the second quarter of the Argeiest Cup," said Vertomina in one breath.

"Excellent, another day talking to fools, I really need to stop this charade...," the King said, with a wry smile on his face.

"Strength and conditioning today?" asked the King.

"Yes," replied Vertomina.

After an hour in his personal training room, throwing rusty iron around with Vertomina, the King washed and then made his way to the dining hall to meet with the salt barons. On entering the hall, the wealthy and powerful barons of the Western salt mines of Traveras and their distributors bowed, keeping their heads down until the King addressed them.

"Welcome my friends, welcome again to the capital, I assume your journeys were pleasant?" asked the King.

"Ah yes, yes," replied a few of the barons, in union.

"Your Majesty," the spokesperson for the Salters stands.

The king smiled, made eye contact, his exterior was cool and welcoming. His mind, however, laughed at the man before him, standing there shoulders back, as if he were all powerful, surrounded by his comrades, both men and women, all equally smug. Another small man, physically gifted in no way, 'a disgrace', thought the King, most definitely of low stock, but sharp of mind and as educated as an ignorant Traveras mongrel could be, given his limited years and inferior breeding. The King cut his inner dialogue short.

"Yes, my friend, what business do you bring before me here today?" The King knew what was being asked, he knew what was afoot, yet as always, he played ignorant.

"The production of salt is up, the consumption of salt is also up, we are making good inroads to all new territories, laying the ground well before military conquest begins and then setting up distribution hubs afterwards...." Turrum took a big breath and let out a sigh, his head turning from the King's direction as his posture contracted ever so slightly.

"Yes," said the King, as he waved his hands impatiently for Turrum to continue.

"However, there has been an increase in the amount of attacks that our distribution waggons have faced. We believe this is due to numerous new religious cults, that are now springing up throughout the empire, as well as an emerging black market. The cults are spreading throughout the empire, as you will be aware, the key components..."

Turrum paused dramatically and looked around at his fellow salters before continuing, "The core message between all these new cults is a warning of the enslavement of the salt. They all, in one form or another, offer a release, a deliverance from the grip of the salt demons and some even offer spiritual salvation. Salvation, they claim that goes beyond this life and into the afterlife," Turrum let out a slight laugh, which was met with smiles from the salters, before continuing.

"Mumbo jumbo, but no doubt a proportion of the dim-witted savages will fall for it. Small numbers just now but the cult of the pine, the largest of these upstarts has seen significant increases over the last year. Their numbers, our intelligence tells us, are almost as large as all the other cults together. They seem to offer a genuine solution to the addiction of the salts,"

The king looked towards Vertomina.

Vertomina instantly addressed the group, "Interesting, yes, we are aware of this, we have a few good people deep undercover. Just now, we are meeting their propaganda with ours, whilst we collect more information about the main cults and their empty promises. As for the black markets, we will look into it." Turrum acknowledged Vertomina and thanked her.

"Turrum, I am a busy King and I am rather hungry and I wish to break my fast, tell me what you want?" The King was now stood directly in front of Turrum, radiating power and staring hard, intensely, down at the small, pale skinned, blonde-haired Turrum.

"Yes, Your Majesty," said Turrum, in a stagnated stutter.

As Turrum spoke, the King called a magical symbol, drawing it in his mind's eye, the symbol so ingrained through repetition, its initiation is triggered by the thought alone. As his vibration changed, his energy centres expanded, as his mind's eye opened. His pineal gland, deep in his brain burst alive with activity, flooding his senses with information, with sight beyond sight. He seen his minions upon the shoulders of every salt baron. The QUAF are attached, slowly leaching life force, 'the barons it would seem, enjoy their own product a little too much,' thought the King.

"We need help to keep our distribution networks open, at the moment your profit is not effected but if the attacks continue, we will struggle to provide you with the same level of turnover from the salt,"

"HAHA business men, blind to everything but that which is in front of your face. OK Turrum, Vertomina will sort out the details, you will have your men, the salt must flow, more now than ever!" said the King.

The King waved the salt barons to leave. When the hall was cleared of their southern stench, the King looked to Vertomina and laughed.

"How ignorant are we, in this continuous illusion?" laughed the king before continuing;

"I look at them like ants, as they miss that which is confirmed to them, they look at the end users as ants ignorant of the truth of their precious salt, yet my people, so righteous in their own beliefs, look at me the same way. But someone has to keep the empire safe." His laughter was deep and genuine. It filled the hall, reverberating off the walls, changing as it echoed again and again.

***

'I WONDER WHAT I am not seeing. If I am an ant to the King and the QUAF, then I must be missing so many parts of the grander scheme. I must see beyond the false summits he presents, that this reality presents, I must work out the long game," thought Vertomina, in a scramble of thoughts that she knew she was not encouraged to engage with. Her concentration now focused within, as she pondered this fresh stream of ideas that now flooded and captivated her mind. Not for the first time, the vague realisation embraced her, that as powerful as she was, she was but an insignificant pawn in someone else's grand game. Someone she never even had a name for.

***

"VERTOMINA, WE NEED TO bring our cult of the pine spies' home, what is the earliest you can get them here?" said the King, snapping Vertomina out of her treacherous, scheming thoughts.

"Six weeks, possibly seven, once their cover is blown the cult will know of your interest in them," replied Vertomina.

"We know what they are doing Vertomina, they are aware of some of the more esoteric uses of the salt. They will be aware of our interest in them but we must know how they re-activate the gland and we must know what techniques they are employing to achieve this," said the King.

The King paced a few steps, stirring up the dust; it sparkled as the morning light pushed through the small round windows, high on the walls.

"We cannot have a free-thinking people, allowed to reach their potential..." said Vertomina.

"Sometimes I wonder Vertomina, why I suffer your inferior intellect, of course we cannot allow a slave to be free thinking. Their pine cone is symbolic of the pineal gland, it's what the gland looks like, the pineal is in fact the chemical gateway to the ether, to the Bar En Dough, as they call it. The pine undoubtedly doubles as a symbol of freedom, of the seed they are planting. A seed of hope that will grow into their precious freedom! The leader of the cult must be a hybrid, educated in biological sciences and magic, someone who understands his potential. We must find them! And we must crush them. They will learn their place in the order of things," said the King.

"Yes, my King," Vertomina took an unsteady step back. For the first time that morning, she realised the sun was trying its hardest to push its glorious fingers through the dark prison of a hall.

"I will make arrangements today to return the spies to the north," said Vertomina.

"Order them, on their exit to secure leaders, someone with an understanding of their inner knowledge, as soon as we have them in our protection, declare war on the pine, storm their buildings, ban their symbols, kill their members publicly, send in the Sun's shadow men, it's always good theatre," laughed the King.

The King smiled, his thick lips glistened in the only prominent finger of sunlight, as it illuminated a side of his face. The King stretched, balancing on the balls of his feet as he rubbed his back against a pillar for relief. The sudden itch made him laugh with pleasure.

"Ok Vertomina, breakfast, let's eat!".

CHAPTER 9 - ΛNICE

"THE MAGICIAN'S CODE: MAGIC is your birth-right, we have chosen you. Magic is never gifted; it requires hard work and commitment. Magic never travels alone; everything is always connected." Interesting ideas, but I am looking for something a little less abstract, something a little more tangible and actionable, thought Anice as she flicked yet another page in her newly acquired Grimoire. "We can liken the mage to a warrior, except his world is the magical arena beyond the physical realm, his sword is the spells he can call upon automatically, his aerobic endurance is his ability to concentrate." 'I am a warrior magician and my battleground is the ether,' mused Anice. 'Why are all these Grimoirs written by men, for men? I need to change this!' thought Anice.

My Grimoire will start: "By the Witch Anice, daughter to no man, daughter to all men, one of the many abandoned daughters of a prostitute. Here is written the magical practice of compassion, the highest and truest form of Magic. The Magic within this Grimoire has the power to transform the world around you for good." 'Yes,' thought Anice, outwardly grinning at her inner musings. 'No warrior stuff, no macho, ethereal battle grounds, no...'

"Gather round," Anice's thoughts turned to the woman now shouting loudly across the town square. She paused and composed herself. After all, this was why she was here.

"Gather round, gather round the great God of Gods, the great King of Kings is amongst us," shouted the lavishly dressed God woman of the Golden Solution. One of the many cults that plied their trade, promising miracles, offering hope in a time of fear and desperation.

"Gather round, gather round the great God of Gods, the great King of Kings is amongst us." The averaged sized, lightly balding, God woman, pumped her fists as hard as she could into the sky, before ceremoniously pointing those same fists at passers-by, as if shooting them with energy she had just collected from the sky. As the dramatic dance continued, so did her words. "Close your eyes and feel its presence, feel its presence. You can feel it, you feel it," shouted the Golden Solution devotee, as she pointed to the two members of the crowd who had now stopped and stood, incapacitated by some unknown force, eyes closed, swaying gently in the light breeze.

"FEEL the presence, allow it to flow, allow it to heal, to energise, to awaken you, to awaken its very presence from within," shouted the God woman, with a renewed enthusiasm.

Slowly the crowd grew, those who would have normally passed on by, who would have heckled, who would have looked the other way, even those folk had stopped. The power of the crowd was too much for their curiosity, stirred by the legions who were now standing still, engrossed in some abnormal group trance, eyes shut, listening to the woman in fine clothes talk them into a silent, stillness.

As time flew past, one by one, they regained their senses and returned to the otherwise bustling square. Each returned smiling, as they emerged from the silence, each and every one of them had a new found glow, an almost visible radiance about them. One by one they skipped back into life and returned to the paths they were on, as if the Golden Solution had never crossed their paths.

"Praise its presence, praise its power, praise and gratitude to its invite," shouted the devotee, as she witnesses the same miracle that those around her had experienced. Anice loved observing the inner thoughts of the religious zealots she used to administer her seeds. As they experienced their God manifest, she jumped into the God woman's thoughts to experience it first hand with her. 'Over ten years I have been a devotee, travelling, preaching and teaching the Golden Solutions ideas. Never have I seen such results. One or two individuals will stop and one or two may even shut their eyes and one or two might then engage me in conversation. But this was truly a sign. Over fifty individuals had transformed in front of me, by my hand, by my devotion to the Golden Solution. The great presence has opened its self to me through these new devotees. Today was a special day. Today was a confirmation of everything I have worked so hard to experience, everything I have longed to experience, everything I have wished was real but had doubted. But today the presence was felt and not just by me, today is the greatest of days. Today we freed lives, we healed lives.' Observed Anice from inside the God woman's mind.

"Feel good now?" The voice was distant, weak, whispered, as it attempted to force itself inside Anice's mind, but as soon as it entered her energetic field, her talismans had begun to autonomously reject the mental intruder. Anice's eyes opened. She spun, looking for the intruder, simultaneously breaking off from all of the minds she was commanding and focused in on the lone intruder's mind. A single mind remained connected, where previously there had been over fifty. He stood across the street, staring straight at her.

***

IT WAS IN THIS instance that Tam realised that the woman's mind he just attempted to overpower, was no newbie playing at a magician. He had entered a thousand minds and every time he had felt like a god, at this moment all he could feel was fear, inadequacy, weakness, rejection and powerlessness. As he entered her mind, the way he had others a thousand times before, he knew something was wrong, that something was very different. As he entered this woman's mind, a monumental pain had exploded in his, leaving him physically frozen in place and unable to move.

"Calm," her voice boomed inside his mind, filling his very being to the core. Instantly his body relaxed, he realised he had no choice, she was in control.

***

ANICE SLOWLY BEGAN WALKING across the street from where she had been weaving her healing spells, unbeknown to the Golden Solutions devotee and her crowd.

"Why? Who are you? What do you want?" projected Anice as she made the first steps towards his position. He stood frozen in place by the corner of the bakers and the old cobbled lane that fed up to the once royal mile.

"I was ...," he began to spurt out loud.

"Project, don't verbalise," projected Anise

"I was just trying to, sorry I was just," at this he stopped, Anice observed him as he became aware that she was in his mind, reading his naked thoughts, unfiltered. As he realised his undisciplined mind was forming its lies, that she too was observing him form his lies. He had never felt so powerless as he did in that moment.

"Calm, I mean you no harm," projected Anice as she delved through his mind, as she continued walking towards him. "Ah, you entered my mind because you just wanted to let me know that you knew that I was a magician? You wanted to observe my energies to see if I was worth robbing. Ah, you weren't aware that I was the one behind the drama in the square. You thought I was trying to enter the minds of those in the trance, fishing for secrets, weaknesses to exploit, sexual memories... I don't think I want to look any further," projected Anice.

"What have you got yourself into, Tam? She just took over the minds of fifty people simultaneously, she must be a level eight," blurted Tam's inner voice, his every naked thought now being observed by Anice.

"Ah, so you thought I was also in a trance, you were attempting to enter my mind to portray yourself as the 'presence' of the Golden Solution! Unacceptable," boomed Anice from inside Tam's mind.

"Why heal them, what do you get out of it?" screamed Tam's mind.

"What do I get out of it? What do we get out of it?" Anice sweeped round, pointing at specific people across the square.

"What is the purpose of life, Tam? What has magic taught you?" projected Anice, as Tam's mind replied with images and experiences of sexual practices, memories he had stolen from others' minds. These quickly cycled into dreams of power and wealth. Anice silenced his mind and continued with her answer.

"Each of those people will leave this square today and they will try their very best from this day forward, to leave the world a better place than the day they found it. Each will do at least one good deed each day, something small, something within their means, and from this seed that I planted here today, the world will change for the better," projected Anice.

"You healed them, made them happy and sent them out to make the world a better place, all under the guise of the "Golden Solution". Why? Why not create your own cult? Hell, there is...," blurted Tam's panicked mind.

"Because there are hundreds to choose from and they all serve my purpose when the opportunities present themselves. Like today, fifty-two re-energised, re-awoken, happy, positive souls, ready to live a life free from the QUAF. Bodies, minds and energies re-aligned, free to leave a positive mark on the world. It is not important who takes the credit for the deed, what is important is that the deed is done. Why? Because we are all one, my brother," smiled Anice from inside Tam's mind.

"They are FREE? You hypnotised them, you fucking hypocrite, you've made them your fucking mind slaves. I just collected folks' memories to masturbate. You, you fucking hypocrite, you're playing grand puppet master and your ego is telling you it's all OK. Yeah, you're the good guy. You keep telling yourself that," blurted Tam's mind, now in full panic mode.

Anice was now standing toe to toe with Tam at the corner on the cobbles. He was short, well dressed, middle-aged, and he smelt foul. He was staring hard at Anice. His eyes were focused and angry, as he stood locked in his position, unable to move under his own will. The surrounding street was once again alive and chaotic after the strange mass silence generated by Anice.

"Silence!"

Tam's mind instantly complied.

"You referred to me as a level eight, in what system are you referring and how many levels are there, who taught you?" As soon as the questions had been formed in Anice's mind, the answers had revealed themselves in Tam's.

"You're a part-time magician, part-time thief, part-time rogue. You follow the Revalo magical teachings of old Namangan origin, but you don't understand them, you skip things that you don't understand, you're more interested in boosting your ego than performing actual magic. You are a level six on the Revalo scale but only by your own evaluation. Your teacher, a Miss Silverton is an eight, hence you giving me that grade. She is a sister of the sun and apprentice shadow. You have never seen real magic or experienced genuine power," revealed Tam's mind.

"From today onwards Tam, you will devote yourself to healing others, to learning how to make life grow, to making life better, to sharing the many gifts that magic can deliver. You will start at the beginning and learn everything again. This time, you will learn everything thoroughly before moving on. Happiness, contemplation, love and gratitude will be your cornerstones, your guiding principles. And you will wash that stink off."

As Anice projected into Tam's mind, he felt himself being hypnotised from the inside, he felt himself becoming happy, wanting to go forth into the world and do good. To use his low-level parlour tricks to help shape his fellow Lanasians into something better, to spread happiness, joy and healing.

"You can feel it Tam, your core is good, it is pure, you were just misguided. I have freed you from the QUAF for now. I have realigned your energy pathways and planted a powerful, hypnotic seed for your positive growth. This will continue for one week and then you will be free to do as you choose. You can regress to the low vibrating, foul smelling QUAF farm that you were or you can continue on the new path. You have the gift Tam and the choice will be yours."

Tam felt his entire inner world open, calmness overwhelmed him as he merged with everything seen and unseen, momentarily.

"Now you know why I healed them," said Anice out loud.

As Anice left Tam, she began walking in the direction of his master's library. There were so many questions that his mind had generated. Including a good few grimoires and magical items for her to acquire. 'Today is a wonderful day,' thought Anice as she walked towards the magician's home, guided by the memories she had hijacked from Tam's mind. As she moved off, normal waking reality, again closed in around her, the bustle of the crowd, the midday sun warm on her bust, the unevenness of the cobbles beneath her feet, the smell of fresh bread from the bakery. Anice disappeared around the next corner, a bounce in her step and a smile from ear to ear.

After a few days' walk and a few small opportunities to do good, Anice caught her first glimpse of the high magician's magnificent home. From high on the crest of the valley, she could see down to the other side, where the grand building sat. It was the only building that was lit up in the fading light of the evening sun and everything matched with the memories extracted from Tam perfectly.

"Finally, I am here, happy new grimoire day," laughed Anice.

"You there, get away from the gates, sex workers enter round back. Don't let this happen again or you will be beaten and recover no pay." The guard was big, armoured and exceedingly confident. Anice weakened her posture, bowed her head slightly and replied.

"Yes sire, thank you." As she moved past him in the rough direction of the back entrance, Anice slipped inside the guard's mind effortlessly.

'Fucking dirty, fucking whore, I will be sure to get a shot on her. Look at those fucking curves, those big titties bouncing on my face. A fucking waste. Look at her, completely unaware that she is never coming out of here alive."

At this very point, Anice glanced back over her shoulder as she continued to progress forwards towards the back entrance. She felt the shudder in his mind as he caught himself thinking. 'Did I say that out loud? That was weird. It was as if she heard me. Weird!'

Anice continued to the rear entrance and the guard promptly regained his posture, sureness of mind and position outside the gate.

As Anice entered the rear entrance, passing another guard, one who was far less interested in her job as she waved Anice in, with a stern facial gesture and swift flick of her head. She was then quickly ushered by another woman, not a guard, this worker was small, petite and carried the traumatic energetic signatures of someone who had been heavily abused. It was like her energy and her body were misaligned, open, vacant. She had definitely been removed from her body at some point and not wilfully, something here was off. Alarm bells rang in Anice's mind as she was ushered into a sizeable side room to meet the Madam. She was an older woman whose beauty still lingered like an echo, pushing through deep wrinkles and harsh sun-dried skin, her eyes where still sharp. Instantly, she stopped when Anice entered.

Anice had probed the madam's mind the instant she had entered the room. As the Madam stood there about to address Anice, Anice was ready.

"Ah she has arrived. Materson has done well, she is glorious. Miss Silverton will be pleased," thought the Madam, observed by Anice.

Anice met the Madam's eyes, bowed slightly, keeping eye contact throughout the movement, then with her eyes and a slight jiggle of her cleavage, she uttered as seductively as she could "Madam".

Anice probed her mind, looking for the directions to the library or magical shrine so she could correlate and compare to the information gained from Tam. The room she was interested in was at the rear of the house and easily accessible. With no time to waste and with an urgent desire to leave this strange home, Anice began a simple reprogramming spell. As the Madam returned to awareness, she looked directly at Anice and barked, "Ok, leave my sight and make sure I do not see you again until tonight!" Anice did as she was told.

The house was old, grand and full of wealth. The walls were loaded with family portraits and exquisite works of art, stuffed animal heads, weapons and maps. As Anice navigated her way to the library, she worked her spell, an inner ritual of symbols that called upon her bound spirits, extra physical beings from some other dimension that she had bound through previous magical incantations. She had sent them ahead of her to find the most powerful grimoires and magical talismans. As Anice entered the library, four books glowed in her mind as she scanned the walls packed with books. Without hesitation, she grabbed them. 'Luckily, they are all small,' thought Anice. Then as she moved towards the door, she felt a great tug from her mind to the deep far right of the library; her bound spirits had found something else. As she placed the last of the four books into her satchel and began making her way to the area at the rear of the library, the main door to the room crashed open.

Anice dived behind the bookshelf in front, from here she could see the glowing talisman. Then, without warning, a great dark entity engulfed her bound spirit, ripping the magical bond from her mind. In that instance, she screamed out both physically and mentally.

"Come out, now," shouted Miss Silverton.

Anice centred her inner self and secured the talisman before walking out from behind the bookshelf to confront her caller.

"Hello, Miss Silverton, I presume?" said Anice. Silverton stood directly in front of Anice, her face contorted in anger.

"Who are you and what are you doing in my library?" shouted Miss Silverton.

Whilst the two sentences of dialogue had been verbalised, both magicians had sent out their feelers to probe the magical potential of the other. 'This was a level eight in the Revalo magical teachings,' thought Anice. She realised there and then that young Tam was extremely self-aggrandising in believing that he was a level six. Comparing Tam to Miss Silverton on any scale was ridiculous. If there was a scale, Tam was a one and just barely.

"As you can no doubt sense, my Magic differs greatly from yours. I use my gifts to spread love and to unlock potential, but do not underestimate me or believe for a second that I will not defend myself if need be. My mission in this life is far more important to me than you. You may have noticed that your primitive dark incantations based on the weak Revalo magical teachings are no match for the abundance of magical disciplines I have at my disposal," Anice stated, as a matter of fact.

Miss Silverton stepped back, and as she did, she looked left and then right, as if looking for an accomplice.

"What are you doing here, in my home? Why are you here? And why on this night of all nights? This cannot be a coincidence. Explain yourself or you will not leave this room alive!" demanded Miss Silverton.

"I travel and visit magical libraries. I am here to look at your impressive library, nothing more, nothing less. Regarding your threats, if I was not sure that I could defend myself, I would not be here," stated Anice.

"I think, that you think, you are better than you are. My QUAF consumed your bound entity! I think you know you are no match for me," said Miss Silverton.

"You sent a warrior to slay a seeker, and you believe that this is a measure of your Magic? The QUAF you sent is not under your control, quite the contrary. You are its servant; your entire magical system is based on the scraps they give you. Your entire concept of what Magic is and what its purpose is, is so misunderstood. You are a servant of the QUAF and your power is an illusion and of no match for me and mine," said Anice.

As Anice finished speaking, Silverton squeezed the talisman held tight in her right hand and unleashed her strongest spell, forcing open a rift to the ethereal dimensions of the QUAF. Her masters heard her call materialising in the ether instantly, as if they were already present. The buzzing came, its intensity filled everything around them. Anice felt the rift tearing across the ether, the instant it began and cast an internal spell on pure instinct, ramping up her vibration, projecting out from her core, a continuously resonating, super-fast vibrational cage that now surrounded her. The low vibrations of dark energy utilised by this fraction of the QUAF could not interact with her in any way. Instead of retreating to the rift in the ether from where it came, it turned and dived straight into Miss Silverton. It had been called to a feast, and a feast it would have.

With a short sharp mental jab, Anice punctured through the now weakened defences of Silverton's mind. At first, she reeled back at what she encountered, Tam's mind was tame compared to this darkness. Silverton's soul, her light was almost gone, her consciousness, her very being, was locked deep within, whilst multiple QUAF ruled the roost, occupying the conscious space where her light should have been. The buzzing engulfed her. Then it made sense, Tam's mind had revealed that she was an apprentice Shadow. She had volunteered herself to the QUAF, to become a shadow. 'Not on my watch,' thought Anice. With every ounce of her will that she could command, Anice forced her way deep into this QUAF infested host, right to the very core, where Silverton's consciousness, she hoped, still flickered. Transferring her own energy into Silverton, Anice synchronised Silverton's vibration to hers, as her vibration increased. The once comfortable, all you can eat buffet venue for the live-in QUAFS closed in around them. As Silverton's consciousness regained enough light to remember, to realise that being a host for the QUAF was not what she wanted. Once again, it fought for its own freedom. The two magicians teamed up against the QUAF. Deep within the mind of Miss Silverton, a magical battle raged for the very seat of her conscious awareness. However, the QUAF were intelligent beings, not the simple dark entities they were made out to be, and as the resistance to their occupation increased, they abandoned Miss Silverton and returned to the ether. The buzzing stopped. Anice cast her spell, leaving another disciple for good as she left the library and then the grounds with her new grimoires and talisman to continue on her quest.

CHAPTER 10
- ARRAN -
ENTERING THE
AURD

THE FIRST DAY TRAVELLING with the small troop up into the Aurd was strange. They knew he was Mertak by title and they gave him the respect earned but the winter traders of the Gavodeon nation were slightly different from the whole. The twenty Gavods and their yaks slowly made their way up into the mountains. The paths were not as steep as the direct routes that Arran had had to take to reach the summits of Theru mountain, but they were steep nonetheless and difficult, more so as he had not yet regained his strength after his month's ordeal.

"So young Mertak, you think you're special? Above the rest of us because you ate some mushrooms?" asked Etive.

"Far from special, all I ever wanted to do was prove to my mother and Irvine that I was worthy of the social sacrifice they had made. I have always been a silence in the song. I just wanted to do them proud. Summit Theru, eat the sun, survive the moon cycle and return. Little did I know that the mushrooms would give me a mission so compelling that I would defy my parents and the elders and set off on a quest to attempt to understand it," replied Arran.

"Aye the Golden caps are powerful, that's for sure. Not everyone has the profound vision shit that you mentioned, but some folk, aye. It's as if the mushroom is some sort of key that unlocks part of your mind or something and for folk like you and Rannoch, the rare few. It gives you visions, powers, purpose. For the rest of us it's just a crazy good time, well sometimes it can be a crazy awful time," says Etive.

"You've eaten the Sun?" Spouts a confused Arran.

"Aye lad many times, every cycle's end but as I said I don't get no crazy visions, etc. It definitely allows me to get in touch with myself and sometime allows me a deeper connection with my music and drumming. I have even transcended my very being and a few times it has even transported my consciousness into the nothing, I think, but it never gives me a purpose. It just lets me know, time and time again, that we, that everything that is, is one and connected," said Etive casually.

"You have eaten the golden capes many times. How can that be? I assumed it was only Mertaks that got to experience eating the sun," asked Arran.

"No lad, the Sun is only one part of Mertak, the initiation, the survival, the will to survive when you're naked, when you have nothing. That is the key. Somehow, you, Rannoch, the late great Coe, you guys are wired differently and the test to summit the peak somehow shines a light on those with the Mertak qualities. By qualities I mean, you will react like a crazy moon man to the powers of the golden capped mushroom. Not like me. I lasted five days on my Mertak, I mentally broke, the cold, the hunger, the physical exertion. I remember it like yesterday. I thought I would make it easily, but when I couldn't sleep because of the cold and couldn't move because I was hungry, I knew the end was near. Add to that seeing my friend being attacked and eaten by a Cassartan, I broke. Five days in, I returned, tail between my legs, ashamed and broken. But that's fine, it's not about me, Mertak is about finding you guys. It's about finding that rare gem amongst us that can focus, that can bend the Aurd to his will and push his mind to places that the rest of us can only sing about. And when you rough diamonds are cut and polished by the ordeal of the Aurd, the golden cap gives you a vision. Anyway, that's my understanding of it, young Mertak," smiled Etive.

Arran looked at Etive and then looked up at the trail in front. The yaks were slowing as the path narrowed ahead. The path they were on was still in the rolling hills and forest base of the Aurd but the majestic highlands were now within grasp.

"We will walk for around eight days Arran, then we will start making contact with the Lammas people and then the Ternakas folk of the Aurd. Both these tribes live their entire life in the mountains, some deep in the valleys and some like you, their Mertaks, live high in the peaks."

"Like me?" enquired Arran.

"Their Shamans, monks, wise folk, some of them live high in the mountains, isolated in strange dwellings that cling to the cliff faces or are balanced atop mountain peaks. I am talking about dwellings that are only accessible by mad folk on a quest for death. I have only seen their homes from afar but the Ternakas have told me that the routes to the shaman's shrines are perilous and induce nothing but fear. They really are a crazy bunch, the Ternakas. I have said it before and I shall say it again, we should all be up here trading with the Ternakas, they are far more like us than anyone else in the south," said Etive.

"So, you think I am different somehow? The Sun is some sort of key that unlocks our potential, the potential born into us and only those born with this potential can ever be a Mertak?" Puzzled Arran.

"Yes, I do. You have more Nencom in your blood than most, and his blood reacts somehow with the mushrooms. The Lamas shamans are the same, I suppose the major difference is in Lamas culture, everyone eats the sun. In just the same way we smoke the herb and drink ale, they eat the sun, it's no big thing. It's where we get Rannoch's supply! The Lamas folk believe that the golden cap is like a special messenger from mother earth, a messenger with its own unique message for every single child of hers, and all they have to do is eat her flesh. They have many stories about the gifts the great mother has delivered to them, from great quests, to magical warriors, from ancient gods reborn, to prophetic visions, to more mundane qualities. Like its ability to break addiction and uncover creative and musical talents, to engage users with stories of philosophical insight and more, but for some she delivers nothing but confusion and fear," said Etive.

Arran was unaware that Rannoch had eaten the sun more than once or twice and that an entire people ate the most sacred Gavodeon artifact as regularly as his people drank ale.

"So, I will be able to trade for some Golden mushrooms?" enquired Arran.

"Ah, now I see you, yes. We buy them at a premium but that is understandable, they are good traders; they understand our culture and know the value we place upon them. They trade them amongst themselves as a fairly inexpensive item, but to us the price is tenfold. They bring the price down to local prices if we are consuming them here in the Aurd but for the supplies I will take back to Rannoch, we pay the premium. Anyway, that is still days away, grab a bow as we are entering Cassartan country. If you see one, fire an arrow in its general direction, a warning shot is usually enough, they are not dumb like wolves," stated Etive.

Days passed as the slow waggon moved forward gradually, climbing higher and higher until all tracks became one single track. It was just after the single track that the first remnants of mountain peoples appeared. The first sign of the Lamas was a few outlying huts, lost in the wilderness, but the first contact with them showed they were friendly and trade was good. They seemed happy to see Etive and his small contingent of Gavods. After an evening trading, we made camp and arose early to make our way to the first real settlement of the Lamas people, half a day's trek from the first outliers. This was not like the previous collection of huts; this was a town. Buildings of various sizes and styles, made of dry stone and exquisite woodwork throughout. Each stood on a bed of rough rock and stone pillars and then morphed into a smooth exterior, painted in bright colours with geometric patterns and strange texts. In the air hung the perfumed fragrances that were being offered up to their deities, mixed with a subtle undertone of burning Yak dung.

Everywhere Arran looked, small colourful flags with geometric patterns jostled in the wind. Arran automatically assumed that the Lamas folk must be very wealthy, for he knew the effort, the labour and resource that went into making fabrics so elaborate and colourful. Arran was mistaken; they were poor as dirt.

As Arran went to offload the canopy and begin building the stall, Etive stepped forward.

"Not today lad, this is a festival day, we cannot trade today. Tomorrow," said Etive.

Arran looked around once more at the town sprawled out in vibrant colour before him. Etive continued.

"We will head to the tavern at the end of the main street, the last place to sell real ale in all the Aurd, join us," said Etive.

"I think I will have a walk first," said Arran

"Aye, there is lots to do here, the street theatre is always a good option," said Etive.

"That sounds good, I will go for a walk and see some of the festival, possibly take in the street theatre and absorb some Lamas culture," said Arran

"We'll be ready, the Lamas stories are something else. I suppose their vast imagination is a product of a nation of Sun users, they see time, space and therefore history differently from the rest of us and their stories are like no stories you will ever hear anywhere else in Lagosia." As Etive finished, Arran smiled, his face lit with curiosity and joy.

Etive continued, "The play in the square is most likely the story of Nencor, one of the greatest stories to ever be told. Their understanding of Nencom the great or, as they call him here amongst the Lamas people, Nencor. It's a tale full of strange stories of ancient slaves, gods, god kings, glorious wars, void travel, etheric farmers and freedom," Etive laughed as he signalled Arran to move on and enjoy.

"I will see you in the tavern soon," replied Arran as he set off towards the main square and the lively theatre at its centre. As Arran approached the entrance to the open space that had been temporarily constructed to house the theatre, with its many brightly coloured tapestries and fabrics. A seemingly random individual stepped forward from the entrance, nodded, and handed him a large cushion. Then in a heavily regional accent of perfect Gavodeon, the cushion passer said with a strange smile and a wink.

"Take a seat, get comfortable and enjoy the show. The story of Nencor is about to begin." Arran smiled, accepted the cushion and made his way to an open spot and took a seat. As he sat amongst the strange yet familiar people of the Lamas, he was passed sweeties and wine and greeted with many smiles and chat. After a short while, a gong sounded.

The announcer walked onto the stage. She was dressed elaborately in a bright orange robe, her upper torso, neck and ears were painted white, whilst her face was hidden under an elaborately carved white mask. Arran sat in fascination as the crowd cheered, then when the audience wave crashed, the announcer continued.

"No greater story has ever been told in the history of Gods, hybrids, slaves and free folk," shouted the announcer. 'It's the same voice that had passed me the cushion,' thought Arran. Then from stage right a tall, powerful male walked majestically to the centre of the stage before stopping and bowing to the crowd. He wore large baggy trousers; his torso was naked and oiled and adorned with many gold necklaces. His face and most of his heavily oiled beard were covered by a flesh covered mask, painted with large exaggerated eyes that seamlessly merged with an intricate head piece. Nencor had arrived, and the crowd went wild with boos. Again, the announcer waited for the audience to wane before she continued.

"He was the first demigod, the first hybrid, a son born of God," as she said God, a colossal male figure entered onto the stage from stage left and made its way to stand towering over Nencor. It was dressed like Nencor, but it was twice the size, with a distinctly larger and more elongated head. As the two actors stood still, she continued.

"The Tenni, our forefathers, were an advanced hominid species from the planet Dogon, which can be found deep in the great night void. Nencor was the first son born of the Tenni Gods..." The announcer paused, took a large exaggerated breath, then she looked left, then right, raised her hand to her mouth and leaned forward just a little, before announcing in a slightly hushed and somewhat uneasy tone. "And a slave". From behind the announcer, a small woman shuffled into the centre of the stage between the two giant men but significantly closer to the actor playing the God. The actress was on her knees, fake shoes stuck to her trousers at the knees in a comical fashion. Her head hung low and her posture was submissive. Yet, in the brief second or two that she looked up to see the audience, her beauty radiated, she lit the stage with her beauty, and in that instant yet internal moment, the world itself seemed like it had stopped. The crowd, in sync with the moment let out a collective breath. The announcer pointed directly at the slave and continued.

"The slave, the original Tenni Uh Akki creation. A mix of gods' blood and the blood of our world's native and true ancestors. The first, the original hybrid, the first of the slaves was grown to full maturation, deep in the belly of the void ship. When the Gods arrived from far across the void, they took their own blood and mixed it with our native Lanasian ancestors and grew a technologically advanced living creation. This monumental moment produced the first native born, conscious life here on Lanasia. The slave is the true ancestor of all of us. We are slave born." The crowd cheered in ecstasy for the slave but not the hero, Nencor. Arran sat up upon his cushion and sucked up the joyous, playful atmosphere that now engulfed the audience, whilst his mind reeled in total confusion. Arran laughed to himself as the realisation that the play had barely even begun and he was already lost.

As Arran returned his attention to the performance, the God and the slave simultaneously exited the stage. Nencor took two steps forward. From behind him, a grand lounge chair covered in gold, slid into position as he sat down. From stage right and left, many servants shuffled in. Again, the actors were on their knees, their lower legs obscured by the baggy trousers and shoes stuck to their knees, denoting their short stature and slave status.

Nencor laughed and pointed and as he did, many things were brought to him, grand goblets of liquid, trays of foods, jewels, slave women, animals, books, mystical talismans and weapons. Again, the crowd booed loudly.

As the boos receded, Arran looked on in amazement as Nencor's story came to life. The music that had been playing all along in the background, had become all-consuming. So much so, that the performers on stage began to move in a strange, impossibly slow dance. They now moved at a fraction of their normal speed, yet they stayed in perfect sync to the music. As if time itself had slowed down for the performers, but not for the music. The music was louder but still at normal speed, yet somehow, they were still in unison. Simultaneously, the stage grew and merged with his awareness; it became bigger and then moved forward till it was only a few feet away from him. The masked features of the actor playing Nencor had morphed into the most realistic stage make up he had ever seen. The actor was Nencor; the stage was no longer a stage and Arran was somehow pulled into this new dream like world, without alarm, with no jarring transition. As another world beyond his normal senses engulfed him, the story continued.

Nencor rose to his feet and walked on the spot, yet he was moving forward. He was now effortlessly walking through landscapes, as he walked on the spot, the backdrops to the play changed. First the stage transformed, now the whole experience had transformed into a strange, flat land, full of strange wonders. As he walked, the landscapes behind him filled with Gods, then pyramid cities, full of slaves and a few Gods. Then deserts full of slaves, then forests full of slaves, then fields and mines and palaces full of slaves.

Like a dream, Arran moved with the narrative and the environments as they changed, from one to the next without acknowledging the significant full sensory changes from the environments he had just been inhabiting. The characters in this play were now real, the backgrounds were landscapes full of features, full of depth, rich with colour, sounds and smells.

As the strange dream like theatre production continued in a time construct of its own making, Arran, a solo observer to the drama, sank deeper into his cushion. He tuned into the narration that carried this now all-encompassing sensory delight into full fruition.

"He was one of the first true god like hybrids, the first ascended slave! A son born of the Gods and lust, of the Original Tenni Uh Akki sweat and original slave creation. He was born into a life of privilege, where almost nothing was off limits. Whilst his brothers and sisters were branded slaves and toiled from sun up until sun down, he travelled far and wide and lived a life of luxury. After seeing all of the pyramid cities of his masters, he ventured far into the south, eventually and finally moving across the Aurd and into what we now know as Lagosian lands." In the new dream like state that Arran had entered, although he hadn't recognised the dream like state consciously, he had become aware of hundreds, if not thousands of eyes now looking upon him. It was as if the many eyes gazed down in collective realisation from the ceiling of a massive invisible dome, only eyes, no faces accompanied them, yet this did not provoke his conscious mind into questions. It did not puzzle him or alarm him. He just was. He let it flow past and jumped back into the narrative as it again unfolded.

"As he travelled solo, deeper into the south, he contemplated the major experiences of his own life, the life of his gods and creators, of his extended family on his mother's side. His life as a being, straddling two worlds and not belonging to either. With time, he contemplated all the big questions: the meaning of life, death, profit, leisure, gold and slavery. He was blessed with God's superior technology, like the magnificent books of golden knowledge and Nencor would regularly be seen debating with himself, as if two or more people inhabited his body. Occasionally, he invited his brother and sister slaves to debate against him."

The crowd let out a slight cheer. The announcer paused, before flying to the front of the scene, gliding to where Nencor stood. This truly was becoming an otherworldly, imagination-expanding experience, yet Arran never budged as she flew around him and then morphed perfectly into an owl, yet still retaining her face, before landing on the shoulder of Nencor. As she landed, she continued the narrative.

"As Nencor passed what is now the large southern desert beyond the location of the now Tanni Ma Barian capital, he seen thousands upon thousands of original slaves, toiling hard in the sun. He took advantage of the privileged non-slave life they had granted him. He had always been told that he was special and that the Gods had granted him this life of infinite possibility. In comparison, Nencor could not but notice all those who toiled in the sun, day after day, with no reality of ever leaving that task. The guilt always left him quickly, as he believed that he was just, God full and blessed. Beyond the deserts, Nencor moved up into the high mountain passes. High in the Aurd, after many months exploring the many mountains, he came across a plateau, the roof to the world. The land was large, a vast flat kingdom, sheltered by the surrounding mountains. Here, he discovered the Golden mushrooms that would change his life. The mushroom acted like a call to self-realisation. It forced open the highest aspects of himself, made him confront his own construct. It broke down all the rhythms and patterns that his culture, his life, his privilege and his education had formed. The golden mushroom stripped everything back, reality was laid bare, without the comfort of familiarity, or the cultural looking glass he was so comfortable within." The owl continued as the environments flowed and ebbed in a strange, gloopy, continuously malleable fashion. Arran's focus and concentration ebbed with the flow and soon he drifted in and out of consciousness as the story continued, yet Arran did not question the strangeness of all that he was encountering, he just went with the flow, until it no longer flowed.

"He lived up there for a few years; eating, surviving, exploring the inner space. Realisation, born through work seen Nencor recognise that his initial ideas of fate were wrong, that the opportunities granted to him by being born a hybrid, half Lanasian, half God, were in fact the very reason why he chose to reincarnate into the shell of Nencor. Why he chose to be re-animated into this slow, sluggish physical vibration. He learnt through the hardest of routes, through death itself, that he had chosen to re-enter this world, that he had chosen to implant his being, his soul, into the first hybrid shell ever created on Lanasia and that he had consciously done this for a purpose. He decided that purpose was to be the bridge between the created slaves and the Gods, he reasoned that everyone should have a say in their own life, especially as their souls were equal. He had discovered on his many journeys to the Bar En Dough that the soul of a being, be it a bird or a God, is equal in the Bar En Dough, all is divine. However, on entering a physical shell, the soul experiences the limitations of that shell, yet always retains the option to realise its full divinity. We are divine. Yet when a soul re-enters the physical space from the Bar En Dough, its vibration lowers, as well as weakens. This is because of the weakened state of the new biological machine housing the soul. So much so, that it temporarily cannot connect with the Bar En Dough and therefore over time, forgets that it can and thereby loses its true nature. Due to the unique life and abilities of Nencor, the solitude and the mushrooms, he was able to reclaim his divinity, whilst still firmly grounded in the physical realm. But that was not enough. He devised a system so he could pass on his revelation. He returned to the pyramid cities, stood against his creators, his masters, his gods, revealed the truth to all who would listen and when enough souls had re-awoken, he re-entered the Bar En Dough once again, leaving his physical corpse behind. The original Gods heard Nencor's truth, felt his divinity and flew back into the void. The now freed slaves went forth and made our great Lanasia."

The crowd cheered. All except Arran, he sat like a lost soul, staring into nothingness. For him, there was no longer an actual crowd. All around him were the scenes of the play. All around him were the multiple layers of the story unfolding, simultaneously. All around him were the Lamas folk, he knew that they were physically near him yet with him, they were him, he was one with them. Arran found himself silently cheering with the crowd, from deep inside his strange shared experience; the now completely synchronised experience that was partially merged with the interchanging, flowing, sensory rich, all-encompassing story. Then the imagery changed, the music that had been carrying everything invisibly and harmoniously in-sync with the experience, changed sharply. The stage re-appeared as a large chess board, full of Gods and slaves. Nencor stood alone in the centre of the board. The owl was no longer; the announcer was the sky, her voice reverberated with the power of the gods of the sky.

"A board game where everyone is being played, Necom's freedom was not to leave the slave cities, not to free the slaves. His freedom was returning from the Bar En Dough to show us all how to leave the game."

The crowd now all-around Arran cheered, they hooped and jostled and whistled. This time Arran was completely absent from the interactions of the crowd.

"The non-time, multi-dimensional game, through which he freed his very being from the grips of the puppet masters............ This is why he can come back. This is why he can return, again and again, from the place beyond death.

But each time he returns, the vessel he chooses does not know that it is Nencor. Rarely does his truth get revealed on the physical plane. Prophecy is told."

The sound of the gong woke Arran into full conscious awareness. The crowd is gone and the theatre company patrons are hard at work stripping the stage, clearing litter and ultimately returning the square back to the town. Arran stood, bent over and picked up the cushion, took a few uneasy steps and handed the cushion to the nearest theatre rep. She was a beautiful woman, with piercing eyes and long black hair, who smiled as she received the cushion before saying;

"Thank you. Did you enjoy the play?" Instantly, Arran realised it was the voice that had narrated the strange inner journey he had just returned from. For a second, he paused in amazement while she stood still with the cushion, awaiting his reply.

"Yes," replied Arran.

"The show was exceptional, probably the best I have ever experienced. I don't really know what the story was about yet, but I am sure its many truths will come to me soon." She looked at him and smiled. "I believe it will, I believe it will."

Arran moved off. After a few paces, he instinctively looked back, to see all of the theatre company had stopped and were looking in his direction, heads bowed. Only the announcer briefly looked up. Arran returned her gaze momentarily, before turning back to the dark, dimly lit, uneven street before him.

Soon after, Arran arrived at the Inn to find the other Gavods still drinking.

"Ah, young Arran, come, sit. How was the show?" Etive smiled and poured out an ale for Arran from the massive jug at the centre of the Gavod's table. Arran was thirsty and quickly picked up the tankard and gulped the ale.

"I don't really know what happened there, but that was the craziest theatre show I have ever experienced. Like nothing I have ever experienced before!!" said Arran, as he looked directly at Etive. He still hadn't put the cup of ale down.

"Aye lad, the theatre productions up here can be wild. I am guessing you accepted some treats from the crowd?" laughed Etive, as he looked directly into Arran's huge pupils, his eyes were like large dark disks.

Arran looked at the other Gavods, as they smiled back and realised in that moment, that the theatre experience, although completely different from the mushroom experience at Theru peaks, it had similar characteristics.

"Those treats where laced with the sun mushrooms?" stated Arran

"Probably not son, possibly a small quantity. The Lamas people are brilliant chemists and botanists. They have many herbs and trinkets for the mind. Most likely, it would have been something of less value, of less potency, after all, it was designed to enhance the show, not obliterate it!! The items we can buy up here are weed, henbane, salvia, ergot, ten varieties of mushroom, a rare cactus, sacred vine and blue lily. The list of what could have been in those treats is endless!! Was it good though?" laughed Etive.

"Good? It wasn't bad," stated Arran with a smile. "I still don't really know what happened. The story was so vivid and so strange, yet so familiar. Their version of Nencom's beginnings had points of similarity, yet points that were so very different, from what I can recall, but to be fair it's all a bit of a jumble at the moment. I recall it being other worldly." Arran laughed as he took another swig of Ale.

Etive signalled the serving man for another jug of ale, as he returned his gaze to the table, Arran began to talk.

"You see, this is the version we all know and the reasons why the Mertak is so important to survive for our culture. Mertak was the slave over lord in the old slave days. Nencom The Great was captured in the outer deserts of Tanni Ma Bar, a place I will hopefully see for myself soon enough. One night, after listening to Nencom talk about freedom, souls, purpose and potential, the guard let Nencom go, turned the key and set him free. Nencom ran through the night and sought refuge in the mountains. From here, he entered the Aurd. As he climbed, his only option of crossing was over and through Theru peaks. Here, while he was hungry and sore, he rested a little. He picked and ate some mushrooms to recover his energy, and the rest is history. The golden cap showed him nature, showed him all other beings live in sync with nature, how they migrate, year in year out, how they sing, how they laugh, how they thrive. The blueprint for the Gavodeon nation was born. We are now the last nomadic people of Lanasia. In fact, we were the first. Our creators gave us society, manufactured us from the wild monkey, ape and from themselves. We were slaves, like everyone else, and then we were free."

"Beautiful Arran, beautiful, we are all master traders of the Gavodeon nation, son. We know the story of Nencom," laughed Etive.

"I know that you know, but how can we, as a nation, just glance over the idea of our creators, creating and enslaving us?, The Lamas version of Nencor explores such ideas," exclaimed Arran.

"It sure does son, anyhow, drink up. It is close to closing time and we have a full day of trading ahead of us," said Etive as he rose to his feet.

The day after the festival, the traders set up their stalls as the first rays of light broke through. The day was crisp and clear and the mountain air was fresh and intense. 'The vibrant blue of the sky seems more intense up here in the mountains,' thought Arran, but he didn't have long before a frantic day of trading begun. The day's trade went well, he helped as they secured speciality

Yak wool fabrics, Cassartan furs, Golden capes, and many dried mountain herbs, roots and flowers.

"I can't believe you want to leave this life, I have rarely met a more natural trader. You value things fast, appraise well, you keep the customer's eye, your warm and pleasant and your negotiation is sound. Aye young Arran, your mind is sharp, that is true," proclaimed Etive with a big smile.

"Thank you Etive, it's the only thing I have ever been good at. Once I learnt the inventory, I relaxed and could be free to loosen up on my mother's stall." said Arran.

"Aye, it's a colossal task for the young to remember all the ins and outs of an inventory. Aye, just think, if you stayed on the trail, like me for another eight cycles, you may have a chance of recalling the entire cycle's inventory." Etive was proud of his accomplishments. "I can even recall the historical facts, cultural practises, past seasonal prices etc for almost every item we sell, in every location, over an entire cycle," Etive smiled and winked at Arran.

"Yes, I agree it was an enormous task but after it was done it made it easier to trade, gave me the freedom to relax and just be with the customer," said Arran.

"What you, you have memorised the entire cycle's inventory?" Etive's voice was almost angry as he stated what he now realised Arran was saying.

"Yes, for every section of the trail, I filed away everything. Just like you, I added information about culture, history, seasons, whether it was food, medicine, culturally important, seasonal, etc, etc," said Arran.

"What do you mean? You filed away everything? You probably have a good grasp of the goods we trade, I am sure, but it takes many, many cycles before you develop the memory recall of a master trader. You probably have a great inventory, but it's missing a good few things, I can assure you of that young Mertak," said Etive.

"Test me," Arran had told no one of his obsession with his inner world and compartmentalisation rituals that he ran through daily, of everything from the trail.

"Ok, young pup. In Lerr, name the six types of roots we pick up from the southern wetlands, their name, their price points, their use, their cultural significance, their name in their native tongue, their colour, their smell and the most common reason for buying each of them?" Etive was sure he would stump Arran with these low selling, culturally specific roots, but without hesitation the information flowed. Time and time again, Etive tested him and time and time again, his answers were flawless. And each time, he over delivered in information, connecting aspects of the inventory that Etive, the Master trader had not.

"I need to pee now; you're working me to hard," Arran winked at Etive as he left the temporary yurt to pee by the nearby bushes.

As Arran returned to the stall, Etive signalled for him to get some long-serrated knives and selection of the lowland root vegetables for a customer, then as if by magic, the entire town stopped. From the other side of the narrow road, where they had set up, a great horn sounded. Etive had not mentioned how revered the shamans of the mountains were, but it was now clear for Arran to see. Everyone had stopped, some bowed, some threw flowers in their path and others burst into tears. All around them, a deeply ingrained cultural dance was taking place and Arran was loving it. As he secured the vegetables and knives from their respective locations, he returned his attention to the vibrantly coloured men and women moving slowly, ritualistically, in his direction.

Etive turned to Arran, "So it looks like they can sense their own." Etive nudged and nodded to Arran, in a strange, 'told you so' kind of manner, as the procession of shamanic monks arrived.

"Let me do the speaking son, they might just want some fabric and some tools," laughed Etive.

"Hello, how can I help you today? Tools, Fabric, Vegetables?" said Etive.

"Thank you, but we are here to start a dialogue with the young trader. It's the first new day of the new heavenly flame, I am sure you are aware? You may have seen her high in the sky last night?" enquired the monk.

Both men acknowledged the fact.

"We believe, as you are probably aware, that everything is foretold by the heavenly flames. This one is significant and a long time cometh. It is the last flame before the great flame." The strange ramblings left the monks' mouth, but his eyes never left Arran.

"You wish to speak with me," shouted Arran, slightly louder and more aggressively than he intended.

"Yes, we do, we wish you no harm, we just want to talk," replied the Monk.

"We are talking now," replied Arran.

"Yes, we are, but it is not I that wishes to talk with you. It is our leader, Lopsangy. He is our leader in all things," replied the Monk.

"And where is this Lopsangy, is he amongst you?" Arran pointed to the monks, all standing still, two by two, bright red robes flowing in the wind.

"No, he is not amongst us here, he is up there," the monk turned slightly and pointed to the mountains away in the distance.

"And from there," Arran pointed in the direction that the monk had indicated, "Are there paths or routes down into the northern lands, beyond the Aurd?" asked Arran.

"Oh yes, there are a few paths that lead to the Tanni Ma Bar deserts, not well-trodden paths but if that is where you are going, then after you have met with the High Holiness Lopsangy, then we will show you the route to the northern desert," said the Monk.

"Well, it looks like you have a deal," said Arran, as he thrust out his hand to confirm. The monk was not sure whether to touch the great Gavod, predicted by the heavenly flame or not, but did not want to offend The Great Flame, so he grasped Arran's hand tight and shook.

CHAPTER 11 - ARRAN AND LOPSANGY

THE GRANITE WALLS BEFORE him rose vertically into the clouds. Arran stood still, swaying slightly in the wind as he looked up at the mountain side in awe.

"Your Lopsangy lives up there," says Arran as he points directly up into the clouds.

"Yes, all of our leaders live high in the mountains, this mountain chose Lopsangy," said the Monk.

"Why?" said Arran still looking up at the impressive granite wall, scanning for some obvious route upwards.

"From the top of the mountain, you can see the entire world and being able to see across the entire world gives a leader, true perspective. It allows our great leaders to see that everything is connected, that everything is one." Said the Monk, Arran looked down from looking up, unable to see any routes upwards. He looked at the monk and smiled nervously.

The last few months had been strange, really strange for the young Gavod. After saying farewell to Etive and the other Gavods, Arran had travelled north with the monks. They'd set a fanatical pace over tough terrain, but he'd kept up, until they'd reached the mountain monasteries. Arran had thought that Etive had been exaggerating the accessibility of the Lamas and Ternakas temples with his "only accessible by mad folk on a quest for death", but he wasn't.

The first leg of the journey to the reverent Lopsangy, left the uneven beaten path for a stair well carved into the very side of the mountain. Unlike a standard stair case, which was by its very nature designed to make vertical climbs easier, this ridiculous step system did not, it was more like a ladder carved into the wall. The first section from the road didn't look too bad, but as Arran scanned the route above, he noticed that the vertical steps stopped and were suddenly replaced with small foot sized holes that went horizontally across the overexposed crux of the cliff. Without a second of hesitation, the monks climbed, one by one they scrambled up the almost vertical rock wall to the beginning of the horizontal walk way. Arran was way behind. He wasn't rushing this for anyone; he took his time, kept his focus on the correct placement of each hand and each foot, and continued on slowly but surely. 'The monks will wait for me', he thought.

When he scaled to the top of the steps, the horizontal grooves awaited him. The sight before him instantly sent fear deep into his very core. The granite wall ahead was completely vertical with only the slightest lean. 'The footholds are only big enough for one foot at a time, but to cross successfully, they would need to house two,' thought Arran. The first monk leaned in tight to the wall, his left ear against it, as he looked toward the direction of travel, his palms pushed flat against the wall. As he faced the wall, his hips were almost flat to the wall, he balanced on the edge of the cliff with his right foot and crossed his left foot over and into the first groove. He then quickly placed his right foot into the next groove along, he was now out over the precipice, unsheltered and unprotected. Again, he crossed his left foot through to the next groove and then the right, all whilst keeping his hips flat to the wall. Arran could not believe what he was witnessing. Were these Monks insane, what logical reason would one have for creating a pathway so dangerous, so fear inducing, so hazardous as this? 'It surely can't be for perspective, we can see the world just fine from here' thought Arran.

As the second Monk began his journey across the horizontal death path Arran thought to himself, "Well, I guess there is only one way to find out".

Before the last Monk set off, Arran grabbed his sleeve.

"You may have noticed that I am not a mountain goat. Do you have any advice for me?" The Monk looked at Arran, he did not hide how upset he was, that Arran had just shattered the monk's illusion of him, as this great, heavenly flame, saviour character.

"Fear death and the route before you will be impossible," stated the Monk.

Arran's brows raised in disbelief of what he heard, was this the best advice this monk had? 'Surely not,' thought Arran. Surely not. The monk, sensing Arran's non amusement at his parted wisdom, tried another tact.

"The path before us," the monk pointed out to the open, unprotected route before them.

"If this obstacle was only one foot off the ground, it would be a fun challenge, easily mastered by any child of Lanasia."

"Ok," replied Arran, waiting for the punch line to this most horrific of jokes, but none came. Then the monk balanced his right foot by the edge of the cliff and like his brothers and sisters, stepped out into the abyss, one foot at a time, across and around the horizontal path until he was out of site, round beyond the wall's end.

Arran looked at the pathway and visualised it being only one foot higher than a grassy field. Instantly his heart relaxed and the fear subdued. The temples were not important, the journey was, thought Arran. These were ways to train out fear. Extreme tests to measure how one masters their own mind, emotions and more.

After rehearsing the moves made by the Monks, Arran visualised the green grass directly below him and moved to the edge of the cliff and began his slow, methodical traverse across the horizontal path of death.

The route to meet with Lopsangy had many more vomit inducing experiences, but time and again Arran adapted quickly, realising the primary cause of fear and rationalising it away.

The temple that greeted him near the peak of the mountain was insignificant. The monks sat outside, each performing an intense rhythmic breathing exercise, legs crossed, eyes shut, steam bellowing from their naked upper torsos. 'How bizarre,' thought Arran.

Arran entered the small shed at the top of the mountain and was greeted by a wiry, middle-aged man.

"Ah, the Gavod, as foretold by The Great Flames, welcome," said Lopsangy.

"Thank you, how do you see the future using the moving lights of the void, or The Great Flames as you call them?" replied Arran.

"Everything is foretold by The Great Flames. They are a map to the choices you made. But that is for another discussion, another time. How was your journey? You're the first non-monk, non-Lamas, non-Ternakas to visit this fine hut," said Lopsangy.

"Aye, it's a fine hut that is for sure, if a bit empty," replied Arran.

"The hut reflects the journey, as I am sure you are aware. One must empty his mind to make the journey to this hut. More importantly, to enter the Bar En Dough, one must empty their mind. When you die, you have a few choices. Be eaten whole, be trapped and dwell on the life you lived whilst being eaten slowly or enter the nothing on your way to being reincarnated, or for the few, there is one other option."

"How can anyone know what happens when you die? We Gavods believe in reincarnation, that those who die are reborn quickly into another Gavodeon body. We believe that we can speed the process up by hacking the body into pieces, which forces the soul of the departed to move into their reincarnation journey as soon as possible. However, I could describe another fifty beliefs about death from the various cultures throughout the south of Lanasia. We believe in reincarnation, but no one can actually know! The only thing I know, is that I don't know with any certainty, what happens when we die," said Arran.

"Wisdom flows from the messenger of The Great Flame," said Lopsangy, with a big genuine smile.

"Sorry, your journey up here must have been thirsty work, can I offer you some tea?" said Lopsangy.

"Tea, I thought you would never ask," laughed Arran.

From behind his robe, Lopsangy pulled a ceramic flask. On releasing its cap, the steam rose and a light pleasant fragrance filled the small hut. Arran found himself unconsciously rubbing his hands together, excitedly. Hopefully they have mixed lots of butter into the tea,' thought Arran. He was not disappointed.

After a small ritual, which Arran observed with respect, he was offered a cup of tea. It was more bitter than the teas he was used to and it had a few flavour profiles that he could not identify, they were new to his pallet.

"This is a rather strange tea, it's like a Lerrian blend, mixed with the teas we trade from the Aromian lands, with a hint of sweetness that is finished with a slight bitterness, not too dissimilar to that of a grapefruit. What do you callllllll.........thhhhhhhiiiiiiisss?" Arran's voice slurred.

The sentence continued in Arran's mind.

"What do you call this kind of tea?" As he looked up from the tea, Lopsangy was no longer in front of him, which was strange but somehow not alarming. Before he could really think about this, he was once again amongst his people in the southern lowlands of the Aurd. Again, for some reason, he never questioned this. He just found himself overjoyed at being back amongst his people. Quickly the scene changed. Now he was being welcomed and celebrated "The Mertak has returned," sang the Gavods on mass. From amongst the song, a silence arose and, in that silence, a single female voice asked, "but why did you leave?" Arran quickly justified his decision.

"I did it for you, for every Gavod...".

As he began his explanation for the fifth time, Arran felt drained. The young girl was somehow amplifying every doubt he had ever had. She was playing his weaknesses for all to see, but Arran was completely unaware. Again, he repeated the defence of his decision to leave, as his anger grew at her unwillingness to listen.

Then from the heavens, as if a great bell had been rung that shook the very skies themselves, Arran heard a voice that swept in on the winds, from every direction. At first it was clear and succinct but it was quickly matched by the repetitive questions from the young, unnamed Gavod. The voice repeated, "enter the nothing", "enter the nothing". Arran asked the young girl "What does it mean?", as soon as he had asked her, she quickly comforted him, but now she was not the young girl, now she was his mother. In his mind's eye he was repeating "enter the nothing", "enter the nothing". Then, the memories of the Gavodeon nation that he had been so fondly remembering slipped away. Arran did not feel fear or panic, just a strange realisation that leaving his mother was difficult, as if she wasn't allowing him to leave. He could feel her sucking his very essence. Now it was just his mother and him. As she forced him to focus on her, the entire environment now echoed and reverberated with "enter the nothing", "enter the nothing".

Arran held his breath and begun his automatic ritual to enter his inner sanctum. In an instant, he entered the nothing and the girl was gone, her pull was gone, his mind was clear once again. As he regained full consciousness and with this he finally realised, he was in his mind and no longer sitting next to Lopsangy. Was he dead or dying? Was he now crossing over? The voice was Lopsangy's, he knew this all along but could not pinpoint it until the girl had gone. With no further hesitation, Arran silenced his mind and focused on nothing. He re-centred and entered the nothingness. Before entering the nothing, the surrounding space expanded until his consciousness was the size of the Aurd and in that instant a bright light opened from the darkness and he was there.

"Where am I?"

"Where, when, what, who, why?" thought Arran.

"All of these questions are slightly different here, as are the answers." The information came at him as a full, single, uninterrupted, burst of instantaneous information from every direction and to every sense at once.

Inside this awareness, Arran understood everything. He belonged, everyone belonged, then in a flash, the entire realm disappeared, the very fabric of this new reality folded in on him. The light flew away from him, to the end of an infinitely long dark tunnel, observed Arran or was it that he was flying away from it, down an infinitely long dark tunnel? There were no reference points. However, it was irrelevant now. All he knew was that he was no longer there.

***

IN THE HUT, MOMENTS earlier Lopsangy opened a small vile of dark purple liquid and wafted it under Arran's nose, then he causally reached into his sleeve and pulled out a second vile with a clear liquid. The contents of this vile were then poured into Arran's mouth. With a lot more haste, Lopsangy began to manually pump Arran's heart. He knelt over the unconscious, lifeless body of the young Gavod and pumped down on Arran's chest, hands locked, arms locked, rhythmically, as he chanted in time with the compressions. Then within seconds, Arran's limp body jumped back into life.

***

ARRAN'S EYES OPENED. HE looked around the hut, drinking in this unfamiliar environment, not sure if it was real or not.

"Welcome back, young Arran," said Lopsangy.

Arran heard him, acknowledged him, but was still groggy and somewhat unhinged.

"How was death? I hope I answered your question about how we know," smiled Lopsangy.

CHAPTER 12 - ARRAN TRAVELS BEYOND THE AURD

DEATH, FEAR, THE NATURE of reality and how his consciousness perceived it, occupied Arran's thoughts since leaving the chaos that was Lopsangy, the Lamas and the Ternakas people. As Arran descended from the high Aurd into the northern desert, after spending over a month with the Lamas people, eating mushrooms and defying death, he still couldn't quite get over the fact that he had died, that he had met death and that this life changing experience had happened just so Lopsangy, the crazy bastard, could demonstrate his point. He kept reflecting on the "truths," opened to him and the possibility that these truths were in fact, bastardisations of the truth.

'Lopsangy told me what to expect from death,' thought Arran, 'and then it happened. Maybe death reflects the beliefs or the expectations you hold of it.' Arran thought about the various religions and paths of the south. He contemplated that if an individual from each of these religions was killed and brought back by Lopsangy, would they see the great deities associated with their belief, or would they see and experience the suggestions implanted by Lopsangy? Or was there only the "universal" truth as Lopsangy said "be eaten, stay locked in the past or enter the nothing". The young Gavod's head was truly pickled. As he walked the paths of the Aurd, he filed these experiences into a new 'room' in his internal library of knowledge under the title. "The illusions of death".

He arrived in the southern Tanni Ma Bar desert range after many months, walking the lowest paths of the Aurd, moving north through the high mountains, preferring the cool mountain terrain to the inhospitable deserts below.

It amazed Arran how sheer the Aurd on the Tanni Ma Barian side was, as if the mountains had risen straight out of the desert, into the clouds instantly, with almost no transitional hills. Like a wall, a significant barrier to the south. As the extremes gradually changed, the desert's heat began. The landscape, from vertical, granite cliffs of almost sheer descent that required both hands and feet to negotiate, to the hard, dry sand that levelled off into the north and west, before turning into massive rolling dunes near the visible horizon.

Arran had filled his canteens with water but as he looked into the distant desert, all he could see was the effects of heat, radiating, warping everything in sight, even his confidence. Yet, Arran knew that the only way north was forward, so he pushed on, into the searing heat. Arran tried his best to conserve his little and precious water, but in these new conditions, without the gradual acclimation that life on the trail offered, and the supply caravans, Arran was useless. He had survived in the snow, in the rain, in the wind, in the high mountain passes and in the eastern desert's sun. His people were experienced in the sun, but here when the fireball was high in the sky, taking up residence directly overhead, its strength sapping powers were immeasurable and soon too much for Arran to bear. He had no answers, no solutions. Here, there was no shade, no Yak to unpack, no yurt to build , and unlike the trail, he never knew the locations of the watering holes, wells or streams.

Weeks of walking north west in the desert had pushed Arran to desperate measures, out of necessity he had stripped out of his clothing. His mountain wear of thick fur was in hindsight the wrong gear for the desert. Using his only shirt, he belted it to his head and shoulders to act as a simple shade, then continued walking. It was inspired by the dress he had seen the Nevarous peoples of the eastern desert wear. His shirt only covered his head, neck and upper torso, but it was the best he could do. For the next three days, his legs burned, as did his arms from the elbow down, his chest, face and his back where his pack gave no protection. The powerful desert winds masked the severity of the burns as they continuously cooled his burning flesh. Then on the fourth day, with no more water, and no more energy to carry on, Arran screamed in desperation before collapsing. Unconscious and unprotected, he lay burning in the desert sun.

Arran awoke, his eyes slowly adjusting to the dark, cool room. He knew many days had passed since he was last conscious, but he could not determine how many, nor was he bothered. The slab of granite he lay upon cooled his skin and the luxurious silk cloth that now covered him, hugged the contours of his thin, red body. As Arran's eyes fully adjusted to the room, he noticed someone stood near the edge of the chamber, next to a large majestic door, ornately inscribed with gems and symbols, the likes of which, Arran had never seen before. The mysterious man dressed in the same luxurious material that now caressed Arran's skin, his eyes met Arran's in the light of the darkness. Two metres from Arran, he lowered his dark hood to reveal his long unkempt beard and then he spoke.

"You are here, not through circumstance, coincidence or chance, you are here because we both agreed that you would be here. Timing could have been better, but the subtle works as it does, we can only guide it," said the bearded figure.

Arran's face twisted with pain and confusion as his thoughts raced. What was this bearded fool talking about? He'd had no choice in being here, wherever here was. Another thought sarcastically slipped into Arran's mind, which made the young traveller laugh, "I guess this was written in the great flames as well". The black-bearded figure closed the remaining two steps, as he stood by Arran. He started a strange breathing pattern, then after a few moments, he placed his hairy hands upon Arran's head. To Arran's amazement, all the pain and heat from his body disappeared. With his hands firmly gripping Arran's head, he started to talk again.

"Arran, you are here, because you have the will to learn our secrets. Through the web of life we broadcast our need for a pupil. The timing could have been better, but you're here now, so we shall begin. Arran, we are the Tanni Ma Barians and you are here to learn our secret ways," said the bearded figure.

Arran could not control his emotional response. A mixture of gratitude, adulation and amazement at what he was hearing and of what he just experienced, was written across his face and wide-eyed gaze.

"Young Arran, you are here to learn and learn you will. Memorise everything my brothers and sisters tell you. For this is the truth of how things are, as we have experienced them." The bearded stranger let go of Arran's head, sucked in a large breath and swept his hands against each other, numerous times and in quick succession, as if removing dirt or sand from them. He then turned and washed them in a large stone basin, by the door. Arran sat up slowly, pain free. He turned to dangle his legs over the edge of the granite slab. The mysterious man by the wall began to talk.

"There is a God, an all-encompassing, unifying force, this God is within, it is within all of us, within everything and this truth can only be verified by yourself and to do that, you must know yourself. The journey of self-mastery will bring you to know, to understand, to experience God, for God is already within," said the man with genuine conviction.

'These arbiters of truth always have conviction, I wish I had that kind of conviction,' thought Arran.

Arran turned to keep his eyes on the bearded philosopher, again Arran turned to his thoughts 'well this is interesting, let's see where it goes'. Arran smiled at the bearded man, and he continued.

"Alchemy is the transformation of lead to gold. We are not referring to the metals but to the characteristics they represent and how these characteristics relate to our soul. Lead is the dark heavy aspects of our soul, desire, fear, greed, hatred. We have to transform these into gold, into love, compassion, unity, acceptance and forgiveness. This transformation of the microcosm will help us transform the macrocosm, awakening all sentient beings upon this planet. This is the journey you are upon, young Arran, this is the journey that every being is on. But on this planet, in this world, there are gods that play God. This country, this continent, this planet is more than just this physical dimension." The stranger bangs against the walls and then the floor, hard, and then waves his arms around, as if caressing, comforting and communicating with the air itself.

Arran raised an eyebrow as his lips tightened into an uncomfortable smile. The bearded one continued.

"There are also energetic and etheric dimensions. Everything is vibration, that is how I healed you. Let me explain. A musician can play a note then play the same note an octave higher and the note will sound like it, the two notes are the same and connected, yet different, for one note is vibrating twice as fast as the other. The same idea is true for the surrounding space, for this very space is inhabited with other beings not of Lanasian form. These ethereal beings are sentient, different cultures call them by many names. Dark souls, light workers, shadows, QUAFS, fairies, trolls and jinners are just some. Most are given names that confine them to the dominant cult or religion of a particular time. However, these beings are just some of the gods that play God here."

Arran smiled, "These demons, these angels, do they glow different colours? Do they communicate with us? I think I may have experienced something that fits into this category," stated Arran, plain as day.

The bearded one was now illuminated fully in the brightest light the room offered. His beard swayed as he shuffled on his heels. 'He looks agitated,' thought Arran. He returned to face Arran, his left hand stroking his moustache. It looked like he was lost. He looked mildly annoyed at Arran's questions; 'he has lost his train of thought,' thought Arran. Then he continued.

"Yes, they are associated with different colours, and they communicate with us, almost exclusively for their own gain. But I digress, there will be time for questions, much time for questions. I must continue."

The bearded healer looked flustered. He took another breath, waved his hands strangely, then stretched them out to the side before raising them up, in harmony with his breath, before bringing them back down to his belly button and exhaling. He looked calmer, 'if that is what the breathing is for, that is a neat trick', thought Arran, Before the healer continued;

"There are also physical beings inhabiting this planet; from distant planets, from far across the void. These powerful beings also claim to be gods, but these gods are not God, but yet they are, as are we; God. You see God is everything, so they are God, a part of God, as we are but the people of Lanasia, the common man who toils the field, who lives to raise farm and family, who prays and adheres to one of the major religions, will pray to one of these false gods, these small gods. Feeding them, instead of praying to the almighty God, the universal truth, the everything, the microcosm which is the macrocosm and feeding themselves. Making themselves God full. You will be God's messenger Arran, you are he," said the bearded man, with such conviction, Arran almost felt himself believing the words.

Arran looked at the man before him as if he just descended from the heavens on a flaming dragon.

"Gods messenger you say?" Arran gripped the silk sheet around his naked body, tucking it in tight before spinning round and pushing off the granite slab. He laughed as he looked up at the bearded figure that occupied this small room with him.

"By your own reckoning, I am no more God's messenger than you are. As you say, God is within, God is everything, everyone is God's messenger." Arran smiled as his laughter settled.

The bearded man smiled.

"These ideas of God are refreshing and as always, when I have time to think about such things, my mind explodes with ideas, each fresh idea in turn birthing another unique pathway of possibility. However, the big God, the everything God, I agree, is within us all. What I have experienced is that the mind is a powerful tool, and with it, we can create unlimited possibilities. Our imagination is unlimited and over time, with focus and determination, the mind truly has no limit to its potential. Just now, I am following a vision, a vision handed to me by the Golden mushrooms of the Aurd, of a powerful man in the north, a King, I assume, maybe. Powerful in every sense of the word, possibly seen by many as a god. In my vision, he surrounds himself with energetic beings that feed upon men like they are yaks, possibly the dark souls or QUAF you talked about. In my vision, this King will challenge the Aurd and go south. I cannot let this happen. I would be grateful if you have any information that could help me in these regards," said Arran.

"Arran, you are God's messenger, and my heart sings with your presence." The man looked into Arran's eyes and smiled, a wide, toothy, genuine smile, full of love and acceptance, Arran felt it, felt every ounce of it, as he relaxed and shared the smile too.

"And another thing, how do you know the common Gavodeon tongue? Is it the common language here in the north?" asked the curious Arran.

"The Gavodeon language is a bastardisation of the common Tanni language which was once universal throughout all of Lanasia, hence us being able to communicate with relative ease. Further north, beyond our main city, it can be a bit of a hit or miss, whether someone will know Tanni or not. Most converse in national, tribal or in the forced Namangan tongue, but most educated, wealthier members of society will speak Tanni, although few will easily understand your thick southern accent," said the bearded man.

He looked at Arran and smiled, "I think you will enjoy your time here Arran. Please stay as long as you wish, and if you decide to stay, we will teach you all we can." He stretched out his hand. "I am Brother Moray of the Tanni. If you need anything whilst you are here, let me know and I will do my best to accommodate you," said Moray.

After only a few days, Arran's skin had completely healed of its burns and his body once again felt strong. The air here in the city was nothing like the desert. Arran decided to stay a while, learn as much as he could before moving on. His new hosts had suggested that he explore the city, get familiar and comfortable with his new surroundings, before they get down to many days of learning. The next morning, Arran awoke early, ready to explore. As Arran left his room, a young man approached him.

"Hi, I am Riley, I will be your guide today," said the boy.

"Ok," replied Arran. The older boy pushed out his hand and Arran met it with a firm handshake. His smile illuminated in the pre-dawn candle light. Then he took off one of the packs he was carrying and handed it to Arran.

"It's just some food, water and some wine, enough to keep you going whilst we are out and about," said Riley, Arran smiled and nodded.

As the duo left the building, the internal lamps gave way to the darkness of the adjoining street. The pair walked deeper into the darkness, ready for the day ahead.

After a time, the day emerged from the darkness. The bringer of light had arrived and with it, the new morning. As the light slowly filtered through the streets, its rays ceremoniously prodding and probing everything into life. With the light, came energy, with energy came heat, noise, sound, and smell. Arran stood motionless, soaking up and admiring the might of the sun, and its life bringing powers. He realised then and there, that the Sun was the true transformer; it was the source of all of life's energy. Arran thought to himself, 'as with most strange things in life, the great answers come from nowhere.' Here it had come from a simple observation of something he had witnessed thousands of times before, yet he had never actually seen it. The sun, it was the sun, as clear as day he seen the light, the bringer of life. Arran stood motionless. It was as if his thoughts had melded with reality to show him this truth. As Arran stood observing, the sun chased the night's retreat from the city and for the first time, Arran seen the Great Pyramid of Tanni Ma Bar.

Before him stood the massive pyramid, it was such a peculiar structure. Arran knew right there and then that he must explore this magnificent structure. As he stood gazing in admiration, the morning light approached and transformed the pyramid. Light and shadow danced and slithered like snakes up the great stairwell as the sun slowly illuminated the majestic structure. Unfortunately, the magic and majesty of the event was curtailed as the narrow streets from where he stood partially obstructed his view.

Arran's mind erupted, how? Why? When? And who? In all his travels throughout the south, he had seen nothing so big, so colossal and he had seen them all, churches, cathedrals, fighting arenas, universities, shrines, merchant stores, palaces but never a building like this. He knew the history of Nencom the great and his choice to leave the slave cities of the Pyramids, but never did he think a building could be so monumentally big. He had always envisioned them to be the size of an extra large communal yurt, but the strange, hallucino-genic theatre show in the highlands of the Aurd had put that notion to rest, but even that paled in significance to reality. 'These things are massive, beyond comprehension,' thought Arran.

"Are you ok Arran," asked Riley.

"I am, I am," Arran looked over to Riley and smiled.

"I have just come across an amazing truth, so simple, yet so profound that it has touched my very soul. Then, as if that was not enough," Arran gestured out his arm towards the Pyramid, "I discovered the city has this!"

Riley smiled "The great Pyramid of Tanni Ma Bar, it's a beauty"

"We need to explore it," Arran's voice was high pitched and excited.

Riley smiled, "The Pyramid is one of my favourite places and lucky for you, we are scheduled to learn about semiotics this week. A big part of semiotics is the study of symbols and their meanings and that's something the Pyramid is not short of!" said Riley, excitedly.

The two young men smiled as they made tracks towards the pyramid. An hour's walk, seen Arran and Riley out in the desert, next to the great pyramid, the pyramid was in ruin. Once, it may have been a glorious edifice, but now it was a sand-swept enigma, from a time long gone.

On the walk through the city, Riley recounted everything he knew about the pyramids. Arran was told of its age, its history, of how they were built as grand tombs for the ancient, powerful Tanni Ma Barian kings. Arran thought this foolish, ridiculous in fact, no man or woman would go to such extreme lengths to bury themselves in such a magnificent feat of engineering. 'How does one even build such a thing,' thought Arran? Arran laughed as his mind mocked the idea of the pyramids being built by Kings and Queens as grand tombs. 'Did these kings live for hundreds of years? Because these pyramids were not built in one man's lifetime,' thought Arran as he laughed to himself.

Arran and Riley explored the exterior of one side of the massive pyramid. Arran wondered at the carved stone bricks that were three to four times the height of him, ten times the width, a surely immovable mass, levered and levied one on top of the other, bricks in numbers way beyond which Arran could count. An unquantifiable amount. Everywhere Arran looked, he saw the strange remnants of a masterful civilisation, its art and culture immortalised in the pyramid and the hieroglyphic symbols, pictures and wall carvings.

The entrance was high on the pyramid's eastern side. Getting there took more effort than originally thought. The blocks were enormous, with the foundation-level blocks being over four times the height of Arran. Luckily, there were only a few levels of these preposterous monsters. The smaller, man-sized blocks acted like giant's steps but not all, somewhere joined and covered with an outer cladding. This flat, smooth, un-textured surface connecting sometimes three or four of the massive blocks together. Arran and Riley, under Riley's instruction, moved upwards, towards the entrance. Arran took it in his stride, to Riley's amazement, but after living with the Lamas people, climbing without the high possibility of death was strangely enjoyable.

As the two men exerted themselves in the emerging heat of the new day, face to face with the stone, they climbed. Arran used the time-eroded surface to plan his ascent. 'The continuous puzzle presented by the climb is strangely exhilarating,' thought Arran. Arran knew this Pyramid was old, older than any other man-made thing he had ever seen or experienced. Arran continued upwards, until they reached the opening to a large, underwhelming entrance to such a magnificent structure. No door greeted the two, just darkness where the light could not penetrate. Beyond the total darkness of the entrance, Arran hoped that there lay the pathways and passages to the depths of the structure, to her secrets. For as far as the light penetrated, the opening was covered in script, pictures and symbols, each delicately, skilfully carved into the solid granite walls, unlike the Tanni Ma Barian script they had shown him. Instantly, Arran knew the pyramid was not of Tanni Ma Bar origin. This was like no art, culture or language he had ever seen. One advantage of being Gavodeon, was travel. All of his life, he had come across and interacted with many different peoples, cultures, languages, ideas and most of them came from somewhere, most of which were traceable and connectable. Arran had seen nothing like this, it did not fit into his Gavodeon way of thinking and Arran thought that was strange. The massive pyramidal structure that looked older than time itself, welcomed the two young men into its underbelly with open arms.

The darkness was all-consuming. A strange low hum resonated, as the hustle and bustle of the city disappeared and the pair slipped deeper into the darkness. Then, with no warning, Riley lit a torch. Neither of their eyes appreciated the sudden change, the deep yellows and oranges of the flame initially burnt so bright it temporarily blinded Arran, masking the corridor that started adjacent to where he was standing.

"Where does that one lead?" asked Arran.

"They all lead to a central chamber, the King's chamber where once a glorious king lay, his body and soul directly connecting to the underworld and the overworld. That was before his corpse was stolen," replied Riley.

"Let's go to this burial chamber, let's do it, I need to see where the rich and famous leave their dead," laughed Arran.

"Ok," replied Riley, his annoyance at Arran's wit and scorn was visible in his voice and body language.

With the guidance of Riley's torch burning brightly, they made their way up the steep walkway before them, towards the King's chamber. As they approached the middle of the walkway, a strange hum began to resonate and quickly within a few steps, it grew louder and louder.

"Is that not driving you crazy?" questioned Arran.

"Is what not driving me crazy?" replied a confused Riley.

"The hum, the low, voooosh, voooosh, vooosh, voooosh," said Arran.

"I hear no hum Arran, just our footsteps as we walk, or breath as we breathe..." Riley stopped mid-sentence as he could see Arran was serious, he was hearing something that he could not.

"Vooosh, Vooosh, Vooosh," Arran stopped and crouched down next to the wall in front.

"Some light please Riley," said Arran.

Arran knelt down with his ear firmly against the wall that led to the King's death chamber. The voosh intensified as he laid his ear against the wall. Within seconds, he was being ripped from his body. As his consciousness left his body, it joined with a great flow that rose along a physical network, built right into the infrastructure of the pyramid, from the grounds beneath the pyramid right to the capstone that crowned her. The energies from Arran's body flowed directly into the King's death chamber. This was the focal point, where all the energy from all over the pyramid was unified, amplified, purified and re-patterned before being beamed directly upwards through the capstone of the pyramid. It was as if it had transported him into a raging waterfall as a fish, but as soon as the water fall hit the turbulent waters below, it somehow filtered back in to the very waterfall it had come from. The energy all around was surging through the pyramid, constantly, continuously but the pathways were wrong, like log jams in the rivers that feed the waterfall. He could sense that the pathways were wrong, the original design and purpose of the pyramid was broken. 'Were these broke by time?' wondered Arran.

"Arran, Arran, Arran," shouted a panicked Riley, as he pulled him from the wall.

Arran's body convulsed as his consciousness came back from the strange, energetic river he had joined with.

"Arran, Arran," shouted a hysterical Riley "Are you there, are you hearing me?" shouted Riley

Arran looked up. His eyes told Riley everything he needed to know.

"What happened? Why are you so panicked?" asked Arran.

"Your face changed, your eyes, your skin, it glowed with lines, bright red lines. They were glowing so bright, as if the torch or red-hot metal was under your skin, illuminating you from the inside. Then you began to shake, to convulse. Your fucking meridians lit up, what the fuck? Healers use them and there are charts and all, but they are invisible, yours lit the fuck up!! How is that even possible? I have seen nothing like that before...," shouted a shocked Riley.

"Wow, neither have I," said Arran "It sounds kind of amazing," he added.

"Why are you laughing, you crazy fuck, that was insane?" shouted Riley.

"I don't know how to react, I never witnessed what you saw. As strange as it was, it gets stranger, because whilst you were panicking over my glowing, pulsing mass. I somehow melded with the pyramid and entered some energetic stream that flows through the entire pyramidal structure, like an infinite looping river," said Arran.

"Em ok, Em. I don't know what you're talking about Arran, anyway we need to get back, like now," said Riley as he turned on his heels and began moving quickly towards the entrance with his torch.

"Hold up, hold up," shouted Arran as he pulled himself together and made his way towards the exit, in the heels of the firelight.

"Wow, that was intense," said Arran as he approached Riley in the warm, direct day light that was now illuminating the pyramid's entrance.

Riley looked at Arran and said nothing before turning and beginning his descent.

Arran followed him. As the pair made their descent down the perilous side of the pyramid, Arran unleashed a barrage of questions. They came thick and fast, "Who built it? How? Why? What was the purpose of the energetic river? What was the energetic river? Why could I hear it and not you? What are meridians? And why did mine begin glowing? Were we more advanced in the past? Did Nencom come from this more advanced race? Where the gods real?" Arran looked down at Riley as he finally realised that all his questions had fallen on deaf ears, Riley was descending rapidly, putting as much space between himself and the bizarre experience as he could. Arran shouted towards his scared friend as he scuttled further and further away, "Well, I hope Brother Moray has some answers," shouted Arran.

As Arran completed his descent, he could not stop thinking about the purpose and potential of this wondrous, mind melding architecture. "And this is just the beginning of this new adventure into the north, what other mysteries lie in this land," thought Arran.

Arran was extremely disappointed when he reached Brother Moray. Moray walked Arran over to an ancient wall tapestry. At the centre of the piece was a magnificent pyramid. It was deep in a valley, high walls of the mountainous valley hemming it in on both sides. A grand river snaked its way through the valley, then down and around the pyramid. On both sides of the river were thousands of men. They depicted the pyramid with an eye a third of the way down, with golden rays radiating out to every corner of the tapestry.

It prophesied that "The pyramids are the key". His fingers ran across the text emboldened on the bottom of the tapestry as he read it.

"Unfortunately, Arran, we know little. They are, in truth, still a complete enigma to us. This is one of the oldest relics connected with that time. The key to what, we do not know. The valley is of the great Ali Ma Bar, our sister city to the north east,' said Brother Moray, before he turned on his heals. As he walked, he shouted back before exiting. "The tapestry is called 'The overseer's' eye," then he was gone.

For many months, Arran explored and learned. The Tanni Ma Bar, after all were an ancient and wise race. Once, they were the rulers of the largest empire Lanasia had ever seen. The Tanni Ma Bar referred to this period of their history as The Age Of Golden, for wisdom was common and man lived to his fullest potential, yet they never once mentioned the origins of their culture, pyramids, or of its strange hieroglyphs. They never ever brought up any ideas of their shared origin, as told by the Gavodeon, Ternakas, Lamas, Biergyen and many other peoples of the south. The Tanni believed they were the beginning; they were the origin. 'Ludicrous,' thought Arran.

Tanni Ma Bar was now only a small city, a shadow of its former self. A couple of hundred thousand or so, Tanni now clung to the stories and glories of their past wealth, their past empire, and the power of their 'original' bloodline. Decimated by time, like all empires eventually, the echo of the great Tanni now survived in the furthest outposts of their once great empire. The greatest population of which, was here in the southern deserts, underneath the shadows of the Aurd, where their empire began. Arran was taught and instructed in many techniques of the mind, his eternal thirst to learn and absorb the Tanni Ma Bar knowledge blinded him temporarily from why he was there. Yes, they rescued him and yes, they had fed and kept him, but his quest to save his people must take top priority. Yet he knew that the longer he stayed with them, the more he could learn. Their knowledge had solidified the identity of his bogey man as the Namangan King. More knowledge could be invaluable to him on his quest to defeat this king in the north and stop an invasion to his beloved south. Arran's mind plagued him with guilt, he could not help but feel that the time he was there learning, he was wasting, selfishly amusing himself with culture and knowledge, relaxing in luxury, whilst the fate of his people hung in the wind. He felt like he was neglecting the great responsibility that life had bestowed upon his undeveloped shoulders.

Five months into his stay, two strangers arrived within the city's gates. Both were Lagosians from beyond the Aurd. One was a huge man, as big a man as any Gavod, one of the barbarian fighting clans, from the north of Lagosia, Biergyen possibly. He wore a loose-fitting cape, under it a simple loincloth and a pair of boots. On his back, he carried an enormous pack, weapons and a goat. The other was a small woman, wrapped in white robes, with a single small pack. Arran recognised her attire. It was from the Zaoists, an old and mysterious, spiritual tribe from beyond the trail, up to the north east. Their people sometimes came to trade at the Bay of Life. But he did not recognise her, she didn't come from the south; 'she's not a southerner,' thought Arran, 'she must be a native of the north.'

Arran was very curious, and he wasn't the only one. The high priests had stopped Arran's council and asked if he would remain in the library and its grounds until they summoned him. For almost a week, whilst the strangers had been in the Tanni Ma Bar capital, the only contact Arran had had was for food, water and instruction in proper reading materials by Riley. Although things were still awkward. Riley joked and conversed but had started to act like Arran was royalty, revering in everything he said. Arran was consumed by the ample learning the library granted him, but things were happening, which Arran sensed, included him, yet he was out of the loop, excluded. Who were these new strangers and why this strange lockdown? What are they hiding? thought Arran.

As Arran spent another day contemplating, reading, learning, Brother Moray entered the library.

"Young Arran, it is time. Your people are our people, the Gavods and the Tanni Ma Barians share the same ancient lineage! Nencom freed us before he left this magnificent city many, many thousands of years ago. He was the strongest of the original Tenni Uh Akki half gods, and the only one, we believe to revolt against his masters."

"You are his descendant, Arran. You have Nencoms blood. God's blood," said Brother Moray.

CHAPTER 13
- LATHORAN,
NANOC AND LOO

NANOC AND MISTRESS LOO's year-long spy camp had come to completion. Lathoran's archives housed much information of the north. Information gained from many sources, information brought in by the brotherhood, sailor's, traders, religious missionaries, gladiators and mystics. Nanoc and Loo spent time and learnt the strange Namangan tongue, culture and religion, as well as the Tanni language, which was similar to the common Gavodeon language used by all traders and merchants of the south. They studied northern maps, tribes and history, as well as fighting styles, military strategies, political systems, customs and hierarchies. Aspects of the archives however, were out of date due to the rapid changes that were now taking place in the north. The Namangan empire was expanding, accelerating its pace, faster now than at any point in history. Entire countries, cultures and histories were being lost to the merciless, progressive and destructive machine they called, The Empire Of The Immortal King. Very few southerners who went to the north ever returned to flaunt their wealth and those who found success, most likely made profitable businesses which kept them in the north. Maybe this was the reason they never returned. Combatants on the hunt for fame and fortune most likely died in the arenas. It was, after all, a hard way to make a crust.

As well as all things Namangan, every day the duo practised their martial arts. Every day, day in, day out, they tirelessly, relentlessly, worked on all aspects of their martial skills; mental toughness, sparring, fitness, mobility, flexibility, proper rest, proper nutrition, unarmed and armed combat drills. Nanoc was also introduced to the mystical energetic side of combat and everyday he practised the basic skills diligently; he had a lot to learn.

As well as learning everything about single combat for the entertainment of the masses, the duo learnt military strategy, battle field leadership, communication techniques and logistics. They spent evenings memorising many key historic battles, and the lessons learnt from them.

The plan for the north was simple, infiltrate the gladiatorial fighting circuits of Namanga, the biggest and most profitable fighting circuit in all of Lanasia and then use it as their eyes and ears. Nanoc was to be the warrior, a prized Biergyen barbarian from the south of the Aurd and Mistress Loo, his trainer, masseuse and manager. And if the opportunity arose, they were to kill the King.

When the day arrived for the two to leave, each of the warriors took some personal time and performed their own farewell ritual. Mistress Loo took time to walk around the complex which had been her home, her school and training grounds for the last year. As she walked, she quietly contemplated the journey ahead and remembering one last time, everything she had learnt here, in this place. Nanoc, on the other hand walked to the centre of the training hall, the hall he had made his own through endless hours of sweat and tears. With a quick and precise movement, he drew his main sword and raised it firmly above his head, simultaneously, he screamed with passion and certainty;

"Summerian, first of your kind, your fate is sealed."

As they left the complex, Lathoran knew that these warriors would be instrumental in determining the future of Lagosia; as a federation of free nations or as an enslaved people, under a tyrant King. All of his personal plans for Lanasia rested on the shoulders of these two Valdaharians. Now all that remained between them and the mission in the north was the mighty Aurd.

As the two warriors left the compound, Loo shook Lathoran's hand.

"Our job seems easy compared to yours, best of luck at the summit of the south, convincing those bastards to do good. I'd rather take my chances with the north and the King," said Nanoc.

"It will be hard, no doubt. But I believe the truth will speak for itself. I will find out in two days' time," said Lathoran, with no expression of confidence.

"The south will be ready," shouted Lathoran, as Nanoc and Loo disappeared into the horizon.

***

SAILING AROUND AURD'S END would have been easier and possibly quicker, but conquering the Aurd, that was a symbol for the journey ahead thought Nanoc.

Cross over the roof of the world, then kill the immortal King. That's how legends were born thought Nanoc.

Nanoc and Loo took over six months to get to and conquer the mighty Aurd. After leaving the training complex, they made their way to the only known pass, which was deep in the mountain ranges, southwest. Their path took them past the sprawling camp of the Gavodeons, where they attempted to purchase a guide for the mountain crossing, but to their amazement the traders of all traders refused to supply them a guide. Time and time again, the traders dismissed them quickly, uninterested in providing passageway through the Aurd, at this time. One trader reacted as if Nanoc had asked to purchase an evening with his beloved yak. He was as tall and thick built as Nanoc, with a beard so black and deep, it was as if his head only had eyes and a nose, his lips and teeth were only revealed when he talked. Nanoc laughed at the reaction and the lack of a trade, as it now seemed there were some things that even a Gavod would not sell, but why? thought Nanoc.

But in true Gavodeon fashion, the skilful trader upsold them provisions and furs for the cold that would soon engulf them. Nanoc, a seasoned buyer himself, stood his ground and would only make the purchases if they had someone escort them, at least to the beginning of the trails that crossed the Aurd. As they did the deal, Nanoc confided in Loo with a raised eyebrow that the strange, hairy, uncultured savages were usually extremely hospitable, hard negotiators but always super friendly. However, this was the first time he had ever encountered them in their own environment, their own camp, 'here in their own territories they don't need to play the salesman's game,' thought Nanoc.

"Aye, seems you can't even rely on great Gavodeon customer service," laughed Nanoc out loud. Loo believed there was something else happening, she said she could sense a strange undertone of fear and uncertainty mixed with excitement within the camp. Nanoc thought she and her senses were full of shit. Yet during his year with her, he had seen her jump so far and high, it was as if she was flying. He had seen her read emotions and he had received more than one of her legendary, energetic attacks. As much as he portrayed that she was full of shit, he knew she was onto something.

***

AS THE GAVOD THEY had dealt with prepared her Yak and her man, Nanoc and Loo prepped their own supplies and then they were off. The sombre feeling that Loo had felt from the Gavodeon camp had lifted as they left their camp, their light and their songs behind.

Not too long after they left camp, Loo brought up the subject with the lead Gavodeon guide. "I felt a feeling of excitement and uncertainty in the camp?" said Loo. The Gavod looked down and across at the shorter woman and smiled. "Yes, your woman's intuition is keen, you read correctly. It is indeed a great time of change for us Gavodeons. Our great cycle has ended and the new one will soon be reborn."

"Ah," laughed Nanoc. "So, there is a beginning and an end to your cycle. I have often wondered about that. I tell you, you Gavodeons are strange. We only ever see you in other peoples' cities, towns and villages. Trading other people's goods, speaking other people's tongues and being extremely knowledgeable about other people's cultures, folklore, health cures and remedies. It's strange to see you in your own home and to be talking to you in your own tongue," laughed Nanoc. "I am learning every day".

As the four travellers continued further along the path, Loo spoke again. "No, it was not a common feeling, it was uncertainty, it was unease, tension, division. Why would you feel such emotions as a tribe if it was something that happens time and time again? No, there is something else, but I will not push, I just wished to speak my mind, one woman to another. I have been lumped with this unfeeling brute for the last year and it is good to have some female company again, even if it is just for a few days." The Gavodeon man turned towards Loo and turned away laughing. "I know how you feel, Gavodeon men are about as sensitive as a lump of Yak dung, that is why I spent years making sure my Ar........." instantly she burst into tears and the yak train came to a halt.

"Viki, come here," said the male Gavodeon, still holding the yaks' reigns as he embraced his lover.

"Please forgive Viki, she has been through a lot recently. Her son, a rare sensitive soul, has left her, left us, left all Gavodeons and well, we are still coming to terms with it," said the large Gavod as he hugged Viki tight.

Loo instantly sensed that this was the emotion, the sentiment she was feeling, that the entire camp was feeling. 'For the loss of one son?' thought Loo.

Nanoc, took two steps forward, to the side of the Yak, where the couple stood in each other's arms and embraced them both. "Aye, I have no words, nor know of your customs, I am sorry for your loss." said Nanoc, with sincerity.

"Sorry, he is not dead, he has just left, he actually walked this path himself," said the male Gavod as Nanoc left the embrace.

"Irvine is just a man but my son, our son, he has become the Mertak. He was chosen through trial to lead his people. He would have only had to walk one more cycle as a Mertak in waiting, and he would have led our tribe. He chose the coward's route, to release himself from these responsibilities and go north into the Namangan territories. His decisions have shattered and divided our people." said Viki.

"No Viki, don't believe their lies, you know Arran better than anyone. He saw something. The sun blessed him with a vision, a calling, something we as non-Mertaks could never understand. He is selfless, he is fulfilling his destiny, and bringing Mertak to us all," said Irvine, the couple's embrace ceased to be.

Viki turned to Loo, "Did you get your answers?" she stated sarcastically, the emotions raw in her voice.

The Yak began to move. Nanoc raised an eyebrow to Loo as Irvine turned towards her.

"If you come across a young Gavod named Arran on your travels, tell him we love him dearly and we will see him when he returns,".

Loo smiled, nodded and agreed, then a silence, an awkwardness, took over the group and they all simultaneously picked up the pace and began marching hard ahead.

Viki and Irvine led them to what Viki referred to as "the only available low-level pass of the Aurd".

After two days trekking, Loo and Nanoc found the term "low level" extremely funny. It was the lowest pass the Aurd offered, but it was still a serious endeavour that led them away up into the snowy peaks, to the roof of the world. The Aurd, it seemed, did not do weakness! Loo observed that Nanoc liked this.

The Gavodeons stopped the Yak. "This is it; this is as far as we go. Follow the path up into the Lamas lands and then up further into the Ternakas Lands, then down into the deserts of the north," said Viki.

"Safe journeys, may the spirit of Mertak travel with you," said Irvine.

As the couple turned to return, Loo shouted. "If we see your son, we will tell him he is much loved". At that, she turned and began moving forward.

Before them, the path opened up into a magnificent vista, dark jagged peaks burst from a snow-covered landscape that surrounded them and continued on into the distance, for as far as the eyes could see. They were now just above the forest line and could see the path before them dip down again, into the forest below, before rising high up once again to the other side of the valley. As the dynamic duo entered the forest, both felt the hairs rise on the necks and arms.

"Nanoc," whispered Loo.

Nanoc scanned the forest in front before turning towards his short companion, "Wolves?" asked Loo as Nanoc sniffed the air. His facial expression told Loo that the scent was not a wolf.

"There is definitely something here, a predator of some kind, but it's not a wolf, it's an odd smell. If I was a betting man, I would say it is a cat, but different and I can't be sure, but I smell more than one of whatever it is," whispered Nanoc as he continued to scan the trees out in front. "Hopefully it's just a heavily scented area, the breeding ground for some mountain cats, lets continue. Nothing to concern us here, but keep your guard up. Those pesky kittens can be unpredictable," laughed Nanoc, Loo nodded.

Three paces after his speech, the scent hit him hard, overpowering in its strength, the pungent musky fragrance was blown in from the right, on a powerful gust of wind. As Nanoc turned to his right to catch a glimpse of the mysterious being that was creating the smell, he heard an almighty hellish roar from his left. Nanoc knew the ambush was coming. As he spun to his left to establish eyes on the roar, his sword unleashed. As he spun to his left, his eyes seen nothing of the beast that had roared, of the beast that should have been in plain sight. In that instance, Nanoc allowed himself to continue his momentum and spin, directing himself down onto his right shoulder and rolling over it. After he rolled, he came up hard, facing the opposite direction, the direction the scent came from, the true direction he believed the attack was coming from. His nose was right. As Nanoc sprung up from his gymnastic tumble, his sword came up and in one majestic, powerful sweep, decapitated the huge Cassartan that was almost on top of him. Without a pause, Nanoc kicked the carcass of the dead beast aside and scanned the area again. Loo stood still, not moving from her original spot. Her heart beat slowly. She was like ice as she watched, as she observed the fine work of her fellow Valdaharian. No more Cassartans arrived.

"It looks like we will feast tonight," laughed Loo.

"A feast for sure but the skins are mine," Loo was shocked at the tone of Nanoc's voice.

"Never come between a hunter and his prize," said Loo, as she looked over to Nanoc and the impressive beast that lay at his feet. "How simple you are, my friend. It makes me smile every time," said Loo.

"The hunt is a sacred thing," whispered Nanoc.

"Not really a hunt, Nanoc. More of a reactionary masterclass but I will not challenge you for the furs of this beautiful beast". As Loo kicked the carcass of the Cassartan, she could feel the tensions between them melt. Nanoc was satisfied. Loo made a mental note that she had to watch out for the strange, cultural triggers that lay deep inside this now trusted ally. For it felt like he would have risked the Valdahar, on the pelt of a dead animal, if she had not backed down., 'How strange cultural traditions are,' thought Loo, as she held out her hand to help Nanoc back to his feet, while he inspected his new furs.

In the next three months, they never heard, smelt or saw another Cassartan or Lanasian, as they completed the cold mountainous leg of their mission north.

No Ternakas, nor Lamas people, as promised by their Gavodeon guides. Their intelligence informed them that the desert they were now entering was one of the last remaining outposts of non-Namangan controlled territories left in the north. Beyond the desert lay the first city of the Tanni Ma Bar, where they would seek accommodation and determine their alliance in the upcoming war.

For three weeks they walked under canopy, fast but controlled, only breathing through their noses. These two southerners both came from hot environments and found the sun no mean feat. As the first day of the fourth week began, the first sight of settlements and greenery entered the warrior's view.

"Look Loo, to the northwest." said Nanoc.

Mistress Loo looked towards the sun; 'it seems that civilisation is getting closer,' she thought. Nanoc was still pointing, way before the city, far in the distance was a goat herder and his goats. After a while, the warriors finally caught up and approached the young goat herder. Loo bowed deep and presented the Tanni Ma Bar greeting. The young herder was visibly anxious, things in the north were changing, strangers were now a regular event and the huge tattooed barbarian did nothing to ease his anxiety.

"My friend, we are travelling into the city. We would be thankful if we could purchase a goat to offer them," said Loo, in her first attempt at the high Tanni/Gavodeon language on this side of the Aurd.

"Oh, your accent's funny," laughed the young man nervously. He continued, "Is he your pet, does he speak?", the young goat herder pointed at Nanoc before continuing again. His words were thick and fast and heavily accented. "Why would a barbarian and a, well, whatever race you are, why would you be performing the Goat Rite? I don't think so, but I don't really care. As you can imagine, in times like these, goats are precious and, well, this herd is my only possession, and seeing that the dirty Namangans bastards will be coming here soon," the young herder took a second to spit on the sands, at the Namangans before continuing. "I am afraid the going rate for a goat will be about fifty gold strips,".

"Let me kill him, we'll just take his goats," Nanoc's eyes were ablaze as he shouted, and Loo could see he was not posturing.

"My young friend, we asked to buy a goat to build a friendship and show respect to you, your leaders and your culture, but I can see things are changing fast here." The herder had heard enough, as he turned to move away, Loo intercepted him, using a joint lock to the young herder's arm whilst simultaneously pushing her etheric energy down through his limbs deep into the ground, rooting him to the ground and immobilising him instantly.

"Beautiful execution Loo, slow but I suppose it's down to those small legs of yours," Nanoc and Loo's eyes meet, as their laughter released.

With warmth and laughter, Loo tried addressing the young herder again.

"Now you might have gathered, that if my friend here had his way, you would be dead already and we would have left your goats for dead. But I know that there is more than you who depend on these animals, so you will give us your best price on a goat and then we will be on our way," stated Loo, as a matter of fact.

"The goat to the left of you" said the herder. Nanoc pointed to a nice plump, marbled goat, a promising beast.

"Yes him, he's my prize, my stud, anyone but him. Five strips, that's a fair deal," said the herder, still rooted to the ground, where Loo had left him.

"Where I come from boy; five strips of gold would buy you a roast goat with tarragon, thyme and rosemary, a flagon of ale, good ale, a few bets on a fight and a good woman for the night. Your goat hasn't even been cooked and you want three strips of gold for it?" said Nanoc, without the slightest hint of sarcasm in his heavily accented Tanni.

"Hahahah," Mistress Loo erupted into a fit of laughter at Nanoc's negotiation techniques, "Three gold strips," laughed Loo. The two warriors enjoy the moment, Loo reflected momentarily on the close bond that had developed between them over the last seventeen months. Whilst the young herder struggled to comprehend what the two strangers were laughing about. Nanoc looked the young herder in the eyes.

"How many in your family, boy? How many children?" asked Nanoc.

"Seven children," said the young man.

Nanoc produced four strips of gold from his pouch. The herder smiled as Mistress Loo released him from the arm lock and waved her etheric energy away, releasing it from his legs. Nanoc selected the second-best goat and slung it over his massive shoulders.

"His father will be pleased. Four strips of gold for a goat is unprecedented, I hope there are many Arenas up here, buying goats at that price, we will be penniless in no time," said Loo.

"Well sometimes, you have to share the love. We will make that back ten times over, the first fight we confirm." replied Nanoc as the two warriors moved off into the distance, towards the city.

CHAPTER 14 - ARMON

"ARMON, TWO STRANGERS APPROACH the city from the south. They were spotted crossing over the outer sand line last night and they will be here soon. One of them is definitely a warrior. We believe they could bring trouble or they might be here for Arran?"

The young monk looked up, waiting to be dismissed.

"Thank you, arena competitors from the south?" said Armon as he stroked his chin.

"Yes, that would be my evaluation," said the young monk.

"Ok, thank you. You are dismissed," said Armon.

As the door clicked shut behind the monk, Armon took a moment to reflect on the information.

'Why do they waste my time with such information? Why do the religious cast find it important to trouble me with the fact that two travellers approach the city, hundreds of travellers enter the city daily, what are they not telling me?' thought Armon.

Armon turned quickly, his eyes scorched with frustration as he shouted. "Riley, summon the high priestesses to my quarters," then realising his lapse in self-control, quickly reflecting on his outburst, whilst observing the shocked and somewhat timid Riley's puzzled expression, like he was in trouble, Armon lowered his tone, meeting Riley's eyes "NOW, lad."

Armon stood quietly, allowing his mind to run riot, as he contemplated the reasons, the possibilities of why this information was important? The King had sent an entire division of his elite guard, his personal protectors to scout the desert's eight moons back and another only two moons back. Both times, the area that the young nomad was found near death and now two travellers, one of which is a warrior, are coming across the same patch of desert from the south? This made no sense, but 'why should it?' thought Armon.

The high priestesses arrived, accompanied by one of the high priests, in particular the specific priest, Brother Moray, the brother responsible for Arran, here in Tanni Ma Bar.

"Thank you for coming" Armon turned as he closed the gap between him and Moray.

"It is good to see you, brother, but why?" asked Armon.

Brother Moray stood, relaxed as he returned Armon's full gaze.

"He is here because there are things you need to know Armon, things that might affect our future, our security as a people, and as that is your department, you must know what is really happening," said Ilera, the lead high priestess.

"That is what I'm trying to figure out. Elite guards, twice, then the strange Gavod, who you and your ilk have been swooning over, like flies to shit and soon, two more southerners will be upon the city. Two strangers who you know something about but have not informed me about. Therefore, I summoned you, to find out if these southerners were here in relation to the Gavod? Why are these two, out of the hundreds that enter the city each month, why? What have your divinations and quackery foretold?" Armon's body tightened up, unconsciously bracing himself to receive a body punch or some physical attack.

"Armon, the two warriors that approach the city are not here for the Gavod, they are, we think, the bringers of war," said Ilera.

"Thank you, sister. Armon, the young Gavod is not young at all, he is the very spirit of Nencop, also known as Nencor and Nemcom. To the Gavodeons, he is Nencom the liberator, Nencom the fearless and most importantly Nencom the transformer. In the fables of Arran's people, he is the greatest Lanasian that has ever lived, within the youthful body emanates an ancient and powerful soul. Arran is here to challenge the Namangan King. It is his fate, if he chooses it. Now, we must choose to assist him or not," said Brother Moray.

"The young Gavod has the power to bring down The King? Every Lanasian born under the glorious sun has that potential, for The King is only a man." Armon smiled through his anger before he continued, "A great soul returned? Where do you guys come up with this mumbo jumbo?" Armon didn't realise it, but he was now shouting, his posture was tense and he was staring down every one of the class of priests before him, his eyes full of contempt. Armon spun, the light in the room catching the warrior's face as he took a breath and continued, calmer this time.

"Arran is just a stranger from a primitive nomadic culture. He is young and determined and this is his first time here, his first time away from his people. He is not aware of our history and culture, he may be coming across all messiah like, but any correlations between him and your prophecy is just coincidence, bias that you have placed upon him to fulfil your assumptions." Armon turned towards Brother Moray, who had let out a short, mocking laugh. Their eyes met and Moray smiled at Armon whilst he kept his gaze. Armon continued.

"The elite guard is here to evaluate our defences, after all, we will be the last city they will need to conquer to claim total control of the north. Our great city would then be used as a base to conquer beyond the Aurd," smiled Armon, as if educating small, simple children.

"Yet, you believe that the King sent his elite guard to find the Gavod because he knows that the kid is somehow a threat to his empire. Or that he sent the warriors of the sun, his elite guard, of which there are possibly under fifty in the entire Namangan empire, to intercept the two from the south. The two you claim are the bringers of war. You realise how ridiculous that sounds!! Bringers of war. The Namangan King is the bringer of war, he has been for over fifty years, in one form or another. OK, when they arrive, I will ask them. The proof of your piss and miss, prophetic mumbo jumbo will be in the pudding," stated Armon.

"You have seen most of it without our sight, Armon." The high priestess returned his sarcasm and disdain, her emotive eyes drilling deep into Armon's.

"Arran needs to be trained in many more things if he is to stand a chance against The King, starting with a realisation of who he really is. We need to get him to Barratash, he is the only one left of our people, who can take him to the next level."

The priestess had not moved. Her eyes stayed tightly on Armon as he paced the room, shaking his head in disbelief.

"Summerian is not sure, this is why he never brought his main armies south. He can feel Arran's growing presence in the web that connects all life but can't or doesn't quite understand what he is. This could be because Arran is still transforming. The two from the south are Valdahars. When we ruled the north, the Lagosians warred amongst themselves, each nation state trained assassins to enter one another's territories, spreading propaganda, collecting strategic information and assassinating enemies. It seems they have revived the practice," said Ilera.

"We have to agree to disagree, I really think that our chances of survival lie in science, engineering and historical studies, not premonition and mumbo jumbo. You say the lad needs to recognise who he is, does this mean that I am some reincarnated soul that has lived many lives but my past beyond the grave was not of significance, therefore I do not need to reclaim my past greatness to play my part in saving my people? No, whoever built the pyramid used science and engineering, not mumbo jumbo. Just like in war, practical experience coupled with historical battle studies and hours of strategy games lays a solid foundation for winning. Thinking of the outcome doesn't make it so, action makes it so. If he is who you say he is, he needs to be trained in the strategies of war, in battle technologies, in tactics and weapons engineering, not shipped off to some quack we have banished because his mumbo jumbo was even too extreme for you crack pots," shouted a frustrated Armon.

The group was startled when someone knocked on the door.

"Yes, come in," said Armon.

"Master the two southern strangers are at the outer gates of the city, should we let them through, they bare the old custom of a sacred goat!" said Riley.

"Yes, take them to the Ten-tiens square and stay with them until I arrive". With that, the young man was off.

"They are here, they have made extraordinarily good pace in the desert, these southerners are strong, fit and it seems experienced in desert travel. Has anyone any suggestion before I leave to meet them?" said Armon.

"We need to engage the southerners with the truth, well most of the truth, we cannot reveal the true identity of Arran until the correct time, for the more people who know who Arran is, the less chance Arran has of defeating the king," said the high priestess.

Armon shook his head in disbelief of what he is hearing.

"Yes, I agree we must be up front, we will need to ally ourself with the south to have any chance of keeping our people and our history alive."

At this, Armon signalled for Brother Moray to follow him.

"Brother, shall we welcome our guests?" said Armon warmly, with no hint of sarcasm or insincerity as they turned to leave the room on their way to meet the southern warriors.

***

NANOC'S IMMENSE GIRTH, HIS weapons and tattoos usually got a reaction, he was used to it but here they just ignored him. They glanced and continued with their business. No one apart from the guards on the outer city gates and the young Tanni Ma Barian in front had said anything. Mistress Loo and Nanoc curiously followed the young Riley to the meeting point he claimed his master would be at. The architecture was old; the streets were uniform and decorative, if not a little faded by time. Sewage and water run off entered drains with metal grates over them. The city instantly impressed Nanoc. After many short streets, and many confusion inducing turns and re-directs, they reached a bridge and a very nice-looking tavern. As the pair looked ahead of them, just beyond the bridge, lay a very open and somewhat unpopulated square. Nanoc was on full alert.

"Is this where we will meet with your master sir?", asked Loo.

"Yes, my Master will be here shortly, I have to wait with you until he appears," replied Riley.

"So, young pup, who is the man you call master? What is he a master of?" asked Nanoc.

"He is Armon, head of the military and ..." Riley's words were cut short by Armon across the square.

"I am a master of many things," completed Armon.

Nanoc turned slightly to lay eyes on the voice. Armon approached quickly and met the two warriors, eye to eye.

"I am Armon and this is Brother Moray and our student Riley, you have met. Welcome to Tanni Ma Bar, friends. I see you have brought a goat. Is it still alive? I could get you a good price for it," said Armon.

"Firstly, my name is Loo..."

"And I am Nanoc."

Armon nodded

"The goat is still alive, and it's a fine beast. I thank you for your offer, but it's not for sale. We have brought this as an offering to you and your people that we come in peace. This here, is the first city we have seen in a month since we entered the desert. We are simply looking to pay for a room, food and a woman for my fighter and we will be off in the morning." explained Loo.

"Ah, you are fighters, heading north to the arenas," Armon looked Nanoc up and down then addressed him directly. "You are in fine condition, a fine specimen. Will you be fighting un-armed or armed in the arenas? I dabbled a little in the arenas when I was younger."

Nanoc closed the gap until there no longer was one and he was but a hair's width off Armon.

"I fight any man who will stand in an arena with me, armed or-unarmed," Nanoc said, keeping his eye contact, as his nose pushed against Armons. Within a breath and a heart beat he noticed a fighter in the eyes of Armon, and a respect was born.

"Aye, you definitely have a warrior's heart, Armon. That much I can tell and you control your energies as well," Nanoc winked at Mistress Loo, "The real question is, what style do you use? How long did you compete? Did you win? Who was the best you ever fought? I love meeting seasoned veterans of the arena, and you are the first veteran of the northern arenas I have encountered first hand. I would be interested in discussing, we," Nanoc pointed to Loo "Martial technique, arena rules and customs, etc," said Nanoc.

"I would be delighted, but if I may, why did you bring a goat? Why did you enact an ancient gesture of kindness? If you were just in transit, two warriors on a long road looking for a bed? Surely by passing this ancient ceremony and using coin to purchase goods directly, would have served you better?" said Armon.

Nanoc looked over at Loo, Loo turned back to Armon.

"A simple gesture of friendship is never to be overlooked. We have just set off on this new journey, a dream of conquering the northern arenas, a dream of wealth and fame. The goat, I agree may be misplaced in its ceremonial value but for us, it was more of a gesture of good trade and friendship, not only to yourselves but to the north as a whole, as we enter this new land beyond the Aurd, ready to conquer her arenas. As you know, not many from beyond the Aurd ever make it to the top of the Namangan circuit. We will garner luck, from any local customs that we can get," said Loo, smiling easily with Armon.

"Interesting philosophy, your way of planting a seed for a positive and profitable venture, a ritual. Ah, you southerners are a strange bunch. Well, I will accept the goat, but I have to be honest with both of you, we know you are warriors headed for the arenas but we also know that you are going north to collect information on the Namangan empire, on the King." Loo and Nanoc's eyes instantly met before realising what they had done, they returned to a jovial bluff like the great actors they were.

"I would like to discuss with you, the possibilities of opening some sort of alliance, between our people and the Lagosians." said Armon.

"I thought it was a bit strange that our goat was not taken at the gate, and that we were marched so far into the city, to such a militarily," Loo paused, as if contemplating her words, her thoughts. She gestured to the surrounding area, hands and arms sweeping around as she spun on her heels "hahaha a perfect place for an ambush..." she smiled as Nanoc's mind began to race.

"Is our cover blown already, how have you come across this information? Many fighters travel north to fight, we could be just another two on their way to the fabled riches of the northern arenas. Is our cover blown? Or have I just blown it," demanded Nanoc.

"When we ruled the north, when our empire was strong, centuries ago, various nations within what is now Lagosia, regularly sent their valdahars into our territory to find out if we were thinking of expanding south. As the Namangans have now conquered all of the north, threatening your people, we bluffed and we bluffed well. We have been truthful about who we are, so we can build a friendship, an alliance, and hopefully also save our people from the Namangans," said Armon.

"How many of your people know who we really are?" asked Nanoc.

"Just us here and a priest and two priestesses," replied Armon.

"If they compromise our identity, I will personally inflict so much pain on them, they will regret the day they ever heard my name," said Mistress Loo.

"Is that clear, Armon? What do you know of the Namangans?" said Nanoc.

"Were do I start?" replied Armon.

"We start by moving out of the sun and into that tavern, or to your quarters." said Nanoc.

"I agree," stated Armon

The four headed for the tavern to discuss the ins and outs of the Namangan empire.

***

As NANOC AND LOO'S first evening in Tanni Ma Bar came to a close, Nanoc informed his new allies.

"I think if we are staying for a few more nights, I will thank you for the insights and the fine food and call it a day. It is now time for me to test out the plumbing of this magnificent city and then get my head down for the night. And this one, she needs her beauty sleep," Nanoc winked at Loo as he addressed Armon directly. Nanoc and Loo retired to rooms above the inn.

The two had agreed to stay in Tanni Ma Bar for a few days to discuss everything that had been brought up in the tavern discussion. Brother Moray had been relentless in his request that they transport the young Gavod to someone called Barratash on their road north. After several days of discussions, agreements, disagreements, fine food and no major exercise, Nanoc decided it was time to leave. Loo and Nanoc committed to memory, everything their new friends had taught them about the north. Nanoc made a thorough note of everything he had heard and in exchange for transporting the young Gavod north, they would make sure his note was delivered to Lathoran, with great urgency.

***

"INNKEEPER," SAID NANOC AS he entered the tavern for breakfast.

"How did you sleep, was everything to your satisfaction," said the small balding man with enthusiasm.

"It sure was. An indoor outhouse is something magical," laughed Nanoc.

"Can I get you some breakfast," asked the innkeeper as he passed Nanoc and Loo the morning menus.

"Thank you. Can you get a message to Armon?" said Loo.

"I can. His student Riley is on hand," said the Innkeeper.

"We will leave today, after the midday sun starts to return to the underworld. So, tell Armon to prepare the boy for travelling. And then bring me one of everything," laughed Nanoc.

CHAPTER 15 - NANOC, LOO & ARRAN

"ARRAN, THIS IS NANOC and Loo, they are traveling the great Northern Road to Yi Ma Bar and beyond. We have arranged for you to travel with them to Um Ma Bar, there you will meet Barratash. He has many skills that the sisters and I believe will benefit you greatly, as you begin your transformation. We have taught you all we can here with our resources," said Brother Moray.

Arran nodded, acknowledging Brother Moray, as he looked across at his new travel companions. The large barbarian and the small woman looked back indifferently.

"Hello Arran, I am Loo and this is Nanoc. No doubt as a Gavod you will have come across my people, the Zaoists. We often trade with your people at the Bay of Life. Biergyens, I assume need no introduction." said Loo.

"Aromia, I thought you looked different? Sorry, that was rude," spurted an excited Arran but she did not look upset by his lack of manners.

"Sorry, thanks for agreeing to walk with me to Um Ma Bar, I look forward to sharing the journey with you."

Arran's destination was around fourteen days walk, about three hundred and fifty miles to the north west via an ancient, yet well-crafted Tanni Road. Arran's new companions were strange, they never talked to him much. If he was more self-conscious of how others thought of him, he may even have thought that he was a burden to them. However, years of being the silence in the song made this a norm. Yet he tried, he was curious why these fellow southerners were also here in the north. Every conversation with the big one, either started or ended with a "silence boy". As the first day of walking with his new companions came to completion, barely a word had been exchanged. As they approached a small watering hole, his new companions unanimously decided to set up camp for the night.

"Exercise then we will eat," declared Nanoc in the Tanni language, which was near identical to Gavodeon.

"Arran, here boy," shouted Nanoc.

"I am no boy," Arran replied in Nanoc's first tongue, not in Gavodeon. He was a bit rusty in speaking Biergyen, but spoke well enough to get Nanoc's attention. Arran took a few steps closer to Nanoc. Now within a few feet of the huge barbarian, the fear began to grow, like a rat gnawing at the pit of his stomach, but he knew he had to swallow it down. There could be no weakness in his voice. This time Arran spoke in Gavodeon/Tanni, for Mistress Loo to hear.

"I am Arran, Mertak, and one day leader to all Gavods. I am young, true, but I am a man and one day a leader of men, not a boy," Arran kept his eyes firmly locked on Nanoc's.

***

MISTRESS LOO SAT RELAXED, leaning on her backpack as she watched, observing the body language and energy dynamics between the two men. Loo seen a strange energetic quality in Arran, something she was not expecting, something she had never expected. She was a master of energetic combat and healing and here was something she had never seen before and something she had no real reference point for. As she concentrated on her energetic training, she could see his base energy centre, just below his bum swell and connect with the ground. The energy then moved upwards, from the ground into him. As it did, it transmuted through him and pulsed, pushing upwards through channels that did not relate to anything she had ever seen or been taught about before. Her mind raced, however a constant ghosting thought clung to all, 'she was witnessing an energetic potential, the likes of which she had never witnessed before. Was there more for her to learn?' Loo felt a rush of excitement. As she concentrated on what she was experiencing, Loo felt echoes of Nanoc's raw thoughts, thoughts of death, of murder, of swiftly and effortlessly killing the boy where he stood. This message was mirrored in Nanoc's face and posture.

"That's enough," shouted Mistress Loo, "Nanoc, exercise!" Loo made eye contact with Arran. As the energy he was building dissipated, she diverted his attention with an invitation.

"Would you like to join us?"

***

ARRAN LOOKED AT LOO, perplexed by the invitation to exercise! He had seen the wealthy traders in the bigger cities run for fun, a concept he never understood.

"Exercise, why?" asked Arran.

"Exercise is one of the keys to life, young Mertak. Health is wealth and if you truly are to become a leader of men, you will have to become strong of body, as well as of mind. Practical strength will help you in every aspect of life. For example, we are travelling over rough terrain for many days; better conditioning in the body will make the long journey easier on the body and on the mind," explained Mistress Loo.

"A strong mind is nothing without a strong body. They should always be in balance with each other," continued Loo, before throwing Nanoc his fighting pole.

"Shoulder press," said Loo.

Nanoc raised the poll up to rest horizontally across his chest.

"Arran," called the huge barbarian, "grab the end, please". With Loo and Arran gripping tightly to each end, Nanoc began his exercise. His raw strength was unparalleled and his endurance was evidently well trained. Arran and Loo were hauled upwards, as Nanoc pressed them up above his head, again and again, ten times in total. It impressed Arran, the strength this barbarian possessed was immense. As Arran let go of the pole, Nanoc shouted "Where are you going? I have another twenty sets to do, get your scrawny carcass back on here." Their eyes meet, this time Arran noticed a sarcasm and a smile "Please," added Nanoc, to Arran's amusement. After some time, Arran felt like he was the one exercising, holding his own weight time and time again.

"Arran, now we do some push ups and squats". After showing Arran how to do push ups and squats, Nanoc went into his own routine of one armed and one-legged variations. After the two warriors finished their exercise, they both spent time developing their martial skills. At this, Arran moved to start setting up his bed for the night.

"Before you retire for the night, young Mertak. Let me bestow some wisdom on you, something for you to dream about," boomed Nanoc.

Arran raised his eyebrows and nodded at the big barbarian, as he continued clearing the ground around where he was about to sleep.

"You, me, Loo, we are simply what we repeatedly do. When you breathe, you do not command your lungs in and out, when you walk, you do not command your legs to place one in front of the other. Your brain, your gut, your heart does that for you. How? Repetition. There is no secret mystery to life lad, the only thing you need to do, to become Mertak, to become a leader, is to define what a leader is and then repeatedly do it. Time and time again, until it becomes unconscious, as natural as breathing. Only then you will be the leader, not the leader you were born to be, that shit does not exist. You will be the leader you have moulded yourself into, through repetition. This is why we exercise as we do, it's why we spar as we do, why we act as we do. I have fashioned and forged this warrior you see before you through pure will. And when a punch comes in my direction, I do not think, I react on instinct, forged by a thousand drills, a thousand repetitions. There's wisdom in these words, son. Now enjoy your dreams. We have an early start tomorrow," said Nanoc as Arran listened intently, nodding to the wisdom being imparted.

The next morning, Arran awoke to loud screaming and his body being violently shaken. "Give me your fucking money boy, nnnow". Then before he really knew what was happening, he was picked up from his sleeping mat and flung across the camping area. In that instance, he knew he had to live. He knew he had to get to his feet, assess the situation, the surroundings, his attackers. As he hit the ground, he tried to roll, but with no practice he just jarred his shoulder into the ground, then the rest of his body head first. As he rose to his feet, he saw Nanoc standing, grinning before him.

"If I was really after your money or your life. You would be penniless and dead," laughed Nanoc.

Arran looked into Nanoc's eyes, unaware that his face was twisted in anger.

"Here is a message from your mum, lad," said Nanoc, his eyes still drilling into Arran's.

In the instant it took for Arran's face to convey confusion, Nanoc's large fist had come up from his side and landed flush on the right side of Arran's face. As his body began falling, Nanoc's kick hit him square in the chest, changing the direction of his fall and pushing him backwards, to crash into the ground once more.

Nanoc stood still and allowed the young Gavod to get back to his feet. Arran was a little shaken, but he stood tall and was ready to stand his ground against Nanoc.

"Leader of people! I think you need to master yourself before you lead folk. I think that's why your Mum was a bit pissed off with you. Yes, your Mum, Viki," said Nanoc.

Arran's mind rallied. How did Nanoc know his mum's name, and what is he talking about? "I am confused, what are you talking about?" blurted an emotional Arran.

"Two things. One, your mum and dad love you and they want to see you return to them, strong and ready to lead the Gavodeon nation," said Nanoc.

As Arran stood there, looking confused, Loo took over "We paid for supplies and a guide into the Aurd. The Gavods who made trade with us, just so happened to be your parents, Viki and Irvine," said Loo, with a sincere smile. "It is a small world!"

Tears came to Arran's eyes as the adrenaline from the attack settled.

Then Nanoc continued "And second, if you are to become a leader of a nation, you best toughen up. That was just a slap I gave you. And yes, we can see that you can take a punch and that your mentally tough, you have a fighter's resolve and a high threshold for pain and great mental control, for sure. But if you ain't careful, especially here, in this foreign land, you ain't going to be leading anyone. That could have been a knife. This is why we train. In my culture, you lead by example. And your people are the same, they trade hard and they don't take no shit from no one. It is a tough gig, rocking up into someone else's turf, I am guessing some friendly and some hostile.

Your leaders are strong. You, on the other hand, your soft as shit, too introverted. We heard all about you from Armon. Anyway, to you it might have been a shock getting a wee kick for breakfast but where I come from, that was my first meal of the day for ten years straight. Learn to defend yourself, physically as well as mentally and you will be the great leader your people and those fucking strange Tanni bastards are hoping for. Until then. Heads up," laughed Nanoc.

"Arran let me translate," said Loo as she moved closer to him, hands clasped in front. She moved slowly with grace. As she reached out to embrace Arran's hand, she continued, "Nanoc wants you to succeed. These methods have worked for him. He shares them with you as he wants you to live. We are transporting you to the north but once there, you will be on your own. No horde by your side. No Nanoc to protect you. Just, keep your wits about you. Be more present, if you wish to survive," said Loo, Arran could see and feel the love behind the words.

Arran stood still as he came to grips with the strange experience. Arran looked at his belongings now spread out all around, as he moved to pick up his kit, his two travel companions picked up their already packed belongings and set off. Arran quickly sorted his gear and set off after the duo. The two warriors set a mammoth pace, which Arran found hard to match, he, continuously fell behind. Foolishly, he assumed they would occasionally wait for him but he soon realised they would not be stopping for him, or slowing down so he ran every so often to bridge the gap. For a nomad, for a man who had spent his entire life travelling on foot, he really was surprised by the pace, drive and stamina of the two warriors, maybe there was something to this 'exercise' after all. After catching up to the two as they bathed in a river, Arran thought his luck was in for a break at last, quickly he unslung his belongings and took a seat, but as soon as his bum hit the moist grass, the warriors had exited the river and within two ticks they were off again. Arran joined them instantly in hot pursuit. As the sun faded, they could see a small town on the horizon. The three travellers headed for the light to seek a tavern with beds.

Nanoc, Mistress Loo and Arran located the only tavern, it seemed in the entire town. As they entered, it was as if the entire town was in the tavern. No one paid any attention to the three fresh faces as they entered. At the furthest end of the tavern, there seemed to be a small fighting arena with a troop of beautiful naked men and women in the ring dancing. Mistress Loo approached the innkeeper.

"Hello sir, I will be requiring a large room for the night" said Loo slowly and clearly, in her best Tanni. Luckily, the innkeeper understood her clearly, which was good as she wasn't ready to try out her basic Namangan just yet.

"Hello Madame, unfortunately Wilmer is fighting tonight and all our rooms are booked, all I have is a stable section." Said the tavern master.

"That will do perfectly. May I ask, has the main fight been or is there plenty of action left for this evening?" said Loo.

"Plenty left, big Wilmer's still eating;" the innkeeper proudly pointed and nodded over towards big Wilmer and his team "The main fight will be in about two to three hours' time. Up until he takes to the pit, we have some excellent up-and-coming fighters for your entertainment. Best fighters this side of the Aurd, guaranteed!!" Loo let out a little laugh, at which, Arran noted, the innkeeper was not impressed.

"Excellent, thank you, sir. All bets with you?" said Loo with a smile.

"Yes, best odds in the house," the inn keeper leaned forward and laughed, "Only odds in the house." At that, Loo purchased two beers and some tea and turned to Arran and Nanoc.

"Well don't just stand there, find us a table," said Loo.

Arran quickly moved to secure a table, Loo and Nanoc followed. As the three sat down at the cramped table, Nanoc stood surveying the room before sitting. 'Odd behaviour,' thought Arran.

"So, there's a small fighting area in the tavern, some action for us tonight," said Nanoc, as Loo passed out the drinks.

"Mindless violence for the sake of it? Vulgar!" Arran's distaste emanated. The many years of being bullied made him tough, yet repulsed by macho alpha males and their need to be the dominant force, in every situation.

"Mindless? That's an interesting concept. That's one of the ideas Mistress Loo pushes and what I was telling you about yesterday. You're a fast study Arran. The art of no mind, the idea that by repeating and repeating your fighting techniques, your reactions become so instinctive that without the interference of the conscious mind, the body can react faster to a threat. Beautiful Arran, I didn't know you were a martial scholar," Nanoc laughed as his eyes met Arran's.

"Mindless, i.e. like an animal, except an animal kills what it needs for food and fights only to protect its territory and family, because it has no higher faculty to reason and negotiate with, no conscience," said Arran.

"Well, I agree with that. Animals are pure instinct, like that fucking Cassartan that attacked us in the mountains. Pure instinct was driving that thing," said Nanoc.

"Yes, but your trained instincts defeated it easily. Did you encounter one of those, Arran, when you crossed the Aurd?" said Loo.

Arran unconsciously began to rub the scar on his face.

"Ah, so that's where that came from," said Nanoc.

"It is," said Arran.

"Well, tell us more, we are listening," said Nanoc. Arran thought it was strange that, for the first time, his new companions looked as if they were genuinely interested in what he had to say. Arran looked across at Nanoc and then at Loo, before recounting his story, of Mull's death, of turning him into weapons, of rescuing his friends, of fighting the cassartans, of surviving.

As he finished his story, Arran looked over at Nanoc, looking for something in the eyes of the large warrior, possibly recognition that he was not as weak as Nanoc had thought, but there was nothing behind the large eyes of the warrior. At this, Arran rose from the table.

"I am off to find the toilet," said Arran, before heading into the depths of the bustling tavern.

***

Loo and Nanoc's eyes met.

"Well, now we know why those Gavodeon leaders are not to be fucking messed with. Fuck, they send their kids into the mountains, naked to fight cassartans. That is seriously fucked up! I don't think we would have survived its attack if we didn't have steel! Crazy bastards."

As they laughed in tandem, Mistress Loo leaned forward. "Nanoc, I was observing young Arran when he stood his ground yesterday, he is very powerful and I'm guessing he is raw and untrained. If he had the chance to fill his potential, this one could be special. I now see what they see!"

Nanoc met Mistress Loo's eyes and smiled as he began his reply "For a moment, amid our stalemate, I felt he was my equal, then my superior, I then thought of killing him but only for a moment, before you distracted me," Nanoc winked at Mistress Loo, with a devious smile.

"For a moment you thought of killing him or for a moment you thought of him as your equal......"

"Look", Nanoc pointed to the other end of the Tavern. Loo met Nanoc's eyes and nodded as she reacted to the sound of many glasses shattering against the hard stone floor. Loo and Nanoc, along with the rest of the tavern looked across to see what the commotion was about.

"Looks like the action may be starting early," laughed Nanoc.

Loo observed the men around the head table, the table where Wilmer, the main attraction fighter was sitting, seemed to be involved in some altercation with a small but vocal woman.

Wilmer's voice echoed loudly. "I ordered rose wine, not ale, you stupid wench, how many times do I have to tell you?".

"The order was for rose wine," replied the server. Wilmer grunted in reply "and there was no need to smash the glasses, who is going to pay for that?" continued the woman. Wilmer's anger flared, then with a powerful backhand, Wilmer sent her flying backwards into the gathering crowd. As she hit the ground unconscious, Arran emerged from the crowd.

***

"Do you feel like a man now?" asked Arran.

"Who the fuck are you boy?" shouted an angry Wilmer.

"I am Arran, who the fuck are you?" returned Arran, with as much venom as he could muster.

"Wilm...." Wilmer found himself answering, explaining himself to this young upstart. As his anger climaxed and in mid-explanation he lashed out. Arran foreseen the strike and moved fast but not fast enough, and not in the right direction. The blow took him clean off his feet. Arran was launched backwards, hitting a few of the forward moving crowd, luckily breaking his fall. As Arran rose to his feet to confront the giant again, Arran found his passage blocked by Wilmer's men. Before young Arran could get to his feet, the barrage of pain began, as the mob punched and kicked him into the ground, all he could do was cover up and take the beating, incurring as little damage as possible, something he was at least fairly good at. As the blows rained down, he curled up tight, protecting himself as he rolled, ducked and dodged, keeping his body tucked tight.

***

NANOC AND LOO HAD stood back watching, observing Arran, impressed with his chivalry, guts and determination to stand for what he saw as right. They liked the character of young Arran, even if they would not admit it, and they liked his bravery. Nanoc turned to Loo and winked "A fight has invited us, after all, we vowed to transport the boy. Can't transport him if he is dead, unless you want to carry his carcass?" laughed Nanoc. The two warriors were calm in the erupting chaos of the now confined area at the other end of the bar, as they entered the action. Nanoc moved right to the front of the attackers and with one great, berserk movement cleared the crowd from the bloody Arran. As Arran rose to his feet, Mistress Loo stood behind him. Wilmer stood and moved towards Nanoc.

"What the fuck, who the fuck are you?" demanded Wilmer.

"This guy seems to only have one question," mocked Nanoc.

"We are just friends of a friend," stated Mistress Loo.

"Ah, you're with the boy; sorry about the beating but in future, tell him to keep out of my affairs," stated Wilmer.

"Unfortunately for you, when you beat him, you entered into my affairs," replied Nanoc.

"Meaning what, you think you're going to walk into Wilmer's bar, on Wilmer's night and fuck with me?" shouted a furious, agitated and aggressive Wilmer. Nanoc looked deep into Wilmer's eyes and with not even the slightest rise in heartbeat to Wilmer's ultra-aggressive attempt to intimidate, Nanoc replied.

"I will beat you here and now, if you don't change that tone or we can take this to the pit? And earn some coin." Nanoc turned his back on Wilmer and began waving his arms up and down, pumping the crowd into accepting the latter. As the masses booed and cheered this potential match and its instantly gripping story line, Nanoc turned back round towards Wilmer.

"Let's give these fine people here a glimpse of the greatest warrior the north will ever, see?" The crowd booed again but the innkeeper, sharp and always looking for a quick coin, signalled towards Wilmer with his thumbs up, as if to say take the fight, we will earn a lot of money.

Across the room, a lone warrior stood. "I am fighting that ugly dog this evening, after I take his soul, you can do what you want with his carcass".

The innkeeper, hot on the action. "If you can defeat Voost, then you will have earned the right to face Wilmer. Not before. We have a ranking system here, southerner."

Nanoc turned his back to Wilmer and the crowd and walked casually up to the table of the warrior named Voost and grabbed the old fighter by the scruff of his caller. As he reacted, Nanoc slipped the advance and applied a nice neck and shoulder lock before escorting him quickly to the door. As the door closed firmly behind them, Nanoc had already gauged the ageing warriors' level, as acceptable by this outback, run-down, shithole of an arena but nowhere near acceptable on the Nanoc scale.

"Old man, maybe in your heyday, but now you have no chance against me. Now I am going to go in there and make a point. I can if you wish, break you first or you can leave," stated Nanoc.

"I can't leave, this is my job, this is my livelihood. I am going to fight because I need to fight and I need to fight in the ring, because I need to support my family. You think I want to still be fighting. I've lost the hearing on my right side, I can no longer bend over or turn my neck to the left, my memory is shot to shit. You young warriors, full of spunk, you have it all to look forward too," said the old fighter.

"I hate people like you, touching on my good side. How many children? How many wives?" asked Nanoc.

"Eight children and two wives, I need this fight," said Voost.

"Ok, put all your money on me to win, and you will make more money tonight, than you would've betting on yourself to lose," said Nanoc.

"Why should I trust you? And I'm not betting on no man I've never seen fight," said Voost.

"Some people, just don't know when their luck is in. Escorting you out, like a disobedient child, was that not clear enough?" said Nanoc.

Another demonstration was required and Nanoc needed it done fast. He circled the old fighter, whose reactions were faster this time. He responded by moving in, judging the gap and moving in tandem with Nanoc. Then he realised the calibre of the stranger. Nanoc moved again, faked the left and went straight in and took him to the ground, simultaneously transitioning to the back control and proceeded to choke the old fighter until he tapped.

***

As HE RELEASED HIS grip, Voost put out his hand, signifying a deal. Nanoc's technique surprised Voost. He had never seen those fighting techniques strung together like that before, the footwork, the control, the precision, the efficiency. He became utterly useless in a matter of seconds; he was now looking forward to his returns.

***

NANOC RE-ENTERED THE INN, walked straight to the bar and rang the bell. The crowd turns and silence becomes. "I am Nanoc, the best of all the outstanding fighters of the south. I hereby challenge you," pointing directly at Wilmer but not making eye contact.

Wilmer laughed. The bar owner called over Voost. After a heated debate, he announced the bout and a change to the odds. "I set the new bout for one hour's time," declared the innkeeper, which made Nanoc smile.

Arran watched as Nanoc and Loo reacted to the innkeeper, signifying it was time, the hour flew in.

"Come with us to the pit side Arran, where I can keep an eye on you," said Loo as Nanoc stood from the table and began the walk through the tavern, towards the fighting area. Arran nodded and rose to follow Nanoc. As the trio moved through the crowd, the shouts began.

"Kill the southern scum, Wilmer"

"No one fucks with Wilmer"

"Booooooooo"

"Wilmer, Wilmer, Wilmer"

As Arran walked through the hostile crowd, he felt their anger, he felt the hostility, he felt his posture weakening. But as he had done a thousand times, he entered into his mind and took refuge from the onslaught. As he pulled himself together, he observed Nanoc. The man mountain, carved of muscle, walked slowly, purposefully, with his head held high and confidence radiating with every step. 'I need more of that,' thought Arran.

The fighting arena was small compared to the arenas Arran had seen down south but large enough for an establishment of this size. The room sloped down gently to meet a roped off ring at its centre. 'The ring is no more than four times the height of Nanoc,' thought Arran, as he looked round from his vantage point beside the ropes. The hostility of the crowd still penetrated his confidence.

"Arran, stay here. Keep your focus on Nanoc, hold your energy. Don't let the crowd intimidate you," said Loo. 'How does she know' thought Arran?

"I will keep my attention on Nanoc," said Arran.

"I must tend to my fighter now," said Loo.

"Best of luck Nanoc," said Arran, Nanoc smiled in reply, before returning his gaze to Wilmer, as the large local made his entrance into the ring.

The crowd went crazy for Wilmer, the boos turned to cheers. The anger and intimidation turned to joy and acceptance. Arran began to relax as the mood in the arena changed.

The innkeeper entered the fighting ring and leant over to Arran.

"What's his name, what do we call him?"

"He is Nanoc," said Arran.

"Nanoc Ranoh the greatest southern warrior of his generation," stated Loo.

The innkeeper smiled in acknowledgement before moving to the centre of the ring.

As the bell rang, the crowd slowly quietened and as it did, the innkeeper bellowed.

"Ladies and Gentlemen, it is time for a clash of titans. As always, the Night Light Inn has put together another spectacular show, worthy of your hard earned money." The crowd once more erupted in cheering, whistling and throwing beer at the ring.

"Hush, quiet," shouted the innkeeper. The room, obedient to his command, quietened.

"From the south, Nanoc Ranoh, the finest the south has to offer," shouted the Innkeeper as he eyeballed Nanoc directly. As the boos erupted, the small innkeeper spun on his heels.

"And his opponent, a man who needs no introduction here at the Night Light Inn, Wilmer The Great. Undefeated in over fifteen years, crusher of champions," shouted a very enthusiastic innkeeper.

Arran had seen many fighting arenas and he had witnessed many fights in the many towns and cities he had traded in but he had never willingly stood by and gave his time to watch. He mused to himself how strange life was as he now stood ringside, in a small town, in a strange land, with two new friends, ready to witness if Nanoc and Loo's claims were true, or just piss and vinegar.

As the Innkeeper's hand came down, Nanoc moved swiftly towards the centre, eager to engage. Wilmer however did not, he back peddled and began to move to his right, maintaining a gap between him and Nanoc. Wilmer raised his arms and waved at the crowd. To Arran, it looked like he was more interested in his cheering fans than the very real threat of the man mountain, that was Nanoc.

Then Nanoc lunged forward and Wilmer had no choice but to engage.

As Wilmer threw his first punch, he began to laugh. As he laughed, Nanoc suddenly stopped moving, then Wilmer turned and looked directly at Arran.

Arran felt his mind being punctured, someone or something was intruding into his personal space, into his inner realm. He had no chance to dwell upon it, for one by one, his own greatest fears began to engulf him. Instantly, he felt his balance leave and he instinctively held out his hand to grab the ring rope to stabilise himself. But compared to the fear caused by the darkness of the forest, this was manageable. As he did, he looked up at Loo, who was watching Nanoc in confusion. Nanoc now stood at the far side of the cage, hands at his head, taking unanswered shots from Wilmer. The local fighter paused every three or four punches to interact with the crowd.

Loo began screaming commands at Nanoc.

"Attack him Nanoc, don't just stand there. You can see those punches coming from the other side of the tavern. Counter them,.... For fuck sake Nanoc, do something..."

The strange vice like grip on Arran's mind clamped down harder, as Arran gripped the rope with everything he had to keep him from falling. He heard Wilmer's voice inside his mind. In that instant, instinctively and with everything he had, he pushed back at the intruder, to his most sacred of spaces.

As his balance returned, the room returned, Arran looked up to see shock and anger on the face of Wilmer as he stepped back from attacking Nanoc.

'He is somehow controlling Nanoc, like The King had done in my vision,' thought Arran. 'Did I stop him? Was that me?' thought Arran.

Then, as if a great restraint had been lifted from Nanoc's body, the barbarian leapt into action. Wilmer fought back with everything he had but without his strange mental magic, it was not enough.

As Arran pondered the strange event, the barrage of Nanoc's fury seen Wilmer crumble to the floor. His corner threw their shoes into the ring, as a sign of mercy. Nanoc accepted and turned toward Arran and Loo with a smile.

"Thank you, Arran," said Nanoc.

"I done something, but I do not know what it was," said Arran, as Loo looked on in confusion.

"Once before, I felt someone inside my mind, that bastard," Nanoc pointed at Wilmer.

"He was in my mind, and you, I saw you, I felt you, you removed him. You made the fight fair," said Nanoc.

"He was in mine too. I just..." mumbled Arran.

"How did you do that? Are you a magician..." asked Nanoc.

"Ladies and Gentlemen, your champion, Nanoc Ranoh, the south's greatest warrior and soon, the north's," shouted Mistress Loo.

Mistress Loo, quick to turn coin and advantage to the situation, proposed a training seminar for the next morning for any interested parties. She promoted it to the angry crowd as an opportunity to learn the superior southern fighting techniques, a sure ploy to advertise and spread the word that a barbarian from the south was coming. A warrior always needs a story! And an angry crowd was always an excellent medium for spreading that story. This evening would be good for his new friends moving north. 'A great warrior's reputation should always arrive way before them,' thought Arran. Arran was glad of the distraction from Nanoc's questions, for he had no answers of how he had done what he had done.

In the days that followed, the intrepid trio travelled further north. They talked much of Arran's parents, fighting techniques, leadership, the strange mental attack and the Namangan King. Finally, after many hills, bridges and floods, they arrived at the village of Um Ma Bar. They followed the instructions and directions, left to them in the note.

"Barratash is the strongest magician we have. He is Tanni Ma Bar's finest, if a little odd, driven and opinionated. Locate him in the Um Ma Bar orchard, by the tree that does not bear sweet fruit, but by the tree that bears the very sweetest fruit, the fruit of the soul. Loo, go alone into the orchard, hand him this small jar of perfume but send out your energy beforehand. Feel for his vibration, he will have no QUAFS on him, if he does, it is not Barratash, he will instruct you from here," read the note.

***

MISTRESS LOO LEFT NANOC and Arran by the entrance to the orchard, as instructed and set off into the bustling mecca of apple trees. After a time, Mistress Loo climbed one of the hundreds of apple trees. From up there, she could see the intended meeting place clearly. As she made her way towards the pine tree, she wondered why they refer to it as bearing fruits of the soul.

"Hello may I help you?" asked the stranger that sat by the assumed meeting place.

"I hope so, I am here to meet a friend of Tanni Ma Bar!" said Loo.

"A friend you say, I am a friend am I not?", the stranger sat bolt upright against the tree trunk, legs crossed and looking, gazing, focusing on some point, out across the orchard. As he continued to converse with Mistress Loo, his gaze did not change. Loo opened up her energy with three breaths and a very subtle hand movement, combined with a complex, yet now routine inner mental instruction. Her vast energetic reservoir stored around her belly opened. With her energy now unleashed and under her will, Loo sent it out to interact with the stranger by the tree.

"Enough, I am Barratash, I am the one Moray has sent you to meet," Barratash was still staring out, away from Loo, as if blind to this world.

"Your energetic field has a volume and density to it that I have rarely encountered and I cannot see through your eyes. A potent? An energy dancer? What do you use? Who trained you?" asked Barratash.

As Loo's energy overlapped Barratash's, she found she could not match his vibration. His energetic field was like nothing she had ever encountered, she didn't even have words to describe it. Strange for a woman who has devoted her entire life to developing the internal martial arts, yet it has now happened twice in the last week. 'Strange indeed,' thought Loo.

"I have trained in many places, with many people," replied Loo.

"The boy will have to wait, it's not happened yet and I have other tasks to fulfil, responsibilities the likes you could not fathom, but maybe one day you will. Send the boy up the Northern Road to Ali Ma Bar. It is a short walk from here, just over and into the next valley. Tell him to head for the city's main square, there is a celebration happening, I will meet him there. Now be on your way warrior, take the Southern Road back to the fork and take the road north from there to Yi Ma Bar. The north awaits you." said Barratash.

"The Tanni Ma Barians specifically told us to deliver him to you, I gave my word," replied Mistress Loo.

"And you have, and I and every free soul in Lanasia give you thanks, he will be fine, but your journey, your role in this grand game must continue. So please instruct the boy and be on your way, and travel cautiously southerner, a storm is coming," said Barratash.

"Southerner," shouted Barratash as Mistress Loo looked back, she saw, for the first time, Barratash looking straight at her.

"Do not eat the salt, keep your vibration high at all times, lower it around The King's guards as they will be sensing for it, teach the barbarian. I wish you every success in your mission sister, for no man or woman, north or south, should be farmed as we are."

Barratash looked away and as he did, he vanished from sight, as did the strange voice that had just slipped out of her mind. A little in shock and full of curiosity, Loo returned to Arran and Nanoc. After passing what little information she had to Arran, the three parted company.

As the two warriors set off, leaving the young Gavod behind; Mistress Loo told Nanoc of her encounter with Barratash, of the strange thousand-yard stare into nowhere, of the voice inside her head, of the idea that Arran had arrived too early for something that had not happened yet, of the energetic advice of a high vibration and finally of the enigmatic phrase "I cannot see through your eyes". Loo and Nanoc talked of Arran, Barratash, Tanni Ma Barians and the principals of energy and internal martial arts as they made for the Southern Road out of the town and again towards the north.

CHAPTER 16 - ARRAN ENTERS ALI MA BAR

A STRANGE FESTIVAL WAS taking place; every street and walkway rammed with a sea of people and colour, bright oranges and purples fluttering through the air, great swathes of fabric weaving and bobbing through the crowds, dancing harmoniously with the excited children who waved them. Arran's eyes followed the children, their bodies moving erratically yet ecstatically to some silent inner rhythm. Arran was spellbound. He had seen many carnival celebrations but never one like this.

Never had he stood amongst a people feeling so unaware, so uninformed. His people always arrived early to the major Lanasian festivals, always knowing all the ins and outs of the festival. Knowledge was profit to a nomadic tradesman. Here, however, Arran never even knew the language, never mind the customs, the importance of the colours, hell he couldn't even recognise the music or the high-pitched monotone instruments that were making the ear shattering noise. As he moved forward, deeper into the parade, Arran realised for the first time since leaving the south, how different the north was and how alone he really was.

Arran stopped by a street vendor, the small brightly coloured man draped in the same oranges and purples as the crowds. He looked him over a few times, 'understandable,' Arran thought, even in the south they would give this 'oh, a Gavod' look, which signified stranger. Arran just assumed this man had never seen a Gavod before. The trader was not indigenous, possibly the equivalent of a Gavod from the North? Arran was a full head and a half taller than the vendor. Behind the short man, hung a mirror, decorated in the same oranges and purples of the festival. Arran took a moment to gaze upon himself. The man looking back was unrecognisable, Arran recalled the last time he saw himself in the reflection of a puddle, deep in the Aurd. The scar from the Cassartan attack on his cheek had now completely healed and below it and around it grew the beginnings of the thickest facial hair the northern vendor may ever have seen. Arran smiled at his reflection, at his transformation and ordered some food but in reply got "High Tanni only little", followed by some quick frantic pointing to what he could only guess was popular local food products. Arran broke the awkwardness by speaking universal trader, he produced some small coin and pointed at the long pastry-looking item and to what looked like the wine jug and nodded, the small trader broke away from his thoughts of wonder and broken high Tanni, and cranked into gear. As Arran relaxed, as a common ground had been made, he was pushed from the side.

A group of men stood scowling at him. Then one man began shouting and pointing. Arran unaware of what was being said, relied again on a trader's cool head, as excitement erupted around him. The man shouting directly at him was clearly angry and drunk, yet Arran still had no idea of what was being said. In-between the local Tanni tongue, there were a few classic high Tanni words, he recognised "respect", "northerner" and "Namangan", but the accent or dialect was bizarre. A small crowd quickly formed around the food stall. He could now sense the unmistakable sense of fear and anger in the gathering crowd. The energies, the vibe around him had changed, the twenty or so individuals around him had now morphed into a single, unified expression of emotion. As Arran made a final look towards the trader, his eyes meeting Arran's briefly before the big sad disks, filled with guilt and sorrow, looked away.

The first cut was strange, the first stab of the blade was even stranger, in the midst of the mob, in the noise, in the moment, time slowed down as the warm, physical sensation made his abdomen glow intensely. Time slowed and as it did, a strange yet familiar lucidity like that experienced at the Lamas theatre or on consumption of the mushrooms encapsulated his body and mind as they separated. Here in this strange place where time had all but frozen, Arran realised the reality of what had happened but more importantly, more fundamental in this state of forced mental lucidity, he saw the strange red energetic entities. At first, he was really unsure of what he was seeing. It's always strange trying to quantify, trying to register a thing that you cannot and have not the vocabulary to contextualise or conceptualise the experience with. Up close they were not the simple red glow from his vision, they were intricate patterns of fluid chaos straddling infinity. As he was forced to look beyond his physical sight by this strange experience, he seen them, not on every man but on most in this mob, and as his energy seeped from the wound that now adorned his side, they moved in closer, leaving their hosts as if vultures to a fresh kill. In that instant, he knew they were the demons from his vision and that they knew that he was aware of them. Then the buzzing began. A noise of a thousand strange voices, all out of sync, all fighting for attention.

Arran's mind reeled back as a solo voice cut through the buzzing of his subconscious mind, "follow me," he did not know where the voice was coming from, or the direction in which he was to follow, as his mind rushed back into its physical meat sack, the pain welcomed him back. The reality of the last five seconds sent his body into a crazed fight-or-flight response. The crowd unexpectedly stepped back, faces frozen in fear, as if they had just entered the strange mental space Arran had just left. Arran glimpsed a strange black-bearded figure, like that of the Aurd. Again, he felt an aspect of his own consciousness communicate with another part of his own consciousness. "This way, hurry" the mental voice said. With no delay and as fast and as energetically as he could, the wounded Arran sprinted off, through the small gap into the crowd, towards the bearded saviour.

Arran was determined not to wake up in a random room, naked as the day he was born. With everything he had, he fought to stay awake, to stay aware. Instantly, he could consciously feel his body wanting to give up, to shut down, to rest. He could now feel the warm blood seeping from his stomach and hear the lukewarm blood in his shoe squelching with every desperate step. Arran moved forward, not really knowing what he was following. After the initial mental flash of the bearded man, he had no real visual confirmation of him. As his mind fought to keep himself conscious, time once again slowed, not to the same extent as when he was stabbed, but enough for him to perceive, to step out and realise a door to his left was shimmering. Without hesitation, and for no reason he could explain, Arran made a beeline for the door.

As the door shut behind Arran, he heard her voice, "This way stranger," that's not what he heard but what was conveyed to him inside his own mind. Her real voice was beautiful, sweet and full of exotic, husky tone. The strange language was like honey leaving her tongue but Arran could not think of such things, or why her voice was clear Gavodeon inside his head, as he heard her speak her native tongue out loud. All he could think about was staying conscious and the warmth that was radiating from his stomach. The pain had now become the norm, as Arran felt himself slip down onto the floor, he felt her warm hands touch his side and her mind entered his thoughts once more.

"Why have you so much power but you can't even use it? I am not powerful enough to heal you but I can guide you through it. Repeat every sound, every gesture, every symbol, your life depends on it," the secondary internal voice said.

"I will," thought Arran.

As pictures, ideas, thoughts and symbols flooded Arran's mind, he felt things he could grasp and repeat and others that he couldn't, that were just out of touch; like on the mountain with the black bearded shaman, things he couldn't quite put his finger on, yet he kept going, repeating the strange rituals that he was shown. Here, inside his mind, he worked this new information, slowly becoming aware of the energy in himself and of the power that these strange words and symbols encapsulated. His mind's inner world opened up, this place being created, here inside his mind was as magnificent as the castle atop the Aurd, as wonder inspiring as the great pyramid in Tanni Ma Bar, as spectacular and homely as every night he snuggled up in a yak hide with his parents. This, he was discovering was the seat of his power, his sanctuary, his source beyond the great door. It was strange finally discovering this place with the female voice present, but if it were not for her guidance, he would not have returned to this strange yet all too familiar place, deep within himself. When Arran's eyes opened, he could see his breath in the now ice-cold room and his wound was healed.

"You're awake!" Again, her voice tickled his ear as a translation echoed through his mind. The young woman stood over Arran as he sat up from the deep seat he was slumped into. "I am Anice, welcome to the north," as she spoke through chattering teeth, she smiled and as the strange new language flowed from her moist glistening lips, Arran smiled, she was the most beautiful, the most intriguing woman he had ever met.

"Your wounds are completely healed, your Magic is extremely powerful, raw and totally untamed," as she spoke, Arran listened with his ears and his mind. His linguistic brain learnt the new language, it was not so different from a few languages of the south, it was her that was magical thought Arran.

"You rescued me, spoke to me through my mind, showed me my black shaman, a shimmering door in a wall, and then opened the door to my inner potential to heal my wounds. How did you find me? And will you teach me?" said Arran.

"I am a witch, a sorceress. I travel, I collect grimoires and magical formulas. About twelve moon cycles ago, I cast a spell from a new grimoire that I acquired. The spell I cast was to find me a powerful magical source, which I was going to use to perform spells that are too powerful for me. Over the last twelve moons, the spell has brought me to a few energy sources and now to you and the rest is history," said Anice as she moved around the room, her thin silken garment hugging her curvaceous body, her nipples erect in the cold air, Arran sat mesmerised.

"What do you know of the demon things, I can't believe I nearly forgot about them? Strange beings made of energy, they looked right at me... It was strange seeing them again," said Arran, exploding the words out in a rushed shout.

"Ahh; The QUAF, The Ingurgitators, soul eaters, demons, the guards, the watchers, the farmers, they go by many names, depends on which people you talk to, but most people are blissfully unaware of their existence. I call them the QUAF. They feed upon the negative energies produced by all Lanasians, like ticks but far more dangerous," said Anice.

Arran sank back into the chair. His world, both internal and external was changing and fast and all he could think about now was Anice.

"Sorry Anice, I am so confused right now, my world is changing so fast," Arran talked aloud but not for Anice, more just to air his thoughts and organise his fast-moving world aloud. "I was kind of fine with soul journeys, spirit flights induced by the sun mushrooms and inner magicians warping my limited view of physical reality. These are all well recorded within Gavodeon and Lagosian culture. Experiencing the QUAF in my dreams and in my visions is one thing but experiencing the QUAF eating the very essence of a person first hand, and connecting with them, experiencing them as they fed. Seeing them in a vision is one thing, but face to face was another thing entirely. They looked different in my vision. Who are the soul eaters? What are they? Are they native? How long have they been here? What does your history and culture tell us about them? What are they actually eating? Are they eating? How much do they need to eat? Are they like ticks, swelling with blood, surviving until their next meal? Like ticks and leaches, do they have some evolutionary tricks to make the blood, sorry, make the energy release faster? Wow, that's just fucking crazy, yet so fucking real. Everywhere I have been since leaving Lagosia has challenged my construct of how I think things are. As a Gavod, I know much of culture as that is my job, but I had never really thought about history. I hadn't considered how culture, it's society, its arts, its language, its laws and its legends, formed, until I got to Tanni Ma Bar. Pyramids with blocks so massive that giants must have built them or they were created by some vastly superior engineers from a time long gone, or by travellers from the void above. Buildings filled with symbols that were both strange and familiar at the .... Arran paused momentarily looking up at Anice.

The symbols were like those that you used to heal me. Is the power locked in the symbols? Are they an instruction set for magic? Is that what magic is? I was thinking about the symbolic language of the Tanni when I merged with the pyramid. WOW. Is it the language that is magic? Who wrote the grimoires? Do you understand the language of the symbols or do you just cast them and hope for the best? ...."

Arran paused, he knew the answer to some questions, he may not have been paying attention or have previously linked the various cultural dots together but now he was asking the right questions and now he could see it so clear. In every culture of the south, there were references to things like vampires, dream stealer's, demons, bogeymen etc, ingrained in every kind of story, told to children to keep them in line, or around particular locations like the Vantera forest to keep people out but that's all they were. Or was this another great lie, built behind a false summit, a truth that was always in plain sight for anyone willing to look and ask the right questions?

"Pyramids? Built by travellers from the void? What do you know of this?" asked Anice.

"What? What are you talking about? I was just throwing it in there, a turn of phrase. For us Gavodeons, the bogeymen are the travellers from beyond the void and when we need to explain something and we can't, we attribute it to them," replied Arran.

"Oh, OK," said Anice.

"What did you think I meant," replied Arran, his curiosity on full alert.

"Well," Anice took a few steps towards Arran. The small room had regained its warmth, the bare and simple space now radiated with Anice's smell. Arran ceremoniously drew in a deep sniff of the fine feminine fragrance. As his heart fluttered yet again, Anice began to talk;

"Arran, have you never looked up at the sky at night, have you never thought what the lights were? The place beyond the sky, where light and dark dance for all eternity. It is not void, it's not empty! Our sun brings us the energy we need to live, the energy our world needs to live. So, each of those lights could be distant suns that are also providing the energy for life somewhere else in the Void. These others have travelled through the void to us. It is said the star-men built the array of Pyramids. They crossed the skies in flying machines, destroyed each other in timeless battles with magnificent weapons to secure our planet's resources. This they say, happened long, long ago, in one of our distant pasts, and some still believe that they are still among us! Dancing in the shadows." Anice was now literally standing over Arran's chair. 'She must be aware of my sexual attraction towards her and she seems to be interested in me,' thought Arran, as he looked up into her eyes.

"I want to contribute to what you have just said but just now, all I can think about is you, your smell, your curves, your large moist lips, your deep brown eyes..." before Arran could continue, Anice stood up, laughed and walked towards the door.

Three steps from the door, Anice turned back around, Arran looked up at her, unsure of what to do. 'What do I say? Do I apologise? Do I demand she loves me? Do I...' Arran's inner world spiralled.

"You are or could be destined for greatness. There is a great war coming, the people are awakening and The King and his armies are manoeuvring. Hell, they are camped outside this great city as we speak and every day, more will surely arrive," said Anice.

"The camps down the valley are the Namangan army?" asked Arran.

"Who did you think they were?" replied Anice.

"I just thought it was an extension of the city. Many cities of the south's true population stay in tents beyond the safety of the main city's walls. Where the workers, butchers, traders live. I just assumed..." said Arran

"Beyond the gates are the Namangan's, and if history has taught us anything, they will not settle for anything but conquest. That's why you were stabbed! The mob thought you were a Namangan!" said Anice.

"I have seen them in my vision, I look nothing like a Namangan," said Arran.

"Because your cultured and well-travelled does not mean that everyone else is. You'd be lucky if any of these natives of Ali Ma Bar had even been to Tanni Ma Bar, never mind travelled north into the Namangan territories. You're different, they are different, they feared you, they attacked. Anyway, we need people with your power fighting on our side, on the side of good. So, stop thinking with your cock. For most men, the meat between their legs rules them. If you can't control yours, there is no hope for you and the potential within you," said Anice, this time there was no flirtation, there was only focus as Arran looked up at her from his chair.

"What do you mean?" asked Arran as he rose to his feet.

"Is it not clear, you are powerful and if you want me to show you, to train you, you must transcend your attraction to me. You must see the world with your mind, with the gift you have been given, not with your cock," said Anice.

CHAPTER 17 –
THE KING'S TRIPLE
EDGED SWORD

THE LAST TIME LATHORAN opened up the great hall of Juy for an event was to choose the Valdahars, the day he seen the south's finest warriors emerge. Today, he hoped that he would see the south's finest leaders emerge. Lathoran pushed the memories of screams, blood and steel from his mind as he prayed that today would not degrade to such violence. However, he knew crowning a leader in violence was always easier than finding a leader in thought.

"Wilsot, have all of our guest's arrived? Has everyone been signed into the great hall? All fees and dues collected?" asked Lathoran as they walked from his chambers towards the main walkway down to the grand hall.

"Yes, everything is in place and breakfast for the delegates is currently being served. We have food, water and wine for up to three weeks if needed, sir. And the fees will give us reserves, if we need to buy more," said Wilsot.

"Let's hope it is not, let's hope the might and minds of the south see through The King's deceptions and unite behind our cause," said Lathoran, as he pushed open the mighty doors to enter the main hall of Juy. No trace of the Valdaharian blood bath remained, now sat hundreds of delegates from all over the south, eating, drinking and discussing the future of their beloved nation.

Lathoran took a moment to make eye contact and acknowledge key ruler's, diplomats and business folk as he walked towards the podium and his table. It sat slightly higher than every other table, giving him a great platform to observe the room this day.

The southern Logosians had met in mass to discuss the Namangan empire, potential trade opportunities and the enticing offers sent by The King, beyond the Aurd. The official offer was brought to the table by the Valdaharian and Golden Transformation priest, Lathoran. This was not something he looked forward to. He was and always would be a representative of the Golden Transformation and was, therefore biased, meaning he probably wasn't the best ambassador for relaying a message to a room full of his political and religious opposition. Today they were all here.

Lathoran didn't take leadership lightly he lived for the responsibility and the life lessons associated with it. This opportunity for personal transformation, he took seriously. Everyone of power was here, no matter of ethnicity, political background, religious persuasion. A meeting of this calibre, on this scale, featuring the most powerful leaders from all of the southern nations had never been done before, well not in his lifetime. An event, two months in the planning would not go un-noticed by the peoples of the land. Before breakfast, Lathoran's men collected the fee, a simple contribution from each attendee to cover the cost of the emergency council. As each delegate sat for breakfast, they were given the proposal document; highlighting The King's offer, detailing the gathered intelligence from the north, sharing some popular proposals and also including a section for them to write their thoughts for submission.

As they consumed breakfast, the southern leaders debated amongst themselves, table upon table of loud, proud voices, confidently stating the correct and proper process for all Lagosians to take on this unsure road. There were some heated exchanges between well-known rivals with deep-seated hatred based on ethnicity, business, personal dealings and love.

As Lathoran took to the podium to chair the event, the first real emergency meeting since the plans for its conception were drawn up. He stood, unaware of how to address the leaders of his beloved Lagosia.

"Brothers and Sisters, the day will soon be upon us, that day when we in this room will have to decide the fate of the peoples we serve. Do we fight to protect our sovereignty or do we concede to the might of the north? For the last one hundred years, every generation of our ancestors has had the same question loom over them. Alas, it falls upon our broad shoulders to deal with the ever-consuming King in the north. We here, in this room, will decide the fate of all of our brothers and sisters." Lathoran stood, his power emanating, his posture straight and his face relaxed. The great glass dome above the hall only brought the dull, grey light of the morning's dark rain storm, as the rain abated slightly, Lathoran read the King's Proposal.

"Brothers and sisters, fellow Lanasians. I, the one true King and master of all Lanasia respectfully invite you, my noble subjects, to formally enter the Namangan empire. Each and every noble amongst you will retain your titles, deeds and respective sovereignty over your domains. The transition to

Namangan customs, laws and taxes will be swift and painless. Join our ranks and let us build a better world together. We, your brothers and sisters of the north, await your reply. Faithfully your loyal master, The King, Summerian the First."

As Lathoran stopped, the hall erupted, full of boos and cheers, of anger and joy. Lathoran realised then that he had misplaced his brother's and sister's disdain for the King in the north. A small, powerful and very vocal contingent had evidently decided that a deal with the King was more advantageous to their interests.

"Brothers and sisters," the small woman stood and struggled to be heard over the rabble, but she did not sit nor stop. "Brothers and sisters, this is not the only proposal". As her words spread like wildfire around the hall, the small, round frame of Alianas Marsek found the entire hall's eyes upon her.

"Brothers and sisters, I fear I am not the only one amongst us today, who has had a personal offer from the devious bastard that calls himself The Immortal King. As some of you may know, but for you who do not, my house, my people, control vast amounts of farmland and produce a fair percentage of the food here in the south. I have personally been offered titles, lands and various immunities and guarantees for the various farms that I control. The King, it seems, wants to conquer the south, to have his cake and eat it. Obviously, it is in his favour to keep producing crops as his armies conquer the south. I am guessing there is nothing worse than conquering a land and having to deal with its poor, broken and hungry people! They have invited me to the north to thrash out an agreeable contract of business. This tells me several things. The King has already planned his conquest in great detail. He knows the lay of our lands and the respective owners. He is feeding some of us with hopes and dreams and others with nothing. I ask each and every one amongst us with a personal offer from the King, to show your cards. For the King is coming south, this is no longer an unknown! The real question is, who will stand with the alien bastard in the north and line their pockets? And who will stand with the south to protect its people against the misery that the north will bring?"

Again, the hall erupted, boos and cheers, clapping and spitting. The game had been played by the King, but now the cards to some of his ploys were visible to all. His offers were fair to those of genuine power and extremely generous to those with limited or no real strategic advantage. The King's offers were sent to divide and create disharmony amongst the ranks of power in the south. Lathoran and Alianas, among others, could see this clearly.

Lathoran, was genuinely surprised to see the split in the room so clearly. As he scanned the hall before him, he could see the many factions forming, nods, winks and other physical confirmations were being communicated between acquaintances and enemies. Up above him, he noted that the rain was finally abating, its constant pounding on the great sky light was now a mere tinkering and for the first time this morning, the arguments within the hall drowned out the gods above. Many voices competed to be heard, cutting in and overlapping each other. Never had there been so much heat in a debate in the south. Arguments of every angle could be heard, the benefits of aligning themselves with The King, stating the inevitability of his conquest. The voices rang loud and emotional, Lathoran observed all he could.

"He will come south and he will conquer! We must negotiate to secure our lands and deeds to protect our national sovereignty or they will leave us with nothing",

"I would rather die than eat from the scraps from the King's table".

"The king cannot conquer the Aurd".

"We will unite as one people, we are the south, if he comes knocking, we will send the northern bastard home in a box".

"We nobles have more in common with the King in the north than with the workers of our lands, or to the mongrel ethnic groups of the south. We must negotiate, we are educated lords and ladies, not savages".

"We are leaders of the poor, the very people, off whose backs we have built our wealth, we cannot abandon them, they may be poor but they are our poor".

"The King brings modernisation, roads, sewage systems and more, he is a man of science, ready to build a unified future".

***

FINALLY, AFTER TWO SOLID weeks of debate, the beginning to the end of the emergency meeting was taking shape. Everyone had committed themselves to making sure their voices were heard, pushing their own twisted agendas, conspiring and lying. Power was a potent drug and the King knew how to make his offers enticing. However, everyone in the hall had now had enough. Three firm camps now swayed the majority of the rooms favour, with one group already set on firm action.

"I, Vantis of Lerr and the representatives for the south are in favour of giving the King a fair hearing. We will head for the north and meet with the King to determine his thoughts, promises and desires first hand. Only then will we be truly able to determine if he will make good on the promises of a peaceful takeover that leads to an autonomous south that pays a little extra tax. We believe this is in the best interest of every one of the south. We have dispatched a courier with word to this effect and we'll leave when we hear word has returned for the meeting"

"Traitors", boos and hisses are shouted loudly.

The divide was so clear, all hope of a united front left Lathoran. Everything he had worked so hard for his entire life was now out of his control and slipping from his grasp. As he looked around the room, he kept his head held high, despite his inner world crumbling. In the hall, stood a clear divide, an ancient divide that had, for many years had a very superficial mask pulled over its ugly head, but here, under pressure, it had revealed itself again. The masters with ties to the oldest bloodlines, those of Tanni Ma Barian heritage, stood ready and prepared to align with the King and his ancient bloodlines over their own people. Lathoran looked on as his last hopes of unity now lay with the sharp mind and tongue of Aliana Marsek.

"How have you represented yourself in the letter? Are you claiming to be representatives of the south as a whole? Of us here! Us, who oppose your ideologies?". As the furious figure of Alianas grew in anger, uncontrollably re-acting to the smug, self-important gestures from the crowd of this new southern alliance, with unity and subservience to the north. Aliana erupted again "I will write my own letter to the King. I will tell him of the truth of this conference, that we, the people of the south, in majority voted against his proposal. That you arrogant fools are not representatives of the south. How arrogant."

The hall roared in resonance with the small rotund woman. Her passion and her anger were clear for Lathoran and everyone else in the hall to see. As she stood there, fending off the last heckles of the opposition, it looked as if the blood from her entire body was now surging through her head, something that had evidently amused Vantis of Lerr noted Lathoran. As her blood flow normalised and drained from her head and her posture relaxed, the makeshift leader of the opposition Vantis of Lerr stood to rebut her argument.

"We wrote our letter from the perspective of a cooperative delegate of the south's most powerful families, landowners and most influential people. This is a fact, that even you know to be true, but none the less, the purpose of the letter, written from a collective representation of the south is designed so The King will bring his best offer to our table. That is not only in our interest but as you can see, if you get down from your high horse, it is in yours as well," stated Vantis.

"You traitor, you do not represent us! Are you so self-important, so blind to the truth of this emergency council? Were these weeks of discussion for no reason, to no avail? You may rely on your wealth here in Lagosia to dominate our domestic politics and commercial interests but we see clearly, your artifi-cial leverage over the common people and events of our land, but this council is clear, you do not speak for us here. Two-thirds of us here are against accepting any form of the devious proposal put forth by Summerian, in the north. You do not represent us and we will make this clear in our own letters," shouted Alianas as the blood rushed once more to her head.

"We will see, we will see," replied Vantis with a grin and a quick raise of his eyebrows.

The hall, full of energy, emotion and confusion seen the newly formed group of unionists gather together and leave. Once clear of the main door, Vantis turned to his long-time business associate and fellow bloodline supporter. "We must intercept their letters to the north; we have a three-week advantage. We must be ready to travel north as soon as the King replies. Have our full inventory and a copy of all supporting documentation at the ready. If you can't beat the best, join them and take them over from the inside!" said Vantis, with a grin.

CHAPTER 18 - THE MEN OF TANNI

"JUST A WARM MALT, extra honey," said Barratash as he slid his coin over the sticky bar top. Barratash then watched as the innkeeper, turned and ladled one out, full to the brim, steaming mug of warm malt.

"Don't forget the extra honey," said Barratash as the innkeeper moved towards him to serve the drink.

"It's just there at the end of the bar. You know where it is. Help yourself!" said the Innkeeper with a smile.

Barratash nodded and smiled back as he took his warm malt from the bar, before moving deep into the tavern. He was looking forward to it, the malt was the traditional drink of the Dancing Star festival and only sold during it. Tonight, he would forget his responsibilities, tonight he would drink malt and listen to his brothers' and sisters as they enjoyed the festivities, possibly for the last time.

This pub was a regular for Barratash when he was here in Ali Ma Bar, it was small, dark, dank, smelly, smoky and cramped. It was rammed to the rafters and as always, it was alive with its regulars. This, and the hundreds like it, were the beating pulse, the true heart of the last free Tanni Ma Barian city before the great and first city of Tanni Ma Bar itself. Today there was lots of gossip, anger and joyfulness to go around, for yesterday had been the start of the festival of The Dancing Star.

Barratash was here to listen and observe and tonight, across from him sat a small group of men, drunk and still drinking, talking loudly around one of the inn's short tables.

"What a blight to our great festival. The poor bastard was just trying to buy a fucking pie and boom. A disgrace I say," slurred Amear, 'the most coherent of the group,' thought Barratash as he slipped into all of their minds simultaneously, gleaming their names, a general impression of their character and a bit of history on each, so not to feel like such an outsider as he eavesdropped in on their conversations. In fact, he had become so good at this, that when he sat in the taverns observing, it was as if he was in the conversation, picking up on everything seen and unseen, by the closest of friends. Observing the conversations from inside their minds as well as externally gave him that vantage. Interesting group, good to hear that the news of Arran's arrival is travelling. Barratash slumped back in his chair as he raised his warm malt to his lips, 'I will listen to this group for a while before securing another malt and moving to another corner,' thought Barratash as he turned his attention back to the group.

"Aye, the attack on the poor hairy southerner was unfortunate! I can understand the anger though," said an equally drunken Farelo.

"Their anger, yes, but not their ignorance. He was a big hairy southerner; the pie man knew he was a southerner!! Mistaken by some dull-witted, uncultured, untravelled moron! A fucking northerner, a Namangan military man. He probably couldn't look more different if he tried. I sincerely hope the southerner survived that, that's not how we greet guests to our great city. As for the fucking Namangans, I hope they all fucking die! The cunts." said Qertus.

"Aye, I agree, if the pie man's story be gospel, then we as a people should be ashamed. Especially on this day, when we celebrate our victory from oppression," said Toigen

"This great celebration, a celebration of the master's return..." Amer breaks into one of his all too familiar monologues about the TRUE history.

"Amer, we are drunk and we are joyous. Do we really need another history lesson," said Farelo.

"History's important Farelo, soon it will be all we have." Toigen slapped Amer on the side of the ear, just the way all affectionate drunken brothers do, and laughed. "Carry on Amer, on this great day and in celebration of the Dancing Star, educate us, your brothers, of our glorious history."

Amer smiled, as did every man around the table, as each man took a drink of their warm malt, Amer began his tale.

"The Dancing Star festival. Everyone knows of the great orange and purple stars that dance in our night skies every ten years around this time. I spent a good hour earlier tonight just observing her beauty. Such a rare sight. Arriving on a streak of light, then steadily pulsing for three months, before returning on her endless voyage across the void. Amazing. Truly amazing. I was also lucky enough to observe the first streaks of light that foretell the dancing stars return just over eight months ago. But why are they significant? Lots of stars dance in our nights sky!" The men smiled, as they relaxed back into their seats, they knew this was not going to be short. Well, everyone but Farelo, who is starting to look annoyed already. Barratash observed their reaction and the acceptance they gave to their brother and smiled, before taking another sip of his comforting malt.

"It started before our time, before our species even began. A strange race came here from those very stars, from deep across the void. They came to Lanasia in the hunt for gold. Obviously they found it, and in abundance, but our world was not like theirs. The air here was harder to breathe, the gravity was stronger than they were used to, and the Sun's rays were too concentrated for them. The masters of the void created a worker to enter the mines and extract the precious yellow treasure. It was hard, manual work retrieving their precious gold, not a job for them! The first workers were the Cassartans, a mix of our great apes and our great cats, strong of body, a tireless worker but with a fleeting mind, too much base instinct intact. They were easily distracted. Before long, the mines ground to a halt. The masters of the void needed a worker that was as much brain as brawn, one that could operate their fancy machinery and perform their manual tasks." As Amer continued, Barratash found himself sitting up nodding unconsciously with the story as it unfolded. He was not expecting this from a pub chat. As misguided as it was, it was refreshing to hear it thought Barratash as he continued observing, malt in hand. "They mixed our ancestors, the native humanoid of Lanasia with their own essence, and henceforth we were created, an evolutionary shortcut to what we may have become! Once all of the gold they came for was mined, they upped sticks and left, leaving us, their loyal slaves to fend for ourselves. After generations, we went forth to create and conquer this great world, our world...." Amer said proudly as he is cut off by Farelo.

"Wow void men, apes and cassartans, gold mines and slavery!! Where do you get this stuff?" mocked Farelo.

"That, my friend was the short version, that was just the overview of one festival, I am drunk and I am merry and I will not bore you with the true details of our history, of how this world, this life really works!" said Amer

"Haha I know how this life works, I work, I drink, I fuck and soon the King in the north will line his pockets with my soul. He, my friend, is the most powerful man here, on this planet," retorted Farelo. 'Agreed,' thought Barratash.

"Ok Farelo, where did we get our concepts of time, of money, law, architecture, agriculture, maths, engineering, music etc, etc. Our earliest sources, the hieroglyphs inscribed throughout our ancient land, on the walls of our great pyramids. These writings tell us everything, they tell us clearly, in our own hand, that the Gods gave it to us!" Amer folded his arms, sat just that little taller, the actions of a man certain he had clinched the argument.

"And I tell you, Amer, you should stop downplaying the significant achievements of our people. We made them, we the Tanni Ma Bar, we built the Pyramids with sweat and muscle, we created language and music and math. Either God gave us these gifts and we are created in HIS image, or we learnt them, we worked it out via trial and error, as we do everything else. Fucking VOID MEN ahhhh. And if you were right, why have the outstanding leaders, our rulers, the actual guardians of our true history in the great TANNI MA BAR, not realised this observation? They have only had the last five thousand years to do so! Ehhhhh," shouted an unsettled Farelo.

"They have ears but they do not hear, they have eyes but they do not see." muttered Amear.

As the two lifelong friends butt heads over their very different understanding of Tanni Ma Barian history, Qertus began to speak.

"I fear you are both mistaken and correct at the same time. But let me tell you this, the real people that run this world, you and I, and the world at large will never hear their names, see their faces or hear anything about them. EVER!! Not the government, not the elite guard, the generals, religious leaders or even The King. The people that run this planet are in places we don't even know exist. THEY call the shots, and you better believe that these people are powerful and out of sight. So don't even think about trying to figure it out, cause you ain't ever going to."

A few raised eyebrows and smirks appeared across the faces of the drunken friends, including Barratash's, as he hid in plain sight, across from the men.

"Everyone has a boss and that boss has a boss and it goes all the way up to GOD! Let me tell you, we are and always will be, continuously controlled by unseen forces." Qertus sat back as he grabbed a breath.

Farelo slammed his tankard of ale hard against the table "Amear, Qertus, you guys need to stop listening to your wives and their crazy stories from the fertile crescent. These tales are made up by irrational dreamers, by weak-minded fools that cannot separate reality from their own imagination!!"

From the table to the left, a tankard of beer hit the table hard as the drinker let out a sigh. His long, heavily waxed moustache dripped with warm malt as he turned towards the neighbouring table. Barratash sat up and slipped into his mind, in preparation for his contribution to the conversation.

"I hear you young whipper snappers. I feel you but you're all wrong, there is nothing, you're all just wrong. Cassartans, secret histories, ancient gods from across the void; where is your evidence? There is nothing, we created all this bullshit to make our lives liveable, that is all."

"He's just an old blacksmith," mumbled Qertus.

"Just, just an old blacksmith!!" The older man stood, his upper torso was massive, the hand on the beer tankard was huge, the wrists that supported the hand was the same width as the entire hand, they both merged into one solid trunk like appendage. He released his malt and leaned forward.

"I rebuilt the mechanisms for the great gate, I restored the great timepiece of Ali Ma Bar. My father cast the finest sword this land or any land has ever seen, commissioned by the great Reteshi. I understand how things work, and I have asked more questions about God, life, death and history than all of you and your brethren put together. Now shut the fuck up and let me enjoy my malt in piece. For this is the here and now, this is what is important, not false promises of a future full of amazing things or factitious, invisible bullshit from a by-gone era."

The group laughed. Friendship, festival, malt and Amear's tales always made for a great time. Barratash stood up, taking the blacksmith's intervention as his cue to grab another malt and another conversation. As the common Ali Ma Barians continued to fight off the inevitable onslaught of drunkenness, dizziness and vomit, the pub's door burst open. Before the morning's light could illuminate the drunken, coalescing mass within, a voice hit their ears. A second later, as their eyes adjusted to the strong morning light, the pub verged on silence. The voice, full of fear and uncertainty shouted again.

"The Namangans have taken the gates, we need every man." The room once again erupted, this time in frantic motion. Barratash, stayed calm in the unfolding chaos. "And now it has happened," he said out loud as he made his way to the door.

CHAPTER 19 - ARRAN IN TANNI

THE PEACEFUL TRANSITION INTO a Namangan state collapsed before the signing of the historic transition treaties ink had dried. As the city celebrated, surrounded by a Namangan army, biting at the chaff for action, a local militia had spontaneously formed, fuelled by malt and the blood of mistaken identity, they marched on the city chambers. The rest was history; as the news reached General Mariehoos, just beyond the city, that the peaceful Namangan ambassadors, as they began the administration duties of new Ali Ma Bar had been butchered, he gave the signal for the onslaught to begin.

In the chaos created by the drunken militia, the forces of Ali Ma Bar's military only assembled fast enough to secure two of the three gates to the city. A thousand of The King's men overwhelmed and surged into the city via the poorly manned eastern gate. The fragile idea of a peaceful Namangan transition instantly reverted back to the tried and tested strong arm of brutal assault and occupation, broadcast Barratash to the minds of his comrades of the The Pine, stationed throughout the Tanni and Namangan empires.

***

ARRAN AND ANICE WERE sheltering in dwellings right at the eastern gate. They heard the commotion outside; they saw the surge of Namangan warriors flood into the city; they saw their expertise and skill, and Arran saw first-hand the horrors of war and the inhuman techniques employed by battle hardened men, as they attempted to conquer the city.

"Why do we stay in here, we should be out there! We should stand with our brothers and sisters against this oppressive regime. What good are our powers, when we don't have the courage to act?" shouted Arran.

"Lower your voice," said Anice, her voice quiet, yet firm and full of authority.

"They are the keys to this," Anice waved her hands around, enveloping nothing and everything.

"If we leave here and stand with our brothers and sisters now, as you suggest, we will be dead soon enough. As will every one of them, who stand with us. You have to learn how to use your incredible power. You need to master your mind, your dreams, your vibration! Then, when we go out there..." Anice was on the verge of shouting, her voice trembling with raw emotion, grabbed Arran and pulled him close, her bust rubbing tight against him, her eyes peering deep into his.

"Then we will stand with our brothers and sisters and not for the small skirmish of one town but for the very soul of every Lanasian," said Anice.

"For every soul of Lanasian? I am not here to save the world. I am trying to save my people. I am just a simple Gavod trying to make sense of a powerful, drug fuelled vision and the subsequent snowball of strange events I now find myself in. I am just looking for answers!" said Arran, his voice full of strain and frustration.

"As am I, my friend, as am I. But you are not like me and I am not like the common woman that walks the streets of this fair city. Neither is the King! The world is full of great opposites, powerful forces that shape everything. Love and hate, light and dark, the KING and YOU!!" said Anice.

Arran moved uneasily and took a few steps back from Anice.

"I am no Messiah. I am Mertak, and my duty is to protect my people, possibly to protect all peoples. I am here, attempting to understand, to learn, to stop, to change the course of the vision I witnessed." Arran's body slumped forward, then as he rubbed his temples, he began again.

"You are right, Anice! I need to learn how to tap into and tame the strange powers of my mind. This is true, but I cannot sit here and see my brothers and sisters be oppressed without at least helping. If I don't help here, then what chance do we have? And if I am a Messiah, as you have hinted at, then surely, I can help heal the sick and master conscious dreaming and other magic tricks, all at the same time? That's if you will come with me and train me?" Arran and Anice locked eyes. As their eyes met and their energies synchronised, from the widest part of their collective, peripheral perception, they realised they are not alone, there was someone else in the room.

"I agree with you Arran, on one level you are right, on another level your actions are wrong," said the stranger.

"Sorry what? Who are you and how did you get in here?" Arran took a step forward to put himself between the stranger and Anice.

"I am Barratash, my misguided brothers and sisters from the mother land requested that I train you. And I will, if you choose to join me."

"Join you?" asked Anice as she secretly began a tried and tested spell to glimpse the magical capabilities of a person. As the inner thoughts and symbols came to fruition, she seen in her mind's eye, the measure of Barratash's power. She catches a glimpse of a man able to control his physical and energetic bodies independently. A man whose soul, as he stood here in this room was simultaneously interacting with the Bar En Dough, as well as with strange light beings that she had no words for. She also glimpsed Barratash's mind, as a great tangle of tentacles, slipping in and out of hundreds, possibly thousands of minds throughout Lanasia. She quietly stood there, lost in awe of what she was experiencing. He could possibly transcend physical reality if he wanted, what is keeping him anchored, is this the true Messiah, was I mistaken? thought Anice.

"Yes, I could and yes, I transcend the physical, and so do you and Arran and every other Lanasian to some extent. All people need is the training! But you are fairly skilled as is." Anice was taken back. She knew as soon as she had cast the spell, as Barratash's potential unfolded, that he must have been aware of her spell, that he was allowing this glimpse into his world.

"Sorry, what?" Arran stepped towards Barratash, a little lost.

"We need to train you, Arran, in the fundamentals of the mind. But as you said, we need to help our brothers and sisters of Ali Ma Bar. Both the Namangan and Tanni need our help. We will heal the sick and the injured! And help the dying pass over safely from this life to the Bar En Dough, then to the Nothing. Both of you follow me, we have work to do!" said the commanding voice of Barratash from deep inside their minds.

CHAPTER 20 - THE KING

"IMMORTALITY. THE GRASS IS always greener on the other side," laughed the King.

"Vertomina, remind me again why we are here in this cesspit? Look at these degenerates, each one of them is a sorry excuse for a Namangan. Some of these people have QUAFS on them the size of horses," said the King.

"We are showing face, which is your favourite phrase," Vertomina let out a little laugh. The King met her eyes with a single raised eyebrow and sarcastically thin smile. They are riding alone, no entourage, no royal protection, through the main streets of Ardeert, a fairly large city within the southern boundaries of the original Namangan country. The day has been spent travelling. The King loved riding his horse along his roads, one of the many engineering scraps he had revealed to this, his latest empire.

The smell of Ardeert in the extraordinary heat of the midday sun had been brutal on entering the city, but now the King's nose had adjusted to the warm, flowing stench of poverty. Its reality is easier and more pleasantly experienced in a letter,' thought the King.

From time to time, The King would be seen walking or riding the streets of the various cities and towns of the Namangan Empire. It was known that if one was to approach the King with small talk or to beg for some pardon or favour, that he would probably kill them where they stood. However, he was known to intervene in skirmishes, in local court, and to reward generously, individuals brave enough to approach him with ideas of value, the King after all was building an empire and industrious, tenacious bravery mixed with risk had to have the ultimate reward, as it had with its failure.

"Vertomina, the schedule?" said The King as he dismounted from his horse. The square before him opened up as onlookers quickly spread word of his presence. As the sun began to slowly tuck its golden rays and radiant heat behind a massive grey cloud, Vertomina replied.

"We have a meeting to address some sewage issues and the new tax proposal by Eferentis"

"Eferentis, the young, bold mathematician, finally comes good," said the King.

"Then..." Vertomina dismounted and moved in closer to The King, as they approached the walkway to the royal court building. In a hushed tone, Vertomina added, "Then we have a meeting to discuss the Tanni Ma Bar invasion, the recovery of a Cult of the Pine magician and the continued subversion of the populace".

"Hahahah," bellowed the King.

"Your awareness, your perception, the potential you bestow upon your kind always makes me laugh. Shout it loud Vertomina. You, my dear Vertomina, are a slave. A small, insignificant grain of sand in the grand scheme, as am I. What would it change if they...," the King gestured up his open arms and swept them in an arc, emphasising the city's people, that coalesced everywhere getting on with their daily lives. The King continued, "...if they knew they are farmed by two species so old, so ingrained into this planet, that they have duped every tribe, government, kingdom and power structure from before your history, as you know it, had even begun, what would your mighty Lanasians do?" laughed The King as he continued to mock all of those around him.

Vertomina looked at The King, fear emanated from her unwittingly, she instantly took control of her energies, the King nodded in approval.

"Yes, my lord, as always you ...," replied Vertomina.

"Do not stand there and play me like some dim-witted fool. Your species is like a parasite, limited faculties by design, with rare individuals capable of wondrous things. But the rare individuals with potential to see the truth are always hindered by time, as well as by the stupid, ignorant masses of the time frame they are born into, making them so easily controlled as well. During my reign, I have had hundreds of Vertominas. Each of your predecessors was clever, physically able, an overseer, an energy dancer and a credit to your people." The King paused and looked directly into Vertomina's eyes. "My seed makes sure of this." The King always monitoring Vertomina's mind, experienced her inner world explode with questions. He smiled at her directly before continuing. "And when you are gone, I will choose again, until the time comes when the war is won and I am given permission to leave this world and go home."

"Your seed?" blurted Vertomina.

"Yes, my seed!" said the King, before dismissing any further enquiries with a gesture of his hand.

"Enough of this, go and make sure my meetings are set up, I will be in shortly".

The King left to walk among the various people working, trading, lounging, eating, training, and debating around the square. As he walked, he made many small gestures of kindness and wealth to the people he interacted with. His generosity of time and coin was always met with smiles and awe. The King returned to the hall.

"Vertomina are the engineers ready?"

"Yes, in the principal room," said Vertomina.

"Some tea and something sweet." Vertomina nodded as the King made his way through the doors to the principal room.

"Hello," The King's voice entered the room before the doors were fully open, catching the engineers off guard as they danced around the great hall laughing and joking.

"Hello," the voices replied, the jolliness had left them.

The silence that engulfed the room was swiftly broken by the creek of the main doors as Vertomina returned to the hall carrying a tray of fresh pastries and tea. The King looked over, acknowledged Vertomina and raised a hand, signalling her to stop before pointing to the small table behind him. Vertomina moved quickly and put down the tray, as she did the King returned his gaze to the engineers.

"My sewage systems have been failing throughout the empire. One key to my great empire is a working sewage system and access to fresh water. We have the water, I commend you on this. But I cannot tolerate a failure in the sewage system. You are here because you are bright, industrious, tenacious, inventive. You may not fully understand the importance of a sewage system, you really don't have to. You just have to build them."

The King turned sharply and for sheer effect, thudded the magnificent ornate table in front of him with both hands, the solid hard wood table shattered into many pieces.

"So, what has been the problem?" demanded the King.

The engineers sat still, unreactive, but the King and Vertomina could sense the inner chaos being unleashed within their minds.

"Look at me, not the floor. This is a table, made of wood, nothing more, speak your mind freely," said the King, with a hint of sarcasm.

The engineers did not know where to look. The lead engineer, as was her duty and right, spoke first.

"The administration is the problem of why the sewage networks are failing, sir. There is too much corruption. We ask for the resources, the bureaucrats look at our Royal seals and then we receive about a tenth of what we ask for. Limiting our access to resources and manpower," said the engineer.

"Bureaucrats, autonomous regions, people forget too quickly what I, the Namangan empire am capable of, this will no longer be the case," said the King.

"Vertomina, assign one company of men to each engineer, draw up papers for the administrators of the highlighted problematic regions. Inform the commander of each company to assist the engineers in securing all that they need for the completion of their work. Each engineer will write a report weekly which will be delivered to the nearest Church of the Sun, for my reading." The King looked back at the engineers, each was notably calmer than they were a minute ago.

"A sewage system, access to clean water, cheap food produce, basic education, an arena, salt production, a road that joins the network to Namanga and a medical facility in every Namangan territory. Any problems, make sure I hear about them. Thank you for your service. Vertomina will see to some tokens for you to enjoy a night of pleasure, excellent food, salt and some fights before you return, refreshed, to your most important works." The engineers smiled, genuinely happy with The King's response.

"Vertomina send in Eferentis." The King sat down to the tea and pastries, as he slowly bit into the cream and jam filled delight, its essence squirting all over his lips and chin, the engineers silently left the hall. By the time the King had finished his tea, Eferentis had entered and taken up a bold position opposite him.

"Eferentis, ever the bold one," said the King.

"No, not bold sire, just cocky," Eferentis laughed. The King shifted his head slightly and looked towards Vertomina, with furrowed brows.

"I have a new tax system to pay for this growing, haemorrhaging empire and of your new southern invasion!" said Eferentis.

"Southern invasion, where did a lowly mathematician hear of such plans?" asked the King.

"I am the master of the financial realm. I understand little of how the empire works, or why you do the things you do, but I understand money in and money out and I tie these too events. By my workings, you will have to increase your taxation of the north considerably, until the newly conquered lands of Southern Traveras, Southern Hetier you know, the rebellious tip, start to balance out the cost of their conquest. I have a full breakdown and costing of the Tanni Ma Bar expansion and some rough numbers on exploring beyond the Aurd. And it ain't cheap!"

Eferentis paused, looked up at The King and continued, "Add to this, the flaws in the current system that allow for enormous sums of money to be doctored from official accounts. I have seen evidence of this financial manipulation from more and more regions. As well as some regions clinging to their cultural persuasions for corruption and the status attached to financial inequalities. This, on a whole, is laying tremendous burdens at the door of the poorest of your citizens, whilst seeing the gap between them and their Namangan overlords grow," said Eferentis.

"We do not need another tax, money is but an illusion, a simple barrier to resources, created by me to keep you in line! Yet it is a time-honoured tradition that keeps a large percentage of the people motivated, inspired, proud and the majority down trodden, sacks of negativity," The King smiled, "Please tell me more, oh wise Eferentis," mocked the King.

The King's mock, bounced off the self-appointed Eferentis, "Currently, we tax everyone in a simple, yet equal fashion but the really poor can't pay and the really rich don't pay enough. I propose we introduce a tax that collects more revenue from the wealthy. We will calculate it as a proportion of their wealth and it will be broken up into categories. We tax income, property, goods and services, roads, gambling and arenas, in accordance with my new guidelines...."

"Eferentis, you wish for me to tax the rich, to give to the poor? I need the poor to stay poor. I need the rich to stay rich. However, this new tax system should create an initial surge in negativity throughout the empire. A peak in base emotions that will be a powerful and rich source of exploitation," The King smiled, the small QUAF on Eferentis smiled back.

"Yes, Eferentis, create your autocratic model, tax them everywhere, apart from the arenas and its gambling. Also create a tax break for any family actively producing children, more babies, we need more babies! Eferentis make sure that you implement this fast, use force, if need be. My next invasions, as you have correctly predicted will be prolonged and very expensive," said the King.

Eferentis was as efficient at leaving The King's side as he was in entering it. As the heavy, ornate door shut behind the ever too joyful mathematician, fresh sunlight illuminated the great room once more, as the sun was released from the cloud's prison. The King once again turned to Vertomina.

"Are the generals next, my Vertomina?" said the King.

"Yes, the generals of the north await sir, on the agenda is Tanni Ma Bar, the cult of the pine and the general increase in religious zealots," said Vertomina.

"Well, send in my generals," said The King as he gave Vertomina a gentle wink and a friendly, all-embracing smile.

Ten generals arrive, ten from over a hundred officers that kept The King's military, a well-oiled machine. They walked with no QUAF attached, all holding their vibrations high. No salts for these men, only daily rituals of the sun to keep their vibrations high and their skills sharp. These men were Kingsmen, these were men of the arena and each had the blood.

"Ah my Generals, welcome, welcome," one by one as they entered, the King shook their hands and slapped them on the back, each a good solid slap. A reminder that the King was the biggest, badest, strongest, fastest, cleverest, most powerful alpha in the room. The gesturing was noticed, recognised and understood but not accepted. Even though each of these military men and women had been brought to the King's personal training room and physically, mentally and or energetically dominated by the King, their life, their biology, their psychology, only allowed for the belief that they were the greatest. As the men and women sat down, Vertomina brought some more tea and sweet pastries to the table.

One by one, the generals stood and addressed the King, updating him with news from their region. Then came the turn of Atal.

"Report," said the King, looking over at Atal, who stood in place of his lead, General Mariehoos. As Atal stood up from the table, the chair fell back, although he did not care, his time to shine had arrived.

"Lead General Mariehoos is still in the field sire," said Atal, The King acknowledged this and waved the man on.

"We have successfully breached the Tanni frontiers. We have secured many towns as well as a non-hostile takeover of Ali Ma Bar, the desert frontier city and the last satellite city of Tanni Ma Barian culture. Once we have re-cultured it, the city will serve as a great base for the invasion of the mother city, Tanni Ma Bar. We secured Ali Ma Bar using new methods, they were very effective, we have spent far less than usual and we have no major casualties to speak of." Atal was proud, this was unmistakable to all in the room as the large, hairless man paced systematically back and forth.

"So, we have secured the boundaries? The people have been broken? They are now eating salt and dreaming of killing The King, before returning to their meaningless lives?" asked the King.

Atal stopped pacing. His posture slouched ever so slightly, enough for every predator in the room to see.

"The town is secured, I guarantee that, the people seem happy. I left soon after the papers were signed, on General Mariehoo's orders, to return to the north, to this meeting. The city was flooded with stories of our superiority, of our previous conquests and of our unstoppable nature." Atal's posture straightenened out as he paced again, "When we arrived, they sent a small force to greet us, General Mariehoos entered the city alone and negotiated a five-month window of adjustment, before our men would enter the city to take over administrative and military control and begin the takeover. I have the legal documents here." Atal gestured to the documents on the table in front. "In six weeks, when I return, the city will have celebrated its Dancing Star festival, after which, they have agreed to peacefully submit to your rule, my Lord." said Atal proudly.

"So, you are telling me, that these proud warrior people, with a culture and history that rivals the Namangans, will sit down quietly after they've had one last drunken month to celebrate their demise? I have really underestimated the great General Mariehoos! His job was to conquer the city. Its location, as you noted, is a key lynch pin in the invasion of Tanni Ma Bar and the south."

The King paused, took a deep breath, as did every general in the room. After a moment, he continued. "Allowing conquered people months to celebrate their origin story, a story that celebrates their ancient lineage from across the void, is in some way going to weaken them? I think it's going to give them strength, give them resolve, give them hope. Let me see these documents." The King was not pleased and everyone in the room knew it. After a few moments, reading the papers, the King's energies had changed.

"Ok, it's not how I would have done it but what is done is done and if Mariehoos's idea of a peaceful legal takeover work, I suppose we will have more resources, which we will need to fight the south," nodded the King.

Atal turned to take his seat. He moved gracefully, making no sound as he picked the chair up from the floor, until his holstered dagger clunked against the wood as he sat, breaking the almost palpable silence in the room. As his bum hit the seat, his head left his shoulders. The others barely saw the King's sword, it moved that fast. Each of the warrior generals sat in silence, their full attention on controlling their energies in the presence of The King.

"Let it be noted, when I summon you to a council of Generals that you come in person." said The King calmly, as Atal's body slumped from the chair.

***

"VERTOMINA," THE KING CALLED as he began walking to the small, almost hidden door near the end of the hall. As he opened it and walked through, he turned to the Generals "Help yourself to tea and food, we will be back momentarily". The small door was rarely used, yet it glided open effortlessly on well-oiled hinges, opening up onto a balcony that overhung the five hundred feet vertical drop off the south side of Mount Menis. The wind was strong here, whooshing directly up from beneath the ledge, the King's hair was blown forcefully upwards, appearing to be frozen vertically at the wind's beck and call. Like every other balcony in the Namangan capital, there was no rail, wall or barrier between the ledge and the abyss. Shouting to counter the noise of the wind the King turned.

"Vertomina, I sometimes think I am losing my way." Vertomina's eyes looked down from The King as he moved to within an inch of the edge and began looking out over the precipice. His hair, face and clothing were now battered hard by the continuous, raging updrafts from below. "In which way sir?" asked Vertomina, as she joined him on the very edge. "Legal settlement. Where is the fun in that? That is not how I built this empire. This is not how the game is played. This iteration of the Namangan empire is born of fearless savages, a culture chosen and moulded for its lust for violence. All the work and plans that I have put into the south, for the great harvest. For the great Ali Ma Bar to be taken over by paperwork. This is not how it's done." The King spun, ninety degrees, counter clockwise and now with one foot hanging out into the abyss he walked the very edge of the ledge, one foot at a time, before stopping on the very edge. He appeared motionless, yet Vertomina knew he was working hard to make his movements seem so effortless in the challenging winds. As The King appeared to stand still, he looked out over the vast lands before him, seeing none of it, his eyes had iced over into his now familiar, thousand-yard stare, his eyes were blank, he was silent, still, meditative, then he was back.

"Vertomina, organise my personal guard, have them ready. The legal takeover has already failed. Mariehoos has been pushed back beyond the river. Decisions, decisions. I could leave now and be there within six weeks to crush the bastards into submission, the good old-fashioned way for a quick harvest." The King turned back to look at Vertomina and then stepped off the edge, took three steps towards the door and re-entered the hall.

"Ok let's deal with this pineman then I will make plans for Ali Ma Bar. Let's see the captive," said the King to Vertomina.

***

SINCE BECOMING A GENERAL, albeit a lesser General, Giat had to attend the Church of the Sun daily, to learn the magical rights and traditions of the secret order of the King's Generals. The other Generals were seasoned, as was Vertomina, but Giat was still relatively new to these concepts of mental training, of energy dynamics and personal energetic fields, vibrations and QUAFs. The day he became a General was the day his mind was blasted open, metaphorically and literally. But here he sat, again in the presence of the King, except this time he had a somewhat clearer picture of the King's potential and of the mystery he experienced when he first encountered the great leader.

They brought in the cult of the pine captive; he had been transported from the middle region of the northern empire. Over eight weeks in a slow-moving waggon, in the Ingurgitator's cage! A small cage laced with salts, the drug was painted onto the cage, in order to slowly enter via the skin and administered via the captive's food and water. They manufactured the cage and its binding to be so small, to make sure of his contact. The captive however, only ate and drank the very minimum, every few days. The Ingurgitator's cage sat in the middle of standard prison transport, filled with vile, ultra-low vibrating Lanasians, criminals and wretches of the most depraved nature. Allowing for the vibration within the Ingurgitator's cage to sync automatically to that low vibration. The magician had been trained and trained well. He held his vibration high and kept his thoughts to a minimum.

The King took a few steps back as the QUAFS shadow men brought in the Ingurgitator's cage. Instantly, the vibration in the room changed. A deep, dense, slow vibration seeped from the QUAF's shadow men, as well as the cage. There in the middle, sitting cross-legged, crammed into the inner cage, was a small man, with long, unkempt hair and a heavy beard. His gaze lost, out into the infinite abyss, beyond his blank eyes.

Besides the transporter, the pine spy walked into sight. He still sported the long hair, tied in a topknot and beard associated with the pine.

"What news do you bring from your time within the pine?" asked the King.

"It took me every ounce of my training to stop them from entering my mind. These sneaky bastards are always poking around other people's minds. I have detailed everything in my report. The key points are, the Cult of the Pine has cells in every major city and town throughout Lanasia. They have even begun expanding beyond the Aurd. They are zealots, fanatics, extremely focused and committed to their path. This, you will know.

There remedies for the salts do work, the ingredients are noted in my report but of how they are put together and in which doses, I do not know. Their systems for finding and training overseers, energy dancers and hybrids are effective and thorough.

However, the key information and possibly the most crucial, is that they have an elite military, an offshoot of the main philosophy. A team made up of thirty powerful members, who somehow link their overseer abilities and work as one? I have seen them train and they have the potential to give their armies an advantage, whilst wreaking havoc on ours. The prisoner was one of these, elite cult of the pine Magii warriors. The good news is there are only twenty-nine of them now," said the spy.

"Tremendous work, Tarbean. I knew you were the right man for the job. Please retake your place amongst the Generals and at your first convenience, sort out your appearance," said the King, with a smile.

"Thank you, my King, it was my pleasure to be of service," replied Tarbean as he bowed, before moving in behind his fellow Generals.

The King smiled. "Hopefully this will be a triumphant day. Is today the day I find a challenger worthy of my time?" the King turned to his Generals. Giat could feel his blood rise, and sense the energy shift as each of his comrades reacted similarly, before consciously controlling themselves.

"At last, we meet a magician of the infamous, secretive Cult of the Pine and a magii warrior to boot," said the King. The man did not move or respond in any way. The King approached the cage.

"Slave, yes you, bow your head, you are in the presence of royalty," laughed the king.

"Remove the cages, free the magician, remove his chains and slay those disgusting excuses for Namangans," said the King.

Giat stood unaware of what he was looking at; not the ominous Cult of the Pine magician, who sat cramped and seemed totally unaware of his situation and new surroundings, but the QUAF's shadow men! In his training of the occult arts, he had learnt of the QUAF and their guardian status, but his mediocre energy control resulted in a very limited first-hand awareness of them. The QUAFs shadow men however, looked as if they were made of swirling dark smoke, so dense that with his limited energetic awareness, they appeared physical. Beyond this energetic representation he could see that they were wrapped in the strange dark smoke, like some sort of physical disguise. On top, they wrapped themselves in black cloaks and wore closed helmets. Giat instantly knew that the QUAF's shadow men were not something he wanted to be a part of.

"Giat," the voice so strong inside his mind, made his head jerk upwards.

"Do not react, stay calm, I will not harm you. If you react, they will kill you! You are not a pure man, but you're not an evil man. Your heart is still radiant, please listen to my words and absorb my experience, we don't have a lot of time."

Before Giat could react to the intruder's violation of his own mind, the stranger showed Giat the illusion as he understood it. Simultaneously, the stranger stood and addressed the King.

"What is freedom? Who is free? What defines freedom? The slave who is bound by a chain with a mind so masterful, so mindful that he can soar like a bird? The slave who has spent years understanding why he was indeed a slave, with such meticulous thought and research that took him way beyond this," the magician gestured at the physical realm that surrounded him.

"The slave that progressed, slowly but surely, to free his own mind. A man who through his own endeavours makes the choice to become a FREE man, one who knows himself, who understands his very being!" The magician gestured with both hands, drawing a strange symbol with his hands over his head and then his heart.

"Or the King who knows not himself or his origin. A King who knows not of his true self or of the potential that lies within him. A man so powerful, he begs for the scraps from their table." The magician gestured to the shadow men and the QUAF, now observing from extensions of the shadow men.

"Simple parasites, locked to the lower ethereal vibrations. A perpetual, energetic warrior born by your people, your ancient forefathers. A warrior that, in its redundancy, after a victorious battle against an invader from the depths of the void, autonomously transformed its self into the parasite before us, to keep itself alive. As powerful as your people were, they could not control their creation as it turned on them." The King reacted as his awareness and concentration fleeted between this realm and the QUAFs.

"Ah, you never knew that? As we suspected, you don't know your true history. They feed you lies and half-truths," the Pine man then pointed right at the King, "You, your Majesty, you are the slave, not I, not we," he gestured to the Generals, to Vertomina. The King let out a mighty laugh, retaking the attention of everyone in the room. Giat struggled with the simultaneous, internal dialogue being transmitted and the outer spectacle taking place, as he attempted not to lose control. Then the King began his rebuttal.

"I brought you here to see how advanced your understanding of the truth has become, before I reset the farm. The way you misrepresent the history of my people and the QUAF, with the scraps you are fed by your crude interactions with the Bar En Dough, tells me much. Now, I only hope your martial skills, with your God given Tenni Uh Akki abilities are greater than your poor understanding of reality," said the king.

"Not today, Summerian, not today. You are a liar. We are of you and as powerful as you. Today is the day I return home. I have opened the gates and I am leaving this farm behind. The QUAF will not feed upon me this day, the nothing awaits," said the man calmly.

"Fight me," shouted the King, as he realised that the cult of the pine hybrid was electing to die, instead of using his gifts to fight. In an unusual fit of rage, triggered by the pine man's unwillingness to fight for his life, the King charged the Pine Magician, the initial shoulder impact taking the small, malnourished man off his feet. Before he had hit the ground, the King had unleased multiple, powerful blows smashing the skull of the magician. His body now lay lifeless where it landed. As his soul left this realm, the QUAF moved in, to feed upon his vast energetic reserve but to their astonishment, they could not. The magician, as promised had moved beyond their realm, the King stood laughing and as the Generals joined him in celebration across the room, Giat stood stock still, unable to grasp what he had just experienced.

Giat's mind was peaceful, like nothing he had ever experienced. The magician was no longer with him, he knew this because he experienced his soul pass over, into the Bar En Dough, and then The Nothingness, first hand. But the calmness of a newly inherited illumination, mixed with a lifetime of information that he could not comprehend. Add to this, a frightening first-hand experience of physical death and its choices, be eaten, revisit the past or ascend. Giat knew that with this new knowledge, he could become a focused target for the QUAF, he now seen them clearly before him. Giat slowly and calmly took control of his energies, his emotions now in check, for if anyone knew that the magician had linked with him, he would not make it out of this room alive and neither would his soul.

CHAPTER 21 - MARIEHOOS

"They have refused Mariehoos," said Sepher.

"When will these fucking Traveran bastards finally realise they have been conquered? You would think they would have got the message by now. Raise the black flag, let us be done with them," said Mariehoos.

'I suppose it was just a matter of time,' thought Mariehoos, he knew the southern Traverans would not bow. He knew there was only one way to bring a Traveran city into the empire, but just once, he thought they might be able to see that history was not on their side. This was the last Traveran city, beyond it was nothing but the cold expanse of the southern tip. The last resistance of the fiercest nation the Namagans had encountered. Nation, Mariehoos thought about that for a while, for all intents and purposes, he used the word nation when describing the Traverans, but after years entrenched in their lands, he knew that was not the right word. He would rather refer to them as separate kingdom of fiefdoms, united under a common goal of fighting off the Namagan empire. But that was not going to be possible, not under Mariehoos' watch.

"Sepher, recount for me one last time what these ice dwelling savages have for defences," said Mariehoos.

"The outer defences start a mile or so from the city, sorry town. Much the same as every other town this far south. They have various land fortifications, including tree houses, large ditches, single file bridges, and lookout posts with fire signals. As we progress closer to the town, a classic wooden fort surround. They have a water well, and ample supplies. There are a number of overseers and energy dancers amongst them as well as a number of warriors of the warrior cast," said Sepher.

This is the last stronghold of Traverans, they know this and we know this, they have dug their heels in and they are willing to die, so we will let them die. 'The QUAF will eat well this day,' laughed Mariehoos to himself.

"Let me deal with the overseers, amass the army, make breakfast and make sure everyone is fed and watered, then we will attack, balls to the wall. As always, we will light their fires for them, we will send panic through their ranks. Their defences are like the last five villages we have conquered, worse in many respects. The plan remains the same, I will enter the minds of the outer defenders, crush them, open the gates and as a whole, we will storm the inner sanctum and kill everything that moves." said Mariehoos.

The sun was just coming up as Mariehoos exited his tent. The morning mist hung over the frost-bitten land as the sun fought hard to bring a much needed warmth to the camp. Ten paces from his tent, one of the group sharpening stones already had queues forming as his men pushed, pulled and ground their blades to perfection. Beyond the hustle and bustle of the sharpening stone, the fires began, pots clanged, water sloshed and smoke began to billow. 'This is life,' thought Mariehoos; this is what it is to be alive.' As he walked to the nearest fire, a sadness took over him, for him this was it. The last Traveran town, after this one fell, who was left to conquer, the Tanni were still there and still to fall but 'there is no fight in the sand hugging bastards,' thought Mariehoos. Possibly the legends of going beyond the Aurd would come to fruition, but time he felt, was not on his side.

This town and these Traverans, these were the last of their kind, the last free Traverans in all of Traveras. Never would he lead an army into foreign lands against such fearless warriors, never again would he know the true spirit of the enemy. Over the years, he had come to grow fond of the Traverans, of their bravery, when compared to the Hetierians and the numerous tribes of the central lands who just rolled over and accepted his hammer. The Traverans were more like Namangans than any other, proud, fearless, relentless, and now he stood on the precipice of conquering the last of their strongholds. Finally, the whole Traveran nation would be integrated into the Namangan empire. 'A man with no purpose is no longer a man,' thought Mariehoos.

"General," said the soldier to his right as he passed some warm salty tea.

"Thank you," said Mariehoos.

"Today, we will flatten the last Traveran town, the last stronghold. Today, we will do them the great honour of fighting as hard as them, for today they will honour us with a ferocity and gamesmanship that only the Traverans and the Namangans possess. So, eat up, the Traveran finale is upon us. Songs of our victory here at Budieta, more than any, will be sung throughout time. Fill your belly, these bastards will not fold easily," said Mariehoos, before bringing the piping hot beverage to his lips. As the liquid hit his lips, his men quietly tapped their swords, thighs and gently tapped their feet. They were ready, as was he.

"Who has eyes on the outer defence Sepher?" said Mariehoos as he finished his tea.

"Batera and Sepasta's men," replied Sepher.

As Mariehoos sat down his cup, he jumped into the minds of both Batera and Sepasta and then from Sepasta to his lead scout and from here, he could see the tall blond haired Traveran standing by the first fire signal. Then Mariehoos jumped from the scout directly into the mind of the Traveran, to his astonishment there was resistance, the savage's mind was fortified, protected, shielded. By the fire, Mariehoos's body sat still, with the thousand yard stare on full display, while his men stood around, ready to protect him from anything and everything.

Mariehoos pushed hard into the mind of the Traveran, digging deep into his mind, he began pulling up emotions, fears, hatreds, memories, then he hit a wall, and felt his mind reel back. His defences were being breached, his mind was being infiltrated, his memories, his emotion, his fears were now flooding his inner world. As his world began to crumble, Mariehoos called out. He had never had to call upon the King, he knew as an elite guard and a General of the Namangan empire, it was something he and every other man with the gift could do in times of need but being one of the most powerful overseers of his generation, he had never needed to, he was always able to crush every mind he had ever entered, but not this one. As the fear engulfed him, he knew that it was not the guard's mind he was fighting, it was another mind or collective of minds that were protecting the guard. As the doubts embraced him, as he felt his mind begin to disappear, The King arrived. The power that surged through Mariehoos was intense, the doubt, the fear, the pain, the feeling of inferiority melted away as it was replaced by power, raw untapped power. From inside his mind, he heard and saw the King.

"Mariehoos," broadcast The King.

"Yes, my King," broadcast Mariehoos.

"The overseer was one of ten, they had combined their strength, they knew we would attack the outer defences with our overseers, and they were ready. A little too late," laughed The King.

"Their last outpost and now they finally changed their strategy. You attacked well Mariehoos, but you were no match for ten of them. I have crushed them all. The rest is yours," broadcast The King, as he left Mariehoos's mind.

Quickly Mariehoos commanded the Traveran guard to light the warning fires and open the gate before he returned directly to the campfire.

"Are you ok sir," asked Sepher.

"I am, I thought I would just slip into their minds, light the fire and open the gates. The Traveran bastards had other ideas. For a moment, I was nearly gone, my mind completely lost to them, but I say this for all to hear. In my moment of defeat, as ten plus overseers combined as one, to attack me, the King, Summerian, first of his name, entered my mind and crushed their overseers. He fought ten at once and never broke a sweat. Even out here, he fights by our side," declared Mariehoos.

Mariehoos stood up, his limbs trembling, his mind still reeling from the attack.

"The outer gates are open, it's time for us to attack. Kill everything, let no one survive to tell a tale of this day. Root out their Gods, their dead, their sacred spaces, desecrate, kill and ravage. Let the world know that to defy the King, is to defy life itself," shouted Mariehoos, turning from the fire, he walked back towards his tent and mounted his horse.

"Sepher, are you ready old friend?" said Mariehoos.

"I am," replied Sepher.

"Then let the carnage begin."

As Mariehoos spurred his war horse on, he rode hard towards the enemy, knowing his men were now scurrying hard to mount their horses to be as close to him in battle as possible.

Within moments of exiting the forest, he was entering through the outer defences and entering into the outer realms of Budieta. Up ahead, a few of his riders were shot down by outliers hidden in plain sight. Mariehoos broadcast far and wide to all of his men, to be aware. He knew that they had changed their strategy. The overseer attack on him was evidence of that but in past invasions, when the fires were lit, everyone retreated to the inner defences. At least this part, so far was true.

A few arrows, a few bridges to be repaired and now Mariehoos stood before the main fortification of the last outpost of Traveran might of Traveran sovereignty.

With everything he had he broadcast into the mind of every Traveran soldier he could see as they stood bows in hand atop their wooden fortress and within seconds, he was fighting Traveran hand to hand in combat, as a tall blond warrior god, attacking his kin, swiftly making his way to the inner mechanism of the gate. From behind the gate, he pushed the bar and the mechanism began to open, from the inside looking out he saw himself through the Traverans eyes, sitting motionless, his dark olive skin glowing in the morning light and then he was back.

"The gate is open; the gate is open," he heard Sepher cry and he immediately spurred his horse into action.

Sometimes he thought that his abilities had made him less of a warrior, that life would be better in a world where there were no overseers, where men and women could simply battle, steel on steel. A place where the most skilled warrior, with the most passion, will and desire to win; would win. But he knew that the victories, the songs and the spoils that were his, would not be his in a world like that. He knew he could wield a sword well but without his overseer abilities, he would not be a General. Mariehoos' thoughts were pushed aside by the unfolding chaos, Traveran men, women and children ran from their houses as his men flooded into the town's heart, steel in hand, dishing death with every stroke.

As Mariehoos slashed and stabbed every pale skin that came before him, he smiled, for he knew he had been blessed.

THUD, THUD. The sound was loud, then darkness engulfed him.

As he came back to, he looked up and noticed he was no longer on his horse. The pain ravaged his mind, his left leg was numb and not responding.

"Shield wall," shouted Sepher.

The arrows came thick and fast, large steel tipped arrows with long wooden shafts that embedded themselves in the shields making them harder to wield and manoeuvre. 'Ingenious,' thought Mariehoos, the movement and feeling coming back to this leg.

"Where am I hit," said Mareihoos.

"Left arm sir, impaled from the side, lucky your arm was there or you would be dead," laughed Sepher.

"What is up ahead?" asked Mariehoos.

"Two wooden towers, at the heart of the town, they seem to have a hundred or so men in each, archers and spear throwers. No way out, a last-ditch dance to the death," said Sepher.

"Ok, tie off my arm. Let's get ready to take those towers," said Mariehoos.

Across from where they now took cover, under the shield wall, his men were cutting down children, women, elderly, dogs, and anything else that moved..

"Bring me the children," shouted Mariehoos, "Let's move this shield wall back beyond their range".

As the thirty or so Namangans, holding up the shield wall moved beyond the arrows, the rounded-up children arrived to the side of them.

"Lash them to the shields," demanded Mariehoos.

The children's screams were loud and continuous as Mariehoos and his men nudged forward towards the towers. As they reached the base of the towers, the arrows had completely stopped.

A single Traveran exited from the door at the base of the tower.

"Release the children and we will come down and we, the last line of Budieta will fight you man to man. Stop being such fucking cowards," shouted the Traveran man.

Mariehoos downed his shield and walked forward, beyond the protection of the shields.

"Do I have your word?" asked Mariehoos.

"You are still alive, beyond your shield," said the Traveran.

"Then we will wait here, until your men climb down. Put down your shields, release the children," said Mariehoose.

Mariehose and his men stood and waited as the Traveran men climbed down from the towers. When the last man joined the ranks of Traveran warriors, Mariehoos gave the signal. Within ten paces, he was in the thick of it, slicing, hacking, kicking, punching, pushing, moving, defending, attacking. 'This is what it feels like to be alive,' thought Mariehoos, as his blade cut through the last Traveran warrior. This is what war should be, brave men and women standing across from each other, giving no quarter, no extra abilities, just steel and heart.

"You Traverans were a credit to all of Lanasia," shouted Mariehoos.

His men by his side, shouted and laughed as the last Traveran battle came to completion.

"Round up everyone left and kill them, desecrate their Gods, deform the dead and burn the houses. I want to return to camp within the hour. Our job here is finally done," said Mariehoose to Sepher.

CHAPTER 22 - NANOC AND LOO MEET CASHEW

THE WHIPPING OF WILMER, as the two now called it, had been advantageous. Up here, beyond Tanni Ma Bar, almost every town had greeted them with local fights, arranged to test Nanoc's claims. The level was not great, but competition was competition, and everything contributed to making Nanoc better. After he defeated every local hero, Loo sold seminars to build more notoriety upon Nanocs success. Travelling towards the Tanni border towns had been slow, but the fame accrued was worth it, as they set off for yet another track towards the north.

The track was long, narrow and sheltered as the steepest part of it now levelled off. The slow gradual ascent up the valley had been tougher than Nanoc first thought. As the more forgiving terrain lead them into the shade of the forest, a very welcome breeze enveloped the large barbarian, making his skin tingle and the hairs rise, simultaneously blowing his hair away from his eyes. Nanoc stopped, released his own energies into the surrounding nature, just as Loo had taught him, his large vascular figure poised motionless as he breathed deep into his abdomen. The energies here were powerful, there was something majestic about this place, 'it is calm and warm and has a homely feeling,' thought Nanoc. The colours, the smells, the soft breeze changing direction on his skin. This he thought, was a good place to have a shit.

***

"Loo HOLD UP, NATURE calls, be back in a moment" proclaimed Nanoc proudly. Mistress Loo laughed and smiled back at Nanoc, with one eyebrow raised. For Nanoc, toilet breaks could at times, be as long as a Kings holiday. Loo took a seat. She watched the large barbarian wade down off the overgrown path into the wild undergrowth of the forested hillside that now surrounded them. Nanoc disappeared quickly, the ground just beyond the road fell away steeply towards the valley floor. Mistress Loo entered one of her many energy building, breathing exercises, her eyes still wide and alert. She exchanged her energies with the trees, with the earth, with the fungus and everything else around her. After a time, she was one with the environment, her physical senses almost completely lost to the ultimate reality of mother Lanasia. Her bosom was so warm and inviting, Loo embraced her with her very soul.

The bushes and trees began to scream. As Loo's senses returned to the physical dimension, Nanoc was charging up from the undergrowth, hacking away at his path to gain speed.

"There's a prisoner transport of some description coming, it bears some sort of imperial Namangan flag. Four heavy horses, possibly a further two or three inside, we should take it. It may have valuable intelligence." Part of their mission in the north was to return home with knowledge, knowledge that would safeguard the south from the north. As a natural dissident, Loo knew that Nanoc loved the instruction to disrupt trade, diplomats and communications within the northern empire. She also knew that if they were to survive the north and carry out their mission, she would have to reign him in at times.

"How far away is it? You're sure there are only four? And of the Namangan flags?" asked Loo.

"They are just down the valley, eight hundred yards max, ambling, they will be here soon! And I am sure my friend, you're not the only one with magical powers. I have the eyesight..." laughed Nanoc.

"Spending three years to empty your bowels, as you ponder your naval, doesn't qualify as magical powers," retorted Mistress Loo, as she signalled him to stop and hide.

***

BOTH WARRIORS TAKE UP their position in the undergrowth, at opposite sides of the road. The thick bush was perfect. After a longer wait than was expected, the first horse arrived, Nanoc leaped from the undergrowth, his immense sword grasped by both of his enormous hands. With near silence and almost no reaction from the horse, Nanoc decapitated the beast. All around them, the carnage began. Deep in the chaos that transpired, as reaction mixed with training and adrenaline pumped, time slowed down. Each warrior's body reacted, fight or flight. Two of the so-called guards jumped into flight, their mind might have been saying fight but their bodies were saying flight and as their confusion slowed either reaction, Loo's blades made the ultimate decision for them. In the proceeding calm that quickly surfaced from the chaos, two men lay dead, one lay crushed under his horse, still unmoving and most likely unconscious, possibly dead. The final horseman stood firm, in front of the cargo he had sworn to protect.

"It's good to see that at least one of you is what you claim to be!" said Nanoc.

The final transporter may have taken it as some sort of consolation before his death, to know that when the chaos was unleashed, he was the only man that had stood his ground, the only one who reacted as his training had instructed . None the less, his skills with the sword were no match for Nanoc or Loo.

The waggon was indeed a prison transport, a black box, sealed tight and void of any light, simply mounted on wheels, surrounded by four horsed men. Nanoc moved from body to body, searching for whatever gold and documentation the dead held, before opening the door to the transporter.

The prisoner reacted subtly to the bright light and fresh air as it streamed into his dark cage.

"Ah, we have a live one," shouted Nanoc. The prisoner, bound in chains, was stood upright and braced across the width of the cell, his thick hands grasping tightly to the iron bars that kept him prisoner.

"I would wager that the pair of you are not from around here! Your foreign accents, lack of QUAFs feeding upon either of you. I suppose that has to be a good thing, right?" said the prisoner.

"A good thing? That depends on you. Chirp like a canary with the sort of information we are looking for and it could be a really good thing. Keep yourself quiet or feed us information that has no relevance and we may not be a good thing for you this day," said Nanoc plainly.

"Well, trust me, I am looking for the good thing. So, what do you want to know, big fella?" replied the prisoner.

Loo took two steps forward. "We are ultimately looking for information about the King, him as a person, his armies, his ambitions, what drives him, his weaknesses. But that is a long shot, so failing that we are looking for information on the fighting arenas. Where are the best arenas to progress a fighter quickly, to make a name that will get noticed, to make big money? Can you provide this good thing," asked Loo.

"So, for my life, you only want information on the King?" The prisoner laughed. Loo looked at Nanoc, raising her eyebrows just as the prisoner began speaking again.

"Aye, I can see the big fella, I see a specimen but I can see you too," the prisoner looked straight at Loo.

"I can see that you are both warriors, and no, it wasn't the blood spray across your face that gave it away," laughed the prisoner again.

"Miss, it is your energy, it is dense, confident, powerful, focused. I have only experienced a field like it a few times before. Impressive. You're an energy dancer!" said the prisoner.

Loo instantly drew her energy in around her, focusing all of her energy around her abdomen. This was the seat of her power, her storehouse.

"Relax, I am not an enemy, remember I am looking for a 'good thing' and it just so happens that I have all the information you require and I love to 'chirp like a canary'," laughed the prisoner.

"I am a political prisoner being sent to the King's dungeons to be interrogated. My crime is simply that I began to awake! I am a proud member of a progressive movement that educates Namangans about the illusion, the true identity of reality and conveniently enough, 'the King'. We actively promote and advocate for a Namangan future, free of the QUAF and the King. We operate in the background, in the shadows of every great city under Namangan control, or soon to be under his control," began the prisoner.

"You are no political, nor are you a religious man! You are a warrior, that is plain as day, in everything you do," said Nanoc. The prisoner looked out from his dark cage, squinting at the bright light beyond its abyss. Luckily for him, the bright light of day was now partially blocked by Nanoc's massive frame as he moved in, to sit on the edge of the waggon.

"I agree, I was once a warrior," then the prisoner paused and looked up to meet Nanoc's eyes directly. "Ok, I am a warrior. Just today, I try not to fight with my hands and feet against my fellow man. I now fight an eternal battle for my very soul, here inside my head against an eternal enemy!" The prisoner, unable to make the gesture he wished, used just a single finger to gesture towards his head.

"Well, that puts our mission into perspective, an eternal battle against an eternal enemy," whispered Loo to Nanoc, with a laugh.

"Ah, so you've been locked up and sent to prison for your first steps on the eternal battle against the infamous eternal enemy," laughed Nanoc.

The prisoner took a seat as best as his chains allowed. "I was once a great arena champion, and after that, I was a trainer of champions but poor life choices seen my many opportunities missed. A decade ago, I got a gig, training warriors, well rich young men playing at being warriors, you know the sort. The money was good; I wasn't complaining." At this, he raised his eyebrows and reacted as if it embarrassed him to admit this in front of other warriors. He continued;

"Through this work, I had the privilege to be present at a true northern feast, where my proteges displayed their skill to their overly enthusiastic parents. It was here, in the fancy stalls of a fancy party that I, whilst pishing their expensive beer into an expensive white marble pot, overheard two Generals of the Sun. They were drunk and arrogant and didn't care, probably never even gave it a second thought, if I could hear them or not. They talked of the stupid peasants, of their addiction to the salts and a passing reference to feeding their gods."

Nanoc turned his head slightly to make a quick, glancing eye contact with Loo, with one look he tried to transmit the idea of "where the fuck is this story going?", he ended up just smiling and winking at Loo, before returning his attention to the prisoner.

"With hindsight, I am not proud of it but I had always been a user of the salts, it was just a normal part of my culture, but to have this physically weaker , this fuck, talk about me as inferior, just because I used the salts! Everyone used the fucking salts, the whole fucking party was using salts, well as it worked out, apart from those in the know. This got my back up and possibly because he was a General, i.e., a former 'King's arena champion' and possibly because I was at a fancy northern feast, for the first time in my life, I controlled my rage and never attempted to brain the cunt, right there and then."

Nanoc smiled, as he found himself nodding along with the story.

"The insult however, fired my curiosity, so I started asking questions and before long, it led me to a meeting with The Pine."

"The Pine?" asked Nanoc raising his eyebrows and nodding towards loo.

"The King has outlawed The Pine throughout his empire. He has called us a cult and banned all mention, interaction and consultation. But it was amongst The Pine, with my awoken brothers and sisters that I was purged of the erosion that the salts had caused my soul and my brain. They answered all my questions and more, they gave me information that, funnily enough re-pickled my head, but in a good way. They even taught me a new martial art, the likes I had never seen, that combined dance, breath and mental training. She, I am guessing knows what I am talking about," nodded the prisoner towards Loo before continuing. "After only two months of regular attendance, the long dark veil that had been upon me, lifted. A veil that I wasn't even aware was there. I began to realise that I was a part of everything and everything was a part of me. I could no longer kill another living thing, violence against it would be violence against me. I was a part, an important part in the great scheme of things. When

I awoke, it was not a return to the place I was before the salts, this was a new inner state of awakening, of spiritual transformation. Soon after, I began to see the QUAF for myself. Do you know of the QUAF? Sorry, I am throwing a lot of stuff at you, this must be strange to hear, strange to be blindsided by." The prisoner paused for a second to gather his thoughts as Nanoc and Loo replied to his questions at the same time.

"Yes, we know of the QUAF," said Nanoc

"Yes, tells us more of the QUAF," said Loo.

"I started to see negativity clinging to my people like a dark viscous cloud. I began to hear it everywhere, I listened and seen it everywhere I looked. Then I began to dream again, something I never even realised had stopped. I became aware of the salt's purpose! It creates a subtle addiction that keeps the common man coming back for more. The salt takes the edge off the harsh reality of life, it keeps the senses dull and ambition neutered. It stops the mind from being able to focus and when you can't focus your mind, you are no longer a reality maker!"

The prisoner smiled, especially happy with this coherent string of consciousness that now flowed from his lips.

"From day one, Namangans are told that we are born workers, born to work, fuck, breed, fight, drink and use the salts. It keeps us down emotionally, truncates our potential and provides a straightforward path, the path of least resistance, right down to the lower emotional vibrations and it's here where the QUAF feed. They built this reality to farm us, to keep us as livestock, to keep us from realising that we are as powerful as them. Breaking this ancient stranglehold on the Lanasian consciousness is the key to taking down The King. The salts are key to The King's empire. We are all the same, black, white, red, brown, Namangan, Hetier, Southern!" The prisoner paused, followed by a short blast of shallow breaths, before looking up to make eye contact with Nanoc. Nanoc returned the eye contact, looking deep into the prisoner's eyes Nanoc started, "We are not all the same...," but before he has a chance to find his stride, the prisoner cut him short.

"We, my brother, are all one, we are all, each and every one of us, born under the sun! Our Sun. We are all, each and every one of us, full of potential, full of LOVE. Brother and sister, that is my story". The prisoner gave two great pulls on his cuffed wrist, the metal doesn't budge, the sound of metal on metal reverberates loudly around the small, wheeled prison.

"So, if you missed it, for those not listening keenly to the smelly, crazy prisoner as he chirped like a canary. To defeat The King, you must disrupt the salt, which will disrupt the QUAF, and therefore The King. Now kill me or free me!" shouted the prisoner.

The decision was instant. As the chains fell from his wrists, the prisoner leaped into the sun and laughed uncontrollably.

"Will you join us as we travel north," asked Nanoc with a smile.

"I will, it would be my honour to be your guide for a while," said the prisoner.

"What is your name? I am Loo and this is Nanoc," said Loo as she pushed out her hand.

"I am Cashew, it is nice to meet you," as he shook Loo's hand and turned to offer his to Nanoc.

"Well before we head north, you best get rid of those rags of the dammed you are wearing. His clothes will work for you," Nanoc pointed to the guard, still pinned under the horse "and I can guarantee that they are better smelling as well," laughed Nanoc.

"Let's push the dead and the transporters over the cliffside back there, and then let us be on our way before dark," said Loo.

After a week's travel, the unlikely three came across the small town of Yi Ma Bar, not historically a Namangan territory but now Namangan run. The town was still adapting to its recent takeover, construction in the name of modernisation was taking place on an impressive scale, significantly of note was the central road, now heavily underway.

"Look at that road, Loo. Now that is impressive! You could march forty soldiers, shoulder to shoulder across the width of that road and still have space to swing a cat," Nanoc stated as he stood mesmerised by the engineering before him.

"Just look at it, it is almost level, all the way to the horizon. You could march a hundred thousand men, thirty miles a day on a road like that. The Namangan empire has roads like this in all its territories?" asked Nanoc to Cashew.

"Yes, it is the first thing The King's men build, after a new territory has been conquered," frowned Cashew.

"Efficient transport and spare no expense, this Summerian is smart," said Nanoc.

The three travellers walked towards the market square, the streets here were still narrow and the road was badly cobbled and covered in dirt. Soon it would be wide and flat. Nanoc and Loo took this opportunity to purchase some fresh supplies for the days ahead. As they approached the first vendor, the freeman spotted a King's guard at an impossible distance, walking near the top end of the new road's main work camp. The King's man began to walk in the general direction of the three. He is stocky and walked with an air of confidence, not born through false belief. Cashew informed the two southerners to "look down and keep your eyes away when dealing with Namangan traders, do not make eye contact and control your emotions! This town is still on edge, it is still hurting. Do not draw any undue attention to yourselves, just act as if you're dumb foreigners, well established in Namangan culture, simply trading". As he finished saying this, he completely ignored his own advice and started shouting out at The King's man. Nanoc couldn't believe what he was witnessing, this new companion, this man who owed them a debt was about to get them all killed. As Nanoc and Loo's bodies jumped into fight mode, as their hearts started to pump, the prisoner and The King's man met eyes and both men began to laugh.

***

"GIAT. A KING'S man now?" asked the free man.

"Cashew!! Hahahah" the two friends share a warm embrace.

"I am, at last I am earning good money and a just living, serving the common good." said Giat, Cashew laughed.

They took their conversation and catch up to a nearby garden, where the two old friends talked and laughed for a time. As the excitement of their reunion wained, Cashew signalled over for Nanoc and Loo to approach.

"Ah, your new student, I presume? I saw you and him on approach through the magnifying glass. He is a fine specimen." said Giat, as he looked over towards the approaching Nanoc.

"Nope, they two are my saviours! I could only wish to have another student as good as you. In the week I have travelled with this one, in the games I play; you know the ones, let me tell you, he is special. A specimen like no one I have ever experienced." said Cashew as he looked out towards Nanoc with a smile.

"Saviours? What trouble have you gotten yourself into this time old friend," laughed Giat.

Giat observed as Cashew deflected, deciding to turn towards his new companions. Even though they were still thirty yards away, Giat observed that Cashew would rather sit awkwardly than answer the question. 'He will tell me when he is ready, he is rubbish at holding secrets,' thought Giat as he slapped his old friend lovingly on the back. As Cashew's two friends approached, Giat instantly knew that they were not from the north, 'well at least the large one is not, the woman could be,' he thought.

"They are prospectus fighters from the South," stated Cashew.

"Warriors," said Giat. As the southerners joined Cashew, Giat began to recount his tales of the arena, glory days of him and Cashew, of adventure and risk and of the twenty-plus years they spent together.

"Every grand champion needs a coach and nowhere on Lanasia will a man find one more skilled than Cashew," said Giat.

Talk turned to where they were headed, and what Cashew was doing in these regions. Cashew, unable to hide a lie from a friend such as Giat, spoke freely.

"Giat to answer your question, you must first take off your hat as a Kings man and listen to what I have to say as a friend, before you judge me." Giat nodded, smiled and gestured that he was listening.

"I am no longer the man you once knew, Giat! I am still the martial strategist but I have awoken, I have begun to see through the fog! I have left that life of violence, greed, anger and hatred behind me. I am at the beginning of a beautiful road to transformation..."

"You are a member of the Cult of the Pine." Interjected Giat as he took a few seconds to dance through the mental symbols of his inner energy work.

"You don't have to answer that, I can see it with my own eyes. No QUAF! A man with your salt background should be ripe for the harvest," Giat then looked around and smiled.

"No QUAF on any of you, and you," Giat addressing Mistress Loo directly.

"Your energy field is like nothing I have ever seen! Not that I am an expert but the Sun's training is very good," said Giat. Loo simply nodded back in agreement. 'She is an energy dancer,' thought Giat. How rare.

"Well, you are correct. To answer your questions, my friend, I was traveling around the south, spreading the word of the pine and recruiting anyone of talent, when I was captured by some elite Namangan spies. No ordinary warriors. However, I was lucky, as they entrusted me to some substandard transport soldiers and well these two made light work of them. Hence, my saviours," said Cashew with a smile.

"Ah, not just a man of the pine but a fugitive of the King," said Giat.

With a short uneasy laugh, Giat boldly confronted the dilemma that he was now a part of. Reveal his card of the chance encounter with one of his oldest friends? A friend, who like him had recently transformed, who had recently had his entire world view blown open. Or bury the strange yet majestic encounter with the pine magician that entered his mind and safeguard his position, his family and his new life at the top of the food chain? His royal loyalty built on fear had truly been blown out the park, when he temporarily crossed into the Bar En Dough with the pine man, the decision was clear.

Giat told the three of his encounters with the pine's magi warrior, of the magician's ability to enter his mind and converse with the King simultaneously, his parting words to the King, his choice of non-violence and his acceptance of death. Nanoc, Loo and Cashew were left speechless by the story, but Giat did not stop there. The flood gates were open and it was time to release.

"You know that each and every royal arena champion is personally invited to the Kings home? It is a test where he humiliates them, before offering the position of General. It happened to me. A sort of psychological leash, looking back at the whole experience, it's actually pretty clever. The King is a very clever man. I say man but I don't think he is a man!" The three warriors sat, ears pricked up, Giat could see that they were unsure of where he was going with his story.

"Have you ever actually seen the King?" asked Giat

No one responded, everyone had seen effigies, pictures and statues of the King but not actually physically with their own eyes.

"Nope," in sync and strangely all together, the three replied.

"I have, not only have I seen him, I have fought him, face to face, belly to belly, sweat of his brow dripping on mine. I have thought long and hard on this and I am now sure that his physical prowess, his magic, it is all too much. He is not one of us. He is not Lanasian. He is from, I think, from the void!"

Giat looked intently at their faces for any sort of reaction as he revealed his deepest observation, before opening up his magical symbols in his mind for a deeper understanding of their reaction. It seemed, unlike him, they were unfazed by such a revelation, 'either that or they control their energies well,' thought Giat.

"I should not be talking of this to anyone, never mind to an agent of the Cult of the Pine!" He gave Cashew and uneasy look. "Since my first encounter with The King, I just can't stop running it over and over in my mind. There were too many anomalies. As you know Cashew, I have wrestled with a thousand different men. I have spent more than thirty thousand hours on the training mat, I know the feel of a man, of my opponent. I know every inch, it is my art, my life. He is not what is presented, there is something very different about our King. He out grappled me, and then made me feel like a novice on my first day. He is far better, far more powerful than his story alludes to. A story which he controls." Giat stood up and looked out beyond his companions to make sure there was no one within earshot, before sitting down again and huddling the group tighter.

"This is going to sound bat shit crazy, but hang with me. I witnessed the death of another man from inside his own mind, broadcast to my mind whilst the King crushed his skull." said Giat calmly.

"You say what? When you say batshit crazy, you fucking mean it," laughed Nanoc.

"That's not even the craziest bit, the QUAF were ready and waiting to eat his soul, I experienced them trying to eat his soul. It felt like bliss, but it's an illusion, a trap. But his training, his calmness and willpower seen him sail on past them into the Bar En Dough, then into The Nothing. And when I say nothing, it felt like an infinite space and time, void of everything, yet full of everything. I have no words to describe it. And I don't think there are words capable of describing it, it can only be experienced," said Giat, quieter this time.

"He was a Pine man, yes?" asked Cashew.

"Yes, he was, a senior, a leader," confirmed Giat.

"We must do our best to spread the word of the pine, the King is now actively trying to crush us. Hell, they captured me near Ali Ma Bar, that's not even Namangan territory," said Cashew.

"It will be soon," informed Giat.

Giat stood up from the huddle, realising who he was, the side he had chosen and how he cannot let the QUAF eat his daughters. He looked at his old, dear friend Cashew and spoke.

"My brother, you cannot talk to anyone of where you came across this information. I have fallen into bed with the enemy and I am at a loss as to how to continue. Your identity is safe, as I am guessing, is mine?" The four acknowledged what had been said with a simple nod of their head.

Giat turned to the southerners, are you travelling to the arenas? "I am. We are." replied Nanoc. "Head to Hetier, we have the greatest warriors! Maybe not the best venues or paydays but we have the finest warriors, us two, can testify to that, even though this one is a dirty Namangan. He lived in Hetier for years." Said Giat as he smiled at Cashew.

Giat slapped Nanoc on the shoulder. "Aye, you're a fine specimen, even if you had no martial skill, a specimen like you should not be fighting at the start of the night". Giat produced a small parchment of paper and tube of ink. He wrote a simple note and then took some ink and covered his ring, pressing it to the paper. "This will get you a good rank, I have vouched for your competency, do not let me down".

"It seems like everywhere I look; I always find awoken brother and sisters. We are the risen, we are the reborn. It looks like it is time to part company brothers and sisters. Remember violence is not the answer, do not feed the lower aspects of yourself and thank you!" said Cashew. The freeman slapped his long-time pal on the back, shook the hands of the two southerners, turned on his heels and headed for the new northern road.

Giat smiled, "It was great to see you once more my friend, travel safe."

***

THE FOUR STRANGERS, THROUGH some random act of universal synchronicity briefly mingled, just enough to unify their cause. From a distance, Barratash smiled.

CHAPTER 23 - JASINO

THE FINELY GROUND MIX of chalk and salt swirled like smoke as streaks of fierce midday sun filtered through it. The climber formed a tight fist with his, freshly chalked right hand. White and tight he thought as he jammed his fist into the crack before him. As it secured his weight, he clenched his left fist, ready for jamming into the crack further up. Again and again, he jammed his tight fists, hanging off one at a time as he climbed, higher and higher. As the long narrow crack in the rock face finished, the climber grabbed tight, desperately tight, to the largest of the small protruding holds available. The rock face was flat, the holds were shallow and soon he would begin the push towards the crux of the climb. The overhang would test him to his limits.

The climber hung upside down, carefree, his legs wedged and supporting his weight as he shook out his arms and emptied his mind in preparation for the intense final section to his route. Far below, he noted some observers, down by the side of the road. The added pressure of an audience made him smile.

The climber re-chalked his hands before securing one of the only two available holds, one of which was superb, the other not so. He could only hold it with the tips of two fingers. "Ok, this is it, relax, breathe, focus. Time to deliver the goods." With his grip sure, he released his first leg, then his second. He had not time, nor desire to dangle perilously high above the exposed rocks, far below for long. Quickly but deliberately, he moved upwards, along the underside of the overhang, along the route he had mapped in his head. Four powerful moves, carrying his entire weight on the tips of his swollen and bruised fingers, seen him in a position to get his legs back into action. As he secured a toehold, he exploded up to the final set of almost non-existent grooves beyond the overhang, he climbs them with masterful ease. The climber gives a tremendous shout, his lungs almost bursting with intensity, as the exhilaration washes over him. Completion of another puzzle was his. He stood tall and enjoyed the view. Down below he saw and heard the observers clapping and whistling.

***

NEAR THE BASE OF the climb, Nanoc and Loo took up seats on a nice rocky out crop. As the two unpacked their food, the climber came into view, whistling a merry tune as he walked around from what must have been an alternative route to the top.

"Hello there lad," shouted Nanoc in Namangan, the language now becoming almost automatic. The climber nodded as Nanoc continued to stuff a whole, smoked chicken breast into his mouth.

"Hello brother, sister. What a beautiful day," the climber continued his whistling, blissful in his success.

"It sure is," replied Nanoc.

The climber looked towards Loo with a smile, "Have we met before? You look familiar".

"No, I'm afraid not, this is our first time here, in the north," said Loo.

"Why do you waste your time up there? Seriously, what kind of fool does what you just did? Is there a golden nest up there, full of golden eggs?" Nanoc smiled, happy with his witty observation. The climber took a few seconds to look over Loo and Nanoc, before looking back up at the cliff he had just mastered.

"Another question might be," smiled the climber, "what fool wastes his time, enquiring why a fool wastes his time?" Mistress Loo laughed, at first just a little, but quickly her laughter became so deep and genuine that all three of them became swept up in it. The laughter flowed organically, building until their faces turned red and teary with joy. As they began to relax, the climber took a seat next to the two southern warriors.

"Ah that was good, I haven't laughed like that in a while," the climber extended his hand in friendship, with a smile. Loo then Nanoc accepted his hand.

"I am Jasino and to answer your question brother, I climb to relax, it brings me calm, it brings me in touch with me, with myself like nothing else I have ever done," Loo continued to smile as she listened to the mad climber's explanation.

"To climb, one must develop strength, flexibility and endurance. One must conquer himself to climb, no hesitation is allowed up there," Jasino pointed to the overhang high above "fear, indecision, hesitation will get you killed up there."

"Now that we can understand," said Loo.

"Your ears are all deformed? From climbing?" Nanoc asked with a frown. Loo seen the genuine confusion written across the large warrior's face.

"Hahah no, from grappling. I work in Aterhamis for the warrior school of Retishie. I am their ground fighting, grappling coach. This is how my ears are like yours!" says Jasino.

"Not just a cliff clinging philosopher but a grappling coach as well, the universe is truly smiling at us Loo," said Nanoc with a smile.

"Join us, some chicken, tomatoes, water," Nanoc opened up their lunch and Jasino accepted graciously.

They ate together, relaxing in the beauty that surrounded them. Tall cliffs, trees and the sounds of the soft breeze made Loo smile as she enjoyed the company of this new strange companion. But as always, the mission lay heavy on her mind.

"You say you are a coach. This is very fortunate for us, maybe you can help us friend. We are looking for the nearest, good level arena. A place where we can make a name, a wave and move onto the bigger shows up north. Does your school have any shows?" asked Loo.

"We send warriors to shows continuously. We are always training for combat, for competition! We have over two hundred warriors in camp at our Aterhamis school," said Jasino

"WOW, two hundred! Any of them top tier fighters?" asked Loo.

"Yes," Jasino smiled and laughed.

"You southerners have obviously never heard of Retishie. We are the largest, non-Royal affiliated school in Namanga. Almost all of our fighters are top tier," stated Jasino.

"Non-affiliated school. We were not aware that there were NON-Affiliated schools here in the north." said Loo.

"Hahah yes, the great Retishie was one of the few people to defeat The King in physical combat. He was the first to be invited for a second round, where he was then defeated and humiliated with magic. On turning down The King's offer of military order, Retishie started a school. Training in all forms of combat, physical and non-physical. The King put out a bounty on Retishie for his betrayal, which seen the initial school driven underground and our art even further into the occult. After a time, the first crop of fighters emerged, they were extremely successful. The new breed of warriors were strong mentally, physically and energetically, with great technique. In the early days, we were near invincible. The King, if anything, is a businessman, the bounty has never been retracted but the new level of combatant the Retishie system produced, instantly forced the competition to get better. The arenas seen a tenfold increase in customers, as well as a marked increase in new schools popping up to provide for the new demand. And of course, it brought lots of new warriors to our doors. Now we are a mainstream school, that has unfortunately spawned many a poor copy. Few are now taught by the great man, and fewer still in his original holistic methods. There are just NO shortcuts to the top," Jasino paused and pointed up at the rock wall he had climbed earlier.

"This Retishie sounds like a very interesting man," said Loo.

"That he is, but like every great man's ideas, his message, his system will become diluted, lost in translation and time. Lost to shortcuts and ignorance of the original experiences that forced the Retishie system to develop strong, energetic, magical and emotional control."

Mistress Loo stood listening to Jasino. She now saw this jovial, kind natured stranger with a different light. At that instant she began to go over the words he used to describe his climbing. Her thoughts processed deep in her mind. Maybe, just maybe, this Jasino was more than Mistress Loo had first given him credit for. Loo performed her inner kata and without indication or hesitation, she attacked Jasino both energetically and emotionally but sent her energetic attack with a warm positive, playful energy. It only took Jasino a split second to react, to counter, to defend, to smile.

"A friendly shot across your bow," smiled Loo.

"A simple test, as you spoke, your previous description of the climb and its importance began to click," said Loo.

"Yes, my friend, the climb is one of the Retishie methods for controlling the body's emotions and energies, as well as an effective system for developing a strong focus and unwavering concentration. His methods either make you strong or kill you," laughed Jasino.

Nanoc nodded in approval of what Jasino had just said. Loo could tell that he knew something beyond the physical had just taken place between her and Jasino, but he did not have the control yet to understand what. She could see that he did want to show his cards, to announce his lack of energetic discipline, by stating it so openly.

"Nanoc here, is still learning our energetic ways," said Loo as she reached out and slapped his arm. "It can be hard for those not born of the energy dancer blood to learn our ways, but everyone has the potential within them and when this brute learns the subtle art, he will be the greatest warrior that has ever lived," stated Loo as she held Nanoc's eyes and smiled.

"Well, if quality training is what you are looking for. Then I know the place." Jasino stood and stretched. "Will you come with me, you can bunk at the school tonight for a modest fee and we have, as I have alluded to, a great training facility, with many high-level fighters. Which always makes for an excellent level of sparring, and quality sparring is a rare thing to find. In the morning, we can have a look at the fighter schedules and see if we can get you matched up for one of the upcoming shows," Jasino gestured for the two to follow. Nanoc and Loo nodded to each other in agreement and followed the thin, wirey climber back to the great Northern Road and once again, they were travelling north with a new companion.

CHAPTER 24 - THE RAGING RIVER

"MAY I HAVE A moment, sir?"

"Yes, Gemaras you may,"

"Thank you, sir."

It has been five weeks of travel in the company of the eminent Vantis of Lerr, and now after so much thought, so much worry, so much pedestal worship, he is finally here, in Vantis's ear.

"Your first boat trip beyond the Aurd to the north, sir?" 'And here he is, mumbling small talk,' thought Gemaras.

"It is a necessary journey, not one I would do for pleasure. The views have been good, but I would rather be in the south. These northern lands are full of savages and wild men," the words seemed to flow past Gemaras' ears, no matter how much he tried to concentrate on the lead delegates' words.

"Yes sir, the views have been nice.... Sorry sir, may I ask you a question?" Gemaras mumbled hesitantly.

"Ask away Gemaras." Gemaras felt the sharpness of his place behind the words that rolled from Vantis's tongue. Yet he would not miss this opportunity.

"We are travelling north, our meeting with the King is in five days' time. I was wondering..." Gemaras stopped, took a large breath, "Can we catch an arena show after the meeting? I would love to sketch one." Gemaras looked down at the stripped, wooden floor of the waggon transporter. Vantis laughed.

"After we have secured the south, if your duties have been performed, you may do what you wish with your time and your money. Like you, I once loved the arenas, my beloved younger brother was a legend amongst men, he lived for the glory of combat and died for it too." Vantis's face was dark, as a vicious explosion of emotion flowed behind his deep blue eyes. "Now get your pen back to paper and get the deeds copied out. One for every delegate."

Gemaras' eyes flicked up only for a second to acknowledge Vantis's words, before nodding and moving back to the table to complete his work.

After an additional fourteen days of travel because of heavy flooding and landslides, the convoy at last, pulled into the royal compound, just forty miles south of the Northern Aurd. To the east, just clutching to the horizon, were the beginnings of the first vertebrae. Like a great spine, the Aurd rose. The great spine of the Aurd, the untameable mountains that decisively divided the north west from the south and the east. Gemaras loved the mountains, not being in the mountains but the vision of the mountains. He sat upon the waggon thinking to himself, whilst Vantis and the King thrashed out the terms to the south. He would have many a day to sketch this majestic view.

The royal convoy arrived early the next morning. The word that came through to Gemaras was that the King was still two days away. The flooding encountered by His Majesty's convoy from the north west had been extensive. It was said that, The King would be here, after he attended to the pain and suffering of his people. The King's men met with Vantis and his delegation, the King was not there but his people were. The first round of negotiations was set for an hour's time.

Gemaras' work was done, he had copied and translated all articles to prepare for the negotiation. He cleared it with his boss and set off to the edge of the compound to sketch. As he got to the edge of the grounds, he thought to himself how much he would rather be here looking at the mighty Aurd, as it hugged the horizon, than back there, bending words and knee to secure power. Gemaras picked up his pencil and sketched. Hours flew past as he sat engrossed in shape, texture and shade, as the light continuously changed, filtered by passing cloud and finally by the sun's fading light. Gemaras loved the sunset. Everyone but him, so he had been told by wise, educated men, seen the world in some mysterious concept they all called colour. These colours were somehow different from the multitude of tone he could create with his pencil. He had thought long and hard on the idea of colour before, but he preferred the colours that his pencil gave him and everyone loved his pictures.

When the day's light started to fade, Gemaras smiled. As his eyes laid upon his last sketch, he thought to himself, 'mother will love these sketches from The North'. On his return, he thought of the mountain of copying that would no doubt be awaiting him.

When Gemaras returned to the delegates' room, he couldn't believe his eyes. It looked like the politicians, learned men and business folk he was scribing for, had somehow turned into a rabble of cutthroat, bloodthirsty killers. Every-where within the inner chamber lay bodies, body parts, mangled sinew, chunks of flesh, naked bone broken free of the flesh and pools of blood. Surely it could not be, but it definitely looked like most of the King's delegation were dead.

"Flee, now, NOW I said," shouted a frantic Vantis, as he single-handedly kept the multitude of attackers at bay, like some warrior god, disguised as a legal book worm. The northern delegation was like a startled herd, consumed by blind panic. Gemaras joined the hysteria train, straight out the main doors into the waggon. As the majority of the delegates struggled to board, the massive wagons began to roll, the horses went into a frenzied panic, bodies unbalanced by the sudden movement fell off. Gemaras struck out and grabbed Vantis, as he made a last-minute dash and leapt for the wagon. As Gemaras secured himself upon the wagon, his mind raced. Could the magnificent beasts smell the blood, or were they simply sensing the dread and panic, so palpable in the air? As these thoughts ran around his head, they were pushed aside by fresh thoughts. His mind was racing, rearing out of control. From his perch on the wagon, he watched and witnessed, the oversized and physically dilapidated 'brains' of the south fail to secure themselves into the waggon without aid. He watched as their power, their authority, their privilege escaped them. He thought: 'how can these men manage the south, when they cannot even manage the simple task of saving their own life, when the chaos had consumed.' As the wagon rolled past the gates of the royal compound at full speed, Gemaras had some sites to draw. Well, if he made it home, that was.

'It is a strange world we live in,' thought Gemaras. 'Here I am, a simple scribe's copier, stranded by flood waters, in a backward northern land with the last surviving rabble of The South's finest and wealthiest bloodlines. We have nowhere to go and no options left as blackness of night encapsulates us.' The night was long. Every sound brought visions of The King's men, but nothing came. After a night with no sleep, no warmth and too much fear, the sun broke the darkness and ushered in the fresh day. Then from nowhere, their saviour arrived. From the last outpost of dry land, he walked down towards their stranded waggon, the morning sunlight illuminating him from behind, 'a vision for the ages,' thought Gemaras.

"Hello, morning," shouted the stranger.

"Gemaras," shouted Vantis, Gemaras jumped up to the lead position and shouted back a reply to the stranger, in the common Namangan tongue.

"Hello, friends. Isn't it magnificent?" the stranger signalled, with a tip of his head, towards the swollen river, while he took a hearty, deep breath. The delegates could see the stranger is strong, well-muscled and heavily scarred. His hands were like spades that connected to his tree trunk-like-wrists. The six delegates who were now left, were on full alert. "The water is big; floods are in full flow. The Yantee is magnificent, is she not?"

"Yes, she is," replied Gemaras.

"Gemaras, ask him if he knows of any boat keepers that will risk the high water. And hurry. The Namangans will find us soon." Vantis could see the fear and shock on Gemaras' face when the words left his mouth. The stranger seen Gemaras' face as well and in that second, the atmosphere between them changed. "Are you sure? The river will kill us," said Gemaras, without form or protocol. Vantis looked straight at Gemaras, the large Traveran was now next to them.

"It is either the river or the King's men! We don't have many options here today. I can guarantee the King's men will be hot on our heels, and our wagons are not going any further in these floods. NOW ask the man?" Gemaras instantly relayed the message.

"Oh, wow, that's a relief. I didn't know what the boss man had said but the way you reacted lad, I thought he had ordered me dead." The stranger let out a big breath. "I am Peroot, and the Void has seen it fit that our two individual missions combine, to see them both fulfilled. Ask and you shall receive, ask and you shall receive," chuckled Peroot.

"Sorry what? So, do you have a boat, and can you take us down the river? We have a boat at the seaport of Aurds End," asked an unsure Gemaras. Vantis' eyes were firmly on Gemaras. His stern look and lack of patience was stressing Gemaras. It was making the whole translation of the negotiation much more tense. As Gemaras updated Vantis, Peroot spoke.

"Ah, you men are wordsmiths from The South, that is for sure! Book readers, pencil pushers, law-makers. Probably as good with a sword, as you are with your pen, but this," he pointed to the swollen torrent, less than thirty metres away. "This, my friends, is no book, this is mother nature, and she doesn't give a flying fuck what books you have read. You are not river people, I can see that, but lucky for you, I am the best of the best. And the only man alive who can get you to Aurds End in this." Peroot smiled and nodded, content with his speech as Gemaras relayed his word to the delegates.

"Ok boy, if we are going to do this and survive, we need some simple commands, this translation back and forth, is no good. That shit will get us killed!! So, when does the big boss man want to leave?" said Peroot.

Gemaras relayed the information again, Vantis told Gemaras to get a price. In the panic, they left with limited funds.

"How much will the journey cost?" asked Gemaras.

"Hahahah, you want to pay me, to paddle the Yantee in full flow?" Peroot began to laugh.

"Tell your boss this lad. I have not found a crew brave or foolish enough to oar my raft on such an epic adventure as this, and I have looked. And here, on the very day we see the largest volume of water of my lifetime, you crazy-ass bookworms arrived at my door, completely set on tackling the river, unaware of how truly crazy it really is. Your motley crew is probably the furthest thing from river men I have ever seen. Not only do you want to run the Sheltered Pass and everything before it, but you want to pay me. Hell yeah, I say. Tell him he can pay me whatever he wants, at Aurds End. If we survive," roared a very excited Peroot.

Gemaras relayed the message once again, as Peroot starts shouting commands. After thirty minutes, the six men under Peroot's instruction had manoeuvred his strange boat to the river's edge.

Gemaras was now scared. The boat before them was like nothing he had ever seen before. It was like a large, squashed ring that had somehow been filled with air. The floor had wooden slats, with many holes throughout.

"Ok lad, tell them all to line up here. I need to get the weight and power right for such an adventure," instructed Peroot, pointing to the water's edge.

"Who is the strongest and who is the weakest, no false vanity or we are all surely dead!" Gemaras did not translate, he simply pointed to Vantis and Mellas.

"Ok lad, who is the weakest?" Gemaras shrugged.

"Ok, the boss man front left, the other strong one, front right, the fat one on the left and the others where they are. You, lad, are on my left at the back." Gemaras nodded and relayed the information.

"Ok boys, it's usually three to four days to Aurds End, we are probably looking at about five hours in this water level," Gemaras' translation began automatically.

"If you fall in, lie on your back, feet first, heading down river, head to the sky. We will try our best to pick you up. NEVER stand up! You got that lad?" Gemaras nodded to confirm he had listened and understood.

"Ok what are your words for forward, back, left, right, hard, hold on, over left, over right and oh fucking shit!!" chuckled Peroot, Gemaras laughed as he informed Peroot of the Lagosian tongue. This man, he thought, was insane.

"One last thing for you to translate lad, I am the guide, my job is to manoeuvre, to drive. I am watching the water, picking the best lines. Your job," he points at the delegates with such conviction in his finger. "You guys are simply the power, you paddle hard, you do as I say when I say, you commit right up to the line, if the coward in you rises up, push him back down. Tell the Boss man to give the men some sort of motivational speech. You are going to need it," laughed a very happy and giddy Peroot.

After the briefest of paddle lessons and a short but rousing speech from Vantis, the unseasoned crew of bookworms and lawmakers hit the largest Yantee anyone had ever seen. As the boat broke free of the bank, the commands came loud and clear. "HARD Fooorward", "Reeht backke", "Hard foooorwahrd". As the raft broke through the eddie line, between the slack water nestling near the temporary bank and the main might of the raging Yantee, the boat angled perfectly and with its fresh crew paddling hard but not yet effectively, the raft began to shudder. It twisted and turned, sank and rose, insignificant to the power of the Yantee, as they crossed the eddie line into the main flow.

"Ok boys hold on to your pants," Gemaras was concentrating too hard on keeping his balance on the edge of the boat, for him to translate Peroot's excited humour.

As the boat made its way quickly down river, into the main current, the Yantee opened up before them and the reality of their undertaking was now fully visible and the fear from the crew was now palpable.

From behind them, a bolt screamed straight past Gemaras, so close it drew blood before finding Tellus's fat neck. Instantly, he lost his balance and the river hungrily swallowed the rotund lawyer into its dark, raging underbelly. Vantis looked back to see where it had come from, his paddle coming out from the water as he looked. Peroot had no time for arrows or non-paddlers, this was the Yantee, in full flow, this was where legends where born. This was here and this was now. In Namangan Peroot shouted, "Get your stick back in the fucking water!". Automatically Gemaras was relaying the message with the rawest of translations, Vantis had no time to react to such a breach in formality. Before them, the river dropped steeply, the entire mass and width of water seemed to constrict about five hundred metres to the horizon. The small raft with six men, attempting to survive, paddled hard and fast into the first rapids between them and Aurds End.

"HARD Fooorward, HARD Fooorward, HARD Fooorward," cried Peroot in broken Lagosian.

"Don't fucking stop, HARD Forward," cried Peroot, Gemaras automatically relayed the command.

The first rapids were a reality check. This was like no boat trip they would ever experience again. In amongst the complete chaos that had engulfed them, Gemaras thought to himself, 'we averted one danger for another but maybe we chose the wrong one.' He didn't have long to dwell upon his thoughts, Peroot's commands flowed as fast as the water. He had never felt this alive in his entire life, every fibre in his body was engaged, every muscle was working, his heart was racing, his mind was sharp, fear and the excitement gripped every breath he took. It was like nothing he had ever experienced. Gemaras was loving it.

"Hold on," shouted Peroot as a monstrous wave, stealthily ripped in from the side, temporarily twisting the boat and sinking the whole left side. As Gemaras performed the task of simultaneously relaying the translation and following the order given, he witnessed Vantis, the only man still paddling, fall into the drink. The others instinctively, and before Peroot's command was given, had held on for dear life, fear driving their survival instinct. As the great wave engulfed the right side and the left side sank, Peroot automatically climbed as high as he could up the right side of the raft, countering the weight imbalance. Gemaras gripped onto the outside rope that rimmed the raft and swung his powerful arm out into the drink, grabbing Vantis by his shirt as he flew past. Vantis got both his hands to the rope, but he was struggling. The water was beating him hard, the under current pulling him relentlessly as he held on for his life. The raft tossed and turned as they entered another set of rapids. This time, they were long constant peaky waves. In the now longer, more predictable movements, Gemaras under Peroot's command, pulled a very shaken Vantis into the boat.

Rapid after rapid after rapid, played with the boat, then to everyone's relief, a long wide flat section opened up down river.

"Ok boys, you have all done well, only one lost, paddling is getting tighter, commands need to be followed, through until the end. Until I say otherwise. I need the power. You are my horses."

Peroot was now standing up, on the edge of the raft, one eye on the horizon down river and one eye on the crew as his intensity increased. "The training is over, the small stuff, the fun stuff," with his paddle at full extension, he pointed downstream, "Sheltered Pass is coming up. Now this is where legends are born and the unworthy die!!" shouted Peroot, with his auto translating Gemaras.

"Harrrrrdddd Foooooorrrwaaaarrrrdddd"

The entire width of the river before them disappeared into a narrow channel downstream. Where the water disappeared, vapour rose from the river, as if it were on fire.

"No one has ever seen this sight before and survived to tell of it." shouted Peroot in Namangan. Gemaras translated through shaking lips. Twenty heart beats later, their raft, full of enthusiasm and fear, entered the Sheltered Pass. Within two heartbeats of entry, the raft was flipped. Every man found themselves deep in the depths of a raging, churning, abyss. Up was down, left was right, darkness from light was indistinguishable, yet the urge to live, the urge to survive, the urge to breathe, forced them to fight against the might of the Yantee, to fight for their right to be, to fight for life or die trying.

Below the fabled pass, six men surfaced, but only three men were alive. Peroot gripped Gemaras by the neck, as he struggled against the torrents and pulled him back into, the now heavily damaged raft. Vantis and Gemaras were both shaken to their core. The river had claimed everyone else.

The rest of the journey, in comparison was plain sailing. When the men reached Aurds End, they had no coin to pay. Vantis offered Peroot a job amongst his estates. Their boat awaited them and the three moved on, to sail around Aurds End and back into The South.

CHAPTER 25 - INTO THE DEPTHS

BARRATASH LED ARRAN AND Anice out into the streets. Beyond the door, the city's vibration dropped. Fear, confusion and anger. Just like moisture on a humid day, the fear hung in the air like a wet blanket, clinging to everything it touched. The streets were narrow and Barratash moved fast. This was the first time Arran had been out in the street since being stabbed and his first time, under full consciousness navigating the back streets of Ali Ma Bar. Up ahead, a Namangan soldier lay wounded, slumped against the wall, blood dripping from his head. While holding his side, he looked up and his eyes filled with fear, then in the same instance, they conveyed the look of inevitability, the realisation that he was too weak to defend himself against the three oncoming strangers.

"Anice, the mob are coming, run to the end of the alleyway, point in the opposite direction and shout. Create a distraction, go, go now," Anice ran down the tight alleyway, towards the increasing noise, straight for the heart of the mob just beyond.

"Arran, speed up your vibration, think of nothing, open your mind and think of nothing," commanded Barratash, from inside Arran's mind.

'Speed up your vibration, how do I do that,' thought Arran as he watched Anice run towards the sound of the mob.

"Concentrate, everything starts with focus. I will lead the dance, follow me as I enter his mind," broadcasted Barratash.

Barratash turned his attention to the fallen soldier. He bent down to one knee and cupped the back of the dying man's head.

"Brother," the words entered the soldier's mind. "You are about to go on a journey, I will guide you into the Bar En Dough. You have had no training; you have one chance to defeat the QUAF and enter The Nothing, beyond the Bar

En Dough. Empty your mind brother, feel the calm I am bringing," broadcasted Barratash.

The soldier's body slumped as he relaxed, free of pain. He now realised, for the first time in his life, the ethereal dimension that his mind now inhabited, his mind has always inhabited. The two helped the Namangan soldier, eased his pain, comforted him as he passed over. He wept as he looked back over his last week, of the carnage he had been a part of, before turning his attention to his sons, sons he had not seen in years...

"No," Barratash pulled the soldier out of the powerful, emotional trap he was now entering.

"Stay in the nothing, concentrate on nothing, feel the peace, feel the love that the nothing has, stay with me." A moment later, the soldier's consciousness disappeared, stopped, transferred, transmuted and slipped into the nothing beyond the Bar En Dough. The QUAF sat just beyond the vibrational shield Barratash had erected. Arran could feel them, they were confused, they were angry and ultimately, they were pissed off that they had lost a meal, they had lost one of theirs.

'Do we belong to them?' wondered Arran.

"Concentrate," came Barratash's voice as he called Anice into their minds, "We must move again, Anice return now, Arran, follow me", on that Barratash set off, Arran hot on his heels and Anice hot on Arran's.

The trio moved fast. In the short time since Arran had become a man, a Mertak, his consciousness had exploded. His perception and observation, his awareness of what his sense, his heart and his head were saying had increased tenfold. In this swift flight of darkness, as he pounded the streets, hot on the heels of Barratash, Arran took time to experience what he was feeling. The city was tense, afraid, in turmoil. It felt jagged; the air was heavy, almost sad. His heart sung out for Anice. What were these emotions he was feeling for her, his first crush? She was beautiful, he observed, however; she was his newest partner in this crazy adventure. In this moment, Arran glanced to the side and smiled, Anice's warm eyes reflected and reciprocated the gesture. Finally, he came to the man out in front, a man five times his age, a man whose brothers had rescued him from the desert and sent him here, via the southern warrior courier service. Arran concentrated, focused his mind, combining some med-itation he practised, with the internal symbolic magic that Anice had taught him, from inside his own mind. As he projected this forward, he felt the answer instantaneously. "We are linked," not in words though, the strange feeling was familiar, as Anice had entered his mind frequently, but different as Barratash's energy was so very different. It was like there was no limit, no boundary, no edge, no definition, even within his own mind, where he could place or pin point the consciousness stream that was Barratash. It was as if he was Arran's mind, a very different experience from Anice, where she was more of a visitor that could be defined, quantified and if he wanted, forced to leave. "Arran, we are almost there". In that instance, the thought of the words and the images, emotions, colours, aspirations, memories and histories were all transmitted, all information came at once. Arran knew that the Ali Ma Bar energy transmitter was just up ahead. Of what it was, he did not know, as the volume of information sent from Barratash had overwhelmed him.

As they ran the narrow back streets, the streets became steeper and steeper as they climbed the inclines and steps, until they emerged onto a long street, the last street of the hill that curved back away from them on either side. Behind them, was the last outhouses of this part of the city and in front of them, an overgrown empty ground that led up to the summit of the hill in front. The hill known locally as, The Law Hill.

It gradually rose from street level, from the roads and houses until finally, near the top, shrubbery and open ground covered its plateau and a small pyramidal cairn capped its highest point. Arran knew from Barratash's transmission that this was not a natural hill, as it now appeared, but a covered-up pyramid that posed as a hill, as it lay in disguise, its secrets sleeping within. A pyramid, similar to the one he had explored in Tanni Ma Bar, but this one hid in plain sight, with only its capstone protruding. Of the many questions that Arran had asked about the Pyramids, 'who built them and why?', was now most prominent in his mind. Even now, with the somewhat elusive and cryptic imagery from Barratash's transmission helping to answer some of the question, he was still lost to its awe. The transmission was intense, cryptic and for all intents and purposes, completely useless, as he never had the resources to decode or to even understand what was being transmitted. The whole thing was flavoured by Barratash's own cultural lens and personal knowledge. It was framed in terms and ideas that Arran had no reference for, yet! Then in that second, Arran's mind flashed back to him merging with the Tanni Ma Bar Pyramid, the energy that pulsed through his body and the fear it conjured on Riley's face. 'Will it happen again' he thought? The thought was a mixture of excitement and fear, the fear of being outcast, again.

Arran kept moving forward, Barratash did not slow down, even for a second. Anice was now shoulder to shoulder with Arran as they entered a small orchard, about a quarter of the way up the hill. The entrance was there, plain for everyone to see, yet disguised, hidden for none to see. Anice did not see it and jumped in shock as Barratash disappeared through the open ground, into thin air. Then Anice and Arran entered. The energies here were strong, the area was bright and the interior was like that of the pyramid in Tanni Ma Bar, yet more refined and in much better condition.

"We are here, not much longer now, just a little deeper in we must go!" said Barratash, fresh of breath, his heart beating barely above normal.

"Where is here? I have walked the Law Hill a handful of times since entering Ali Ma Bar four moons back, I have marvelled the void from her capstone and all this time she was hollow?" said a confused, angered and somewhat bemused Anice.

"It's similar to the one in Tanni Ma Bar," said Arran.

"What's similar?" asked Anice, with a genuine air of amazement.

"We are inside the Ali Ma Bar pyramid. It seems that the first two great cities of the north I have visited have a pyramid, some visible, some not. I wonder how many others there are? Of what their true purpose was, is? Barratash?" prompted Arran "I got an underlying idea from your broadcast that they are some sort of power transmitter, but I don't understand what power or a transmitter are? But I think it must have something to do with the way these pyramids focus energy, like the rivers of energy I encountered in the Tanni Ma Bar pyramid, but that one felt broken, as if the flow was jammed. This one almost doesn't feel as if it has energy at all, but I would wager that I can't feel the illusive pulsing energy because I am standing directly in the flow," said Arran.

Barratash laughed uneasily, "You can feel the pyramids energy?"

***

ANICE LOOKED AROUND UNEASILY. 'They have been communicating with each other,' thought Anice. Communicating within each other and they have left me out, am I not part of their exclusive club? Why are they now communicating via the word? wondered Anice. As her paranoia began, Barratash entered her mind. "We will join, all three of us, as soon as we reach the main chamber. I will give all the answers I have." This time, the message was not in words, the whole communication was just an impression of information that streamed into her consciousness and made complete sense. It was instantaneous and complete. This was the first time she had been on the receiving end of someone with true power. On the rare occasions when someone attempted to enter her mind, her defences were often too strong for them to continue but Barratash's power, she was learning, was far greater than hers.

***

THE THREE OVERSEERS ENTERED into the main chamber. The heat hit them, it was body temperature thought Arran and as promised, Barratash stopped. Up till now, there had been a glow, an energetic light to guide their inner journey through the narrow passages, towards the pyramid's centre. It emanated from the walls, just as it had in the Tanni pyramid. Here, there was only darkness, a space so dark that their eyes could not adjust. As soon as their minds grasped the foreign concept of the complete absence of light, the couple became aware of the absolute absence of external sound. In the nothingness, Arran thought he could hear his own lungs. As his breathing unconsciously sped up at this revelation, the noise of his lungs, wasn't all he could hear inside of him. In the infinite darkness, as he screened out Barratash and Anice, he became aware of his body's internal processes, the sound of his body digesting food, of his heart pumping rhythmically, the movement in his joints.

Then Barratash's voice boomed around the large cavernous space.

"For years and years, almost every culture dedicated to unlocking the mind and its secrets have created systems of meditation, chanting, fasting, rituals, hallucinogenic consumption, drumming, pain, sex and more. All with the goal of mastering the mind and entering into the deeper realms and unmasking its secrets. Those afflicted with this insatiable curse will go to any lengths to understand how the mind works and to realise the other dimensions that it may access, the other realms that may exist within. Lucky for you, my knowledge is built upon the shoulders of the most magnificent minds and what you are about to experience here, would take twenty years to master through meditation. Arran could hear Barratash move, his feet shifting his weight and his arms slowly waving, he could feel the slightest disturbance in the air. He could not see him but he knew that Barratash was pointing to the grand room they now occupied.

"This is one of the powers of the pyramid. It is the perfect incubator for accelerated access to the Bar En Dough. Anyone entering this womb can enter the Bar En Dough, it's a miraculous piece of engineering. In almost every culture, they find the darkness in a deep cave to simulate what we have here, but there is so much more to this than just the darkness. And we are so lucky that we now stand here, in, to my knowledge the last of its kind. Are you ready to begin?" asked Barratash, with excitement.

"Yes," came the reply from Arran and Anice, simultaneously.

In that instant, Barratash instructed, verbally, for the two youngsters to strip naked and lay down upon the floor.

Time froze, as the three lay naked, with no discernible, external sensory stimuli. There was no clearly defined separation between their bodies and the ground, because of the ambient temperature of the room. In this strange space, their minds quickly and easily merged with the infinite everything that always has been and always will be. As Arran merged completely, his body now at one with the darkness, his mind now free from its shackles, Barratash began transmitting information. The information came thick and fast, acting internally like vivid memories, a complete world emerging instantly full of light, colour, taste, sound, touch, emotion, interaction, connection, thought, compassion, vibrancy and bias. As it flowed in, as the slower, conscious brain tried to interpret the unlimited data via its usual pathways, Arran began to forget himself, to leave the 'I' behind and merge with the collective information that he was now experiencing, as it filled his being with unlimited, full sensory immersion. One by one, questions formed and one by one they were answered.

As Arran lay on the floor, completely unaware of his physicality, lost in his conscious mind, navigating, observing and reacting to, and with the imparted life works of Barratash, as he attempted to rationalise, categorise and conceptualise the information received.

The message from Barratash was so much more, observed Arran. As soon as he attempted to conceptualise it, to contemplate it, his conscious mind reduced it to the singular, to the restrictive aspect of verbal communication, even here, inside his mind. He unwittingly and unwillingly had limited this vast encyclopaedic transmission to the descriptions available to him, based upon his own life's experience. This transmission was from Barratash, it was from his experience, yet, Arran's understandings of the transmissions were constrained within the primitive linear language-based thoughts that shaped his own inner world. This was not a spoken language. Arran needed to change his thought process to understand the information. Just as he had done a hundred times before on the trail, he needed to adapt to the culture. He had almost completely and automatically limited his thinking, his analysis of this multi-faceted information transmission, to the one-dimensional communication sphere of the word, limiting the external sensory inputs and emotions, even though they were the keys to Barratash's truths.

"By limiting the information to the verbal word," came the booming voice of Barratash from inside Arrans mind.

"The conscious brain loses its ability to perceive the truth of reality, the wholeness, the intangible depth of the truth. The word is the worst possible way to transmit truth, one cannot grasp truth this way. It must be experienced. How does one grasp the truth that we are everything, that we are nothing, without the experience? Release yourself Arran, release yourself."

The information broadcast was omnipresent, multi-layered and persistently intrusive. Arran's brain continued to rationalise, to de-fragment the myriad onslaught of new information invading and consuming his very being, and then, his mind fatigued and he released himself and merged with it, disappearing into the abyss, into the nothing.

CHAPTER 26
- ATERHAMIS
SCHOOL

AFTER TWENTY LONG, INTENSE days, the two southern warriors were still having fun training daily, in their new friend, Jasimo's martial arts school. It was located a few hours' walk from the small, Namangan town of Aterhamis. The two warriors had stayed a few weeks to regain a resemblance of fighting shape whilst the opportunity presented itself. The long days of walking, training on the fly, and fighting easy, local shows were slowly but surely changing Nanoc's physique. He needed some hard combat training, rounds of sparring and combat drills to replicate an actual fight to get his mind back in the game, for soon enough the Royal arena would call.

Nanoc's days were filled with daily strength and conditioning training, hard sparring, technical sparring, technique drills, strategy theory, physiology and anatomy classes, massage classes, combat energetics, magical skills, cooking and nutrition, breathing master classes. They covered almost every facet of the martial arts curriculum, even military tactics like battle formations, group fighting, communication techniques and more. From the outside, the school was large, old and ornamental. It looked like a well-maintained stone building from a time long gone. It stood proud, rugged and alone, completely out of place, set in its own grounds and fortified by a wall and moat. No one knows for sure why it was built but it had definitely been a monastery of some sort and a prison. The solid stone structures were strategically built alone, atop an artificial mound, raising it up from the otherwise flat floodplain between the mountains to the east, and the great grass pastures, before the salt producing Traveras lake far to the south west. Inside, was a raw place where men and women were mentally, physically and energetically broken. A place where brutal training regimes tested a warrior's heart, skill, endurance, confidence, worth, value and every other core aspect of themselves that they held dear and stretched it till breaking point before rebuilding them afresh. Here in this former prison/monastery, warriors came face to face with the greatest challenger of all, themselves! It would reveal their inner heart, the measure of the warrior taken, Nanoc and Loo were in love with the place!

Most Lanasians would never understand a warrior's heart, a heart that was filled with joy, with fun and elation at finding a place like the Retishie school. Another bonus for the southern duo was the skill level, for the first time in a long time, the duo's skills were not night and day to those around them. They were still superior in their respective specialisms, yet the Retishie system worked, breeding legions of well-rounded warriors, disciplined and adept at all facets of combat.

As a hundred plus warriors trained inside, their hard work creating clouds of sweat infused fog, the weather outside was changing. It was intensely dark for midday. High above the gates, a multitude of interchanging layers had replaced the usual big blue sky, dull dusty greys and dark royal blues wrestled for position. The air by the gates was wet with a refreshingly warming smell to it. A young but seasoned warrior stood, a lone sentinel at the outer gates. The storm was moving his way. As the hours rolled past into evening, the sky grew more turbulent as the winds brought it closer. Heavy rain, created long crystal like shards of water that drove deep into the ground so hard that they bounced back up from it. The area just above the ground temporarily disappeared from sight under such heavy, driving rain. As the evening faded, the last rays of sunlight made a last-ditch attempt, it fought hard to pierce deep into the rain, as it sunk beyond the horizon. As the rays painted a multitude of rainbows, fracturing the full spectrum of light every which way through the rain, a lone figure appeared and approached the outer gates of the Retishie compound.

"Sir, sir... please, please come in out of the rain." The young sentinel tasked with securing the entrance, dashed out into the rain, momentarily leaving his post. In one smooth, precise Movement, he removed his cloak and used it to shelter the old man before helping him into the drier part of the gate.

"Thank you, young man, thank you. The great blue has opened up, she cries tonight, tears of joy I hope," said the old man.

"Yes...... yes, she does," replied the young sentinel, who wasn't too well versed in small talk or socialisation. He therefore, jumped straight into his enquiry.

"Old man, where are you off to in this?" he pointed to the fast-approaching storm. Before the old man had even the chance to reply, the young sentinel spoke again.

"Old man, it is six miles to town, you will stay here tonight. I will see you get a bed and a meal. This is no night for an old yin to be out," proclaimed the young warrior.

"You honour an old man such as me with your generosity but I have no coin to pay." In this instance the young warrior observed a shift in the old man's posture, in his energy, his emotions, and adjusted his energies accordingly "and even if I did, I would not want to sleep in a place that smells as bad as you do!!" shouted the old man.

The sentinel smiled, "Old man, I will make sure the room is free from odour, I can only apologise for my smell. As part of my duties I may not wash, I am ...", the old man cut him off with a wave of his hand. The young sentinel, composed himself, "Sir, we have many rooms in our school, the guest quarters ..."

"The fresh winds brought in by today's storm, have broken the stale warm air of the past month, yet you have ruined its freshness with your ungodly smell. Have you no dignity? No pride? When I was young, I was taught that cleanliness was next to godliness". The old man looked the young man square in the eyes, before looking down his nose in disgust at him, dismissing him rudely and purposefully, before spitting in his direction. The sentinel did not react.

"What is this school you speak of? Is this a house full of uncontrolled and repressed sexual urges, where men and women sweat, hug and fuck on the ground like animals? A place where men and women train to kill, to maim, to push fear, whilst they explore their most base and animalistic urges. I think I will continue on my way, young sir. There is no honour, nor pride here." The old man spun before moving towards the line of the gate into the open storm. As it hit him, it swept him from his feet. Without hesitation and before the old man could physically fall, the young sentinel had caught him and quickly carried him back to the inner sanctuary the gate offered from the storm.

As the young sentinel helped the old man to his feet, a warmth came over him. It glowed from deep inside his stomach. The heat rose, a warm strong inner glow that pushed out from the depths where it originated, moving up and down his energy pathways, his veins, his nerves, until it washed over his skin like the finest silk until his whole body ballooned, not physically but energetically and mentally, and in that second, he realised that the old man was his Master, he was the great Retishie.

"Thank you," said the old man, stay strong my brother as he turned toward the main building. This time, as he entered the storm, it was if the storm was absent from his path. The old man moved gracefully towards his school. The young sentinel smiled as he turned back to his post.

Unannounced the great Retishie entered his southernmost school. He walked through the entrance hall, unchallenged and unrecognised. One by one, he passed by the very students who hailed him as a god amongst men. Jasino and Wilsonyan, the schools most senior practitioners sense their master's presence, the unmissable presence of nothingness filled the full sensory and ethereal spectrum. Each of the senior disciples independently stopped their tasks and stood tall, patiently waiting to greet their friend.

*** *** ***

FOR HOURS, LOO HAD been aware of the presence. She had put it down to the evening's meditation but as soon as they had uncloaked their energetic self, Loo had been aware of their presence. Loo experienced many subtle differences in this new energy field, yet she found many parallels with the energies now surging all around the school to the strange energies of Barratash from Um Ma Bar. The supreme absence, the control of emotion, of all thought, it was similar but more than that, it had the familiarity of the grand Abbots of the Wu Da Ning monastery, where she was taught.

The silent figure bowed and gave respect to the school as he entered, moving past the first pillar and over the line into the senior warrior's section of the hall unchallenged, and unnoticed by the administrators who were tasked with keeping the areas strictly organised by rank and experience.

Loo's eyes stayed upon the silent figure. She observed that she was alone in her fascination of this new arrival as he moved graciously through the crowded school.

The old man glided, as if walking on air, his motion was smooth and un-natural, which Loo thought was strange. As she continued to monitor him, as he glided further into the hall, a strange yet unfamiliar knowing of the man flooded her awareness. Loo felt like she knew him. A strange, distant smell of wet blood, mixed with an intensely fragrant herbal smoke, were some of the strange fragmented familiarities that emerged in her mind as the old man approached her directly, ignoring everyone else in the room.

"You have come to me, my sister, and I have come to you. It has been too many years. I am Retishie," said the old man.

Mistress Loo stood, frozen in place by his words. Somewhere deep within, she knew that what he had just said had a lick of truth to it, but her warrior's mind could not accept something so preposterous, so unsupported and mon-umental without proof. Her gut, her heart, and her mind were all pulling in different directions.

"I see you understand deep down, that I speak the truth but you cannot accept it. You need verification," said Retishie, with a smile.

"Verification, you are at least fifty years my senior. There is no way that you can be my brother. I can see a physical resemblance, and your energetic signature is well... strangely familiar. Is this some northern trick, is this a clever martial strategy you have developed to unsettle an energetic warrior?" Loo took a step back and instantly brought her energies into play, creating a dense cocoon around her and Nanoc, poised ready to unleash a tsunami of energetic fury.

"Relax my sister," said Retishie calmly and slowly, sending out ambiance and calm with his words, Loo felt the calm like a well-needed breeze on a stuffy hot day but she fought it and kept her energies up, ready to defend, ready to attack.

"Let me in and I will show you, direct from my memories, I won't force this upon you. I could, but I will ask your permission and all the answers to your questions will be given, instantly. It is so good to see you Mary after all these years." Retishie smiled with a great warmth as he took a simple step back, before lowering all his energetic defences. He was energetically naked, a signal that was clear as day to Loo.

"How did he know your name?" asked Nanoc quietly as he stood behind Loo. Loo could feel him poised and ready for action. No matter what Loo did next, she knew Nanoc would be by her side, this filled her with a confidence she didn't know she needed but welcomed gladly.

"I suppose there is only one way to find out," replied Loo as she turned her head back towards Retishie.

"Share your memories, old man. If you attempt any funny business, there will be a lot of deaths here today," said a very confident Loo as she let the old man's energies push past hers, directly into her mind.

In an instant, his story unfolded. In that instant, the story represented like a children's picture book. The complete story was instant, yet chronological. 'How bizarre,' thought Loo as she observed and experienced the story, her story.

"The old Retishie appeared in her mind as a younger, more powerful warrior who looked remarkably similar to Loo. A ferocious battle between two warriors with exceptional skills battled all around her. She was in the fight, she was looking directly at the Immortal King from Retishie's eyes, as the experience unfolded, as the fight unfolded. It was dizzying how technical, fast and powerful the young Retishie was, and for everything he was, the King was more. The fight was like nothing she had ever seen or experienced. It was fought on three planes simultaneously; physical, energetic and mental, each level working interacting and weaving between the other two independently. Then the memories cut directly to Retishie being defeated in the rematch by the King, the superior warrior, more specifically, the superior energetic and mental skills.

Then the memories cut straight to a heated argument between the King and Retishie, as Retishie point blankly refused to join The King's military. The story moved to Retishie, sat in chains in a dark, damp hole, as he experienced day after day of mistreatment, torture and other pains that he held back from the vision. The King wanted more than victory, he wanted to break Retishie's mind, but he found after months of torture that he could not, so he let him go.

Retishie's body was weak, physically drained, dehydrated, malnourished, physically broken, yet his mind was still strong and his mission of returning home to his family was unshakable. It drove him during the hardships and the tortures and it drove him as he walked, the eight months plus it took him to travel back to his family. As he travelled, he saw his strength return as he used his deep esoteric knowledge to pay for his passage, healing himself and others, predicting rains & fortunes, teaching martial science, protecting villages from bandits, fighting outlaws and more. Time and time again, on his route home, he worked with strangers, mainly local villagers for food, water and shelter.

Then Loo experienced Retishie's return to his family home, she felt herself tense up; she was apprehensive of potentially seeing her never-been-seen-before family. Memories of Retishie's family flooded Loo's, laughter, names being shouted, food being eaten, lots of noise and the hustle and bustle of eight distinct voices from a lifetime ago. As he entered the door, a silence enveloped her. Then came his realisation that something was wrong, the panic, the lack of control as his world unravelled. As the first of his family came into sight, his heart beating faster, his eyes filling with tears, his throat closing over as an uncontrolled shriek and then a desperate call for his family rose, unrestrained from him. Swirls of powerful emotions flooded Loo as it struck home that The King's assassins had been following Retishie all this time and they had massacred his entire family, their entire family, slaughtered. Their corpses were still fresh, no more than a day before his return, and it was his fault, his stubborn fault, all this pain could have been avoided if he had just accepted The King's terms. The King would not break him, then or now. Then, from amongst the death, from amongst the chaos of Retishie's mind, rose a small bundle of innocence, cute, wide eyed and oh so young, covered in blood from head to toe. From amongst the death, rose his salvation.

'Is this me? That is me,' Instantly Loo knew that she was looking at herself, the large birthmark shaped like a strawberry covered most of her stomach, as it still did today.

Retishie grabbed the young Mary and pulled her tight. The dead family faces and his memories of them flooded Loo's mind one by one. Their voices, their stories, their laughter and their love for her. It overwhelmed Loo.

Then she is whisked off into the rain, destination after destination, Retishie travelled far and wide with his sister in tow, never leaving his side. Always on edge, always vigilant that the King's assassins could be close by, watching, tracking, but if they were, he would be ready this time. He was looking for a safe place for him and his sister, and teachers, so versed in the magical realms of combat, something that would give him and his baby sister an edge, which would allow him and if it ever came to it, her, the abilities to defend herself and if possible, defeat The King. Loo found herself laughing to herself, it seemed that she has been destined to fight the King since birth.

Finally, she experienced visions of the strange pair arriving far to the east of Lanasia, beyond the Namangan borders. Up in the mountains, isolated by desert, forest and mountains, he found the Zaoists, a wonderfully strong and wise people who lived high in the mountains. Their customs were strange and complex. Now this place was familiar. As the memories showed her home, Loo smiled. Familiar dress, smells, tastes and faces flooded her mind. Faces that she considered family. Then she saw him; she remembered him; she remembered Retishie. She was young; he was a kind Monk, the kindest of monks who always made time for her, always took a keen interest in her development, when she was young. Then he had left, left to go on a pilgrimage and she, over her time, had forgot of Brother Shie.

Loo turned to the old man that stood before her, her eyes full of tears, her posture slumped, as if she had been through the wars. With one large step, Loo embraced her long-lost brother.

"I am sorry, young one, to learn the magical systems that I had gone there to learn, I had to make the ultimate sacrifice, I left you, my sister, to their care. My life was not one for a young one, and the King could not know that you were alive. Their training consumed me, as I see it has you. I've always known you were alive, I have been with you many times and I knew our paths would cross, I am so thankful for that. You must have many questions?" said the great Retishie.

CHAPTER 27 - THE MESSAGE

As ARRAN LAY NAKED, next to Anice and Barratash, deep in the underbelly of the ancient camouflaged pyramid, his mind soared untethered, lost in the infinite nothingness of The Nothing. Lost to its embrace, then without warning he was suddenly and unceremoniously snapped back into his full awareness once more, by Barratash's voice.

"Think of the Bar En Dough as the conscious mind of God and The Nothing that lies beyond the Bar En Dough, as the unconscious mind of God. The information from the Bar En Dough comes from the minds of the millions of souls who have travelled her depths, each with their own truths. To start with, I will be your guide. I have spent many years probing the minds, both past and present, of our creators, the Tenni Uh Akki.

There will be many terms of reference and words that you will not understand from the vast technological and scientific terminology of their world, but as I recount the many stories I have experienced, I will transfer my understanding of the terms, so you can comprehend. However, just as a library has many books on a given subject, each with truth and expertise on that subject, rarely does one book hold all of the answers. The knowledge we gain from the Bar En Dough is very similar, one's truth will almost always be incomplete and almost always biased! We must seek multiple experiences and expressions but as you are about to experience, the Bar En Dough is not structured like a simple library," advised Barratash, before vanishing from his mind.

Then the Bar En Dough engulfed him. His mind merged with the Bar En Dough and then he was the Bar En Dough. As the information became him, consumed him, Arran's conscious mind fought to regain its individuality, to process, to categorise, to analyse the information it was consuming. Each time it did, he momentarily phased out of the collective whole that was the Bar En

Dough. As the information permeated his being, Arran alternated between his conscious mind and the collective mind of the Bar En Dough.

Instantly, Arran knew thousands of new things. He now understood the underlying principles of the Cult of the Pine and its strange, pine cone emblem. Of course, it was a worship of the brain's very own multidimensional gateway to the Bar En Dough and the Nothingness beyond it. They'd chosen the pine cone that was so iconic of the cult, for its visual resemblance to the strange part of the inner brain which allowed them to enter the multidimensional oneness, to enter this inner space he now inhabited. The same gland that is coincidently overly sensitive to the salts of Traveras. The very salts used by the King and the QUAF to shut down the multidimensional functionality of their slaves, creating a subtle addiction and over time, eliminating our natural ability to connect to the Bar En Dough and The Nothing. But how does one describe 'nothing'? How does one describe an experience of the 'nothing', an experience so beyond words? How does one convey colour to a man who does not see in colour, or to a man who has no eyes and who has never seen a single thing in his life? Or the sound of laughter or dimensions of classical music to a man who has no hearing? How does one convey an absence? Even here, he was struggling to convey these concepts to himself, to his own conscious, language-oriented mind. This experience, which he was simultaneously experiencing and analysing went way beyond and surpassed everything that he had ever imagined was possible.

'The brain, it seems, has way more potential than most of us give it credit for. We have limited ourselves. Our cultural patterns have kept us from discovering our full potential. We got caught up in ourselves, so deep and for so long that we forgot who we were. But like all learnings of truth, this truth can only be experienced. We cannot communicate it via the restrictions of the individual physical sensory and communication channels,' thought Arran.

In this moment, Arran realised all truths, all paths to all the religions, the spiritual paths of his own people and that of the multitude of cultures he had learnt about and interacted with throughout his life, trading in the south. And in that moment, he realised that no word, no scripture could ever do the truth justice. The truth, as he was experiencing it, was universal in how it translated into words via the language, culture, historic lens and life experience of the individual experiencing it. These factors warp the truth into its own unique interpretation of that truth, an interpretation that is just as valid as the initial truth, making it just one more truth in an infinite sea of truths.

The sheer amount of information being transmitted from the Bar En Dough by Barratash, quickly overwhelmed him. It felt like a tidal wave crashing in on him, time and time again. And whilst this deluge of information raged all around him, sweeping him with it, in the torrent, in the chaos, he had to find calm and focus on just one piece of information.

"Focus in, on just one of the millions of connected slivers of information. Focus on their history, this is where we will start. We must know our history" came the voice of Barratash. Arran concentrated hard to penetrate the overwhelming, omnipresent information. As he focused on the Tenni Uh Akki and their history, it slowly came to the forefront. Arran relaxed into it as the wave of information swallowed him up.

"A long, long, long time ago, the Original Tenni Uh Akki's travelled across the Void and the Bard En Dough simultaneously to exploit and steal our planet's resources. They mined our rare elements, especially gold, and drained our abundant water supplies. They were a small contingent of nomadic business folk, looking to stake a claim on a new, unexplored planet and profit from its untapped natural resources."

This time the information came, in part, via the same all-encompassing voice that Barratash would project when he entered others' minds, accompanied with layers of visual and sensory data. The combination consumed him, like the most intensely vivid dream.

"The Tenni Uh Akki's view of life encompassed more than the physical, they experienced a life that goes beyond the simple, single linear birth and death. They experienced a cyclical existence through many incarnations until they mastered the Bar En Dough. 'I don't know what is beyond the Bar En Dough, all I know is, it is something I cannot comprehend, we call it The Nothing, as do they. This is the same Bar En Dough they use to communicate with us, the same Bar En Dough they use to transfer their consciousness across the void, across time and space. With their advanced technology, they created us, created us to work their mines. We were designed to work. I, you, we, were designed and refined over many generations, perfected through many failed attempts until we became such effective workers, while varying permutations were further engineered and specialised for specific tasks. We are a sophisticated and skilled manipulation of the ancient, native hominids of Lanasia, their native adaptation to the planet's biosphere, gases, light spectrum and gravity, formed the base, this was then crossed with the non-native blood of the Tenni Uh Akki to produce us. The first attempts to cross-breed the great ape with a heavily restricted version of the Tenni Uh Akki's far more advanced blood, or as they call it 'genetic code', created mass deformities. This led their scientists to engineer us with their full underlying 'genetic code'. The newly engineered workers' potential was then switched off on mass, limiting large swaths of their new workers' potential, of our potential. They suppressed most of our Tenni Uh Akki abilities. They limited our senses, strength, intelligence, and our ability to access the 'Bar En Dough', our ability to reproduce and more subtle restrictions, like our appetite for leadership, our potential for disobedience and our desire to be curious. Hundreds of years later came the hybrids, a sexual biproduct of the Tenni Uh Akki overlords having sex with their slaves. These second or third generation hybrids created bastard slaves with more access to their underlying Tenni Uh Akki abilities. The new hybrids had more of 'God's' makeup and were promoted to administration and management roles of the vast populations of workers that they had created, that now lived here on Lanasia. These workers were our ancestors.

That was over fifty thousand years ago. The original Tenni Uh Akki is long gone now. In that time, we, their creation, have split into many peoples, races and ethnic groups. Some groups still have a bastardised understanding of the importance of genetic lineage or bloodlines, but most are unaware of the past. Most are consciously and unconsciously intimate with the hidden truths that transcend time. We transmit these through myths, legends, stories, religions, cultural taboos and folklore. The vastness of fifty thousand years has given those bloodlines with a higher concentration of Tenni Uh Akki blood and knowledge, the time to develop their Tenni Uh Akki traits, be it self-awareness, intellect, physicality, longevity, health as well as energetic and mental powers. But we digress, let's get back to the Tenni Uh Akki originals. They had become settled; they had now lived, worked and grown accustomed to this world, as well as too many other worlds.

"Wait," shouted Arran's mind. "So, if they created us, the physical us, as some advanced machine to do their work, then what is our soul? What is our consciousness? This thing we are now? The "I" that can move beyond the physical and interact with others in the mental space, like we are doing now. Where did it come from? Did they create this too?"

Arran, the I, the inner mind, the conscious thing which we use to identify ourselves as ourselves. The very thing that gives us our unique individual perspective, is in fact birthed by the same technology that made the 'workers'. Our consciousness is possibly a sophisticated and complex set of instructions that allows us to control the physical aspects of our created "worker bodies," combined with an echo of the Tenni Uh Akki's own consciousness being produced by their underlying and untapped potential. We are born and just like the Tenni Uh Akki, we make a connection between us and the Nothingness beyond the Bar En Dough, our soul, our mind, our essence is just some by-product of the machine they created to work their mines. But once we become aware of our mind and of our connection to the Bar En Dough and the Nothingness, we, like the Tenni Uh Akki can transcend the initial machine that birthed us and transform into something beyond the initial casting they formed us in. Hence my ability to enter your mind. We are like a caterpillar that has the potential to turn into a butterfly, but we must comprehend that we can be a butterfly before we can transform into it. If not, we stay as a caterpillar and when we die, the QUAF eat us.

Ok, back to the Tenni Uh Akki, as I am sure you will have a million questions by the end of this day and you will have the rest of your life to seek the answers.

Then from somewhere deep in the void came a blind attack upon the Tenni Uh Akki by another technologically advanced race. A race built for war, sent to claim this planet's unique resources for themselves, for the same reasons the Tenni Uh Akki had crossed the Bar En Dough and the Void. Everything the explorers had available to them failed to hold back this invasion. Then with no other option, they broke their original mining contracts by contacting Tenni Uh Akki Prime, before delivering payments upon the original mining loan being secured. You must comprehend that Tenni Uh Akki Prime is millions of light years away, across the void. It is so far away, it is literally beyond comprehension, but it can be accessed easily, via the Bar En Dough. The Bar En Dough connects the known universe, everything in the Void, instantly. They made the right choice, as this was not the only distress call received by Tenni Uh Akki Prime. The invaders had raided thousands of other planets, each time the unknown alien invader had bested the settlers of that world and their super advanced Tenni Uh Akki technology. Maybe even hundreds or thousands of times, as most of Tenni Uh Akki's new world explorers did not return and most would not contact Tenni Uh Akki Prime because the contractual obligations to repay the original loans were too high.

Tenni Uh Akki Prime listened, they reacted, and they sent a brilliant engineer by the name of Gilanite to help the explorers of our world. He was an outcast, an uncommon man amongst uncommon men. He projected his consciousness into a newly grown Tenni Uh Akki hybrid Lanasian, just as every explorer before him had done, with one exception. All past explorers had their own DNA, that is to say, they had an original copy of themselves sent out via their void ships. They had their own purpose-grown clone to call their consciousness home from across the void via the Bar En Dough. Without it, the consciousness would have been pulled back to the original body. Our bodies and our souls are linked, bonded, across all of space and time. The original explorers, off world contracts, allocated a precise number of Tenni Uh Akki shells that could be grown per contract, the explorer's DNA is in most cases, was a one use only deal. These early explorers were not immortal like Summerian is now, they never had his resources. If they died, the rights to their allocation, to their contract, were sold to the next highest bidder.

They loaded each ship with the Tenni Uh Akki DNA technology to make an army of workers, but they restricted this technology in such a way to make sure that they can grow no more Tenni Uh Akki shells. Insurance on their loans being repaid. Gilanite was the first to travel from Tenni Uh Akki Prime to Lanasia since the original explorers' ships touched down all those years ago. Gilanite was forced to enter a hybrid. An impure, inferior shell. Gilanite was the first Tenni Uh Akki to ever enter a biologically engineered, non-Tenni hybrid body, directly from the Bar En Dough, a magnificent feat in its own right. He was a weapons specialist, overseeing fleets of Tenni Uh Akki military vessels that secured the Tenni Uh Akki Empire's dominance across the millions of planetary bodies they controlled. He came to experience the Anti-Mass-Voiders first hand. He set about configuring key components from the now ancient, void ship the explorers had arrived in. His tests then quickly determined that the invaders' consciousness, memories and emotions or as he called it, 'raw computational power' were strangely straddled between our physical reality and the cusp of some other quasi-dimensional-reality. Something akin to the Bar En Dough, yet different, very different. It was slower and denser in vibration and it originated in The Nothing. They were like icebergs, with only their tip in the physical, their genuine power came from this strange, ethereal dimension.

The Quantum Uncertain Autonomous Fighters were Gilanite's answer. They were designed and manufactured as a simple, limited, autonomous warrior, programmed to attack the main anti-mass of ethereal energies of the invading species. The first generation of QUAF were limited, just as we were when they created us. As the invader pushed forward, gaining ground against the Tenni Uh Akki, the decision from Tenni Uh Akki Prime was given to allow unprecedented autonomy to the QUAF. The young engineer pleaded that they must keep control of this new intelligent weapon, that under no circumstances should it be given free rein. There were no precedents set for this form of weapons technology.

The military engineers on Tenni Uh Akki Prime, under intense pressure to provide a solution, to develop an effective weapon against the Anti Mass Voiders, squeezed by invasion on many fronts, ignored the shunned expert and his warnings. In a last-ditch resort, they tested their new weapon at full power. In this war against the "Anti Mass Voiders", the young Gilanite was inevitably sidelined by his superiors. After a fairly short time, the new, fully autonomous QUAF, quickly identified that the Anti Mass Voiders' emotions and consciousness were directly related to the physical performance. Soon after, with very little resistance, it successfully defeated the invaders around Lanasia's biosphere. The QUAF were like a virus, a virus that they had no natural immunity for. As the 'anti mass voiders' fell, they cut off their opening, the access to the ethereal Bar En Dough like dimension and as they did, their technology ceased to work. The potential dangers of the QUAF'S full autonomy was glimpsed and unintentionally ignored in the heat of glorious victory.

As Gilanite's models predicted, their intelligence grew enough to seek out the invaders' weakness and with it, achieve victory, but as he feared, they did not stop there. The QUAF'S intelligence, awareness and understanding of self grew and as they consumed the ethereal emotions and memories of the Anti Mass Voiders, which were absent in every model, they were in fact being imprinted by echoes and fragments of 'The Voiders' very essence. Consuming the essence of the enemies' souls, accelerated their concept of self.

The QUAFs understanding of self-grew, fired by months of abundant energy resources, they could not switch the thirst off, the autonomous warriors made a collective decision to override a command from the Tenni Uh Akki to power down. To voluntarily make themselves redundant. However, they hid this from their Tenni Uh Akki creators. They played their card like the intelligent warrior they were, faking every test, every command until their former masters believed that the QUAF technology was successfully neutralised and safe. From the depths of the ethereal dimensions surrounding Lanasia, they observed, they waited, they learnt. Barratash's broadcast finished, as it did Arran's mind began to ask questions.

So let me get this right broadcasted Arran. If I had this technology, I could replicate myself, then send myself, via a yak to the Gavodeon nation, then at will, I could jump between my body here and this new copy of my body on the trail? And the QUAF, they are just a fancy weapon, designed to win a war for the gods who made us? And all of this is taking place here and now, simultaneously across the void? And we are just an insignificant, lowly world, one amongst millions. To use your analogy of the library, how do you know that the books you read were the correct books? How do you know that the librarian has not curated particular books for you to read and purposefully held back key books of opposing thought? As soon as Arran's mind stopped broadcasting, Barratash's began to reply.

These are good questions Arran, which I and many other members of The Pine have asked many times. In truth, we do not know if the information we receive from the Bar En Dough is manipulated, I am sure it is possible. For us, we can connect and listen but the Tenni Uh Akki, they use the Bar En Dough, it is a tool, a part of their consciousness and a part of their technology. We are discovering our first words, in comparison to a culture that has been reading and writing for hundreds of thousands of years. Who they are, and what they are is truly beyond our comprehension? All we know, for certain, is The King is not one of us. However, I am not finished. Our shared history does not finish there.

CHAPTER 28- THE MESSAGE PART TWO

DEEP IN THE ALI Ma Bar pyramid, the information did not stop. Fuelled by Arran's curiosity and led by Barratash's thirst to share his life's work and direct the narrative, the bombardment of information continued. At first, Arran's mind likened it to a tornado. It felt like a tornado, like a storm, like the chaos inflicted by a storm. It felt like, whether or not you accepted it or not, it was still going to rip right through the very heart of your camp and leave its mark. But this barrage of information was not like a natural force. It was powerful and chaotic, but it had intricate, rhythmic patterns and unlike nature's tempests, these patterns could be manipulated, they could be bent by one's will, controlled and refined. At first, it felt like a tornado, but the longer Arran stayed in its path, the more he believed he was in control. He relaxed back into the storm and allowed himself to be engulfed by all of the information, stories, visions, emotions and physical sensations relating to the QUAF and the Tenni Uh Akk history. This time it overwhelmed him. There was too much, every thread spun off into a hundred more, repeating into infinity. Once again Arran felt Barratash in his mind. "I will narrate our history, you can return at any time and dive deeper, but as you are now understanding, the Bar En Dough without a guide, can be intense," Arran accepted and relaxed into the soothing tones of Barratash and the history of the Tenni Uh Akki.

The QUAF adapted. They did what they were designed to do, they adapted to their new environment the best they could. They identified the closest thing to the energy signatures of the 'Anti Mass Voiders' within the Lanasian Biosphere. Low frequency, dense, negative, emotional energies seeped from many of the

Tenni Uh Akki workers like a fog, and in abundance, these low vibrations became their new, self-modified, attack parameters. Slowly, methodically, they began latching onto and feeding upon our ancestors.

The rushed creation of the QUAF, combined with a team consisting of mining explorers who had little to no grasp of Gilanite's advanced science, or of what he needed from them, was the Tenni Uh Akki's saving grace in containing the QUAF. Gilanite's limited preliminary research into the new ethereal dimensions beyond the Bar En Dough, in this quadrant of the void, prior to manufacture, was woven into the time-pressured designs. This restricted the QUAF to remain within the original gateway of the 'Anti Mass Void Gate' that was opened within the upper levels of the biosphere of Lanasia.

The original Tenni Uh Akki used advanced technology everywhere within their society. They used large transmission towers to transmit the power needed for their mining enterprise, as well as information between the various industries. These transmitters were also used to keep the workers in line, transmitting propaganda continuously. They were also used to amplify transmissions by the Gods and overseers when blanket broadcasts were required, right into the minds of everyone, all at once. The same transmission towers were also used to relay information and control the invisible legions of nanobots that continuously operated throughout the mine. Some of these nanites were augmented within the slaves to give temporary, extrasensory perception, strength and intelligence, if and when they were needed.

These transmitters gave the Tenni Uh Akki the remote ability to keep their workers docile, subservient and under control. When the QUAF feasted on the slaves, the Tenni Uh Akki created and transmitted a perimeter shield to protect the slave workforce, to protect their investment. The slaves ran on base emotion, their communities rife with lust, fear, jealousy and desire. Just as the Tenni Uh Akki had manipulated their creations to harvest the gold from the mines, the QUAF quickly learnt to harvest the uncontrolled emotions, dulling and weakening the slaves further. The energy drained by the QUAF made the workers more docile and lowered productivity. As the Tenni Uh Akki had strict quotas to meet, they created shields to protect their workers and their productivity.

After a while, the fattest, most energy rich of the QUAF realised that with enough energetic accumulation, they could generate mass, they could make a limited physical form which could interact at the physical level. As the energies required to make physical form were enormous, the QUAF made use of their collective energy reserves to transport portions of their collective intelligence into the physical dimension. Slowly, with the help of their followers, who understandably perceived them as Gods, they created buildings of worship, from which the QUAF used to safely emerge into the physical world.

The Church of the Sun was born, a strange cult with outlandish claims ignored by the Tenni Uh Akki. To them, it was just another crass, limited attempt by their slaves to understand their existence, to give purpose to their harsh existence. Slowly but surely, the QUAF's followers grew, unaware of the truth, unaware of the true nature of that, which they worshipped. As their temples spread, their physical assaults on the Tenni Uh Akki also grew and through time, many thousands of slaves became devoted Sun worshippers. When the time was right, the QUAF's minions attacked the technological heart of the Tenni Uh Akki's defence against them. That day seen a coordinated attack, and the transmitters fell, their signals stopped, their shield collapsed. Slowly, the QUAF had become a technological bastardisation of the Voiders they were designed to eliminate.

The original Tenni Uh Akki were unaffected by the QUAF. The way their cloned bodies vibrated differed greatly from the slave cast or the Anti Mass Voiders, but the QUAF were now affecting the production levels of the mines. On fulfilling the minimum contracted quotas to Tenni Uh Akki Prime, the Original Tenni Uh Akki decided to call it quits, shut up shop and return home. They sent their mined resources back across the void in the original void ships, ships that were so large, they would dwarf the Great Aurd mountains in size. As their ships left our skys, each would-be God individually left their physical Tenni Uh Akki clone and returned home to their new clones instantly, via the Bar En Dough.

The Tenni Uh Akki left the planet to the QUAF but as they were firmly aware of the QUAF's new ability to make physical form, they made a final gesture to their most beloved creation. They destroyed every physical Church of the Sun and lanced every worshipper of the sun, forcing the QUAF to start again.

As much as we were created as a simple slave by the Tenni Uh Akki to perform demanding physical labour, they made us in their image with their own blood. They had sex with us, and some of them loved us! In their eyes, there was a massive difference between us, a simple biped with unlimited potential and the QUAF, a reluctant technological necessity, created in their darkest hour. They sped up our vibration, making it harder for us to fear, to experience and dwell in the negative emotional space, passing the information beyond the physical to all those within transmission range, essentially taking away the QUAF's immediate food supply. But the QUAF adapted, that is what they do.

After the Tenni Uh Akki left Lanasia, the many thousands of slaves of every class, bred, evolved and created new hybrids, new ethnic groups, new bloodlines. These new groups emerged through the slow march of time as they travelled far and wide, throughout the varied landmasses of Lanasia and beyond. Whilst the hybrid slaves evolved and adapted to the illusion that they were free, creating cities, cultures and religions, they were unwittingly watering down their true history, until only a few knew the truth. The QUAF also adapted and developed their own societies and hierarchies. As they grew, their need for an effective balanced strategy to farm, to maintain their resources, manifested. They selected individuals with the highest content of original Tenni Uh Akki blood and began a programme to manipulate them. They revealed themselves to these hybrid descendants as Gods, defining these hand-picked individuals as chosen ones, saturating them with energy and using them as pawns to manipulate and manage their farms. They farmed us. They still farm us. Throughout time, their pawns spread the story, spread the lies, reshaping history for one that favoured and fostered a complacent, compliant, apathetic, un-ambitious livestock. One that is content with its physical lot in life, content with their God and his commands.

Throughout our history, many have awoken from the farm, be it through spiritual practises, drugs, pain or near death. These awakened men and women, from the many cultures of Lanasia, awake to the simple truth that the rest of their brothers and sisters are still asleep. To make sense of their new reality, most discuss it openly. We label some mad; we celebrate some as messiahs; we ignore most others. These truths are often documented and through time, some of these shards of truth have become religions. Others became the foundations of secret mystery schools.

Even rarer still are those who awaken within a system and get a chance to build their experience onto the knowledge of those who had come before, like the Pine followers.

The QUAF were often too elusive to be challenged. By the time it took a new, awoken Lanasian to find and train someone else, to the stage where they could enter the Bar En Dough, it had become a myth. Or its essence, not experienced became lost in translation, watered down through the rudimentary and limited physical language of sound vibrations. Over time, the truth of their purpose faded.

Over time, we lost the original knowledge. One individual's power to transform the masses was something the QUAF had encountered many times, over the last forty thousand years. Once someone had entered the Bar En Dough, they changed and this ignited their biological potential, their underlying superior, Tenni Uh Akki blood. The QUAF likened those awakened Lanasians to the long-gone Tenni Uh Akki, our potential awoken and profound. For most who awaken and return from the Bar En Dough, it becomes their mission of their limited time left within the biological machine housing their soul, to pass on the truth, to open up the minds of all of their Lanasian brothers and sisters, to transform them.

Before the Cult of the Pine was founded, and they began efforts to reawaken us to our potential, before us, the last great awakening was in the Age of Golden. It was then that the great Nencom lived; he was the catalyst for that age. Tens of thousands of years after the original Tenni Uh Akki had left. He was a trader, no special augmentation flowing through his blood in any significant quantities. He had a brush with death, which forced him into the Bar En Dough, where he passed beyond the QUAF and entered into The Nothing before returning. Overwhelmed by his experience, he obsessed over ways of returning to the Bar En Dough and The Nothing from that moment on.

As he returned, time and time again, he mastered the Bar En Dough. He mastered entering the many minds of those who transited the Bar En Dough. He learnt from the Tenni Uh Akki and other advanced races that transited the void. Once his dormant genes and abilities were reactivated, he became a master of the mind, the body and its energy. He learnt everything he could, everything he could grasp. He then built the first pyramid transmitter, where the Tanni Ma Bar one now stands. It was small, only twenty feet tall, but it was large enough for him to broadcast his message to the entire town. As hundreds from his tribe learnt of Nencom's truths, they too went in search of the Bar En Dough and were, one by one, awoken. Their message spread quickly, faster than at any other time in history. Soon, there were thousands upon thousands amassed in the lush valley below the Aurd, the area that is now the deserts of Tanni, to build the first and largest pyramid transmitter. The pyramid served three purposes, one was to amplify the dormant Tenni Uh Akki abilities and allow for mass transmission. Two, to serve as a bridge to the Bar En Dough. Three, to serve as a physical time machine, an immovable mass that would stand the tests of time and be able to transmit truth. This truth is still being transmitted via the math ingrained in its dimensions, the hieroglyphs of its walls, the curiosity of its existence and for some, by direct transference via the transmitter itself. Nencom's vision was that never again would the Lanasians forget their potential. Once built, many more arose, all over the north, and after a while the QUAF found it almost impossible to feed upon the people. The people had reclaimed their power; they were like the Gods of old. Previous tactics used by the QUAF of creating physical beings and manipulating followers would not work, as the population was now aware of that trick. For thousands of years, the people of Lanasia reclaimed their true Tenni Uh Akki heritage as powerful beings, as creators, and they roamed the planet and the Bar En Dough as wise emancipated souls.

The next thousand years or so was seen universally, across almost all cultures of Lanasia, as The Golden Era. An era where enlightenment and wisdom flowed, great architecture rose, wealth flowed, as did art, poetry, music and a systematic approach to peace and love overcame all.

The QUAF were dying off from a lack of energy. We had defeated them. We had freed ourselves from them.

Then, The Great Dark Age began. An original Tenni Uh Akki returned, the one we now know as Summerian. He landed in his void ship in the north. He returned to strike a deal with the autonomous warriors, whom his people once created. The Tenni Uh Akki now needed the QUAF, as the AMV had returned, easily conquering many of the outlying Tenni Uh Akki worlds in this region of the void. He promised to crush the Lanasians, offering the QUAF feeding grounds all year round, and freedom from the constraints of the Lanasian biosphere, all in exchange for their compliance and their alliance in fighting for the Tenni Uh Akki, against the AMV.

Summerian promised he would return the Lanasians to low-vibrating energy sacks, that he would keep the QUAF fed year after year, in between the rich buffets he offered off world, in the battles with the AMV.

From that day forth, the QUAF have been his prisoner, and his client. Summerian became the farmer. He has played many roles, spanning thousands of years. Today, he plays the King of the Namangans, as he does his best to harvest our energy and souls for his clients.

During the many thousands of years of Summerian's rule, he systematically attacked the pyramids. Their remains degraded, beaten by weather, ravaged by time and by locals, for building materials. Summerian changed the game by introducing the salts into the diets of the Lanasians. In prolonged doses, it affects our very ability to transmute energy, it shuts down and weakens the body's natural ability to receive transmission frequencies, thereby negating our inherent Tenni Uh Akki abilities, whilst simultaneously making you feel mildly euphoric.

Summerian manipulated the salts, he then changed the cultural limits of its consumption and made it desirable, accessible and valuable. The salts did the rest.

The QUAF had found their ally.

But just as Nencom awoke, so did Tenderas. And with him, hope once again began to slowly drip feed, back into the veins of the once great Lanasians.

The Cult of the Pine was founded over three hundred years ago by the great Tenderas. He awoke early, after a large consumption of a rare, square-rooted plant he named Salvia Maria, which he was forced to eat to avoid starvation. His solution was to form a secret club, with the purpose of producing a series of young masters so dedicated, so adept, that one day, they could potentially transmit the universal truth via the pyramids built by Nencom, to a salt free congregation, and start the emancipation of the masses from the control, the slavery of this parasite and of its reality. Yet, they first had to be cleansed to allow them to receive this divine communication.

Then the transmission changed. It no longer engulfed Arran completely but faded. The images, the scenes that had consumed him, the smells, and emotions faded to black. Then all that remained, in the infinite blackness, deep in the belly of the Ali Mar Bar Pyramid, was Barratash's voice.

"They store this information in the Bar En Dough, or more accurately, I think, they store it in the Tenni Uh Akki, who transit the Bar En Dough. The Tenni Uh Akki still use it to travel across the void, and we can tap into them and glimpse aspects of our shared history as they travel and connect to the Bar En Dough. You must master the Bar En Dough, for what you have experienced is just a glimpse of a super structure that has so much information, so much knowledge that it cannot be described or imagined and therefore becomes nothing, it is The Nothing. There is nothing we cannot imagine therefore there is truly nothing. There is no distinction between nothing and infinity, the Bar En Dough is The Nothing, the Bar En Dough is infinity, the Bar En Dough is the mind of GOD," stated Barratash.

"I feel like a blind man that has been stood before a great artistic masterpiece whilst the artist describes every aspect of the art, forgetting that I, as a blind man, have no concept of shape, texture, depth, light or colour. If all that is said is even remotely true, then Summerian really is a God and we are fucked," said Arran.

CHAPTER 29 - EYES OPEN

As MUCH AS PEROOT was surely the most fearless and skilled river man that had ever lived, he was not a man for the open seas and here, on deck, amid a small storm by any seafarer's measurements, he stood poised and ready to vomit, again. The mild storm was nothing untoward and for a seasoned sea traveller like Vantis, it was just another day. The storm to the north that had opened up during the previous weeks, spreading havoc in the southern Namangan lands, was now pushing south into the sea at Aurds End and now Peroot had found himself directly below it.

The big river man had been relaxing the best he could. It wasn't a fear of the water; it was the rhythm of the waves. It was doing something strange to his balance and something even stranger to his stomach. Time and time again, he felt himself retch, time and time again he felt nothing come up from his now empty insides. 'How long must this continue?' he thought, as he stood with the fresh sea air and driving rain as a gentle distraction to the revolt his body was staging. As another wave of nauseating stomach cramps gripped him, he again moved the two paces to the edge of the boat and gripped the guide rail tight. As his head came up from yet another dry boak, he saw young Gemaras and Vantis coming up from the main cargo hold below. Now was his time for answers.

"Vantiiiiis," shouted Peroot with his right arm high in the air.

Vantis turned, smiled and walked towards his unsung hero.

"Ah, so a river man, is not automatically a sea man?" smiled Vantis, as he slapped Peroot on the shoulder in mid-turn as the green river man bent over the guard rail once again to release yet another phantom vomit from his now aching belly and throat. From his position close to the rail, Peroot nodded to Gemaras.

"Translate for me young Gemaras," stated Peroot and automatically and efficiently Gemaras jumped into action, translating Peroot's message to Vantis.

"Aye, it's true, the river ain't like the sea. The river is beautiful and full of pleasure. This bastard has no soul, even if she has a little of the Yantee in her!!" Vantis and Gemaras laughed as Peroot raised a solo eyebrow on his solid brow line and upturned his lip slightly, almost into a smile but it conveyed all the warmth of a man who lived and loved, someone who could convey that kind of power and humour without words, even with the thinnest of smiles.

"Boy, ask the boss man, what the fuck happened back there? Why were the dirty Namangan bastards hunting you down? Those on horseback at Theo's Point, the ones with the crossbows, those were elite soldiers. I have seen them many times in recent years, well trained, horsemen able to tackle any terrain and that crossbow firing woman, wow. I caught just a minuscule glance of her, nevertheless, she could ride the rough terrain of Theo's Point, balance on the back of that powerful beast and still shoot accurately, taking out the big fat lad and my ear. As I said, Elite!! And you and him are bookworms. What the fuck happened back there?" Peroot's eyes looked up to meet Vantis, he was not looking away and he would not allow for anything but the truth, Vantis could see it and Peroot made sure that Vantis could feel it.

The waves and the rain began to break and a fresh wind parted clouds, high to the southeast, inviting the last rays of sunshine to illuminate unhindered. Vantis smiled, nodded at Gemaras and began.

"Unfortunately, I was had. I thought I was far more important, far more valuable, far more cunning than I actually am. We played chess against my noble enemies in the south and the Namangan King. We came up short against both. I have learnt one of life's most valuable lessons and the price I paid was high. Back there, we lost some of the finest minds of the south and many of my dear friends." Vantis poised for a second as Peroot and Gemaras looked towards him in puzzlement.

"We went to the north to convince the King to favour us, to tie him into many legal contracts to protect our lands and lineage. The King had other plans and we played right into them. He knew we would betray our people for the crumbs from his table. He knew it, and he banked on it. What happened you ask?" Vantis looked down, then looked away sheepishly before bringing his head up once again to lock eyes with Peroot. The last rays of sunshine illuminating his face from the side brought warmth to a sad and beaten man, struggling with the weight he now bore.

"The King outplayed us all. He sent his delegates to discuss terms and make laws and write deeds. He also sent guards with them. Guards, who without provocation or notification began silently and efficiently killing their own delegation. And then in the chaos of such an event, I heard shouts declaring that the northern delegates were being assassinated by the southern scum, but in truth, they killed their own and then attacked us as we scrambled for our lives. By the time we got out onto the waggons, all of their political delegates were dead and at least five of ours."

"Why?" interrupted Gemaras, "This makes no sense. Why would they kill their own?" asked Gemaras.

"They killed their own to create the perfect storm. A storm that will unify the different, competing nations, factions, political opposites and great houses of the Namangan empire and give them reason, false reason but reason nonetheless, to unite and invade the south," said Vantis, his eyes driving home the weight of the message, his slight drop in posture showing his belief that he and his arrogance had now doomed the south.

Peroot began to talk but Gemaras was stood in silent shock, "Translate for Peroot" snapped Vantis.

"It is not so easy to see, not even for the many educated and powerful people of the north. The King is a man possessed and power is his addiction, it is his salt! His power flows like a river, it flows slowly, continually, eternally but in the end, everything always bows to the might of the river, it washes over everything in its path. You know he is fuelled by the most vile and evil of all the spirits, he has done a deal with the dark demons and in turn for his power, he must repay them in full, always in full. We call him the KING, yet he is not even a KING of himself. Life is the most precious resource of all, so precious that we must live it with every breath. He and his minions want to take that from all people. Work, sleep, debt, repeat, that is all his empire offers. The south is an untapped resource that will feed his masters for years to come and therefore that great resource has to be conquered," said Peroot.

***

"Evil spirits?" Vantis looked up at the sail as the wind changed direction, momentarily dropping the sail and then again filling it back up again. As he watched, he thought to himself of how his people once thought that the wind itself was a god that could be bargained with, if one simply attained the trinity and laughed. As he looked down from the full sail fluttering in the wind, he made eye contact and nodded to Gemaras.

"In the initial attack, I thought I saw something and felt a coldness pull at my very being, but until you spoke, I had not given it any weight at all. Yes, there was something very otherworldly about the slaughter." Vantis slowly spun, counterclockwise on his heels, lowered his chin and waited for Gemaras to finish his translation before beginning again.

"But I think that was just adrenaline, shock and fear!! In Lerr, we have many myths of Vergen, a sort of soul sucking tick, as well as many mountain, water and snow deities. It was once believed that if you could achieve the trinity of mind, body and energy, you could conquer these gods, but we have, for many hundreds of years, moved beyond the superstition of primitive, tribal shamans and followed a more rational perspective. I think the King is just a narcissistic maniac, driven by power and success. I think he is very similar to myself," Vantis dropped his head in shame.

"No narcissist would ever reflect the way you have," said Gemaras.

"Let me tell you, as a man who has died and been close to death so many times, all in the welcoming bosom of the mighty Yantee. That death and its path beyond is full of spirits, deities, gods and other powerful beings that take turns to pull on you, in many different directions. In that strange watery place beyond this." Peroot put his hands up quickly and allowed his fingers to gently, subtly, tactilely grasp at the surrounding air, as if feeling for something, something that was not there.

"It feels as if they are all your friends, they all want you to go with them, they all promise you they are your friends, your family, your god. The Yantee shone through and true every time and pulled me back to her watery embrace. But she was competing against others in that realm beyond life." Peroot closed his eyes and continued his strange, slow sweeps of the air. "I do not know what happens, with any certainty, if, when death is near you make one of the many other choices." Peroot's eyes opened and he suddenly grabbed Vantis's wrist, Vantis's natural and well-trained reflexes rotated to the thumb to break the grip, but Peroot's years on the river had developed a grip, the likes he had never felt before. As Peroot pulled Vantis in close to him.

"There are many games of chess being played by the bastard King in the north, and it is part of the same long-term game being played by his overlords at death's door," Peroot released Vantis but did not move back.

"Do you think the south could unite a strong enough force to defeat the Namangan bastard?" Vantis met Peroot's eyes, "I do not know, but I can assure you, I am going to find out. The peoples of the south are far more fractured and numerous than the north, but we could be a force if we united." said Vantis, through Gemaras.

"My great grandfather's generation stood with King Edvar. He gave his life to the greatest Traveran army to ever assemble. For my great grandfather, I will take up your offer, I will travel with you to Lerr and I will assist your south, in any way I can. My beloved Traveras has already fallen, and I would not wish the Namangans on anyone. That is no way to live," said Peroot.

Peroot shook his head intently and as he did, Vantis, then Gemaras slapped the large river man on the back.

"Thank you, both of you. For saving me and for showing me that there is more to this life than privilege, title and deeds. The south will eternally be in your gratitude." Gemaras quickly translated before Vantis, began walking with purpose, back towards the entrance to the ship's lower deck.

"Gemaras," Vantis nodded to the scribe, signalling that he was going below, Gemaras quickly followed with the sunken Peroot, a few steps behind.

The three men entered the main cargo hold of the ship, where most of their co-passengers were already. The space was tight and the air thick with moisture; it was still cold down there, in the belly of the ship, but there was no wind or rain and that made all the difference. As they found a space to sit, their body heat radiated outwards, spreading water vapour into the surrounding air which added to the thick hanging moisture clouds. At the other end of the large room, the livestock moaned and groaned as the ship pitched in the choppy waters. Nearby, a mother soothed her crying baby, as the three survivors looked around, they could see, hear and feel the hustle and bustle of everyday Lanasians, North and South, going about their lives.

The three were closest to a group of Gavodeon-like traders as they took stock and made notes. On the other side of the three, a mother tended to her family.

All around them, folks went about their business with certainty as the ship continued to bank and pitch.

"Gemaras, did you secure a journal?"

"Yes, it's somewhat wet, but I can work with it."

"Ok, please take note." said Vantis.

"To all of my brothers and sisters of the south, I, Vantis of Lerr, apologise. I was gravely mistaken and have come to learn the truth of the King and his true intentions in the hardest of ways. I can confirm with certainty, after our meeting in the north, that the King indeed intends to conquer the south and only on his terms. Nobility, lands, ancient lineage, titles and deeds mean nothing to him. My entire life, they have meant everything to me. However, in the eyes of the King, we are all common folk, who will only survive if we give fealty to the King in the north.

I have never had this perspective in life. I have been nurtured from youth, to be the leader of my house, to always see the benefit others could do for me, as I am the eldest Lerr. Recently, I was put in my place, my eyes were opened and my perspective flipped. Again, I apologise to all that I have subjugated.

I know that I, Vantis of Lerr, have let down so many people of the south over the years. I understand now that there is no bargaining with the north, that our only chance of survival is not by dividing the south by bloodlines and wealth, as I previously thought but by uniting all of the south under one banner, no matter what colour, creed, race or religion. If you were born in the south or even in the north, this is of no actual concern. The only concern that we should have is that we, who are opposed to the King's rule, will unite to fight for our freedom, to fight the King and his ambitions to conquer our lands and confine us all to his system, to his rule.

Why have my views so radically changed? After all, I set off to strike a bargain with the King, to underpin the might of a unified south to secure title and deeds for myself and my kind.

The King set a trap in the north; he did not attend the meeting. He sent his negotiators to meet with us. As the day progressed, we reached significant inroads and had secured many beneficial deeds for our party and all those that we represented. Then out of nowhere and with no warning, the King's delegation was systematically slaughtered, by their own elite guard that had been present throughout. In the chaos that followed, which can now only be seen clearly with hindsight, this event was orchestrated so we could escape, he wanted survivors. I can only surmise as to the purpose of such an event, but I believe that the purpose was to instil a sense of unity to the fragmented and culturally diverse north. It is not confirmed at the time of writing but I believe that the official narrative of this monumental, yet falsely inflated meeting of the north and south will be propagated through the north as 'The south came north with deceit in their hearts, they were given every guarantee and the generous hospitality that every northerner is proud to give. In return, the southern barbarians executed our delegates. The south has sent us a clear sign that they not only defy The King and the peoples of the Namangan Empire but that they are not willing to honour the age-old traditions, by which civilised nations act.'

I believe this event that we recently witnessed was indeed a false flag, designed to unite his people against the last and only formidable opponents to his empire.

But as we, the south, currently stand fragmented and fractured by our own greed, differences and lack of a shared goal, we will surely have no chance against the King's armies, especially when they are potentially now unified and ignited by revenge.

It is now, in this time of great mistrust that we, the many peoples of the south, must unite, if we are to have any chance of surviving.

To show my commitment to this cause, I will allocate fifty percent of all of my current food stores, as well as fifty percent of all future food production from my lands and one hundred percent of my weapons stock to a new unified southern army. I will eliminate all taxes to any and all Lerrian, or other who moves to Lerr to join the war effort, or to any other location that a council of the south agrees upon. I am committed to serving the south.

My only regret is that my eyes were not opened sooner and that my actions, thus far, have not been in the interest of my southern brothers and sisters. For this, I offer my sincerest apologies.

Please join me in one month's time, at the great Hall of Juy.

Your friend

Vantis of Lerr.

Vantis looked towards Gemaras and nodded. He then took a deep breath, stood up straight, and in three quick movements, he swiftly swiped a few creases and marks from his clothes, before straightening up his heavily beaten clothes.

"Gemaras, as soon as we dock at Mantis point, we will go straight to the embassy of Lerr. After securing funds, you will buy supplies for our forward journey, then you will copy out your letter and have it sent to your assistants back in Lerr. Have them make copies and have it sent to every major southern family. This has to be of a far greater distribution than the original meeting of the south. Incorporate smaller families, nomads, corporate leaders, lesser nobles, criminal families and more. We need everyone on board, if we are to defeat the north,".

As Gemaras nodded in acknowledgement of the task before him, Vantis again swiped at his clothing, straightening up his shirt, then like a man possessed, he threw his shoulders back, puffed his chest out and took two steps forward.

"Ladies and Gentlemen," Vantis began confident but apprehensive. His voice was audible, barely. He knew if he was going to get the attention of the folks within the belly of this ship and compete with the noise of the driving rain, waves and sea outside, then he would need to project his voice with everything he had. Vantis, with a few eyes on him, cleared his throat and began.

"Ladies and gentlemen, may I have your attention, please. What I have to say is very important. Please come forward, come forward." His hands danced, waving his fellow shipmates to come closer as his eyes made contact with each and every one of them. His confidence, born from a life of nobility and physical gifts was always magnetic. As the crowd began to gather and close in around him, he began.

"My name is Vantis of Lerr, I know I do not present myself today as a wealthy noble of Lerr, please accept my apologies on my appearance. I am unfortunately, the bearer of bad news." The crowd was waning already, and a few had begun to return to where they had been settled.

"The King in the north is coming south, he plans to conquer the south and this cannot happen. I will be investing in a united southern army to defend us all against the might of the Namangan army". The crowd who were still listening were now laughing and smirking in unison. Vantis angered quickly, but then he understood why they were smirking, it was ridiculous, what he was proposing was completely outlandish, it was the rambling of a madman not a noble, especially one supposedly of Lerr. An army, a unified army, an army large enough to defend against the King in the north. Everyone on this boat had been to the north, some were even northerners, everyone on this boat was unlike most in the south. Here, in the belly of this ship, folk were educated and aware of the genuine power of the Namangan empire. Some may even work for it! Some will have undoubtedly experienced its unwavering unity through brutality, as well as its cultural and engineering takeover.

"Yes," Vantis smiled and joined the crowd in laughter. His face was light but still soft, with a tint of the seriousness he had to convey.

"Yes, it is outlandish, but it must be. Many months ago, the south's wealthiest families met in secret to discuss offers sent to each and every family of southern power. These letters were sent by the Namangen King. Have I got your attention? It was the first part in the King's plan to take the south. As you may be aware, he usually precedes war by buying the elite in the nations he is getting ready to conquer. I say with a heavy heart that I went to the north to represent the Noble houses, to negotiate various offers. Unfortunately, I found out the hard way that the King in the north is only interested in building his empire. Us so-called nobles of the south, are in fact, no more noble than any other man under the great sun above, in the eyes of the King in the north. In a selfish move to protect my lineage, my wealth and my nation, I, Vantis of Lerr, will use my vast resources to unite the south into one grand army, an army strong enough to defend against the north.

When we land in the south, please spread the word that Lerr is offering any man, woman and child, a good daily wage, a uniform, paid training, a weapon, shelter, food, as well as a basic education, to join this new southern army. You are welcome to join us too. If interested, just join me at the harbour when we dock and after registration, I will pay you from that day forward.

The north is coming, will you stand together with every race of the south, well trained, strong and confident in your skills to defend your family, your lands, your culture? Or will you see the enemy and feel your heart burn with regret that you have only two options; die by the King's hand or bow and be his slave?

Join me and employ option three, and I will train you to fight for your very survival."

The crowd did not laugh, some jeered, some mocked, a few clapped. Vantis turned on his heels to see Gemaras finishing up his scribbles.

"Were you scribing my speech, Gemaras?" asked Vantis.

"Yes, more than just these fine folk must hear your speech. I will copy it out and send it, with the original letter to Hardeaf. I will get him to have it read out in every town square of the south. We will create a mass migration to Lerr, or wherever the southern army will be based. We will build our army and we will repel the demon in the north."

Vantis smiled as his eyes met Gemaras's. *The young scribe has come of age. The sights in the north have changed him, have given him resolve. We are three and soon we will be thousands.*

CHAPTER 30 - DEFENDING THE GATES

IT HAD BEEN A blur, a strange blur of sand, sun, some green, more sand and now grey. The last twenty plus hours had gone past, fast, as he clung to the reins and whipped Mathewes, his poor beloved horse, his favourite horse, his trusted friend, to work harder than he had ever worked before, harder than he would ever work again.

"I am not a cruel man," said Armon to Mathewes, "but sacrifices must be made my dear friend," he leaned forward and affectionately slapped the neck of his horse three times, as the great dark beast sucked in air, like it was life its self. His ribs contracted hard, time and time again, the veins on his neck pumped intensely and his great legs trembled. "Your life, my life, Tanni life, Namangan life and many, many, more will be lost before the great balance is fulfilled once again. My friend, your sacrifice is as noble as any that have come before you," Armon said to Mathewes, as he crested the top of the ridge and looked out over the emerging battle field in front.

Here, at the peak of the southern mound, he got his first true glimpse of Ali Ma Bar, beyond just the capstone of the Law Hill. Now, he could see the mighty perimeter walls and also got his first view and measure of the Namangan armies. They were like ants sprawled out beyond the horizon, far to the north. No siege was underway, he expected the entire northern perimeter of Ali Ma Bar to be alive with projectiles. He expected the Namangans to be making ground towards the walls, testing Ali's various land fortifications around the northern gate and beyond. He expected them to be systematically sending small raiding parties in, to test the various defensive structures before committing the mass of their men. Knowing the calibre of this hardened, battle tested army, Armon expected the Namangans to be continuous, and relentless. But they were not. There was no real action in the valley below. A large force of Namanagns, north of the river and a smaller force of Tanni south of the river. 'Bizarre but good,' thought Armon. The Namangan's seasoned armed forces were spectacular, and if it was not his brothers and sisters who were under attack, he would have sat back and watched the spectacle unfold. But he was not here to spectate.

From the top of the valley, Armon scanned along the valley, far into the distance, at the top end of the northern valley before it rounded off to the west and disappeared before the mighty Aurd. There were no more Namangan troops approaching. Across the valley, there were a few groups meandering on the western side of the valley. The eye was clear. To the southwest, as it flattened out all the way to Aurds end and the sea beyond, Armon strained hard, looking across the vast flat landscapes, straining his eyes and scrunching his tired face as he scanned across the depth and breadth of the landscape. On the horizon, to the south, a flock of birds moved in unison, 'no, they are not birds, they are ships. Hopefully not Namangan ships,' thought Armon.

Mathewes was enjoying the short break, but unfortunately for the beast, its job was not done. Armon pulled hard on the reins and kicked another punishing heel into his side. The beast snorted, reared and broke into a three-beat gait, not nearly as energetic as it had been, but still faster than Armon could carry himself. As he continued towards the outer perimeter, the terrain steadily descended. As the descent finished and levelled out completely, Armon could no longer see the army coalescing in the north. Before him, the Assante bridge, a vital and strategic point, greeted him, yet it was neither guarded, nor under attack, which Armon found very bizarre.

Armon jumped from Mathewes as his trusted friend stumbled and fell from exhaustion, just beyond the bridge. 'You did me well old friend,' thought Armon, as he bowed and lowered his eyes in respect to his old friend. He had reached the southern wall of Ali Ma Bar, the main defensive wall of the southern side. The last wall and to his surprise, totally unhindered, unchallenged, possibly unseen and annoyingly, taking no fire. 'Who exactly is in charge up there?' thought Armon in a flash of anger, 'the Namangans are the very best army ever to attempt the walls of this great city, complacency and a belief in the ridiculous ancient myths of the city's impenetrable walls, is the fastest way to get everyone killed,' he said to himself, as he ran along the side of the wall.

It had been a good few years since he had been back to Ali Ma Bar. The outer walls were magnificent, the original blocks at the base of the wall where he now ran, were enormous, interlocking megaliths. All over one hundred tonnes a piece, each had between six and fourteen sides but to the untrained eye, or to those viewing it from a distance, they just looked like regular rectangular blocks. Each megalith was manufactured and cut so precisely, that when stacked upon one another and interwoven, one could not even pass a Tanni hair into a single joint, or the tip of the sharpest Tanni blade. As it had many, many times over the years, Armon's mind filled with awe at the engineering before him and how these masterful skills had been lost to time, like almost everything great that his people still clung to. As he was drawn towards the largest of the megalithic stones that made up the wall, his mind filled with fond memories of Mathewes, his sacrifice, and then it erupted in anger. A giant stone with thirteen sides that wove in masterfully with all the blocks surrounding it but especially with one smaller block on its left. The small stone was strangely out of place. It was small, only by this wall's scale, the width of two men, and stood as tall as three. In a land of giants, it was completely misplaced. A strange stone in a strange wall. Armon pulled out his sword with effortless efficiency, bore from repetition, and with one mighty strike he thudded the hilt of his sword hard to the centre of the small stone. It rang true, as the resulting vibration and piercing ringing noise subsided, Armon looked up.

From seventy feet above, a head peaked over the lip, then the small stone vibrated more clearly, and loudly, as if a man were somehow trapped inside it, "Who are the Tanni?", came from the vibrating stone. Armon replied "We are all Tanni, we are the first, we are our master's image," "and who are you," bellowed the strange rock, "It is Armon of Tanni Ma Bar, first son of the military." In that instant, a rope ladder descended. As soon as Armon started ascending the ladder, it began moving swiftly upwards. He was being hauled upwards from above, rapidly, and then the movement stopped, ten feet from the lip of the wall.

A head popped over the wall and looked down at Armon. "How do we know that you are from Tanni Ma Bar? And how do we know that you are not with the Namangans, who are currently banging at our front door?" With the authority that only a master of the military could command, combined with anger at how easy it was for him to approach the southern wall, unchecked and now with this incompetency and deviation from sacred protocols, Armon commanded. "I, Armon of Tanni, am here to take charge of the city and if you do not want to die this day, you will pull me up this wall, now," as Armon climbed the last ten feet, another few heads looked out over the lip, one making clear eye contact and then the rope ladder moved again.

A priestess of the order stood behind the men and nodded as the soldiers showed their respect for her. As she approached, Armon finished hauling his exhausted carcass over the lip.

"Armon of Tanni Ma Bar, we thank you for your assistance, we were expecting you," said the priestess,

"Expecting me?" replied Armon, with a frown that could have been construed as confusion or annoyance.

"These women will escort you to the war room" said the priestess, as she gestured towards the women standing directly behind her, "We are happy that you came".

As Armon moved towards the women, he stopped and looked at the four men who stood on this side of the wall.

"Get up on that lip and let no man, woman, child or horse get within one hundred paces of the wall. These walls are not impenetrable, this is war and we are children, with their first fucking stick. The Namangans out beyond the front gate are fucking warrior gods by comparison, don't make it even easier than it has to be for them," bellowed Armon.

The war room was tense, everyone in that room knew who Armon was but no one was willing to just let him walk in and take their authority. This was their people, their city and they were ready to defend it. Well, that is what they thought, Armon had other plans.

"Who is in charge?" bellowed Armon.

As the Ali Ma Bar's first daughter of the military turned in reaction to the question, Armon continued.

"What is the plan? Why did I make it to the talking stone unchallenged, no warning shots, no challenge of any kind? I had my signal flags, but they were not needed," shouted Armon, his tone and volume still full of angry undertones.

The first daughter of the military looked down, she had been caught off guard and now publicly shamed. Armon knew that, like every other woman and man in the room, she was well versed in all aspects of military strategy, protocol, theory etc. Armon looked around the room, realising that this room, was full of folk who had never expected to ever put their education and training into practice. The things they had learnt, the things they had been taught about war and strategy and leadership, were just that, things, distant from their reality but now they were here. Now it was reality and she and her team were not ready. Armon could see it; he could feel it.

"I am Gail. I am in charge. I am sorry but we are not ready, we had a plan but the Namangans are not reacting to anything we have done. Regrettably, we had decided to bow to the Namangans might and save the lives of the people we serve." Armon shook his head in disapproval, his lip turning up into a snarl, his eyes locked, unwavering focus on the first daughter of the military.

"We signed various agreements, and the Namangans left, to give us time to put things in order before they returned to begin their administrative takeover of the city." Armon, again looked at the room and all in it, one by one and showed his disapproval.

"You can stand there, all high and mighty, but we heard what happened to the southern Traveras cities of Terenca and Budieta. Terenca complied and now they thrive. Budieta fought their very best, came up very short and every single person was slaughtered, every man, woman, child, dog and cat. They even destroyed the statues of their sacred gods, dug up their ancestral graves, they fucking dug up their graves, their elders. Then they pissed on the corpses and beheaded the dead, the very worst humiliation one can bestow upon a Traveran, nothing is sacred to these bastards. Budieta is no longer, yet Terenca is thriving. They have new roads, buildings, trade, arenas, running water, plentiful food, sanitation...." stated the first daughter firmly, her confidence returning with the authority it knew well.

"I understand sister, your interests are of the people. I cannot judge on that; I have thought over the same conundrum many times, as has every official that has had the Namangan boring down on their front door. But this does not explain what is happening now." stated Armon, without the same edge of anger and volume as before.

"The Namangans left after the negotiations, the dancing star arrived in the sky and the great festival began. Our reports of the precise details from here in are hazy, but the general theme of what happened was; a southerner was mistaken as a Namangan, he was attacked and killed and the mob, fuelled by their success and hatred of Namangans, grew unrestricted and then by some comic synchronicity, the Namangan delegation was, at that exact same time, leaving the administrative district, adjacent to where the southerner was killed. When the mob spotted them, they swarmed them, lusting for more blood, they slaughtered almost all of them. Word got back to the Namangans and now all deals are off. We are now at war," said Gail, the first daughter of the military.

"A southerner, mistaken for a bloody Namangan, poor bastard," said Armon.

"He was a Gavodeon, of that we are pretty sure, thick beard, tall..." said Gail.

Armon sank, "You are sure he was a Gavodeon, killed? Was he young?" he asked, with urgency in his voice.

"Yes, stabbed many times by the mob. The report came straight from a Hetier food vendor that was serving him. We are so ashamed, as this is a huge dent in our cultural pride and especially on that day..." Gail was mumbling as Armon turned away from her, towards the priestess that had met him on the wall.

"Your chosen one, the prophecies. And he is dead all ready?" demanded Armon.

The Priestess met Armon's eyes and then lowered them as if defeated.

"What do we do next, Armon?" urged the Priestess.

Armon looked down at the clay model of the city, its walls, the grounds and the fortifications that surrounded her. "Bring me something to mark and identify the models, bring me paper and ink, bring me some food, and some strong tea, please," instructed Armon in a slow, almost beaten voice.

"Gail, we have some quick but thorough thinking to do, and everyone in this room must turn on. If you come up with something, I want to hear it I want to hear the flaws, I want to hear the holes in the plan. Don't just stand there, if you have something to say, speak." Armon walked the room, carefully eyeing everyone again.

"Who is well travelled in Namangan territories?" asked Armon. A few Tannis stepped forward, six in total.

"You six are now Namangan, it's your job to counter everything we do, it's your jobs to think like those Namangan bastards, it's your job to find the holes in our strategy. Do you understand me?" Yes, came the reply, uniformly and with passion.

CHAPTER 31 - ROTATING THE CROP

THE CHURCH OF THE Sun's main temple was invisible on the horizon, but Summerian knew exactly where it was. The entire temple was carved from the surface down, directly out of the solid rock, four levels of inner chambers, a large congregation hall and an entrance bridge, dug out from the ground, dug out from solid granite, it was a magnificent piece of engineering. To any Lanasian who came upon this place and knew anything about anything, they were always left in awe. It boggled the greatest engineering minds of the era, time and time again. Modern day worshippers of the sun had no answers, leaving only divine acceptance to explain the construction of the Ketesa Temple of the Sun. Or as Summerian, the immortal King liked to call it, the dinner hall. It was the King's technology that made this apparent impossibility possible. Just one of the many gifts he had given his clients over the years, ten thousand years by this planet's time frame. It had been an interesting farm that he had created here, the only QUAF feeding station in the entire void, but like everything in agriculture, the crop must be managed, cultivated, rotated and the only thing that never changes over the years is the fact that everything always changes over the years.

Summerian dismounted from his horse and descended the first few steps in towards the entrance, towards the first underground bridge to the mighty inner depths of the Ketesa Temple. As he approached the first gate, it opened. As he walked over the first bridge, he raised a hand and acknowledged the QUAF that crammed every possible inch of four-dimensional space, between every corridor, courtyard, every volumetric inch of the underground space that had been removed from the hard rock, as well as the space occupied by the rock, they were everywhere. The Lanasian worshippers of the QUAF scuttled about, wearing their black robes of the sun religion and completely unaware of the millions of QUAF that inhabited every inch of the surrounding temple. They were not absent gods.

The King stopped in the very centre of the bridge; he did not like the ornamental hand rail, its craftsmanship was exquisite and awe inspiring, but it was redundant. The King preferred his adopted culture's approach to bridges, the Namangan style made use of no handrails.

The King stopped. From above the thirty feet of granite walls far to the east, the sun was pushing hard through the clouds, however down here, in the tight angles of the underground, only glimpses of the sun's light, ironically, filtered beyond the bridge that the King now stood on.

"Let's make this brief, shall we." He offered out his hand's palm, with warmth and formality, in his business-like tone.

From deep within his mind, he heard the chatter of the hive; the factions began buzzing and then came the first audible tones, projected clearly into his mind.

"Summerian," buzzed the voice of the QUAF hive.

"Is it time again to rotate the crop?" asked Summerian.

Again, the buzzing began, before the millions of voices of the hive replied as one. "Yes, we wish to feed upon something a little lighter. We wish to change the ratios of light and dark. We propose you plant the seeds for another Golden age," said the voice of a million QUAF in unison.

"Are you sure? You know what happened the last time? These Lanasians are fused with my own blood. Given enough time to create, to think and read, to be, they will grasp their predicament and build a solution once again. The pyramids they built in the last golden age nearly killed you. Luckily, I arrived when I did. Luckily for you, I disabled them. Ok, if a golden age is what you want, a golden age is what you will get. You will have at least a few hundred years before it blossoms and I will be ready to crush it before it does. But why? You can assimilate these dark energies better?"

"It has been so long since we experienced the light", came the buzz from one faction, followed quickly by another faction in harmony, just out of phase with the first. "It is our choice. It is for you to fulfil. No questions needed, only compliance." Then came a third wave of chaotic buzzing, overlapping the other two factions. "We must have gold."

"Given enough time, I can shut this farm down and rotate the crop. If they attempt to build another pyramid transmitter, I will destroy it. OK, it would not be my choice, but ask and you shall receive. The south is already set to begin the process. They have not been fed upon in almost a thousand years now. I will plant the seeds," stated Summerian.

Excitement could be felt amongst the hive, then came their response. "The price, what is the current price for a one-thousand-year crop of golden Lanasian souls?" enquired the hive.

"The price is the same as it was the last time, negative energy, positive energy, specific bands of emotions, vibrational states etc, it does not matter to me, I can farm these Lanasians any which way you want. The price, even though you always ask and even though you always receive the same answer from me, never changes, for you it always stays the same. The price, as always, is your eternal assistance in the ongoing Tenni Uh Akki war against the 'Anti Mass Voiders'. The original contract has not changed," advised Summerian as the buzzing all around him intensifies.

"We created you to defeat them, you have not. Until then, we offer up the carcasses of this world that we have made redundant for you, to feed, for you to stay ready to be deployed to fight the AMVs as we see fit," said the King, who was the only original, full-bred Tenni Uh Akki on the landmass of Lanasia.

"We agree, we will pay the price," buzzed the QUAF.

"Then I shall plant the seeds and get the farm ready to grow the finest golden crop. Soon your diet will be filled with love, compassion, kindness, sweet arts, songs and poems. Your guise will be of white beings and mystic visions, I assume?" laughed Summerian.

"An autonomous drone ship from Tenni Uh Akki prime will be arriving within the next seven months,' Lanasian time, as it does every decade. You may have seen the first trails of the light gate engines firing up last week in the sky. Again, it will open up a portal to the frontier lands, we estimate around eighty percent of your brethren will be needed in this, it's no longer a skirmish, you are going to war!! Make sure you are ready to be separated from the hive," commanded Summerian.

The buzzing began again, loud, frantic, chaotic.

"There is not a problem is there?" checked Summerian.

The buzzing spiked again, louder, more frantic.

"The price will be paid," came the many minded voice of the hive's response.

"I will prepare one last feast of the current crop, a feast fit for gods, and then when your bellies are full, the skies will open and you will go and fight." laughed Summerian as he turned, changed his vibrational state so he no longer saw the QUAF masses before him, and walked out, the way he came in.

CHAPTER 32 - FINDING HIS POWER

THERE IS SO MUCH information, and so much of it makes no sense, thought Arran.

"Barratash, you say that this information is from the Bar En Dough, but how do you know it is real? I have heard many versions of the truth. Why is your truth real? Why is this truth real and all the other truths I have encountered false?" challenged Arran. As he stood up, he was disorientated in the complete darkness of the inner chamber. As Arran dressed himself, Barratash replied.

"You are asking the right questions, Arran, and only you can answer them. The way to truth is long and the path is short. We live for seventy years, the QUAF and the King live for thousands. We must claim what is ours, we must become more than what they have allowed us to be, if we are ever to see a future where all our brothers and sisters walk free from the QUAF and their overlord," said Barratash as he began putting on his clothes.

"Did you transmit the same information to both of us," asked Anice.

"Yes, the information transmitted is the same, but what you chose will have been different. Every experience of the Bar En Dough is different. From the torrent of information that bombarded you, there will have been much that drew your interest, information that held answers for you, information that you naturally gravitated towards. From this, you will have selected items relevant to your journey, to your experience, to the questions you hold dear, to your story. Our brains and our senses are continuously bombarded by information daily, so much so that we develop filters to bypass all that we deem to be irrelevant or of no use.

A woman will begin to see pregnant women everywhere, once she, herself becomes pregnant. A trader hears stories of products and profit everywhere, a warrior sees potential contenders. A musician hears sounds and tones in the forests, in the sea and communicates with other musicians about music, art and passion. We filter, it's what we do. So, what you understood from the transmission will be so very different from how I experienced the Bar En Dough and from what Arran perceived from the same experience," explained Barratash, his voice loud in the infinite quiet of the inner chamber.

"That sort of makes sense, I think," replied Anice.

"My mind is mush," laughed Arran.

"I hope not, young Arran, for our training is just beginning," stated Barratash.

"Both of you, link into my mind and follow me," said Barratash as he moved off into the darkness, guiding the two initiates through the corridors of the inner pyramid. As Arran walked into the darkness, his other senses once again compensated for his lack of vision. He noticed the difference in temperatures as they entered different corridors and ascended stairs, the air flow on his skin, the smell of stagnant air, previously undisturbed for months, maybe even years. Then the light came. Even though it was soft, it was the brightest light Arran had ever seen. It felt like the Sun itself was bearing down upon him from the end of the corridor up in front. The glimpse of Anice's face in the dim light confirmed she was experiencing something similar. Then, as the light grew brighter, his eyes adjusted. The three emerged into a chamber that was stocked with some modicum of furnishings and, to Arran's surprise, supplies. Food, clothing, sleeping cots, water and more.

"What is this?" asked Anice.

"This is where we will live and train whilst we are here in the pyramid's belly. This is where we will learn and refine our skills. Entering the minds of others, entering the Bar En Dough and finally, how to unleash your energy to power others, to guide them past the QUAF at death. Here is where you become, here is where you go beyond the basic programmes and parameters of the farm. Here you become a true Tanni, here you become Mertak," said Barratash in his most serious and formal tone that always still had a hint of sarcasm and lightness to it.

"Well, I am ready, there is a battle raging outside and I need to learn how to assist those that die in crossing over. I need to learn to fight and I need to learn this mind trick you both do so well. Can you teach me to control another's mind, not just enter it as a visitor? But control their body, experience with their senses. How many minds can you enter at a time, can it be done anonymously......?" blurted Arran, before Anice cut him off.

"You can enter their mind anonymously and control them physically, but just small things, as they are always under their own control, but we can capitalise on the shock of the first experience that allows us to manipulate them. So, you can make people freeze, walk, talk etc and you can plant seeds that will flower into new ways of doing things. But that is about my limits. It's a subtle art, it's not a sledgehammer. I have used it mainly for good, to plant seeds of hope and inspire good. You're not going to be controlling a full army of mindless warriors," laughed Anice.

"Yes, you are right, Anice, but there is so much more. I have witnessed and experimented with full take over, making an individual my puppet, making them walk and talk to my command. But it is a violation of everything I stand for. For me, the best use of the Overseer ability is for observing, gathering information and guiding the dead," said Barratash.

"So, you can enter another's mind, take it over and make them into your slave, of sorts?" asked Arran.

"A very powerful overseer can, but ones with that kind of power are rare. It is also uncomfortable, for the overseer to do. It would take a lot of practice, years of practice with willing participants at first, before developing the skill of brutally forcing an individual's mind to bend to your will," said Barratash.

"But you are powerful? ... Overseer?" retorted Arran immediately.

"This is the name that we have given to the ability. From what I understand from the Bar En Dough transmissions, the Hybrid overseers, or slavemasters, could jump in and out of all the workers' minds. It was a way of monitoring the work, seeing the progress through the mines, even in the deepest depths of the mine, without having to leave their location. In occasions when it was needed, i.e. times of danger, like a mine shaft collapsing, a slave fatality or revolt; the overseer could enter the mind and take over the body, whilst looking through the eyes of many more to give the best advice on escape etc to the workers. It was a way to monitor the workers. We were designed and manufactured to work," summarised Barratash.

"So, you and Anice are Hybrids," asked Arran.

"Hybrids? Well, that is a question, whatever we are, you are one too!! And you may have a greater amount of original Tenni Uh Akki blood than both of us combined!" said Barratash.

Arran blushed, then awkwardly looked away from Barratash.

"And what does that mean," asked Arran.

"It means..." said Barratash.

"That you are very powerful," blurted Anice.

"You are young. These abilities usually only manifest in fully grown adults, as the role of an overseer is one for adults. But we can forcefully awaken your abilities, as they are already blooming. But it may be traumatic," cautioned Barratash.

"Yes, my ability only flowered within the last few years," said Anice, nodding in agreement with Barratash.

"I may have seen it." said Arran.

"Seen what?" replied Anice.

"For many years I have had the most bizarre, prophetic dreams and night terrors, and I have had visions granted to me by the golden cap. In them, I have seen many times, powerful overseers take over multiple minds and command them to fight, like they were their own private army," said Arran.

"You have seen this? In your dreams?" quizzed Barratash.

"I have indeed, namely the Namangan King and a great pale skinned King with blond hair called Edvar. If my visions have any bearing in reality. Then the King can easily control legions with his mind and make them do his bidding at will," said Arran, almost ashamed at his ridiculous claims.

"There have always been rumours of this level of ability. The great Tenderas, founder of the pine, wrote of this in some of his more obscure texts. A few of my brothers and sisters of the pine have had similar visions and experiences to what you have just described. But I have never seen it, and I have, as yet, never met a more powerful overseer than myself. Those brothers and sisters of the pine broke away years ago to develop a way to unify their minds and use the overseer ability in combat. They call themselves the Magii Warriors Of The Pine. But I have not been in touch with them for years now, and they block every attempt I make to observe them. It's hard when they play by the same tricks I taught them," laughed Barratash.

"An offshoot of the Pine? I thought you were unified. Unwavering in your knowledge of the truth?" said Anice.

"We are, the core understanding permeates everything. The group of thirty are, for lack of a better word, of a 'military' mind, believing that for us to defeat the King, we must train the overseer skill for that very purpose. But from the Pines' main perspective, the ability to fight is not as important as the ability to crossover after death, or as important as helping others crossover at their death," explained Barratash.

"It seems that even the Cult of the Pine, has various interpretations and understanding of truth," said Arran.

"Everything does. Why would the Cult of the Pine be any different?" said Anice.

"True," said Arran.

Barratash looked across at Arran and Anice with a big warm smile, his large moustache twisted and spun upwards showing his rarely seen teeth.

"Arran, you have become a leader of men at an early age. But before you were, were you ever shunned by your peers?" asked Barratash.

"I am the silence in the song," said Arran quietly as he reflected on a time which felt so long ago, yet was not so long ago in truth.

"I have been shunned my entire life," said Arran.

"We have an innate ability to find the hybrids among us. The other Gavods, even from an early age must have sensed your difference, not in a conscious way but in a subtle knowing that you were different. You might have had an inkling of this yourself?" laughed Barratash.

"Most cultures don't have a word for hybrids but recognise and ostracise us nonetheless. Some cultures embrace us. I believe you have met Brother Lopsangy, the Lamas and Ternakas peoples?" said Barratash with a smile.

"Ok, I am different, that is old news. How do we force this ability open; how do we force any and all of these abilities open?" asked Arran with a strange, weak voice as his shoulders slumped, visible exhaustion on his face.

"You were born an overlord, with the blood of the hybrid, you may even be a direct descendant of the Tenni Uh Akki originals, or of Summerian the Namangan King. Act like the man you are to become and the training will begin. Act like an outcast boy and you are no help to anyone. Am I clear Arran?" checked a very firm Barratash.

"Are you ready to begin Anice?" said Barratash.

"Yes," said Anice.

"Enter Arran's mind, Arran, do not resist her as she enters your mind," said Barratash.

Anice slipped into Arran's mind. Without words, he felt her presence deep within him.

"Anice, anonymise yourself, make yourself as undetectable as you can," said Barratash.

As all awareness of Anice slipped away from the forefront of his mind, Barratash spoke.

"Arran find her, resist her and eject her from your mind. Anice do not let him," said Barratash, with a smile.

From deep within his own mind, Arran knew that Anice must be there, he knew that Anice must be observing him. She had entered and at Barratash's command had gone into stealth mode. How do I evict her? How do I find her? How do I find someone who has not alerted me to their purpose? Instantly, Arran began his inner work. Focusing on his breath, he found his rhythm and entered his inner sanctum. He began his test, a self-imposed test, a self-imposed challenge that had become the sentinel to his inner world. He retraced the entire six-year cycle of the Gavods, day by day, checking and filing every nougat of information in its place, and there, like a misplaced fruit in amongst the vegetables was Anice's mind, attempting to hide in plain sight. Arran grabbed her with every ounce of will he could muster and ripped that fruit from the stall and threw it out from the stall. Anice's presence was felt instantly, then from inside his mind and externally Arran heard her scream.

"You are OK, Anice, find yourself, relax," said Barratash from inside Anice's mind. Anice's screaming stopped.

Arran stood still, shocked at Anice's response to the eviction.

"I am sorry, Anice, I did not mean to hurt you," said Arran.

"She is OK, just a bit of a fright. It seems your abilities are stronger than we first thought," said Barratash.

"Now it is my turn, find me and evict me if you can," said Barratash.

CHAPTER 33 - VERTOMINA

"Vertomina," shouted the King.

The doors into the room were gently pushed open, Vertomina walked through, strong, well postured, head held high, with a demure smile.

"Yes, my King,"

"The plans for the south have come to fruition early, however, I am about to change the entire game as you know it. A truly one-off event, not witnessed for thousands of years," said the King.

Vertomina felt confused but did not show it physically or energetically. She was in control.

"I see it, Vertomina. However, I must commend you on your control. In all the countless years I have been here playing these roles. You have been one of my very best students, you are strong, intelligent, quick and loyal." Vertomina was aware that the King was making sure his eye contact with her was being acknowledged, she could feel the warmth behind the eyes.

"And it is very much appreciated," said Summerian.

"Thank you, sir," said Vertomina.

"You have probably added two and two together and got four, I will not insult your intelligence. But I think it is good for you to hear it from me," said The King.

Vertomina met his eyes, her large eyes sinking in sadness as her mind raced at the potential of what her master was about to reveal.

"Yes, my King," said Vertomina.

"You know I am a God and that I am immortal and that you, Serena of Laternas were made Vertomina at my command. You know that you were taken from your mother and ever since, you have been my right hand, my confidante, my secretary, my everything. You are my everything. You are my daughter; you are the direct descendent of a Tenni Uh Akki original and a strong blood line." Summerian smiled.

"You are my father?" blurted Vertomina.

"I am," said Summerian, before continuing;

"I am the...I am the keeper of the Lanasian farm, the QUAF are the Tenni Uh Akki empire's clients. I will continue my service here, in this world for many, many more years and take many more Vertomina's over that time. However, every so often, the farm changes crop. You are lucky enough to be a part of it," smiled Summerian.

"Thank you," said Vertomina.

"I only tell you this because we are about to go to war, it will be the largest, most horrific slaughter of Lanasian livestock I have ever produced in this cycle of your being. And then I, on request of the QUAF, will change the crop. Moving the farm to the south, to give the north time to recover again. As you have given me unconditioned loyalty throughout the years, I will give it back," said the King.

Vertomina nodded in agreement, but internally her mind reeled with complete confusion.

"You have already given too much, it is time for you to leave and start a family. I will make sure you have wealth, honour, stature, land, etc. The coming war will create a lot of chaos, before the dust settles once more," said Summerian.

Vertomina looked up in shock. She had devoted everything to The King.

"I want to go with you, fight by your side. I am, after you, the very best physical, mental and energetic warrior in all of Lanasia. With me by your side once more, this will be another quick battle and then we can return, and build your ideas for the south together," pleaded Vertomina.

"Unfortunately, not. This is a changing of the crop. I will decide for you this final time, my trusted and valued Vertomina. After you have done the errands I have for you this day, I will sign over one half of all my property and stock to you, I will assign ten guards, one platoon, much coin and then you will leave. I would suggest as far north and west as possible, to the islands just off the main landmass. And there, you will begin a new life, a life of your own design. I am grateful for all you have done; it is time to live for yourself. Now I need one last thing," said the King.

"Yes, anything," said Vertomina, holding back the tears.

"The false flag in the south worked, now we need to use it to galvanise the various competing factions of the empire as we go forth into war. We are going to take the road south to Ali Ma Bar. At the same time, as I rally and galvanise all who are true to the Namangan empire, I need you to galvanise all of those who hate us. Those from the south, the Traverans, Hetiers, the Tannis, Namangan dissenters, anyone and everyone, so that, by the time I arrive in Ali Ma Bar, there is a mighty army ready to oppose the greatest Namangan army ever to stand," said The King.

Vertomina nodded whilst being in complete confusion and bewilderment at what she was hearing.

"I can do that, but why?" asked Vertomina.

"As I said, it is a once in a lifetime event and the crop is being rotated," smiled the King.

"I need you to supply our enemies with weapons, food, and hope, via any means necessary, use whatever resources you see fit, the royal coffers will stretch to whatever you plan. I want the largest standing army this generation has ever seen, standing toe to toe across the battlefield, ready for a one-off dance to the death," laughed the King.

"Conscript every male of ten and above. This will force the masses to either bow to our will and fight on our side or rise in anger and join the opposition. One way or another, they will join my war," smiled the King.

"Can you handle this, Vertomina?" asked the king.

Before Vertomina could reply, the King continued.

"And as soon as you have planned a way to amass the hundreds of thousands of warriors for either side to meet at Ali Ma Bar, then you can take your leave. You will then be free; take all the riches you wish and leave." The King walked forward and hugged Vertomina with a great strength. As he rubbed his chin against hers, he smiled and whispered. "Thank you, my daughter."

"I understand, may I speak freely," said Vertomina.

"Of course," said the King.

"By changing the crop, you are referring to a change in how the QUAF eat? Your changing corn for potatoes? Why do you do this, why?" Vertomina held her hand up as if to say do not answer that, then she began again.

"It's like their harvest festival, this is a feast for them, the last feast before we plant the new crop," cried Vertomina as the walls of her illusion broke down all around her. Everything she thought was reality but was not brave enough to accept was now hitting her true and hard.

"And the battle is the last feast. Yes," said Summerian.

"Will I be feasted upon when I die?" said Vertomina.

"Will my children be?" continued Vertomina.

"You are of my seed, you possess more capacity than every other mortal breathing air in Lanasia," said the King.

"Is that your way of saying I am immune to the QUAF," said Vertomina.

"Just as you are in life, you will be in death. You can and do choose to be QUAF free, death and your transition to the Bar En Dough is no different. I have given you everything you need; you are well trained. You just have to decide and make it happen," said the King.

"Obviously, I know the QUAF and that they feed upon us, but I have never really thought of myself as being within the farm. I have always seen myself by your side, and somehow outside the farm. To realise that I am just as insignificant as everyone else is strange. I just assumed that your control of them would have extended to my soul when I died. They are under your control and why should I worry about such things. I am protected. It is hard to come to terms with." said Vertomina.

"Nothing is given, everything is earned. You know this," said Summerian.

"This is true and I will earn my entry into the Bar En Dough. OK, I will. I will begin preparations for the war, but this will take me some time. I will use all of your resources to make sure that the largest standing armies ever amassed stand against each other at Ali Ma Bar. Shall we say six months' time?" said Vertomina.

"Six months it is," said the King, with a smile and tip of the head.

CHAPTER 34 - GIAT ARRIVES

THE GREAT NAMANGAN HIGHWAY now progressed for sixty miles beyond Yi Ma Bar, the small outlying town that once marked the very edge of the Tanni Ma Barian empire. The great road now connected almost all the nations of the Namangan empire. Connections to Namanga in the north, Traveras in the southwest, to the borders of Aromia in the west, and deep in to the Lagosian deserts, skirting the most northeastern edges of the mighty Aurd and as well, to Giat's homeland of Hetier, in the far west by the sea.

The sea air, the local wrestling fares, his family, his children, all gave him feelings of nostalgia. 'It has been too long since I have seen my children,' thought Giat. The regular letters he received described life back home and the wealth he had sent, had given his family every opportunity to build and prosper in his hometown of Hebaras. But home is far away, thought Giat as he climbed hard, tooth and nail, the final ridge to look down upon the battleground. He could hear the grunts of his men behind him, he could feel the pain in the tips of his fingers and the sweat lashing off his brow. 'This climbing lark was harder work than I've ever given it credit for,' thought Giat as he summited the ridge. The sprawling encampment below covered a considerable patch of the northern fields beyond the great city of Ali Ma Bar. The scene before him was split in two by the mighty river Ali. Giat led from the front, as all King's generals did, his men following his route loyally. The final descent down into the green pastures of the open lowlands took Giat longer than he expected, the land was deceivingly rugged, from atop the last hill, or Nencom's eye as he would later learn it was called, the whole southern expanse below it looked relatively flat, he now knew it was not.

Giat and his small entourage of just over one hundred men were challenged as they attempted to enter the north-western boundaries of the Namangan military camp. As soon as Giat's documents and seal were acknowledged, his men could cross the narrow bridge that led over the river Ali, allowing him to access the valley floor below. A rider took the message ahead of Giat, delivering his arrival swiftly to General Mariehoos.

The camp was ordered, well maintained and busy. As Giat made his way through the tents, towards the centre where Mariehoos was camped, he took time to talk to the men and women, starting conversations about the weather, the food, the terrain, difficulties encountered so far, the fortifications of Ali Ma Bar, supply levels, moral and more. The relatively short walk from the entrance of the main camp to Mariehoos's tent took him over two hours. When he finally entered Mariehoos's tent, he could see he was visibly angry.

"What the fuck took you so long? Did you stop and talk to every fucking man, woman, dog, cat, horse and QUAF in this entire fucking camp before coming to my tent?" roared Mariehoos.

Giat kept his eyes low and his energies controlled, inside he felt himself laughing. With the slightest hint of that laughter spilling over into his voice, Giat calmly informed Mariehoos that he was now in control.

"I apologise if I have offended you in some way Mariehoos, I was just collecting some information from the men and women who will soon fight and possibly die at my command," said Giat, as he raised his eyes until they were level with Mariehoos.

"Until the King arrives, that command is mine to give and you, with your Hetier smugness, will show me the fealty I deserve," barked Mariehoos.

"Unfortunately, not this day. I will however, give you the respect I give all my brothers and sisters of the Namangan empire who stand with me against our common enemy. But from this day..." Giat removed a short roll of paper, sealed with the royal seal, and passed it to Mariehoos.

"I am in charge of Ali Ma Bar," said Giat as he handed over the parchment.

Mariehoos had been a general of the sun for over three decades, he was seasoned in many wars; it was his army that first invaded Hetier. He read the parchment, sighed, and then, with everything he had, he began his attack.

Before him, Giat stood still as the room started glitching, as if the visual information from his eyes were broken. As Giat stood squinting, attempting to see clearly beyond the visuals his eyes were relaying, the room expanded. Where Mariehoos once stood, only feet away, he now stood hundreds of feet away. The tent was now as large as the valley the army occupied. A rush of fear ripped through Giat's mind. What was happening? Then he realised he was under attack. In that instant, he began his inner rituals, took back control of his concentration and began to defend against Mariehoos' overseer attack.

As Giat pushed back his perspective, the warped reality his eyes were relaying to him normalised once more. As it did, he could see Mariehoos standing before him grinning. But just like all other forms of combat, Giat learnt fast and he was diligent in his practice, with the single-minded pursuit of excellence. Then, like a sledgehammer to the head, Giat was returning the attack, entering Mariehoos's mind. No subtlety, no finesse, just brute force powered by rage. Giat observed from deep inside Mariehoos's mind as a great fear grew, emotions that he had suppressed for years, of his defeat at the hands of Traveran overseers, of the helplessness he felt then, combined with the guilt he felt at all the slaughter he had inflicted. As it began to bubble up from the depths of Mariehoos's soul, Giat exploited it. As Giat continued his attack, Mariehoos continued to fight back against Giat's emotional manipulation, sending out more tentacles of overseer energy into Giat's mind. Physically, the two warriors stood five feet apart, in the comfort of the finest tent, in the middle of the largest army ever amassed as they battled hard against each other, in the depths of each other's minds.

"Ok, ok, I will step aside. I am not as powerful as I once was. That is clear," said Marehoos as he released his attack, Giat felt his victory and stopped his attack.

Giat's face contorted. He was in the middle of a fight for his life, his first true overseer fight of his life, and now it was over. His body was shaking, adrenaline pumping and his was heart racing. It had been a long time since his body reacted to combat like this.

"I do not know what the King has planned, nor what he sees in you. I will let you know that I think this is a grave mistake, to hand such a crucial battle over to such a non-experienced general. However, I have doubted the King only a few times in my time and he has an uncanny knack for making excellent judgement calls," Mariehoos stepped to the side and presented to Giat, the sword of the first general.

"I thank you for making this as easy as possible," said Giat. "I will not be requiring you to leave, I wish you to stay, I am no fool, you have one of the finest military minds in our great army, possibly the most seasoned military experience among us all and you must work with me as we build and fortify for this battle to be victorious," said Giat.

"Thank you Giat, I was going to challenge you, which is my right, but as soon as I entered your mind, I knew that would be a mistake. It has been so many years since I was as good as you are now. So, I will gracefully step down and take my place as an adviser," said Mariehoos.

Giat smiled. The wind outside buffeted the tent, and then the rain fell once again. Torrential rains, the noise from it was so loud, it almost drowned out the two generals as they discussed the various orders Giat had been sent to deliver and enact from Vertomina, much of which he did not and could not make sense of, but this was not for him to ponder.

"So, you are telling me, we have to recall our scouts from the lands to the north, west, south and east of Ali Ma Bar. Absolute folly. Craziness, I tell you, son. Leaving the routes to the east open, why don't we just send the bastards in Tanni Ma Bar a fucking invitation to come and defend their city, whilst we are sending invitations out, why don't we send one to every disgruntled bastard we have conquered and tell them to unite behind the Tanni cause." Mariehoos' head was shaking furiously, small white pockets of foam forming in the corners of his lips. Giat could see he was not pleased with these strange orders from the King.

Mariehoos stopped shaking his head and burst into a strange maniacal fit of laughter. "We have to scout, but not engage, if we see bands of the enemy as they come from all over to unify behind the Tanni cause. This is not right. This will just encourage the enemy to amass," shouted Mariehoos in a nervous laughter to be heard over the rain.

"The only way this makes sense is if the King is planning a great slaughter, if he is planning a great land war to feed the QUAF. Or, he is willingly stacking the odds against his army to give him the challenge he needs. It makes no sense. But he has done stuff like this before. My grandfather fought for the King as a young man against the great Traveran overseer King, Edvar. He was one of the few survivors in battle that seen tens of thousands die. Summerian allowed Edvar to amass an army over months until his might was as strong as the Kings. Then, the two great Kings fought a true magical battle as their armies clashed in the physical. My grandfather, when drunk always told the story of how the Traveran God, Val Drack entered his mind as he stood ready for Summerian's call to charge. How his mind filled with fear, uncontrollable, endless fear, the kind that grips you from the bottom of your toes to the hair on your head. He always recounted that Traveran God, Val Drack, stood so clear in front of him, filling him with fear, sapping his strength, his will. Then he saw the King, one hundred feet tall, rush forward and behead the Traveran God. He then turned and gave the signal to charge. The battle was fast and hard, and the casualties were enormous. Maybe he plans something similar here?"

"This was all inside their minds? The Traveran King broadcast to an entire army at once? He filled an entire army with fear at once? That is incredible. Are their people so powerful?" asked Giat.

"Our King fought and won against an overseer of such power. He fought Edvar in his mind, and in the mind of every Namangan soldier before they had even charged," said Mariehoos.

Giat began laughing, "Now, I understand when he said that he had defeated me easily,"

"Yes, there are levels to the magical abilities, we are like gods to those with no abilities. And those with great lineages are like gods, amongst gods."

"I am just happy to be on Summerian's side. As these bastards have some strong overseers. Nothing like the great Edvar, but we know of the pine men and someone has been working hard against me and my men, as every time I probe into the minds beyond the city walls, I meet a shield that I cannot penetrate," stated Mariehoos.

"I thought that we would encounter the Pine here. I am with you brother, I am glad Summerian is on our side. However, no matter the Kings plans, we will make plans to win, no matter who stands against us. Now let us talk of the battlefield and the strategies that we can control," said Giat.

Mariehoos nodded, the rain eased, the lighter rain allowing for some form of coherent conversation to take place. Mariehoos walked over to the large, yet simple table, poured two cups of beer, picked up the long simple map pointer and began.

"We are here," the end of the pointer defined the Namangan army's current position, with four cubes each cube representing a Namangan fighting unit. Each unit had two thousand soldiers, made up of a mixture of well-trained novice and experienced infantry, archers, spearmen, cavalry, suppliers, medics and engineers. Each was under the control of a single General of the Sun, and each could act autonomously, or in unison with any other unit in the Namangan empire. These autonomous units had evolved over hundreds of years, adapting to different foreign terrains, different armies' sizes and different strategies. Occasionally over the years, they were defeated, but the Namangan's great strength under Summerian, was resilience. Any time they had been defeated, they went back to the drawing board, revised, adapted, and came back stronger.

"Currently we have four units, I will assume that reinforcements will arrive steadily over the next few weeks until the King arrives. Let's assume forty units in total. You came in via Nencom's Eye? Us normal, civilised men descended the main valley," laughed Mariehoos.

"Nencom's Eye?" questioned Giat.

"Yes, the hill up to the west of here, across the Antara bridge." Mariehoos pointed in the direction even though the two generals were enclosed in the tent with no visual reference to the direction he was pointing in.

"Yes, I came via Nencom's Eye," said Giat.

"So, you've seen the terrain for yourself, I thought you would have. She's beautiful. Just to recap what you saw, and what we know. We are here," Mariehoos pointed at the four cubes.

"The Valley is hemmed in on the east and west, with Ali Ma Bar built into and onto this large hillock directly south and west of our camp, here." The stick pointed at the twenty cubes and many short rectangles denoting the troops and walls surrounding Ali Ma Bar.

"From north west to south east, the River Ali cuts across the bottom of the valley and divides our current camp and the outer armies of the Tanni. The river is extremely high just now, bursting its banks here and here, which gives extreme importance to us securing the bridges." His pointer rapidly hit the three bridges before the tip finely traced out the length of the river, highlighting the bridges again in more detail.

"Antara, the most northern bridge, you have crossed Antara," said Mariehoos.

"I did, barely room to swing a cat, two abreast, no more, or a single horse, made of wood and easily destroyed. Foundations are old and the water there is deep and fast flowing. Easily destroyed, if need be," said Giat.

"Yes, good for a few men, however, we must control it. Across that bridge is the high ground leading up to the Eye, we don't want them raining arrows down on us and we don't want them controlling the Eye, that vantage point is too crucial. We will have eyes up there that we can look through, for a real time perspective of the entire battle. Hence our station there," explained Mariehoos.

His pointer moved rapidly from the tip of the Eye, down her southwest slopes, along the ridge of the high pass that paralleled the entire valley, all the way to Ali Ma Bar.

"Here, there is a route from the western side of the Ali Ma Bar to the Eye, it's rugged and the entrance to the city from there, for us, is suicidal, steep cliffs, single file staircase to a drawbridge, none the less, we must control it." Mariehoos' stick started moving again.

"In between us and them, the Ashar bridge. The main bridge, the lifeblood of Ali Ma Bar, good for transport, trade, mass movement and our victory in this war. Solid stone, four archways, forty feet wide and one hundred and sixty feet long. Currently being held by the Tanni." Mariehoos tapped the bridge drawn on the map vigorously, before it moved again, winding east with the river, before darting south to the last bridge.

"The Assante bridge crosses over to the eastern hills, leading a path up and over, straight to Tanni Ma Bar herself. A place we must control as well, for victory to be secured," said Mariehoos, tapping his stick repeatedly.

"Remember, we have to keep that passage open, we have to allow them to amass an army," said Giat.

"I took that from Vertomina's commands as well, but it just makes no fucking sense. I am all up for giving the enemy a fighting chance. It makes it better sport, but we are not all immortal fucking beings!" shouted a very angered Mariehoos.

"I know, I know, but all will become clear when the King arrives. OK, tell me of Ali Ma Bar's fortifications and give me the backstory of what has happened so far. I was led to believe that initially they were the first major Tanni city to sign over legally, saving their citizens' lives, handing us the keys without all of this," said Giat, waving his hand, gesturing at the armies beyond the tents.

"We did the deal, gave them some breathing space to enjoy some shitty, sacred, backwards festival, then some drunken revellers decided the deal was not in their interest. They savaged our diplomats, and this was followed up by a short retaliation. The engagement took place within the outer, inner Ali Ma Bar city walls. They overpowered us and they pushed us back to here. We were only one unit, they stopped at the bridge, we lost three hundred men," said Mariehoos. Giat nodded as he stood over the topographical map of the valley and of Ali Ma Bar.

"When the second and third units arrived, I began peppering their defences with projectiles, and scouting but when the fourth unit arrived, with General Hasim, he had orders to stop any further attacks until notified. I was to build and assess. Then you arrived, with your new commands, bullshit if ever I have heard it. So that is where we are," said Mariehoos.

"This city is the very best fortified city that I have ever come across," said Mariehoos, nodding rhythmically to himself in appreciation of what Ali Ma Bar was.

"It sure looked impressive from up on Nencom's Eye, an outer keep and an inner keep, surrounded on all sides by steep banking, making access and attack only viable from its northern side." said Giat.

"Yes, it is ancient, the walls are tall and thick, it was designed and built for fortification. The location was chosen carefully, let's just hope those in charge up there are absolute fucking fools!" laughed Mariehoos.

"It won't be the first time," laughed Giat.

CHAPTER 35 - ARRAN BECOMES

THREE MONTHS OF SOLID training, day in, day out. Eat, sleep, practice, repeat.

Living weeks at a time, locked in an airless, stone room with the complete absence of external wind, rain and natural noise was just too much for a nomad. Even as he experienced the outside world through others' minds, experiencing it via other people's senses, the inner chambers of the pyramid were beginning to grate on Arran. Every week or so, he would take a walk up to the top of the pyramid and pace around the capstone, observing the city and the armies below.

"I am going for a walk, get some fresh air, see what's happening out there beyond the walls, with my own two eyes." said Arran.

"A short break, yes, it is maybe for the best, you have been working hard. You both have," said Barratash.

Arran grabbed his small pouch and some water and made his way out of the pyramid, through the concealed exit and out into the fresh Tanni evening air. The night was here. It occurred to Arran how strange it was that the passage of time had been noticeably absent from his life these last few months. He started moving up the side of the hill, remembering the words of Nanoc about the importance of exercise, another thing that had been absent from his life whilst he mastered the overseer ability. As Arran walked up the hill, he wondered where Loo and Nanoc were, as he caught his first glimpses of the lights out across the valley. As he made eye contact with the capstone, Arran marvelled at the invisible pyramid, hidden as a hill, right in front of his eyes. Upon reaching the apex of the Law hill, only the small capstone of the pyramid hidden below protruded, as if it was just that small, pyramidal capstone that had been hoisted here to ceremoniously acknowledge the height of the hill, Arran laughed.

Then he gazed out over the Namangan army, from the apex of the pyramid, he could see right across the valley. The complete darkness of a cloud covered sky was broken by the distant wisps of the moon's silvery light and by the multitude of campfires that lit up both sides of the river.

'Oh, it's real,' sighed Arran, 'it's all too fucking real,'.

Arran sat back and recalled his first walk up here, after experiencing the Bar En Dough and learning of his overseer ability. Sitting atop the pyramid, he reached out to the minds of his mother and Irvine, knowing no matter where he was, he could now always experience home. As he entered their minds, the intrusion overwhelmed him, the guilt he felt at entering their minds uninvited. And then by the reality of entering the mind of someone he thought he knew inside and out, yet in reality only knew externally from the outside of what they showed him. He took warmth from the exchange, but did not probe his mother's mind. He did not want to startle her or Irvine. It was then he seen Rannoch through Irvine's eyes and made the leap to enter the shaman's mind. He was greeted like he had just walked over physically, waving and shouting Rannoch's name, before their eyes had met. The embrace was warm and full. Arran talked and Rannoch listened. The memory was fresh and vibrant and gave great comfort to Arran as he stood upon the pyramid once more.

As Arran brought himself back to the moment, he looked out across the darkness and camp fire light, he thought to himself that this was as good a place and time as any, for him to consume the last of the Golden mushrooms, the sacred contents he had been carrying since he acquired them from the Lamas people all that time ago, high in the Aurd. 'A Mertak must have his visions to guide him,' thought Arran. So much had changed since then, since the Aurd, since his childhood laughed Arran, as he removed the mushrooms from the small pouch, gripping them tight as he took a seat against the pyramid's capstone. Arran took a moment to look out over the valley one last time before making preparations for his last vision quest.

The night was dry, one of the few dry days since the day he had entered Ali Ma Bar. He was glad of it as he sat at the apex looking out over the valley in front, before turning to look down over the sprawling city of Ali Ma Bar. Sitting on the ground, with his back propped up against the capstone, Arran relaxed, and calmed his mind, ready to ingest the mushrooms he gripped tightly in his hand. Then he heard the voosh, similar to the voosh of the Tanni Ma Bar pyramid, but this time it was thinner, subtler, more refined. 'Does this Pyramid work? Does it transmit?' thought Arran as he shut his eyes, mushrooms still tightly grasped in hand.

Before his eyelids connected, Arran heard the voosh again and again. The voosh rapidly intensified. Within seconds, Arran was ripped from his body, his conscious, energetic mind was sheared from his dormant physical body, violently, like skin being ripped from a dead animal. The energy of his consciousness viewed by him, in a strange third-person perspective was a magnificent array of rainbow-like diamonds, that in their millions of miniature reflecting and refracting lights, formed a strange double spiral as it circumnavigated and penetrated through his physical body. It then descended instantly from his head to his toes, before exiting his physical body and being reformed into the single point of consciousness, the consciousness he now was. As his consciousness left his body, it joined with a great flow that rose from the apex of the pyramid. His consciousness entered and flowed along a physical network, built right into the infrastructure of the pyramid, from the capstone that crowned her to the ground beneath the pyramid. Then energies from Arran's body flowed directly into the King's chamber, the very chamber where he had been training, this was the focal point where all the energy from all over the pyramid was unified, amplified, purified and re-patterned, before being beamed directly upwards through the capstone to the apex of the pyramid and beyond. It was as if it had transported him into a raging waterfall as a fish, but as soon as the waterfall hit the turbulent waters below, it somehow filtered back into the very waterfall it had come from. The energy all around was surging through the pyramid, constantly, continuously, 'this pyramid worked' thought Arran. The revelation hit him like a Yak kick to the head.

Then and without warning, the multifaceted, multi coloured, energetic aspect of himself soared up from the capstone of the pyramid towards the sky, into a void of complete and utter darkness. Arran had a fleeting, yet distant comparison to the inner chambers of the pyramid before his consciousness and his thoughts merged seamlessly with the void, the sky, the wind, the mountains, the rivers, the land, the warriors' minds encamped throughout the valley and the citizens of Ali Ma Bar. Then light, great chasms of ever-changing, multifaceted, geometrical, three-dimensional light, in every colour, shape and pattern conceivable, embraced his full being and every sensory experience he could muster in this strange, ethereal, energetic space beyond time, space and physicality. He was, he knew, the universe, God, one with everything and everything was one, not absent from it, not external to it but always, all of it.

As Arran experienced an infinite bliss that lasted for, what felt like an eternity in the full spectrum embrace of the void, he noticed a small ball of glowing red light grow, before consuming all of his awareness. As it grew in size and stature, it became conscious, eyes appeared, two piercing red eyes entered his nonphysical, omnidirectional sight. With the being that was out in front, came a strange sense of danger, a similar feeling to that which Arran had experienced before his first trip on the golden mushrooms, the danger he felt when he realised, he was not the hunter but the one being hunted by the Cassartan. Behind the danger, he sensed fear, not his own fear but the red beings' fear, fear of loss, fear of imprisonment. Behind the fear, Arran seen a strange energetic chain, like the being was a mighty guard dog, chained to the sky. Then again, his omnipresent visual sense caught a brilliant ball of glowing white light, that again started small and grew until eyes appeared, two piercing white eyes appeared, it floated as the opposite and in balance to the red being. Again, it was chained to the sky in Arran's awareness. However, the same sense of danger that accompanied the red being stayed and intensified with the white being, and again, behind that, he sensed its fear and its tether to the sky. All around, Arran could feel his energetic body tingle as it slowly but surely leached away from him, like water being spilled onto a sloping table.

His very essence was being drank, consumed. Both entities smiled, both entities filled him with warmth and calmed his panicking mind. Arran fought the calm and then fled the beings with urgency. Fractals of light patterns emerged everywhere and as Arran's consciousness flew down unlimited pathways of energy and light, he had the unmistakable feeling that all his efforts were futile. Panic and fear grew as the unlimited options of escape opened to him in this unlimited space, continuously, time and time again bore no fruit, bore no relief from the fear, from the danger, from the red and white beings. Like an infinite prison that self-generated continuously to encapsulate the prisoner, the guards always being present was the last thought Arran had, accompanied with levels of fear he had never thought imaginable.

Arran's eyes opened with an almighty shock, his eyes taking time to adjust to the dim light above the capstone as he lay slumped against the capstone, staring mindlessly into the void above. Barratash and Anice stood over him. Arran began to sit up.

"Are you ok?" asked Barratash.

Arran just looked up blankly, his expression was vague, there was nothing behind his eyes.

"You were away for hours," said Anice as she reached out to Arran before continuing. "We couldn't find you in the mind space to communicate with you, you were blind to the overseer ability, it was as if your mind was no longer accessible, which is very strange as we have been dancing in each other's minds for months now and well, we panicked," said Anice.

Arran looked up, regaining his wits.

"I merged with the pyramid. It felt like only minutes had passed, yet I know I was away for years! I merged with God, with everything, with nothing, with the energies, with everyone, for all of eternity backwards and forwards. Then, I came upon a red energetic being and a white energetic being. These were both chained to the sky. I felt in grave danger in their presence, I tried to escape them but they were everywhere, and then I slowly lost awareness of myself and of the rest of the vision," said Arran.

"You merged with the pyramid? No one has been able to do that since the last golden age. The other bits. It sounds like you were being fed upon by the QUAF. The chains represent that the QUAF are prisoners here on this planet. But how is that possible? Your salt free, your vibration is high, are you sure you are recalling your vision correctly?" asked Barratash, with alarm and confusion in his voice.

"It was just a vision, it felt like the visions granted by the golden caps," laughed Arran, holding his hand up, showing the mushrooms, misshaped and moulded to the form of his inner fist.

"Your Golden caps, I have never eaten of their flesh, but I have experienced many herbal helper fuelled visions. They are never just a vision," said Barratash as he helped Arran back to his feet. The three overseers took a moment to look out over the valley as the rising sun brought everything back to life.

"I have encountered the QUAF many times," said Anice, to the shock of Barratash and Arran.

"Encountered?" queried Barratash.

"Ok, communed. You were in contact with the QUAF, that is for sure. Most Lanasian contact with the QUAF will experience the BUZZ, but once, I never heard the buzz. And that once was when I was close to death's door," said Anice.

"Why, would you have gone out of your way to have multiple contact with the QUAF?" quizzed Barratash.

"Life was not always this glorious. My youth was hard and very dark. Being brought up an overseer, or a witch as I was called, in a travelling brothel, I seen my fair share of pain. And in every brothel my mother worked in, the QUAF were present. The perfect feeding grounds, one may say. Over the years, as my gifts developed, they would communicate with me. And I with them. They are not all the same. There are thousands of different voices, groups and factions. They are curious, intelligent, devious, power hungry and very different from us. I believe they can present to us in whatever form we think will be best serve their purpose. To you Arran, it was the two opposing lights that you described from your original vision. They are crafty like that," said Anice.

"Wow, the student becomes the teacher. I would love to hear more of your experiences with the QUAF," said Barratash, with genuine zest.

"It would be my pleasure," said Anice.

"Tomorrow, you will train us. Until then, I will resume the role. Are you up to some training now?"

"I am," replied Arran.

"Yes," said Anice.

"Let us train some of your overseer abilities over short line-of-sight distance. Anice, Arran," Barratash stood in the middle of the two as they looked out over the Tanni and Namanagan armies amassed below, in the Valley of Ali Ma Bar. From inside Arran and Anice's minds, Barratash directed their vision towards a Tanni soldier, driving a horse and cart up from the eastern edge of the valley, around the perimeters of the outer walls, past the great flooded areas to the far east where the river meandered before hitting the solid cliffs of the eastern mountain that hemmed in the valley. The cart was pulling materials for the Tanni soldiers encamped on the southern side of Ashar bridge, the last open land defences against the Namangans. Barratash slipped into the driver's mind, subtly, anonymously, gently, his path in was quickly exploited and followed by Anice and Arran. As the cart driver continued forward, Barratash asked questions to his two apprentices.

"What is he thinking about? Emotional state? Where is he going? What does he think of the upcoming war? Who does he love?"

The answers flowed as mental images, emotions, voices and memories back to Barratash from both Anice and Arran as they performed the tasks asked of them.

"Now, make the leap, if you can, into the mind of his loved one. Then jump back," suggested Barratash to his apprentices.

An instance later the Tanni man, now known to the three as Alved looked up, looked back then erratically stood up, still holding the reins of the galloping cart, before letting go and jumping free, as he hit the ground hard, he rolled and was back on his feet, still running hard.

The communication between Arran, Anice and Barratash came thick and fast.

"We spooked him, he experienced the three of us inside his mind, he thought he was being possessed by the Namangan QUAFs that he keeps hearing people talk about. He panicked and jumped from the cart," communicated Arran, in one solid burst of information.

Simultaneously whilst transmitting to Anice and Barratash of Alved's reactions, Arran, with no thought for himself, only of saving the precious cargo that Alved was delivering to the Tanni soldiers on the front line and on pure instinct, reached out unconsciously, physically to lay his hand atop the pyramid. Instantly he felt the surge, 'Voosh, voosh, voosh' as it consumed him, he jumped back into Alved's mind, this time with tremendous force, overwhelming the Tanni man's panicked, chaotic instincts. As a wave of calm enveloped Alved's mind, he found himself moving, changing direction and sprinting hard after the run-a-way cart.

From inside Alved's mind, Arran heard Barratash's voice saying,
"You tried, but he cannot catch it".

In that instant, Arran pushed harder than he had ever pushed before. As he pushed, he filled Alved, filled every muscle, every fibre, every ounce of blood, with his energy. Arran was relentless, as he focused in and lost all notion of self as he joined with Alved's consciousness, as the two, with everything they had, chased the cart. Alved was now full of energy and, for a brief moment, felt like a god, like a Tanni of legend, like a super Lanasian. In the moments that proceeded the joining, the two minds inside the one body charged after the cart, before making a leap of over twenty vertical and thirty horizontal feet to land back on the cart, before taking it back under control. As Alved and Arran landed on the cart, they realised it was too late, they were going too fast. Up in front, in the path of the stampeding cart were a number of foreign soldiers, coming to join the Tanni ranks. Before the horse, cart and Alved could impact them, simultaneously Arran entered every one of their minds, over three hundred individuals and with his sight, manoeuvred everyone, instantly and simultaneously to safety as they, in mass ducked, dived, jumped and rolled out of the way of the carriage, as he worked with Alved to bring the rampaging waggon to a halt. Then Arran exited all of their minds as sharply as he had entered.

Back up on the hill, back in their own respective bodies, Barratash began to talk.

"What happened there? How did you do that? What did you do? You gave that cart driver energy, you gave him strength and power, you manoeuvred a hundred plus people from danger... It was amazing!" blurted Barratash.

"All I know is that we had the impression that Alved's supplies were crucial in Armon's plans for the defence of Ashar Bridge, and that I had to correct what we had done. Unconsciously, I was pulled by the pyramid to make contact and when I did, I just knew that I could do it, that I could physically strengthen a man with my abilities. Then, as soon as we were on the wagon, I knew I had to save the soldiers. It seems there is so much more to what we can do with these gifts." said Arran, as if what he had done was normal.

CHAPTER 36 - THE SOUTH UNITE

THE GREAT HALL WAS once again full of delegates from all of Lagosia, the room was loud, the passions were fierce. A lot had changed in the months since Vantis of Lerr had led his traitorous rebellion to the north. But everyone in this room was here on neutral ground, to discuss, barter and bargain once more, to secure their future in the upcoming mess that may or may not unfold.

Lathoran took to the podium and rang the gong.

"Hello my fellow Lagosians, please be seated for the day is about to begin," said Lathoran with a smile.

As the room slowly quietened, Vantis of Lerr took to the stage. As soon as he was noticed, the room erupted once more, hisses, boos, whistles and cheers filled the room. Cups and other projectiles accompanied the noise, Vantis ducked and parried all incoming projectiles, his head slightly bowed, as if acknowledging the projectiles' sentiments.

"Hello brothers and sisters, I am here today with some grave news, news that unfortunately took me a lifetime to reflect upon and realise. Truths that were hard to acknowledge. But true they are. My class, the ruling class, we give not two fucks about anyone but ourselves. I thought I was worthy of council, with The King in the North, but I found out like so many people I have slain or ridiculed over the years, that like them, I was not even worthy of an audience. The King killed his own delegation to create a powerful uniting force for his people to come south and conquer our home, Lagosia. We cannot let this happen." The emotion, the rawness, and the passion was all clear in Vantis's voice.

"Today, I stand before you, not as the wealthy Lerr you all know and either love or hate but as a fellow Lagosian, proud of the diverse culture, history, and peoples of the south. I am here today to persuade all of you in this room to join me in creating a unified army, a force great enough to repel any advances by the King," said Vantis.

As the crowd again erupted in both cheers and boos, the great hall doors opened, and in walked a hoard of Gavodeons. A familiar sight to all in the room, but so completely out of context and character, the Gavods never entered into the politics of the south. They traded, they moved, and they traded some more.

Rannoch walked through the hall, to his own rhythm, oblivious to all the eyes upon him approaching the stage, before walking up onto it.

The hall fell silent, Vantis and Rannoch exchanged words briefly. Then Vantis stepped to the side and Rannoch took the podium.

"Hello my fellow brothers and sisters, today I come to you with the gravest of requests. Up north, beyond the Aurd, in the city of Ali Ma Bar a great battle is about to be fought. I recently received communication that Summerian is amassing his largest army to date and that this battle will be the defining factor in whether Summerian, the King in the north comes south or not," the crowd booed.

"I am here to ask you to join us in going north. We need ships, weapons, supplies. We plan to travel via ship around Aurd's end, then take the river up to Ali Ma Bar. Our Mertak, who will be joining us, has requested this," said Rannoch.

The crowd laughed, jeered, and pointed.

"A fucking Gavod, entering the great hall and acting like he is a missionary from God. Hahah," shouted one man standing close to the podium.

Vantis stepped forward.

"I will hire every boat available at Aurd's End, I will head my own personal armies and the new united army we have been building and anyone else that wishes to come. If the Tanni are ready to fight and we can stop the Namangans north of the Aurd then this is the real chance we have been waiting for. Who is with us?"

Again, the hall erupted. Those that were for and those that were against. But one thing was clear, there were enough powerful players in the room to support Vantis and Rannoch's plan to send an army to the north.

CHAPTER 37 - ARMON AND THE WALLS

"REPORT!" SHOUTED ARMON.

"We have secured the Ashar bridge for the meantime, but our elite troops have not yet reported back from their mission to destroy the Antara bridge. Communications with our scouts to the east have the main bulk of the Tanni Ma Bar armies at just over one week away. However, soldiers, farmers, and many more from across the Namangan Kingdoms are arriving daily, signing up to fight with us against the Namangans. The Namangans themselves are staying put. We do not understand why, but they are, and with every passing week, their numbers are swelling--at last count they have over thirty units. Luckily the flood waters are still high and they are being forced to stay up in the north east of the valley, on the firmer ground."

"OK, good," said Armon. The room fell into silence. It lacked the energy of a war council, he thought. "My fake Namangans, come forward." The six Tanni, tasked with defeating Armon's strategy stepped forward. "Before you, are our plans, the Tanni plan. What have you come up with?"

The six Tanni looked over the table, picking up a few pieces, conversing rapidly between themselves, before finally, Aidena addressed the room.

"We struggled with this," she said as she looked to her fellow Namangan stooges, and to the wider room. "Everything the Namangans have done so far is unprecedented in our observations of Namangan warfare. Opening up negotiations for a peaceful surrender, a first in a new domain. Then their small forward army being pushed back and held by the non-surrendering city. Finally, no regrouping of strength before a quick retaliating attack, but a decision to stay put on the high ground whilst their numbers grow, squandering their own supplies, staying put, even when they begin to outnumber the opposing armies... another first.

"However, we think it is a possibility that the Namangans are looking for a large land victory, in open battle. We believe the whole Namangan war machine is simply waiting on the King. If they defeat us, then this would be the largest land victory the Namangan empire has ever achieved, as well as the final linchpin in controlling the north. History teaches us that he did something similar in securing Traveras, many years ago. Also, the floods have been even worse further north, this we believe is the reason the King is not here and why the Namangans are still camped."

"Ok, we know this," said Armon. "What are you going to do when the King arrives?"

"We are going to kill everyone," said Theodore from behind Aidena. The room erupted before silencing itself.

"Firstly, we have control and or access to both the Antara and Ashar bridges. We have not been sitting idle, we have stripped the north eastern forests bare and manufactured everything needed for open land and siege warfare. Initially, we will send two units totalling four thousand troops to control the eye, the high ground on the west side, as well as the western gate access, reducing any ability for the Tanni to use the western gate as a means of warfare, supplies or communication. Simultaneously, we will send two units up the steep eastern valley to traverse the treacherous terrain there before descending further south to destroy the Assante bridge, limiting its access to the Tanni Ma Bar armies, making it harder for Tanni Ma Bar to help Ali Ma Bar. Simultaneously, we will also use our superior war machines to decimate the Tanni armies camped near the Ashar Bridge. Soon after, we will secure the south side of the Ashar bridge. All this without incurring many losses on our side. Once the Ashar bridge has been secured, we will lay siege to the northern gate of Ali Ma Bar. From here, we will take our time, your supplies will dwindle and fear will sap your discipline and desire. We will poison your wells, cut off your food supplies, send you a barrage of deadly fire, decaying corpses and rats, all day and all night. Once the walls come down, we will enter. We will not stop until every Tanni bastard is dead. Man, Woman, Child, Baby, Cat, Dog, Horse," said Aidena embracing her role as Namangan war chief.

"Good, Good. Ok, so we need to secure the bridges, hopefully we will hear soon if our efforts to sabotage the Antara bridge has been successful. Depending on that success, we may need to deploy several units out towards the westerner valley to secure the high ground and the western gate. Assante bridge and the passageways to the east must be secured. We need access to

Tanni Ma Bar," says Armon as he moves the carved wooden troops around his map.

Aidena and the others nodded.

"I see a few options here," as he tapped the wooden pieces representing the northern Namangan armies.

"One, we secure the bridge, we limit their ability to enter the south side of the river. We do not want to give them the opportunity to make this a long siege, as they will win, eventually. We can hope that the floods stay high and they get bored and leave." Armon looked up and smiled.

"Two, we destroy the Ashar bridge and buy ourselves some time. The waters are high and it will take them time to construct a bridge over the river. Up north, beyond the Ashar bridge, before the terrain moves into the northern Aurd, there is only one more bridge. From here, it would take them forty miles to get back to the eye and the western side.

Three, we take the battle to them, we secure the walls with minimum numbers and then we look to fight the Namangans in open warfare. The hope is that we can kill the King and somehow their armies without their leader will just disperse." laughed Armon.

"The armies from Tanni Ma Bar are bringing some new weapons, a new javelin which we believe will give us the edge over the phalanx style of open land warfare, preferred by the Namanagans. Like most javelins, it is designed to pierce a body, but we have also designed these to penetrate shields, and once there, they are almost impossible to remove, hindering further and proper use of the shield, hopefully, allowing holes in their wall to appear. They are rarely ever met in open warfare, the Namangans have been so dominant for so long that they are now so used to siege warfare, they have rarely been tested in land warfare. That is their weakest game," said Armon, matter-of-factly.

The bustling energy of the room was momentarily interrupted when the main door was knocked and the guard entered. He closed the door behind him and walked directly up to Armon. Lifting his hand up to cover his mouth, he whispered.

"I have just been informed that the first unit leader, Elia Wilson, has just re-entered the top western gate. They successfully destroyed the Antara bridge, securing the Eye. However, she is not alone, she is requesting that her new allies from the north, a general by the name of Retishie and his two hundred soldiers be allowed to enter," said the guard.

At once, Armon's face twitched, his eyes burned brighter, and a smile formed across his face.

"Yes, yes, yes. Let them in and have Elia and Retishie escorted here as soon as you can," said Armon. The guard did not hesitate, he was spinning on his heels and making for the door in an instant.

"Ladies and gentlemen, it sounds like we have some new allies, and some good news. We have destroyed the Antara bridge. For the meantime, the Eye and the western side of the valley secured," said Armon with a smile.

"Hahahah," the laughter was loud and forced, the room breaking into smiles and chat at the fresh news. Armon however, turned towards Aidena and Theodore, who were still laughing.

"A mountain ravine to the Tanni is a severe challenge, but to us Namangans that come from the pine and needle mountains of central and northern Namanga, we have made ravine bridges there for a thousand years. In some places, we even knit them together out of grass! In other places they are as simple as a single rope. We do not fear the ravine, the mountains, the heights, we embrace them. We will have three new crossings across the Ali ravine by the end of the week. Guaranteed," said Aidena.

"True, I have read many tales of the terrain in the far Namangan north, of the rope bridges made of grass and their ridiculous tendencies to run towards fear, however most of the army," he tapped the map with his stick.

"Out there, on the northern side are not native Namangan, most are from the Namangan empire, or from the Namangan lowlands or cities. Times have changed, the hard northern bastards that built the empire are now few or soft from the spoils of their victories. Well, we can hope that they are few and that they are soft." Armon laughed.

The door knocked again and the same guard once again, made quick steps towards Armon, raising his hand up and whispered.

"I have a Barratash waiting at the outer office. He claims you know him and that......" the guard is cut short by a wave of Armon's hand.

"Yes, send him up at once," said Armon as the guard once again exited efficiently.

"So, it seems this night is getting even more interesting, brothers and sisters of the great Tanni empire, the leader in our very own brand of bat shit crazy, spiritual fuck wittery is gracing us with his presence, this should be fun," said Armon as a smile creped upon his face, his eyes creasing with enjoyment as he stared at the sisters of the sacred order. In that instant, Armon heard a powerful voice, an impossible voice, a voice that was not his, resonating deep inside his mind, "Thank you, we will be with you shortly," said Barratash.

Armon stood frozen in the middle of the bustling room, his stick resting on the northern side of the valley.

"It is true, the legends are true, there are mystical beings amongst us," thought Armon.

Again, from inside his mind, he heard Barratash's voice. 'Armon, keep control and keep calm, we are here to help.' The door opened again, this time Barratash, Arran and Anice walked in.

"Hello Barratash, now get out of my head and never enter it again without my permission," said Armon aloud, to the room's astonishment.

"As you are now understanding, there are many mystical arts, as you call them and some of them are indeed true, many are not," said Barratash as he walked further into the room, followed by the tall scruffy Gavodeon and the curvaceous and graceful Anice. In that moment, Barratash scanned the room for QUAF, to his amazement, the room was free from them.

"May I introduce to you, Anice and ..." Barratash was cut short as Armon closed the gap towards Arran.

"Good to hear the rumours are for once not true, you are alive, Arran, Mertak to all Gavods," smiled Armon as he shook the young man's hand, before turning to Anice and offering her his hand too.

"So, what other tricks can you do?" said Armon.

"Armon, we can enter many minds, we can gather intelligence, we can influence and we can keep the dead from being eaten," said Barratash.

"I am sorry for the intrusion," said Arran.

Then simultaneously, every voice in the room rang as one. "I can manipulate many minds as one," came the voice in unison.

"We can change the emotions of many," said Anice, as everyone in the room smiled.

'Child's play' broadcast Retishie to everyone in the room.

The door once again opened, Arran and Anice left the minds of those gathered. Armon stood and watched as an old man walked in, followed by the guard who had greeted them, followed by Elia, still bleeding lightly from her skirmishes with the Namangans. Then, in walked Nanoc, covered in dry blood and Mistress Loo, her white robes also covered in blood. In that moment, Arran crossed the room and embraced his fellow southerners.

"Ah, the young Mertak, the leader of all the Gavods, is here as well in this most monumental of times. A man true to his words. It is good to see you. It feels like it has been ages since we dropped you at the orchard, at Armon's request." Nanoc slapped Arran hard and affectionately, before, Arran turned to Loo and embraced her.

Retishie stood in silence, as did Barratash throughout the strange southern reunion in the heart of the Ali Ma Bar war room.

"Looks like everyone knows everyone?" laughed Armon as he stepped forward to shake hands with Nanoc and Loo, before moving back towards the map and the strategy board in the centre of the room.

"Ok, let us get some resemblance of order here. This day has turned into a strange, who's who of powerful folk that want the king dead," said Armon.

Retishie stepped forward towards Armon and addressed the room. "I am Retishie, my fighters are renowned throughout the many arenas of the north. This is Nanoc and my sister Mary Loo, we are here with two hundred of my finest warriors to join the fight against Summerian," said Retishie, the room began to chatter.

"Why did you broadcast child's play, as we demonstrated the overseer ability to Armon and the others of the war council," said Arran.

"Because it is child's play. The King is the most powerful, sentient being on this planet. If you think you can broadcast, control or plant seeds into the minds of his armies then you are greatly mistaken. He can make a thousand warriors fearless in an instant, he can and will imbue his generals of the sun with tremendous power. If we are to win this battle, we need to know how far you are willing to go. We need to know how many overseers are amongst us, how many warrior cast are amongst us, and how many energy dancers and hybrids, are amongst us. Only then will we be able to combine our powers against the King. And let me make it crystal clear, we need to kill the King or everyone here and everyone you care about is dead," said Retishie.

Nanoc found himself cheering with a light-hearted "Death to the King". Loo smiled and looked over to share the moment with Nanoc .

Barratash stepped forward. "In my experience, there is... archetypes of the original slave. The enforcers who became the warriors imbued with stamina, muscle, heart. The overseers who became the mystics, imbued with enhanced mental and psychic abilities. The Potents who became the energy dancers and healers, imbued with immense vitality and energy. The workers, the mass of all Lanasians, those who were blessed with life and who gave us everything of worth in our society, and finally the hybrids, direct descendant bloodlines who have a mixture of various archetypes and traits. Summerian is a full Tenni Uh Akki, from a warrior cast. But we can bind together. We can fight as one." said Barratash as the room listened intently, as if a subtle knowing of these archetypes had always been known or experienced in society.

"There is one other tool that we have, the pyramids. The Zaoists of the Highlands of Aromia, far to the north east had a pyramid, slightly different in design from the ones here in the south. Still, an ancient thing, built thousands of years ago during the last Golden era. The Zaoists believed that it was a time machine, as well as an advanced communication tool, built by the first people.

The pyramids, like the one found in Tanni Ma Bar etc are all surrounded in mystery and confusing folklore. However, the Aromia pyramid comes with a story that is inscribed directly into its walls. It tells of a time when a young singer, wearing the skin of a cat would become one with the pyramid, amplifying his powers, allowing him to fight the QUAF head-to-head in the ethereal dimension where they live," broadcasted Retishie, to an utterly amazed room. To most in this room, mystical arts, golden ages, QUAF and pyramids having a function was redundant chat for wackos and drunks. Now, we have tasted a glimpse of these strange mental powers, in a room where warriors of the various lands of Lanasia had somehow synchronistically met without direction or coordination by some impressive feat of coincidence, through a vast web of subtleness. Eyes were being opened to a possibility. 'The King and pyramid transmitters, as far-fetched as they once sounded, were now sounding possible, if not plausible' thought Armon.

"I am confused, we need to keep this simple and actionable if we are to defeat the Namangan army on our doorstep," shouted Armon, attempting to regain some sort of control over his war room.

From the silence created by Armon, Arran took to the centre of the room.

"I am Arran, Mertak and one day leader to all Gavodeons. Unfortunately, this is not a simple affair. I have travelled here from beyond the Aurd. I have met many people on my journey and experienced many strange and wonderful things. I have been told so many conflicting stories about the King, our origins, gods, QUAFS, the void, the Bar En Dough, the farm, death and more. I do not have the answers, I do not profess to claim what is true and what is not, or whether there even is a truth. All I know is that, if we wish to live and be free, we must kill the King, he is the only constant. Staying here, in this fortress, whilst thousands die, thousands of Lanasian brothers and sisters, is no solution. Meeting the King in open warfare is also not in the interest of the common man, who just wants to live, who does not want to die for another man's greed, legacy, lunacy or for the nourishment of some false god. I propose we challenge Summerian to a fight. Our champions versus his, winner takes all," said Arran confidently to the war room.

***

"Naïve," broadcasted Retishie into Arran's mind and in that instant, he felt Arran's raw power as Arran ejected him from his mind, with such force that the old hybrid stumbled backwards, before falling and being caught by Loo.

"How did you do that?" blurted Retishie.

"I just did, I just do," said Arran, plainly without emotion. The rest of the room acted like the strange interaction between the oldest and the youngest in the room was normal. The room was adapting fast to the strange and bizarre.

"If not one on one, then our best versus his best. We meet him on the open battlefield, we meet them in the middle, we defeat him. Release his men from any obligation. We then broadcast on mass, a truth and plant a seed to awaken, to leave the salts, etc. Then we join as one and fight the QUAF," said Arran.

"Kill the King, then fight the QUAF, what are they fucking feeding you young one," laughed Nanoc.

"A lot has changed Nanoc since you left me all those months ago. I accidentally started the rebellion, the fight back against the Namangans, by being stabbed. I was then trained by a master of the overseer ability. I have spent the time since we last seen each other vigilantly training my new abilities from the dark depths of a hidden pyramid, and now I believe I have awoken to my full potential. I have touched God, the void, the Bar En Dough, the QUAF, death, the depths of my own mind, as well as the depths of thousands of my fellow Lanasians' minds. Before I crossed the Aurd into this new life, I had spent my entire life accumulating vast quantities of information, categorising it, filing it away, making sense of it. With everything that I have experienced so far, I believe that the best way forward for all Lanasians, is to kill the King. This is his farm, we need to kill him and then find a way to starve the QUAF, but I am not sure starving the QUAF is as easy as we have been led to believe." said Arran, radiating like the leader he was prophesied to be.

"And killing the King is that easy. What's this talk of QUAFS and farms? What are you not telling me," blurted Armon.

"What do I know? Could you grasp what I know, if I were to tell you? Our understanding of reality is so very different. I will do my best with a twist on an old Ternakas piece of wisdom. If I were a slaver and I captured and took a Cassartan into the arena to fight, if I were to show it the bars, the brothels, theatre performances, religious ceremonies, grand buildings, roads, blacksmiths forging steel, before returning and releasing it back to the forests of the high Aurd. Now given that the Cassartan are a primitive society, living their entire lives in the forests and mountains, when asked by its fellow Cassartans "What was the city like?" It would answer 'the city was big, it was loud, it was busy, they made the ground of stone,' for they do not have any reference points, from which to describe the religious ceremonies or the musical performance or the roads, grand buildings, the culture, the society, the politics, the technology, etc. And with that in mind, if I were to tell you that..."

In that second, everyone in the room received a broadcast from Arran, precise, concise, and instantaneous, complete with images, sounds, smells and personal experiences.

'This is what I know. On one level we are GOD, we are energy, we are every-thing, we are infinity. And on another level, we are finite, we are contained, we are Lanasians. We live on a planet, deep in the void. There are other sentient beings inhabiting this vast void. Two of these beings, both of which are far older than us, pretend that they are our gods. They are not gods, yet they are a part of GOD. The first of these powerful beings, the original Tenni Uh Akki. They created us to work the Lanasian land, mining ores, precious minerals and for profit. At some point, our first job, 'the work,' must have been accomplished as the original Tenni Uh Akki left.

However, one returned, he now calls himself Summerian, and he has been here, on this planet ever since.

Our life cycles are short, we live for only seventy years, and from this perspective we never see the long game. This one who returned, he is the farmer. He is not the only immortal entity on this planet. His clients live here too. These are the beings of light that appear to us in visions, meditations, spirit quests, religious ceremonies, spiritual practice and magical rituals. They take many guises and in every form that they come; they are all the QUAF. They feed upon us. Day by day, they nibble upon us and when we die, they feast upon us. We are like yaks to them, as yaks are to us. And even if we know that we are on the farm, and that we are being farmed, and even if we can spot the farmer and the client for whom he works, we have eternally struggled to comprehend our situation. Our lives are short, and this compared to their's makes it easy for us to collectively forget our true history and quenches our desire to be free, in confusion. We come from the Original Tenni Uh Akki, made in their image, with their potential trapped inside.

In this time, in this life cycle, this original Tenni Uh Akki plays the role of a King. I am guessing that he has played many roles, over many generations, spanning thousands of years. I would wager that he is many of our great warriors and many of our great villains, one who appears in every great saga our combined histories have recorded. He is the farmer and the QUAF are his clients. I do not know what the QUAF trade for us, for the King must receive something in return, a farm of this complexity, on this scale, must have value.

So, what can we do? We can, with all our resources attempt to stop the farm and if we fail, we must communicate this message to the next generation, so they can at least have a fighting chance. In this, the cult of the pine have shown us how. But ultimately, we must kill the King to stop the farm, then we must starve or poison the QUAF to have any chance of gaining our freedom from this eternal prison. Many Lanasians will fall, but if we succeed, the generations after might live and die in freedom. We are fighting for our eternal souls; we are fighting not against other Lanasians, but against the oppressors. Freedom, by freedom I mean either entering the Nothingness on death or some entrance into the Bar En Dough under full consciousness. Freedom as in, not eaten by the QUAF when we die. This, I believe is the challenge that lies before us. This is the battle that we must fight."

Arran continued talking as if he had not casually broadcast an explosive information packet to everyone. "Would you have the reference points and experience to understand it?" asked Arran casually.

The room was visually split, there were those who had received and decoded much of which Arran had broadcast in that briefest of gaps before continuing his sentence and there were those that QUAF, ancient races, soul eaters, and the true fight of what happens at death had just simply flown directly over their head. For they did not have the reference points nor the experience to comprehend the information, and then there were those who just refused to accept information that was at a tangent to everything they held dear about the nature of reality.

Then, from the silence, Armon cleared his throat, rubbed his face, slapped his cheeks hard, as if he was awaking from a long night's sleep, filled with nightmares and began to speak.

"This day has been both fascinating and completely baffling. How do you know what you transmit is truth? I can't believe and will not believe everything that you overseers transmit, it is not in my nature. But you have my attention. Yesterday, I thought Barratash and his ilk were wastes of fucking space, now I realise that he has been fighting some unseen battle this whole time. For this, I commend you sir," Armon turned towards Barratash and nodded before continuing.

"The QUAF, have you attempted to communicate with them with your mind transmissions? And the King, have you tried him? And how far can you transmit, can you send it to our armies and their's? And this communication of information that must survive through time and communicate truth to the next generation, it has failed. Are we sure that is its purpose," laughed Armon, nervously, as if losing his sanity and everything that he held dear about reality, all in one lucid moment.

"I believe there is a way that we can rival the King on the battlefield. The rest will be down to our skill on the day," said Arran, looking at Nanoc and Loo.

"It is always down to skill on the day," grinned Nanoc. Arran nodded in acknowledgement and continued.

"The ancient Lerr religion of the Lerrians of Lagosia, up beyond the Aurd focuses on the trinity. There, life is about energy, proper mind and physical health. And a lifetime of practice to combine these three to balance and unity. Once that is achieved, anything is possible, even the ability to defeat the Vergen, which is their version of the QUAF. From this new perspective, I would like to try and unify myself, Loo and Nanoc into a warrior so strong, we are able to defeat the King and the QUAF. A trinity of the three archetypes.

CHAPTER 38 - THE KING ARRIVES

BEHIND GIAT, THE NOISE of the army was immense. Thirty units, sixty thousand men, women and children. Some were career soldiers, but most were conscripted. The King had now entered the northern camp, flanked by a sea of loyal subjects. The camped army cheered, drummed and blew horns, the King had arrived and soon, so would war.

The valley was now a campsite for the Namangan armies; the camp swelled and flowed outwards across the valley in every direction, wherever the ground permitted. Within hours, the seasoned campaigners amongst them had set up camps and began preparations for the showdown to come.

This was one of the largest shows of force the King had ever mounted. The day was late and before long, the valley was full of camp and cooking fires, dancing in the blackness of night, only the moon and dancing star for company.

As the King's modest tent was erected, Giat and Mariehoos waited patiently for a signal to enter and commune with the King.

The tent was modest, a bed, a wash basin, a pit latrine, a desk and a large central table with various maps and figurines. In the corner, a mannequin stood with the King's armour and next to it, a simple stand with his sword. No tapestries, no servants, no Vertomina, no luxuries of any kind. Giat's own tent was far more splendid, 'it was war, not hell' thought Giat as he entered.

As Giat and Mariehoos entered, the King gestured the traditional Namangan gesture for hello, Giat and Mariehoos reciprocated.

"Tomorrow, we go to war, make sure everyone is ready. How large are their armies? Report," said the King.

For a moment, Mariehoos forgot his place and began to speak, before correcting himself.

"Your Majesty, currently...Ahhhh. Old habits die hard. Please accept my apologies, your highness, Giat...?," prompted Mariehoos.

"Your majesty, currently they have around sixty units, twenty or so native of Ali Ma Bar, thirty from Tanni Ma Bar and around ten from the new influx they have been receiving steadily. Em sir... Can I ask you why you have allowed them to amass an army?" asked Giat, using every ounce of control to show no weakness in front of the King.

"Sometimes you need an opponent worthy of battle. Did you not wish for an opponent of your equal, is this not why you left Hetier and sought out the Namangan arenas? Is it not why you accepted my challenge, as warriors we like to test ourselves? Victory is always sweet, but it is sweetest when the battle won was against someone worthy of your time and sacrifice. No?" tested the King.

Giat nodded, he knew exactly what the King was saying. 'The King wants a challenge; and because of this, so many are going to die,' thought Giat, instantly regretting the thought and doing a quick inner ritual to retake his emotions.

"The only other thing to report is that Tanni riders entered camp under a flag of truce and left this letter for you." Giat pulled the letter from his belt and handed it to the King. The King turned slightly, flicked off the wax seal of the Tanni empire with his thumb, and shook the letter open. Then he began to read aloud, to Giat's and Mariehoos's surprise.

"We, the free people of Tanni, propose a winner takes all. We will put up our best warriors against your best. One solo or up to one hundred. This will limit the amount of life that has to be lost. Do you agree? Signed Armon, leader of the Armies of Tanni," said the King, bemused.

"Ah, the free folks of Tanni wish to limit their deaths, they wish for only a mere handful of their bravest to die, whilst the weak live off the backs of their hard work, like ticks. I do not think so. I have promised the QUAF a feast and a feast they shall have. Death will come to all the Tanni soon enough," said the King with a grin.

"Mariehoos, pen and paper. Write my words," Mariehoos moved over to the desk and sat, pen in hand, parchment waiting.

"I, Summerian, King of all Lanasia, grant you your wish. We shall meet in the centre of the battlefield two days hence. One hundred of your finest warriors versus one hundred of mine. Winner takes all. Make sure your people know that when you have been destroyed, they will lay down their weapons and bend the knee. If they do, I will spare them. Let the best side win," said Summerian, with another grin.

Mariehoos looked up, made eye contact with the King and invited him to sign the document, before rolling it up and sealing it with wax.

"After we destroy their finest, be ready to run through the rest of those bastards like a hot knife through butter. There will be no surrender for the Tanni that day. The date is set, in two days we will have our victory. Many thousands of Tanni will die, and then everything you know will change," laughed the King.

"Now Giat, if you would be so kind as to deliver my message to the Tanni's door," said the King.

"At once my lord," replied Giat, with a bow.

CHAPTER 39 - GIAT AT THE BRIDGE

"A GENERAL OF THE sun approaches the Ashar gate, with the white Namangan flag of open communication, I do not wish to enter his mind at this time and alert him to our overseer strength. I think we should go to the bridge and receive his letter," said Barratash, speaking through his thousand-yard stare.

"Nanoc, Loo, Arran, come with me, let us see what the King has to say to your proposal, young Mertak. Elia, ride south, take your most trusted warriors and determine who is upon those ships," instructed Armon.

"It is our brothers from the south," said Arran, with excitement.

"I have been impressed by the magic you few possess, but that does not mean I will let thirty years of military training slip. Especially in times such as these. If those ships are full of Namangans, the tide of this battle has turned. Elia, confirm that they are our friends. Take the names and descriptions Arran gave earlier and confirm their identities," said Armon, before turning to address the room.

"Everyone please continue with your tasks, there is still much to be done before the battle begins." Then Armon turned once again and headed towards the door, Nanoc, Loo and Arran following tightly behind.

The massive wooden cross bar that reinforced the door was lifted by four guards, the deadbolts were then released via a pulley system. The first gate was then winched open, its massive rack and pinion system only allowing the gate to open one click at a time. As soon as it opened fully, Arran, Nanoc and Loo followed Armon into the waiting chamber, most often called the death chamber as the outer portcullis rose slowly. Finally, the second door's deadbolts were released and then it opened.

'Odd how different the experience of entering the city when the gates were open and the people were flowing, was to exiting it' thought Arran, as the group that now formed an integral part of the Tanni war council walked the winding road downward, towards the Tanni armies, and the lone horseman standing by his stead on the Ashar bridge.

The journey to the bridge took longer than usual, Armon walked with pace but took the time to acknowledge the soldiers he passed, give comforting words, slapping backs and nodding with confidence. The monumental sight of Nanoc by his side, a foreign-looking warrior god, was well received by the subconscious confidence of every man and woman they walked past, Arran noted as he slipped into every mind he passed. This fascinated Arran.

As the four approached the bridge, Giat stood next to his horse, alone, muscular, powerful, self-assured. No weapon, just his flag and his letter. As Armon took lead and stepped forward onto the bridge, Giat began to laugh, shaking his head in bemusement. Armon looked round at Nanoc, Loo and Arran for some sort of explanation.

"We have met this Heitier before, his name is Giat. He is a King's General but he could be an ally. We met him with a member of the cult of the pine, Barratash's people, who was his friend." said Loo as she pulled out Giat's seal from her inner shirt and waved it at Nanoc. Arran kept quiet, observing the conversation, observing the three as they all moved closer to the Hetier warrior, who stood at the centre of the bridge.

"No rain, it has been a good few months in the works," laughed Giat as the four Tanni representatives approached the last ten feet.

"Ok, that's close enough," said Giat.

The four stopped. The rain may have stopped as well here in the lower valley of Ali Ma Bar, but it had no bearing on the volume of water that was now pumping down the river, directly under their feet. The multiple archways of the Ashar bridge that usually stood thirty feet clear of the river now stood only five to eight feet clear. The noise of the river as it embraced the supports of the bridge was loud, turbulent, violent and hard to hear over.

"I am Armon, first son of the Tanni. Are you delivering your reply to our proposal?" shouted Armon.

"I am, the King's reply is here," said Giat as he waved the parchment in his massive hand.

"Giat, why do you still serve the King? You have experienced the QUAF attempting to eat the soul at death first hand. How can you still serve the King? Make the right decision. Join us," shouted Loo.

Giat let out a laugh, a strong, long, genuine laugh.

"I have made my bed; this is my lot in life. There always has to be at least two sides to truth, to war. If we win, my daughters will be safe, their lives will continue without disruption. If we lose, my daughter's lives will be harder, without me and without my protection, their lives will most definitely change for the worse," said Giat passionately.

Arran stepped forward, "If you have experienced the QUAF at death, then you must realise that your motivation for choosing the King's side is wrong. For if you win or lose this war, your daughters will still have to face the QUAF one day. Would you not rather they enter the warm embrace of the nothing, of GOD, when they die? How could you not desire that for your daughters? Join us. We are planning to kill the King and then defeat the QUAF. I plead with you sir, join us," said Arran, standing shoulder to shoulder with Armon, only feet away from Giat at the centre of the bridge.

Giat began to laugh, and as he began to talk, the laughter spilled out into his words.

"Killlllll the QUU ahahha uaffffffff, what have you been smoking young man? They are fucking gods, true gods. The kind of Gods that live for eternity. They live in the sky, in the mountains and in the rivers. You cannot kill the Gods. You can only appease them and hope that they show you leniency when it's your turn to meet them," said Giat, with a seriousness that took over from his laughter.

"They are not Gods, they are customers, they are the King's customers. They do not have another option; the King is their only supplier. He controls the market. He controls the life and death of the Namangans, as a product and he has forced them to respect that agreement with some carrot, that I have, as yet not fully understood. It is your choice, we can either work as one people to starve the QUAF, like our ancestors done before, or we can fight and die on the battleground. No matter which side wins that battle, the King and the QUAF will win that day, and for all the days following, unless we find another way to defeat him and the QUAF," shouted Arran.

"Well fuck me sideways, you wee shit-stirring know-it-all. You think it is as easy as killing the King and starving the QUAF? And then we all just walk off, hand in hand, into bliss? Wake the fuck up, kid. Unlike you, I have faced the King, and no mortal man is killing him, not today, not tomorrow and definitely not in two days' time in the middle of that dammed field," sneered an angry Giat.

"It has been done before. The age of golden, thousands of years ago, during the time of the pyramid builders, the time before Summerian. We, the united people of Lanasia, defeated the QUAF. We had almost starved them into extinction. But Summerian returned, and broke our people, reintroduced war and greed, hid our knowledge, our truths, drugged us on mass, and now we have a chance, once again to defeat him, and defeat them. It won't be easy but we have to try, we have to try for all of them." Arran swept his arm out, pointing at the southern armies, then to the northern armies.

"I have felt the Bar En Dough and I want to join you more than I can say, but the King, the King is too powerful. Ah, enough of this horseshit," Giat launched the parchment with impressive control, the perfect throw, and Armon caught it effortlessly.

"We will meet you on the battlefield north of the river, one hundred of your best versus one hundred of ours. Winner takes all. You have the King's word and I will enforce it. Time for less mumbo jumbo and more action. I will see you on the battlefield, Nanoc. I look forward to the challenge," shouted Giat as he remounted his horse and rode across the bridge.

"Well, that went well," laughed Nanoc as he watched Giat's horse ride off to the end of the bridge before moving slowly over the softer ground and disappearing from sight, behind his entourage.

"I rather liked that man the first time I met him, I feel slightly saddened that I will have to kill him soon," smiled Nanoc.

The four stood at the centre of the bridge, taking time to look out over the Namangan armies to the north.

"So, you believe this is not a simple Tanni vs Namangan, the people vs the King. You believe this is once in a lifetime battle for our very souls. So, if we kill the King, how do we defeat the QUAF?" asked Armon, somewhat amused at what he just said.

"I believe the answer is in the pyramid, it can give us the ability to broadcast a powerful message across the entire battlefield. Then, as we build more, potentially we will be able to broadcast across the entirety of all lands. But as Giat just proved, knowing some truths is one thing, believing that the King can be killed, and we can defeat the QUAF is another. The pyramid can give me the ability to contact the QUAF, I have experienced them via it once before. But I have been too scared to try since, but just like the darkness on the first night of Mertak, I will conquer it," said Arran, self-belief returning again.

"Contact the QUAF," said Loo, realising he was pulling strength from some event in his past.

"Yes, we understand what the King wants, but I think we should talk to the QUAF directly and see what role they really play in all of this," said Arran.

"Rather, you than me, lad," laughed Nanoc. "Aye, that is some real wizard shit right there. I'm just off to merge with my pyramid, then mentally connect with the demonic, soul-devouring gods that have been eating the souls of our people for all eternity, to ask them to give it a break. I'll be back soon, don't let my dinner get cold," laughed Nanoc.

"It definitely seems like the weight of the world is bearing down upon your shoulders, young Arran," said Armon.

"I believe in you," said Loo, quietly listening and observing up till now before continuing.

"We have some monumental challenges upon us, kill the King, defeat one hundred of his finest in open warfare, contact and negotiate with the QUAF. The latter, I have no answer for, you are on your own their Arran, but the other part. Can we handle it, can we defeat one hundred versus one hundred, sure? I am confident. But can we defeat the King? Giat was convincing, and he is a seasoned arena champion!" said Loo.

Armon was still looking out over the northern armies, waving his hands, drawing imaginary lines across the terrain before turning to Loo, Arran and Nanoc once again.

"If we defeat the King, or if the King defeats us, we must be ready to fight our armies, one against the other. If he defeats us, he will not stop. If what I hear is correct, that he is some sort of farmer that supplies our souls to his customers, then all of this makes sense." Armon looked out, waved and gestured at the grand sea of Namangan armies camped to the north.

"This is a great harvest; this is debt being paid. A contract being fulfilled. This is a feast. I do not believe the King has allowed us to a mass such a strong opposition, nor broke with traditional battle tactics for any other reason. He plans a blood bath. He is confident that he will defeat our best, then as the will of our army is broken by it, he plans to slaughter everyone before expanding south. It's the only thing he knows, it's the only logical understanding at this point," said Armon.

"But if we kill the King, if we kill him dead, then Arran broadcasts his seed to everyone, it may be enough of a shock to stop everyone in their tracks. To make everyone see it," said Loo.

"If I can open one, I can open them all. We will kill the King," said Arran defiantly. Arran then pivoted and looked out at the Namangan army and the red haze that now permeated the camp, the haze of the QUAF, as he had now come to understand it.

"Sorry," said Arran.

As he continued his stare out over the battlefield, Armon's mind was seized by the vice like grip of Arran's. Instantly, Arran projected Armon's mind through Arran's eyes, through Arran's sight, beyond the physical. In that instant, Armon seen the battlefield, he saw the clouds of red, the individual eyes, the mass coalescing as one; he heard them buzz. He experienced the QUAF. Then Arran left his mind.

Armon stood motionless, looking out over the Namangan camp.

"If I can force one to see them, I can force them all to see them," said Arran.

"I do not know what you did, but if everyone has to go through that for us to live a life of true freedom, then as brutal as it was, it is a small price to pay," said Armon, still looking out over the Namangan battle field.

"We will need to fight as one," said Arran to Nanoc and Loo.

Both Nanoc and Loo looked at Arran, as the young nomad that they first met was no longer. The leader of men, the Mertak had arrived and they could feel it.

"We need to fight as one hundred, we need to get back there, pick our best and make a plan," said Nanoc.

"No, I mean, we have to fight as one. I mean you Nanoc, you will fight, you are the one, you will kill the King. And myself and Loo will assist you. We, the three of us, need to fight the King as one, simultaneously, in unison, my mind, your body and your energy. That is the only way we stand a chance against the King," said Arran.

"Agreed," said Loo.

"Well, if you want me to stand in the centre of the battlefield and go toe to toe with the King, then I am game. Shit, that's the reason I fucking came here. Now we are talking," shouted a very energetic and excited Nanoc.

From a long, strange, trance, Armon emerged transformed, like a butterfly from its cocoon.

"Nanoc is right, we need to return and prepare." Armon turned towards the Tanni side and began walking towards the three southerners. As he passed them, they followed. As they left the bridge, entering the Tanni camp, the rain began again.

CHAPTER 40 - ARRAN AND THE QUAF

As THE FOUR RE-ENTERED the inner-city walls, Arran turned to Armon, Loo and Nanoc.

"We will train tonight, see if it is possible to combine our mind, body and energy for battle with the King," said Arran, calmly, with authority.

Then from inside their minds, he broadcast to them, 'I must go now and attempt to contact the QUAF, as soon as I have any information, I will return to the war room. I will see you soon my friends.'

Arran smiled at the three warriors, closed his eyes, lowered his head and turned sharply, before moving off at pace, towards the north-eastern district and the Law hill.

As Arran ran off, in the pyramid's direction, all three of the seasoned warriors in their own way, gave thanks and wished Arran strength.

'It feels good returning to the pyramid,' thought Arran. It was, after all, the closest thing he had to a home, or something he could identify as homely, even familiar here in this still foreign land. As he reached the top of the pyramid, he noted the difficulty of the climb and the fact that it did not grow easier with repetition. Yet, he was happy. In front of him was the capstone, out across the northern valley is where they had met with the King's representative, and now he must travel to meet with the QUAF, if that was even possible.

Arran lay back and touched the capstone. He slowly sat down and rested his back against the capstone and concentrated on the QUAF. The now familiar voosh began, instantly he was ripped from his body, his mind floated free up above the capstone. As he looked down, across the valley with his ethereal eyes, he could see the QUAF everywhere. Unlike the last experience with the pyramid, this was not a vision-like experience, he was fully lucid, fully in control. 'That's a relief' thought Arran. 'Well, here goes nothing' he said to himself. And with his will, he flew straight toward the QUAF.

Like almost all the strange events that Arran was now a part of, he took flying in his ethereal form, in his stride. The whole nature of reality, as he knew it, was really bound to a physical body. Here, in this strange, ethereal dimension, everything was different. Colours, smells, touch, time, thought, boundaries between consciousnesses. There was so much to learn.

"I am here to talk to the QUAF, I am Arran, Mertak to all Lanasians. Speak with me," broadcast Arran into the conscious cloud of coalescing red. Instantly the buzzing began, instantly it filled his head with the echoes of a million or more independent voices, all vibrating as one. The buzzing grew louder and louder as the red mass swarmed around him.

"We are hungry," came the collective voice of the hive as they moved in around him, millions of them latching onto his ethereal form. In one massive push, Arran sent out a scream as he visualised himself cutting the QUAF anchor points from his ethereal being.

"I am not your meal," screamed Arran, as the massive cloud repulsed back from him.

"I am here to speak, to trade," broadcasted Arran.

The buzz grew louder once again. The hive was fluid chaos; it was factions upon factions; it was unity and discord; it was beyond intense; it was extraordinary.

"What does the King have over you?" broadcasted Arran.

"The King has nothing over us," came the buzz of the hive.

"So why do you feed upon us? Why do you not feed upon the Anti Mass Voiders?" asked Arran.

The buzzing grew even more chaotic, then returned to calm, before erupting again and again.

"The Yak does not speak to the Gavod," buzzed the largest faction of the hive. Then, almost simultaneously a smaller, yet more dominant faction began to buzz.

"Does the Yak know it is a steak, that you farm it on mass for its milk and meat? How do you feel about this Lanasian?" buzzed another faction of the hive.

"We don't want your souls, we don't want your energy, we want AMVs. Can you imagine a thousand lifetimes feeding on only milk? You would be weak, your bellies would scream for sustenance, for meat and vegetables, fruit and grains, spices and sweetness. We do not want more milk," buzzed yet another faction of the hive.

Then the first faction of the hive re-emerged. Its collection of buzzes was unique, identifiable, like a voice within the swarm.

"We will soon, after the battle, after we fill the hive with the scraps from Summerian's table, eighty of us will leave through the King's gate and again, we will do what Gilanite designed us to do," came the buzz of a million minds. The buzz conveyed authority, happiness, duty, unhappiness, possibility, conflict. It was the most bizarre communication that Arran had ever experienced.

"We farm many animals, but we must live?" said Arran.

"So must we," replied the many factions of the hive.

"Does the yak know that its life serves one purpose and one purpose only?" said one of the smaller factions of the hive.

"OK, I get it, everything eats something. Is there a way that all of you can leave and get to the AMV's. Why only eighty, there are millions of you. Why don't you all go?" asked Arran.

"Summerian controls the King's gate," came the buzzing in union. Anger, fear, loyalty, and hatred swept through the hive in waves, like a living, breathing firestorm.

"What if the King were to die, what would happen to the gate?" asked Arran.

"The King's gate must be opened by the King, he alone controls the gate," came the smaller, dominant faction again.

Arran felt the QUAF direct his mind towards the dancing light in the void sky.

"That's his power," said Arran.

"The gate, the King's gate, eighty must enter after the feast, one hundred want to go, but only eighty, then the gate will shut," buzzed the hive.

"If I kill the King and open the portal, will you all leave, all one hundred?" asked Arran as the hive grew with excitement.

"Is one hundred all of you? One hundred percent of you or one hundred factions of your hive," asked Arran.

"We want nothing more than to leave this place. We are hungry. Your energy is bad, the Anti Mass Voiders is good, unlimited, boundless, infinite. We have been locked here to this planet for an eternity," buzzed the hive with undertones of sadness and anger.

"If you do not feast on the dead, if you stand back and allow my brothers and sister free passage to the Bar En Dough, I will find a way to keep the portal open long enough for you all to leave. Deal?" asked Arran.

"We do not feast on your dead; we survive on your dead," came the loudest faction of the hive.

"One hundred, deal, if not we will eat every last one of you, then eighty will leave," buzzed the smaller more dominant faction of the hive. The hive began to hum and buzz, the QUAF were very excited.

"Deal," broadcasted Arran.

The silver umbilical cord that connected him with his physical body lit up like an electric snake and in that instant, he was back in his body, sitting atop the great pyramid of Ali Ma Bar. As Arran's eyes opened once more to the physical world around him, he looked up at the lone dancing star, high up above in the sky and knew he had to make contact with the King.

'If I contact him from here, he will know of my potential amplified by the pyramid. What if he already knows of my power? What if the QUAF tell him?' The questions, the doubts, the paranoia came thick and fast. It was as if echoes of the energy the QUAF had been feeding on, had somehow entered into his mind.

'I must communicate with the King, I must show my strength, I must be cocky, confident, sure and I must make sure he does not see through the illusion. Make it a deal for him to add the portal to the table," thought Arran.

Arran jumped to his feet and began running down the side of the Law hill. His feet were going so fast they were almost coming away from him. After a short while, he was once again at the Northern gate. Without Armon though, exiting was not so straightforward. After a few moments of respecting and entertaining the guards at his expense and still being refused passage through the gate, Arran took measures into his own hands. In one seamless broadcast, every guard around the gate jumped into action, like puppets being played all at once. The beams, the gate, and the portcullis, one by one were opened by the strange autonomous soldiers under Arran's control.

"Sorry," said Arran as he began running towards the outer gate.

This time, he did not wait to be asked for papers, to be refused permission to exit. This time, he quickly entered the minds of all those around and again forced the gates open.

Then again, he was off, charging down the steep road outside the walled fortress of Ali Ma Bar. As he approached the camp of Tanni soldiers, he observed that they were now a collection of soldiers from all over, strange ethnic groups he had never encountered before as he ran past them, following the same path he had taken earlier. As Arran seen the Ashar bridge once more, he recalled the vision of Giat, standing there upon it and with everything he had, he began to reach out to Giat's mind, on the off chance that he would be in the vicinity of the King, he was in luck.

"I am Arran, Mertak to all Lanasians," came the voice as it ripped its way out of Giat's mouth, Arran fighting hard for every syllable.

The King turned from his desk, where he sat musing over military maps and documents. Instantly, he began his inner rituals.

"I am Arran, Mertak to all Lanasians," came the voice from Giat's mouth, this time more fluent as Arran dominated the inner battle against Giat for complete control of the warrior's mind.

"You are Mertak to all Lanasians, how interesting Giat," said the King, mocking the intruder.

"In two days' time, we will meet, winner takes all. I have heard you are a betting man; your Namangan empire is built on the bets of other men. I wish to make a wager," said Arran, using Giat's eyes to look directly into the eyes of the King.

"A wager, you have nothing to wager with. Everything you know, everything you think you know, everything you could ever know, is mine. You have nothing to wager with." The King, keeping Arran's gaze, began to laugh as he probed the perimeters of Arran's mind. Arran stopped running, he had made the Ashar bridge, he stepped up onto the bridge and grabbed onto the railing.

"You have my full attention now," said Arran as he pushed back against the King's mind. The King was now pushing past the edge of his mind's awareness, before continuing.

The King was strong. Arran had repelled Barratash, Retishie, Anice, Giat but the King's mind was different. As Arran met him in an invisible battle, here in his own tent, doubt, fear and pain slowly burrowed into his mind. The King's mind was slowly, yet surely making inroads to his mind, like icy fingers that burned as they penetrated deeper and deeper.

"I wager the QUAF," proclaimed Arran in a strange fit of desperation and then just as the King's attack had begun, it stopped.

"You can't wager the QUAF, they are mine," said the King, with a snort.

"They are not yours; they are your client. You have a simple business relationship with them. If we win this battle, we will win that contract. Winner takes all," said Arran with confidence, he was in his element now, a life of trading and bartering had trained him well. There was no weakness, no bluff, no false claim detectable in his voice as it left Giat's mouth.

"Hahahha hahahha, in all my years. Never has someone been so bold, never has someone been so forthright." The King stood and shook his head, a large grin adorned his face as his head and shoulders moved in the rhythm of his laughter.

"The portal to the void, the one the QUAF call the King's gate. If we win, if we kill you, the portal lets through all of the QUAF. If you win, well, you do as you wish. But at least it was a bit more exciting, I guess," said Arran, with nothing more to offer.

The King's right hand came up to his face, his eyes closed as he began to rub his beard. Gentle and thoughtful, when his eyes opened, he pushed hard at Arran's mind. On receiving the attack, Arran tried his very best. He pushed back as hard as he could, but it wasn't enough. Pain flooded his awareness, an unimaginable pain searing through his senses, lighting up every sense with agony. His blood boiled, his skin burnt, his bones exploded, his ears rang, his tongue burned with the most violent spice, the brightest light blinded his sight and the foulest smell permeated his nose, on and on it went. Full sensory domination. On the bridge, his hands gripped the railing as hard as he could as his body began to fit.

Arran, on the very edge of conscious control, pushed back with everything he had; nothing was held back but it was futile. The King's mind was like nothing Arran had encountered, it was vast; it was fortified, it was focused, it was anchored. Then Arran felt Giat's mind break free of Arran's leash. He was no longer fighting him; he was now assisting Arran, then from the outer realms of his awareness, like ghosts on the wind, he felt the pain ease as Barratash's mind, Anice's mind, Retishie's mind, Lopsangy's mind, and the mass of the unified Majii warriors joined the fight. Then, he felt Rannoch's mind, as the old shaman's body slipped in behind him on the bridge, linking his arms under Arran's armpits, his hands gripping the railing tight, allowing Arran's body to let go of the rail and slump into his arms.

The many minds worked in union; the many minds pushed hard against the pain of Summerian's attack. Then it stopped. The King's mind stopped attacking and Arran, once again, looked through Giat's eyes, this time with Giat's permission. The King looked directly at Arran, with such intensity he thought he felt him physically. In front of the King, a strange opaque glass-like apparition appeared, various symbols flashed on and off, then as quickly as it appeared, it disappeared.

"You have your deal, young Mertak. The portal is set to open in two days' time. If you win, you get everything you've asked for. Just promise me you fight this hard on the battlefield. I want to remember you in years to come, as I build future farms. Your story will live on for millennia. The bold Mertak, the powerful overseer that challenged the King for the world and lost. I will do wonders with that," said the King.

"How do I know you will keep you word on death?" said Arran, through Giat's mouth.

"Hahaha, if I die, the portal will open and the QUAF will leave without me to limit their exit. If I live, the portal will open and I will limit their exit. For the ultimate prize, you must take the ultimate risk. I look forward to doing battle with you," said the King as he bowed with a genuine respect. As Arran left Giat's mind, he apologised for this most sacred of violations, before his mind had left Giat's, Giat's head rolled from his body.

CHAPTER 41 - THE PLAN IS FORMED

As Arran looked up, Rannoch stood over him smiling. As their eyes met, their minds met and Arran cried. As he did, a great warmth flooded his body. The old shaman's admiration, love and acceptance could be felt in every fibre of his body. As Rannoch helped Arran to his feet, soldiers stood around looking at the strange nomads, a young man, and an ancient relic.

Then the small crowd parted as Nanoc stepped through, placed his hand on Rannoch's shoulder and with one swift motion, hoisted Arran up into his arms and turned. Arran fell back into unconsciousness.

***

As the massive warrior walked towards the waggon that was just arriving, Arran in arms and Rannoch two steps behind, his anger grew at the Tanni army as they mucked around, pointing, laughing, jeering. To them, the scene was wholly bizarre. It unfolded with the strange-looking, hairy nomad that had earlier accompanied the first son of the military himself and his strange uncoordinated run through the very heart of the Tanni camp. He then continued toward the bridge, before stopping to attack it. From their perspective, it looked like he was at war with the bridge, trying his very hardest to rip the banister from its berth. Then, after struggling for twenty minutes, he lost the battle with the banister before being assisted by yet another stranger, hairier nomad. Now, his unconscious carcass was being lifted onto a cart by a huge warrior, again one who had accompanied Armon earlier that day. Months of sitting by the campfire, readying for a battle that had not come, this had been the best entertainment the soldiers had had in ages, short-lived and strange as it was.

"If only you knew the sacrifices this lad has made for you," said Nanoc quietly as he lay Arran's still unconscious body on the cart.

As the cart pulled away, up towards the main city, Rannoch and Nanoc sat with Arran until he regained himself. By the time they entered the city walls, Arran was sitting up once again. Now that Arran was awake, the waggon picked up speed.

***

"FEELING BETTER, LAD?" ASKED Nanoc, genuinely concerned for the young Mertak.

"I am, thank you," said Arran as he looked at Nanoc and then to Rannoch, still in shock that the leader of the Gavodeon nation now sat by his side, here in the northern lands, beyond the Aurd.

"Rannoch, thank you," said Arran.

"Hush now my son, rest, recover. I am not going anywhere," said Rannoch, with a warm smile.

"Now the next time you want to go off and fight the King one on one, how about you don't. That's my fucking job," blurted Nanoc, with frustration born from protection, covered with a laugh.

"You will have your chance to fight the King soon enough Nanoc, soon enough," said Arran with a smile that conveyed the weight of a million souls upon it.

As the cart arrived at the entrance of the war room, the four southerners exited the cart and made their way up to the war room.

As they entered the room, Retishie, Barratash, Armon, Anice and a few others clapped. Most stood in silence, unaware of what they were clapping at. Then Armon took to the centre of the room.

"Once Arran is ready, we will hear what the QUAF, and the King had to say. Until then, we need to decide who our finest one hundred warriors are. Please prepare your recommendations," said Armon.

The war room was now busy with representatives from each of the major nations, houses, clans, factions that now made up the oppositions, Tanni, Traverans, Hetiers, Namangans, Gavods, Lerrians, Biergyens and more. Each put forward their best warriors, each willing to sacrifice all against the opposition.

From the crowd, the new arrival, Vantis of Lerr, stepped forth, "I have brought many warriors from the south," said Vantis.

"I thank you," said Armon.

"I have brought five of the finest warriors of all of Lagosia. We wish to be part of the one hundred," said Vantis.

"Unfortunately, we have no prior knowledge of your skill, and in these times, we must make sure we send only our very best. We appreciate the south's assistance and in the battle that follows, we will need every one of your men," said Armon, the stress showing in his voice and his demeanour.

"Armon," said Nanoc.

"If this is Vantis of Lerr, then we should be honoured to have him and his men be part of our one hundred. His brother was a magnificent warrior, and Vantis was his senior. They are one of the few real nation-states of the south who have a full-time army. He has trained since birth. As good with a sword as he is with a pen. I vouch for this man and the calibre of his men," said Nanoc, as he nodded towards Vantis.

The room weighed up and finalised the one hundred. Each name was hand-written to a board and displayed next to the topographic map of the battlefield, their skills etched beside their name.

As normality returned to the room, the door once more opened. In walked twenty-nine cloaked individuals, silently, uniformly, sucking in the surrounding atmosphere. Armon raised his sword.

"Stop, who are you?"

"We are the Magii and we are here to assist Arran," said the group as one, twenty-nine voices, in perfect synchronicity.

"Good to see you again, good to have you here," said Barratash.

"The Magii? The who? And how do you plan to assist?" said Armon, sword slightly lowered.

"We are no threat, Armon; we are of The Pine. Each one of us is a former student of Barratash. But we have militarised the overseer's ability. We are warriors of the mind. We have many skills that you will need. For example, we have been shielding the city from the King's overseers for months now," said the group as one.

"Ok, I can work with that," replied Armon.

"Armon, I will not be joining you on the battlefield, I wish for Rannoch, Anice, Lopsangy and the Magii warriors to join me," said Arran.

"The Magii warriors will join with you when the time is right," said the group as one.

"We need to kill the King, it is the only way we win," said Arran.

"That's the plan, lad," laughed Nanoc.

Arran smiled at Nanoc as he took a few steps towards Armon, in the centre of the room.

"Today, I merged with the pyramid and made contact with the QUAF." In that instant, the experience was broadcasted to everyone in the room.

"Then I took over one of the King's General of the Sun's minds and bartered directly with the King," again Arran broadcasted to the room.

"Everything relies on killing the King, that should be our only play, it should be one hundred versus one," said Arran to the room. Most folk in the room were still grappling with the young Mertak's broadcasts, half were in shock and half were in awe. Reality and the strange war they had entered into was now strange beyond measure.

"I will join with the pyramid and then with Nanoc and Loo and between us, we will fight the King energetically, physically and mentally simultaneously. He thinks he has the better of me, he is wrong. We will kill him, we have to," said Arran.

"I agree we must fight the King mind against mind, steel against steel, energy against energy. I propose that I lead the attack. For I am the only man alive who has ever defeated the King in physical combat. Yes, I was in my prime and yes, I stand no chance of recreating that feat. I also held off his mind for months. The King is a sentimental fool and he will love the fact that we have rested our entire hope on an old warrior that had once defeated him. I will surely die, but I have lived a good life and have been reunited with my sister once more. But before I die, you will see a truer glimpse of his abilities against me, than against any other foe. That will be your one and only chance to learn and prepare for your joint attack," said Retishie.

The room broke into dialogue; the names were listed, a resemblance of a plan was formed, all that remained was a day to prepare, and then the final battle for the soul of every Lanasian would be upon them.

CHAPTER 42 - THE BATTLE

FROM ATOP THE PYRAMID, Arran, Rannoch, Anice and the Magii warriors could see the one hundred strong contingents of the allied armies begin their slow march over the Ashar bridge. Behind them, the rest of the Tanni army followed. From their vantage point, the grass slowly turned red, brown and grey, with occasional sparkles of sunlight reflected from sparse pieces of polished armour.

It was noon by the time the armies had entered into position; the sun was high above; the rain had stopped the day before and sky was now clear, possibly the first clear blue sky that the numerous men and women of the valley had seen in months. Surely an omen to all who seen it as such.

From the northern side, a solo figure walked out to the centre ground between the two great Armies. Flanked by ninety-nine of his generals of the sun, each a decorated, royal Namangan arena champion, each to varying degrees able to control aspects of their energy and the overseer ability. Each wore a uniform of the finest lightweight armour, opposing them by comparison, stood a rabble.

At the centre of the opposition stood Armon, with his traditional Tanni armour and long curved sword. To his left, the great Retishie, wearing a lightweight chain mail and similar curved sword. To his right, stood the mass of Nanoc Ranoh, claymore sword in one hand and a small spiked targe shield in the other. To his right, stood Mistress Loo, with her long-curved sword, similar to Retishie's. To her left, stood Vantis of Lerr and the five warriors of Lerr, all in full suits of lightweight armour, every piece reflecting light. Each stood with their claymore sword and shield. Behind them, stood hordes of warriors, weapons ready and there, in amongst them all, stood Barratash, unarmed, eyes closed, ready to assist all.

Arran stood by the apex of the pyramid, careful not to touch it. He relaxed, looked out over the battlefield in front, took a last breath, and dived straight into the first of the King's entourage. One by one, he entered the minds of the Generals of the sun who surrounded the King, as anonymously and inconspicuously as was possible. As soon as he entered, he shouted through their mouths, "Open the portal, be a man of your word," then before the King could attack, he left and jumped into the next mind, then again and again and again. The King began to laugh. As he did, the strange display appeared before his face once more and in that instant, the sky opened up. What was once the dancing star that many cultures worshipped, the heavenly body that periodically streaked across the open sky, began to pulse, to glow, to grow and then, with an almighty boom that shook the ground, it opened. High above the battlefield, a rift between this world and somewhere far beyond opened. Arran observed the QUAF launch upwards all at once, some invisible barrier in the sky repealing all of them simultaneously.

Then Arran was flung from the minds of the Generals of the Sun as the King broadcast through all ninety-nine at once. In unison, they spoke.

"If I die, the force field holding back the QUAF will fall, if I live, all of you will die," said the King, through the combined voices of the Generals of the Sun. Arran was ready.

"Maggi warriors, enter the minds of the Generals of the Sun, find and amplify their fears, their doubts and crush them from the inside. Anice, join with me and we will probe and find the deities, warriors and totems that our armies need. Be their Gods, whisper to them, fill them with hope, with confidence, with belief. Rannoch join with Nanoc and Loo and give them the sight they need to observe the fight between Retishie and the King." said Arran.

From the top of the pyramid, the overseers went to work. Down below, Retishie charged from the centre, Armon stood still as his men charged right past him, in behind Retishie, as they met steel to steel, eye to eye with their opposition across the battlefield. In the first few moments, many fell. The initial impact of the battle was fast, violent, bloody, chaotic, loud, exhausting. Within minutes, over sixty percent of the warriors on both sides were dead, incapacitated or heavily wounded.

Retishie, after cutting through several Generals of the sun, could finally attack the King.

'We meet again,' broadcasted Retishie into the King's mind as he leaped forward with incredible speed and agility. Retishie's attack was layered, attacking simultaneously with energy, mind and sword. Drawing upon a lifetime store of energy, he concentrated it into his chest before pushing it out from his solar plexus, like an explosive wave of ferocious, energetic fury. As his energetic blast flew forth, his sword came down directly behind it. The King's own energetic shield was in place and as the torrent hit him, it buffeted the onslaught, then he used the energetic attack to fly backward, like a giant magnet being repelled. As he did, he parried the very end of Retishie's sword attack before it found his neck. As the King landed, Retishie was charging forward again.

To the many Lanasians who stood only forty feet away, the scene of flying men, lightning-fast charges and impossible skill, was a spectacle to witness.

Vantis of Lerr and his men took up position in front of Nanoc and Loo, cutting through everything that came their way, giving them the time and opportunity to observe Retishie and the King. They looked on, observing what was happening as the two legendary warriors went toe to toe, in a war of mental tricks, energetic attacks and physical strategy. Vantis and his men stood tall in the chaos and reigned down relentless violence as the Generals of the sun attacked again and again and again.

Within a minute, the men of Lerr were down to their last man. Vantis stood alone and he was struggling. His armour, more and more, instead of his sword was parrying the attacking strikes, as his arms and legs gassed out, he fumbled and as he did, Armon slid in and took up his mantle. A new energy began to flow through Armon and Vantis, revitalising the pair. The Magii warriors were with them now. The two men, the two leaders, stood shoulder to shoulder and cut down everything that moved. Then, as quick as it seemed to begin, it was over. The great Retishie was flung back by an invisible force, an energetic attack of extreme magnitude, it flung him twenty feet across the open land. As he flew backward, the old man hurled through many other warriors in the midst of action. Before he could roll to his feet once more, he found himself caught up in the action of four others, each fighting hard for their own lives. As he parried the first attack, he jumped back, creating distance from the chaos he was now a part of. As he looked around to see where the King was, one of the men severed Retishie's lead arm from his body.

In the middle of the chaos, the great Retishie stood still, calm and controlled as his arm pumped blood uncontrollably. In the chaos, he began his final mental attack on the King. With all the pain that his mind could muster, he charged, as he charged, his mind unleashed a furious assault, hammering itself against the mental defences of the King. For a moment, the King almost looked beatable. However, before Retishie's charge could finish, his head was leaving his body, and the King was once again, back in the thick of the action, cutting through the Tannis finest with ease.

Before him, the King could see that they now outnumbered him. He could hear the Tanni army cheering as if they had already grasped victory. There were only him and twelve of his men still standing, and at least thirty of the Tanni rabble were still on their feet. In that instant, the King entered the minds of his men and at once, took them all under his command. The King and his men now moved forward. They all moved independently of the King but with the King at their centre, they cut their way through the remaining Tanni quickly and efficiently.

At the back of the Tanni mass Barratash stood still, unmoved, eyes shut, jumping into and out of every mind on the field. Creating mental shields to those who could not. Calming the minds of those who had recently died and helping them transition into the Bar En Dough, calming the injured and doing everything he could to assist all of his brothers and sisters as he could. As the King and his ring of cat's paws cut forward.

Barratash broadcast to Arran.

"The time is now,"

Arran opened his eyes, atop the great pyramid, took one step forward to stand directly behind the apex of the capstone, and then he leaned forward until his entire torso was against it, his arms hugging the capstone. The pinnacle of the pyramid finishing at a perfect point, just below his jaw. He now lay at an angle, both hands in direct contact with the stone of the pyramid. In that instant, his whole being began to glow, the lines of energy he once experienced in Tanni Ma Bar now illuminated his body, like some luminous dancing tattoo.

"Rannoch, Anice, join with me, observe, keep me safe. Magiis keep Vantis, Armon and Barratash safe," said Arran.

Voosh, Voosh, Voosh.

Arran once again, was ripped from his physical being. As he flew forward from the peak of the hill, he summoned Nanoc in his mind and instantaneously entered the warrior's mind. The entrance was smooth and welcoming, as Nanoc stood calm, heart rate barely beating, like the perfect warrior god as the chaos of the battle thrived all around him. It was just as they had rehearsed the day before. Then Arran entered Loo's mind. As he entered her mind, she began pushing every ounce of her energy into Nanoc. Vantis, Armon and a few of the remaining warriors took up positions to protect Loo as she stood motionless, in a strange trance-like state.

Nanoc's body surged with power, his mind expanded, touching everywhere at once. The whole battlefield was his, every move, every heartbeat. It took him a moment to adapt to the new power that surged through him, to pull himself back, to once again enter the moment. He had a mission; he was here to kill the King. As he formed that thought, his eyes made contact with the King, who stood only forty feet away, as he did, he sensed the King's mind, then he charged. Arran, amplified with the pyramid, pushed hard against the King. The King pushed back. Then to the surprise of the King, his twelve cats' paws stopped moving to his command and attacked him. Fortunately for the King, their attacks were orchestrated by Arran and they were pitiful at best.

"How, how is this even possible?" shouted the King un-amused, however, his attention was only lost for a second. In front of him, Nanoc Ranoh charged forward, sword and targe in hand, now flanked by the King's remaining cats' paws. And then, with one mighty leap, he covered thirty feet and many dead bodies, to bring down his sword and then his targe spike, in a beautifully controlled attack, with a force and accuracy the King had never felt before.

The King blocked both of the attacks and in that same moment, formed his own charge forward, slashing high, then low, then thrusting forward, each of his attacks being deflected, and defended skilfully by the huge barbarian. As the two massive figures danced, weaved, bobbed, cut, parried, rolled, tumbled, crunched and slashed at each other, the great armies on either side cheered.

The King began to surge his energetic powers and with one confident release, he flung everything he had at Nanoc, but to his utter surprise, the big barbarian just flew backwards, repelled by the attack. 'How could one so physically gifted be such a powerful energy dancer, it's not possible' thought the King.

Then, as Nanoc charged once more, his movement was smooth, coordinated and balanced as he covered the distance to the King. But the King had a surprise for the warrior. The King leapt forward, with his mind first, like a spear punching through the outer perimeter of Nanoc's mind, searing pain penetrated deep into Arran, Nanoc and Loo's minds. But then the Kings attack was met with a barrier, to his amazement the barbarian's mind was completely unattainable. Doubt, for the first time in tens of thousands of years, swept in. The King rallied his energies once more and attacked with his mind again, this time holding nothing back, this time he unleashed everything he had in one last desperate panic. As he unleashed his mental attack, almost everyone on the battlefield fell to their knees, crushed by it. As his power surged, he lunged forward with his sword. This was everything he had, yet the barbarian met him toe to toe, energetically, mentally and physically.

As the doubt within his mind rose for a second time, the King's focus was momentarily divided, as he found himself in a predicament he had never trained for, never accepted was even possible. That second of doubt was all that Nanoc Ranoh needed. As the King's head left his body, the buzz of the hive grew in his mind. Nanoc fell to his knees beside the corpse of the King and grabbed his own head with both hands. The buzz from the hive grew louder and louder in his mind.

Nanoc looked up, through Arran's eyes to see the millions of QUAF depart their hosts on mass, like millions of childrens' lanterns being released simultaneously from the thousands of soldiers throughout the valley and beyond. The red mist flew directly upwards to the strange, glowing dimensional portal in the sky. This time, however, they were not repelled, this time they entered.

From inside Arran's mind, one of the more dominant factions of the QUAF broadcasted.

"Now we feed,"

Then the buzzing stopped, and the portal closed behind them.

BOOK 2 INTRO

VERTOMINA'S MIND CRASHED LIKE a tsunami against the shore, violent, relentless, it washed over everyone in our unit simultaneously. Her pain was now our pain. The vast waggon train shuddered to a halt, in the chaos some veered too close to the cliff's edge to be swallowed by the abyss below. Vertomina's waggon shuddered chaotically to a halt as her driver's well-trained instincts gripped the reigns and pulled hard. Her horses were the best trained in all of Namanga and they reacted well, but they too felt the anguish, the pain, the grief, the shock as it was broadcast far and wide. Ashman, the seasoned royal driver, no longer able to hold off the attack, grabbed his head and began to scream.

Agera, still cool as ice, grabbed the falling reigns and wrestled the waggon and the horses to a halt. He was the lead General of this unit, and finally the moment he had worked so hard for, had arrived. He was the last line of defence, he was the shield, Vertomina's shield. He held on tight as the now stationary horses bucked and kicked in panic, the tight winding mountain track that hugged the cliff forced the horses to stop, but they were far from calm. Vertomina's entourage blocked the narrow road in front and the same behind. Agera knew what he had to do, he had to get to and protect Vertomina. With the horses still panicked and Ashman still out of commission, Agera tied the reigns off and jumped-up top of the waggon. He was not scared as he looked out over the river meandering softly at the floor of the valley far below, his heart rate barely rising. The wheels of the waggon below teetered dangerously close to the edge of the cliff, as the horses once more came to life, jerking the wagon forward once more. However, these narrow mountain roads that were just wider than the waggons that traversed them, clinging tight to the cliffs, were his home. To him, these were just the standard roads for a man from the Northern Namangan territories. But this was the first time he had to navigate them, whilst fighting an overseer attack, wilts simultaneously balancing atop an uncontrolled, driverless waggon, but there was no one more equipped for the job. He fought for balance atop the waggon as he focused his mind, trying his hardest to filter out the mental attack that was upon him. He was a General of the Sun and now more than ever, the training he had received to fortify his mind was needed. Just beyond the lip of the ornate decoration atop the oscillating waggon was open air; one wrong step and death would be upon him. Agera smiled as the wagon stopped once more.

From atop the waggon, Agera captured in his mind's eye, then aimed and focused on a small landing area at the very edge of the cliff and jumped from the top of the waggon to the ground in one seamless, well-balanced leap. For a few seconds, Agera was like a bird soaring high above the valley below, on hitting the ground, the edge of the cliff that made up sixty per cent of his landing zone, crumbled on impact but he wasn't there long enough to be taken into the abyss below. Then three swift steps later with his torso leaning more over the abyss than over firm ground, he was entering the rear of the waggon, dagger in hand. As he flung the door open, Vertomina lay slumped over, grasping her head with both hands, in between the luxury seated sides of the inner compartment. As he leaned in towards her, fighting the crushing pain of her broadcast. She raised her head and looked deep into his eyes, piercing deeply into his mind.

"Summerian is dead, my father is dead, the bastards have killed my father," screamed Vertomina out loud. The broadcast was so powerful that he unconsciously and defensively gripped his head and screamed as her voice, fuelled by raw emotion ripped through his best defences.

Agera stood grasping his head, as the pain left his mind, as the pain left everyone's mind. The shock of the revelation hit him. The immortal King was dead.

"Turn the unit around. We are going home to claim my throne," screamed Vertomina.

ABOUT AUTHOR

I am Robb Wallace, author of SEO A Layman's Guide, Smartphone Smart Marketing, Health Made Simple & Steak Bake. These books can be found on Amazon, Apple Books, Google Books, Kobo, B&N, Appsumo and more.

Professionally, I work in marketing. I am an award-winning filmmaker with over fifteen years of experience in marketing, video production, photography, social media, SEO and the digital frontier.

I am currently working on more epic fantasy novels, novels that I hope you will love. Please feel free to get in touch.

All the best, Robb.

PS: Sign up for my newsletter to keep up to date. Delivered once a month.

https://www.robbwallace.co.uk/newsletter/

PPS: A review would be awesome.

Printed in Poland
by Amazon Fulfillment
Poland Sp. z o.o., Wrocław
18 September 2022

20069b78-caf8-43f8-b734-bb0f8e12a65aR01